In praise of *In the S*

"Settle's novel tells the story of long-ago Florida as seen through the eyes of Dr. Drew Duncan, who first comes to the state as an Army volunteer during the Spanish-American War. From Tampa he goes to Cuba, then back to his hometown of Baltimore. After earning his medical degree, he decided to make Florida his home, and he eventually established his permanent medical practice in Moore Haven. The novel paints vivid pictures of south Florida people, places, and things. The climax is reached with the 1926 hurricane that wreaked such havoc on the Lake Okeechobee area. *In the Shadow of the Lone Cypress* is educational as well as entertaining."

> **Patrick D. Smith**, named in 2002 as the 'Greatest Living Floridian' by the Florida Historical Society

"In the Shadow of the Lone Cypress was so interesting that I could not put it down until I finished reading it. I visited the tree many times and wondered, if the Lone Cypress could speak, what would it tell me? Would it say that Oca-loosa-hatchee (Someone omitted the 'O'.) is a Choctaw word that means, 'dark water'? Would it tell me about all the strong winds that have twisted it through the years and seems to point in the direction of the Oca-loosa-hatchee's current? Sally tells the rest of the story in a way that I felt I was there seeing it all happen -- the dreams, the adventures, the struggles, and the tragedies.

> He-tho-pick-chee (Very good.)
> Sho-na-bi-sh (Thank you.)"

> **James Billie**, Former Chairman of the Seminole Tribe of Florida

"Best book I ever read."

> **Rowena Spear**,
> Survivor of the 1926 Hurricane

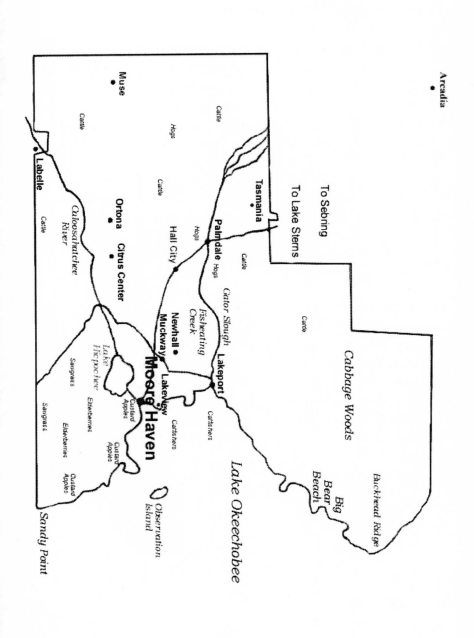

In the Shadow of the Lone Cypress

One Man's Florida

Sally Settle

In the Shadow of the Lone Cypress, One Man's Florida
copyright © 2007 Sally Settle

ISBN: 978-0-9798087-0-8
Library of Congress Control Number: 2007932568
Published by Global Authors Publications

Filling the GAP in publishing

Edited by Kathleen Walls
Interior Design by KathleenWalls
Cover Design by Kathleen Walls
Front Cover Art by Mary Hubley

Printed in USA for Global Authors Publications

DEDICATION

This book is dedicated to the memory of Dr. Duncan Draughn and the pioneers of the muck lands of the Florida Everglades.

FOREWORD

At the turn of the twentieth century, south Florida was on a collision course with what was to become her future. This land, the first in the continental United States that the Conquistadors set foot on 400 years before, was the last to be explored.

Most of north Florida was considered part of the antebellum South. Citrus and cattle drew people to the northeast and central part of the state. Cities like Jacksonville, St. Augustine, Fernandina, and Palatka drew winter visitors because of the mild winters. Henry Flagler's railroad had reached Miami and hotels along its route beckoned visitors southward. Henry Plant built his railroad through the central part of the state to Tampa and on south to Punta Gorda. His hotels also welcomed northern winter visitors.

While both coasts of Florida were becoming well known and populous, very few visitors set foot in the south central part of the state, between Tampa and Miami.

Things changed, though, in the late 1800s when people began to realize that the land around Lake Okeechobee was probably the most fertile in the world. If more land could be made available to farmers by draining some of the low-lying land, it would be an enormous boost to the development of Florida.

To get to the rich soil, the Everglades had to be drained. Subsequently, the dredging of canals began and the water level of Lake Okeechobee went down. Land speculators bought and sold land as they had on the coast. Farmers, mostly from the Midwest, flocked to the area.

Moore Haven, on the southwest corner of Lake Okeechobee, became the largest town in south central Florida.

Today, the ever-shrinking Okeechobee muck lands yield mostly sugar cane and citrus. The small truck farms of the first half of the 20th century have given way to conglomerate agri-business interests.

Because of flood control measures, drainage canals, and chemical fertilizers, the Everglades – the world's most unique ecological system – has been on the brink of extinction for years.

This book is not to glorify a generation who were the first to destroy this pristine land. It is for those who follow to understand why the muck lands were desired by so many.

TABLE OF CONTENTS

Chapter 1

DREAMS IMPLANTED
Tampa, Florida
Spring 1898

La Hacienda de Cuba Libre' was typical of the bars and bordellos which surrounded the Army camps on the outskirts of Tampa. The dark and dreary front room was filled with smoke from cigarettes and the pungent odors of the handmade cigars rolled in the nearby factories of Ybor. Those smells mingled with the scents of cheap liquor and the reek of soldiers who had worn their woolen uniforms much too long in the late spring heat of Florida.

The soldiers were waiting for orders to depart for Cuba, where they would join the Cubans in their fight against Spain. Visiting La Hacienda was a nice diversion from the boredom.

Drew Duncan, a young medic stationed at Camp Libre', had been persuaded to visit this immoral spot in the Cuban community to partake of all of the refreshments which were available. No one had to twist his arm to get him to leave the hellhole of a camp in which they lived.

The soldiers found a table in the back corner of the jammed room. Waiting their turns to go into other parts of the establishment, they shared a bottle of Cuban rum.

After consuming most of the bottle, Drew asked, "I got a new supply of French secrets today. Does anyone need...?"

"No, Duncan, I think you set us up the last time," smiled Jim, a young sergeant from New York whose face glowed from the effects of the rum he had consumed.

Jim had taken a handful of the "protectors" from his friend on their last visit, just to appease him. He had disposed of them later, unused. The way the others around the table smirked, he knew they had, too.

Drew also noticed his companions' expressions.

"I am as tired of treating syphilis and gonorrhea as I am dysentery and malaria," Drew sighed as he looked around the room, seeing many faces he had treated in the past and knowing he would soon see many of them in the medical tent again.

They had finished their bottle and were trying to decide who would buy the next when two strangers approached.

"Mind if we join you Army boys?" the tall one asked. "We'd be pleased to share our Scotch. I'm Hathaway an' this here little midget is Billy Joe."

The two sat down before they could be refused.

While all drank in silence, Drew scrutinized the newcomers and was fascinated by them. They were nothing like the pale soldiers he had been surrounded by for the past six weeks who had never been out in the sun before joining up with the Army.

These unshaven men had rough, coarse, sun-baked skins. They wore broad-rimmed hats and high boots. At their sides hung Colt six-shooters. Drew's instincts told him they could also handle the guns with great skill. He hoped that he wouldn't be witness to their use that night.

No one around the table talked as each man seemed hell-bent on consuming as much liquor as possible. Each was also waiting for one of the girls to approach to say it was his turn to go upstairs. About the time the Scotch was depleted, the liquor coaxed their tongues loose. Hathaway began the conversation.

"Where you boys from? Billy Joe an' me call home a ways south of here on tha prairie near Arcadia. We're cow hunters jest like our pappies. We was two of tha lucky ones who got to work for Jake Summerlin, God rest his soul. Ran cows all over this here state - from St. Augustine to Punta Rassa."

Drew interrupted, "Who's Jake Summerlin? The way you said his name makes me think he's someone we should know about."

"Jake," said Billy Joe, "were 'bout tha greatest of all cowmen that ever lived; lest ways, he were in Floridy. Why, he supplied tha Great States of tha Confederacy her meat during tha war."

He beamed with southern pride in the midst of a room full of men wearing the blue of the U.S. Army.

Hathaway continued.

"Jake sold beef to tha Cause until his contract ran out. Our pappies wuz with him when he snuck past tha Yankee blockades of Cuba an' sold to tha Spaniards. They loved tha way Floridy beef tastes like venison an' they paid top dollar fur hit. Jake an' his hands came out on tha top end 'cause tha Spanish paid them in gold. That thar gold were good long after tha Confederacy notes were good for nuthin' 'cept startin' a fir."

"We got better pay than most cow pokes in these parts, 'cause our daddies worked with Jake," added Billy Joe. "He took us on as soon as we could crack a whip. We been hirin' out to other bosses since Jake died, but thar tain't never gonna be another Jake Summerlin."

Drew listened to all the two cowmen said. During the past six weeks, he had formed a strange connection with Florida. This conversation was adding a new dimension.

The men continued with tales of their lives and their work as Florida cowmen. Drew never realized how big - and wide open - the industry was here. Fascinated, he refused to follow his friends when scantly clad girls appeared to lead the soldiers away.

Soon the only female left was Salieta, a buxom, black haired, black-eyed young girl. When she saw Drew her disposition changed from somber to jovial. The young medic had come to the cantina only a few times but she had fallen in love with him the first time they met. She found fault with all the hundreds of men she had been with but there was nothing about Drew that displeased her.

She loved his wavy reddish brown hair and his sparkling blue eyes that reminded her of a clear summer sky. He was much taller than her five feet. When they danced, the tip of her nose touched the third button on his shirt - just the right height for him to kiss the top of her head.

She loved being close to his slender, firm body. There was not an ounce of fat anywhere on his entire torso.

His smell was sweet and clean, unlike other men she had been with. Most of her clients had not had a bath in months. Most wore clothes that had not been changed since the last bath. His marvelous smell lingered with her for days after his visit.

Salieta also favored Drew because he always paid the most. Drew smiled when he saw Salieta and physically he ached to be with her. He was torn between going to her room and staying to hear the cowmen's stories. He decided to wait until later for sexual pleasures and he turned away from her to the men around his table.

Salieta tried more than once to divert his attention. Obviously, whatever was being said at the table was more important than she was.

Although Drew knew Salieta was displeased because he refused to go to her room, he was enjoying the cowmen's stories far more than a romp on the bed. He paid her what she was expecting and dismissed her.

Seeing the way Drew hung on to their every word, both men talked faster and louder, drawing a crowd of listeners from around the room.

"Now, believe what we say," said Billy Joe. "Thar's a lake that we crackers call tha inland sea. Hit's so big that you nary can see acrost hit. Hit's plum mysterious. We jest seen hit with our own eyes last week."

"When we got done with our last drive ta Punta Rassa, we wuz right there on tha Caloosahatchee. There wuz a steamer gettin' ready ta go up tha river ta tha big lake. We'd jest been paid tha most ever so we decided we'd go see hit.

"Yes, sir," continued Hathaway. "I thought I was seein' another ocean when we got ta tha tall flat topped cypress at tha edge of tha lake. You can't even see tha shore when you're in tha middle of hit," repeating himself. "Tha shore's lined with woods an' vines. One of tha purtiest things I've ever seen is tha white flowers of tha moon vine at night on tha edges of tha water. They's reminds me of large white plates. And they shore smell purty."

"Lake's chock full of tiny islands that's covered with thick bushes an' vines."

"Tha fish's so thick that you can sit in yor boat an' jus' scoop 'em up in a net. You don't even hafta hook a bait."

"Yeah, thar's so many fish, thar ain't no room for tha water."

At this point, Drew knew they were stretching some of the stories for his benefit, but he was intrigued and wanted to hear more.

Hathaway continued, "South of tha lake thar's tha 'Glades that extend all tha way yonder to tha bottom of Floridy. Hit's a heap different than what most people think; hit's not all marsh and swamp. Thar's a lot of dry land."

"You mean it isn't just grass and water?" asked Drew. "Isn't that where Jackson and Taylor chased all the Seminoles? I thought it was a place only for Indians, thieves, and pirates."

"Thar's plenty of them ther', but tha 'Glades is a hell of a lot more than jus' marsh."

"Thar's thousands an' thousands of birds. Sometimes tha sky's so covered with birds that you'd think you is in tha middle of a snow blizzard or under a night sky. Thar's deer, otters, panthers, bears, turkeys, an' a bodacious 'mount of other animals. Thar's nothin' in this here world like hit."

"Don't leave out tha snakes, gators, crocs, and tha bugs!"

"And what 'bout your skeeters?" asked a sergeant from Louisiana. "They's big as ours?"

"They're probably bigger. Thar's a blue million of 'em. They's no bother 'cause you can protect yourself with clothing, bear grease, an' mosquito bars," answered Hathaway.

"Jackson an' all those others ran those Injuns down into tha swamps but I think tha Seminoles got tha last laugh. No one knows how many escaped goin' to tha Indian Territory. Now thar's no danger of 'em being sent away. They's free to trade with tha white man. Some even act as guides for hunters, surveyors, an' anybody else who wants to explore tha 'Glades."

"Mind if I join you, boys?" asked a tall, burly stranger who had approached only moments before. Without waiting for an answer, the new arrival, whose nose looked like it had seen many a bar room fight, sat down. He extended his large, calloused hand to Drew and to the others.

"Name's Seth Paterson, I couldn't help listenin' when I heard you talking 'bout the Okeechobee. I spent two years of my life down there working on dredges an' I can tell you a thing or two. I dredged a river - the Caloosahatchee - for a man named Hamilton Disston, at one time the largest landowner in the United States."

Hathaway interrupted, "Disston followed Jake an' his men up the river. If twered't fur cowmen, you wouldn't had known where ta go. My pappy useta tell how he an' his friends waded in mud an' head high sawgrass fur days ta set tha flags fur tha dredges ta follow. Pappy told howd fellers drownd in tha swift rapids tryin' to set tha dynamite ta blast tha falls. He said hit t'were tha most dangerous job he ever did."

Paterson grunted under his breath and continued his story. "Disston had a sugar plantation up on the Kissimmee and he wanted a way to get his sugar to the Gulf. That's why we dug the canals."

"So," asked Drew, "is your assessment of the lake area about the same as these fellas?"

Paterson said he agreed with most of what the men had said concerning the big lake, but added that the canals that had been dredged had caused Lake Okeechobee's water level to drop.

"That's left good bottom soil that will be great for farming," said Paterson. "Kinda like the Mississippi Delta, I suppose."

He paused briefly, then continued when he knew his audience was still with him.

"Disston shot himself in '93 during the Panic. They say that he was behind in payments and his heirs let most of the land go back for taxes. That was a downright shame all around. Disston had bought four million acres for twenty-five cents an acre from the Florida government right after the War Between the States. Florida was about bankrupt because of the war. Another man, named Henderson, got thousands of acres south of the lake for surveying the land Disston bought. Now, they say, that land is about to be drained, too."

The bartender who brought more bottles interrupted the conversation.

"Did I hear you mention Disston? Folks 'round these parts get furious when they hear that name. They don't like the fact that the state sold four million acres of land to one man. They figure that between him and the land given to the railroad guys, homesteading is a thing of the past. 'Stead of working the land to own it like we could, we will havta buy it from the rich folks to make them even richer."

Hathaway cut in.

"Yeh, I'd always figured that I'd get me some land like my grandpappy in South Carolina before tha damn Yankees burnt him out. I didn't figure on buying hit from no rich Yankee. I always thought I would be able to homestead some myself an' then after seven year hit would be mine. I guess after a few more drives I'll buy me a small piece of tha black dirt they say is goin' to be fer sale oncest they git all tha water drained.

"They say tha land has the richest soil in the world."

The conversation once again came to a halt when girls appeared.

"It's been good talkin' to ya, but we're not skipping what we come here fer," smiled Hathaway.

Drew watched as Salieta and the other girls led the cowmen and dredge operator away.

Later that night Drew lay awake staring at the white of his tent. He was intrigued by the night's conversations. He wondered how much truth there was in their stories.

He thought he already knew a lot about Florida.

A number of his school chums had family connections with the railroad magnates who had been instrumental in developing Florida.

Henry Flagler and Henry Plant had both come to the state after the War Between the States and bought up all the bankrupt narrow gauge railroads.

In order to expand their commercial empires, they laid standard gauge tracks to tie in with the lines from the north, enabling not only marketable products but also people to be more easily transported.

Flagler had tracks down Florida's east coast. He was building hotels to house winter visitors from the north.

Plant's tracks ran down the west coast where he also was building hotels.

To assure that new track would continue to be laid into new regions, the State of Florida promised additional land to the railroaders, who grew wealthier and wealthier.

Once partners, Flagler and Plant were now in intense competition, each trying to best the other. Plant's enterprises also included railroad tracks into the interior to ship out the phosphate being mined there.

Drew also knew that Thomas Edison, the inventor, had his winter home in the small settlement of Fort Myers on the lower west coast.

And then, there were the tales of the mosquitoes. On more than one occasion, those who had spent some time in the state had described the mosquitoes in Florida.

His great-grandfather's shipbuilding company in Baltimore, for instance, had built *The Flirt*, a Boston Whaler that ended up in a squadron of Navy vessels sent to aid Jackson in the First Seminole War in 1837. The squadron was christened "the Mosquito Fleet," for obvious reasons.

Drew believed more what he had heard from family about the blood-sucking insects than what the cowmen had told him tonight. It was highly unlikely, he felt, that one could not be bothered by mosquitoes. Those who said the little pests could cover every inch of exposed skin within minutes of walking outside rang more true. The fact that one could slap hard and leave a bloody impression of his hand, along with dead mosquitoes, was something he would have to see for himself.

Was this area of Florida he had heard little about before tonight as much of a paradise as the cowmen had said? Was there really more to it than desolate swampland, good for nothing but runaways and outcasts from society? Even if most of the descriptions were from drunken talk, Drew was fascinated.

His Florida experiences were certainly a transformation from the college life he had left such a short time ago. He was pleased with the change.

He fell asleep dreaming of tropical birds and beautiful sky.

Chapter 2

GREAT EXPECTATIONS
Baltimore, Maryland
Summer 1895

"Thomas Drew Duncan, III, Phi Beta Kappa, Bachelor of Arts in the College of Arts and Sciences."

Drew rose to his feet and crossed the stage to get his diploma. He hadn't yet celebrated his twentieth birthday and he was graduating first in the Class of 1895 from Johns Hopkins University. Minutes before, he had delivered the valedictory address to his peers. The speech was almost identical to the one he had given three years before when he graduated first from the Baltimore Boys Academy.

"Never before in the history of the world have men accomplished and invented more than they have in the past twenty years," he had said. "Look at the comforts we have that our grandfathers never imagined."

"We have spent the last few years of our lives learning about the great composers, great philosophers, great writers, and great ideas of the past. Now, it is time to make use of our knowledge as we prepare for the duties that will be ours in the future."

"As tomorrow's leaders of our communities and our country, we are judiciously prepared to be the helmsmen of our ship of state - our nation - as it steams into the twentieth century."

"Challenges yet to be taken; obligations yet to fulfill; destinies we cannot foresee, lie before us."

"We, the class of 1895, are ready to assume our new positions! We are prepared to make an impact on the world and on the century ahead of us. May God bless us all as we begin that work."

He thought about his speech as each of his classmates walked across the stage. He knew his words were the ones parents as well as professors had expected to hear. And, he knew his words might inspire some of his classmates. However, the words did not reflect what was in his heart.

Although he knew what was expected of him, he wasn't sure what he would do. He wondered how many of his classmates were thinking similar thoughts.

He thought of the letter of acceptance that was in his front pocket from Yale's School of Medicine. It was expected that he would follow in the footsteps of his father and his grandfather. All three had the same name and Drew, like them, was expected to attend Yale and add "M.D." behind his name. He had been groomed to be a doctor since he was twelve, when he began working with his father after school, on Saturdays, and during the summers. He watched, helped, and absorbed. Although he had much more practical experience than most graduating from medical school, Drew wasn't sure that he wanted to be a doctor.

He was young and it was the dawn of a new century. Drew wanted excitement. He wanted to play baseball.

His love for the game had started when he was seven when his grandfather had taken him to his first Oriole's game. From the time he had walked through the front gate of the ballpark, he knew he would never be the same. The smells, the sounds, the excitement, everything had hit him at the same time. His passion for the game had not waned over the years.

Drew had played with his friends in the empty field by the grammar school for years. He went to see the Orioles play whenever he could. During his last year of secondary school, he got to play on an organized team for the first time and for the past three years he had been the star catcher for the Sigma Chi's. He enjoyed the intramural games but he wished there were baseball games between colleges as there were football games.

His interest had taken a different turn in the spring when a scout for the Orioles had seen him catch. The scout told Drew that he was good enough to play in the minor leagues and that he should try out for the team. The following week he heeded the scout's words. He was good enough at the tryouts to win the number two spot as catcher.

But playing baseball was not part of the plan that had been laid out for his life. What would his parents think if they knew of his dream? Why did he wonder? He already knew.

He had tried to broach the subject every time he had eaten a meal at his parents' house for the past month. Somehow, he knew he would have to deliver the news within the next few days because the Orioles were holding a place for him until the first of June.

Drew's mind returned to his graduation when the name, Jon Zinger, was announced. Following the ceremony, he and his parents walked to the President's home where a brunch was served to the graduates and their families.

Afterwards, Drew and his father escorted his mother home in the family carriage and then proceeded to the downtown section of Baltimore. Dr. Duncan stopped the carriage in front of the Chesapeake Club and turned the reins over to a delivery boy who took the horse and carriage to the club's stable a few blocks away.

Drew had seen the outside of the Chesapeake Club dozens of times during his twenty years, but he had never been through the heavy mahogany doors where men in his father's social circle gathered regularly for fellowship. Many of his classmates were also going into the club for the first time.

Being admitted to the Chesapeake Club was a rite of passage in Baltimore society. When a young man graduated from college, he was invited to become a member. It was almost unheard of for anyone to procure a membership card without a college degree and a family connection.

Drew followed his father up a wide marble staircase to the mezzanine where he was greeted by several of his father's friends. They went up another flight of stairs to a large open room lined with massive bookcases. Leather chairs and sofas were placed in conversational groups. A variety of gaming tables awaited participants and a well stocked bar, the length of the back wall, offered the best and richest labels.

As he looked around the smoke-filled room, Drew studied the faces of his father's associates. These were men he had known all of his life - from school, church, his father's office, and social visits with his family. Yet, in this room, the men seemed very different. Many were the leaders of the Democratic Party. Those he recognized included state and national senators, former governors, and leaders in the political arena of the City of Baltimore. All over 50 years of age were veterans of the Confederacy.

A short time later, all conversation stopped when Judge Adolphus Cramer stood up and called for their attention. The judge's booming voice vibrated off the walls of the stuffy reception room.

"I want to welcome the six young men who have just graduated this morning from Johns Hopkins. Let's see, we have three going on to Harvard to get their law degrees, two going to Yale — one to be a doctor and another a lawyer, and one who is about to be commissioned in the Navy. It looks as if we of the older generation can rest assured that this new generation will continue in our footsteps and the world will survive without us."

"Now boys, that degree was just the first step to a successful life. Membership in the Chesapeake is the second. Marriage to a good woman is the third step."

After the laughter died down, the judge called out the names of the graduates and presented each with a membership card to the club, a fifth of aged single malt Scotch, and a box of fine, expensive hand-rolled Cuban cigars. Established members shook the hands of the new affiliates. It seemed to Drew that he received a hundred slaps on the back - in the same exact spot. A steak dinner followed the initiation. Drew was uncommonly quiet but with the noise in the room, no one seemed to notice.

Drew ate in silence and reflected on his current position.

"So is this what it means to be a member of the most elite group in Baltimore?" he thought. "Is this the place where I will spend my life when I'm not working? Will my social life be full of cards, smoking, and drinking? Is this what it's all about?"

Somehow, he just couldn't imagine treating the colds and the headaches of these men and their rich families. There had to be more to life than that!

Drew knew that he wanted more. Uncle Tyler had broken away. Could he? He wondered.

Drew had first met his uncle when he was nine years old.

Tyler had gone to the Oklahoma Territory to live shortly after the war. He had, by a hand of fate, ended up working in a Union hospital, and was, thus, labeled a Yankee. His father had disowned him. On his deathbed, Tyler's father sent for his son to ask for his forgiveness.

The reunion between Tyler and his family had been joyous. During the visit, uncle and nephew had formed a lasting friendship enriched by a constant exchange of letters in the years that followed.

It had been such a shock to Drew when his grandfather died. In his nine-year-old mind he thought that his uncle had been sent for to cure his grandfather with the medicines that Tyler had learned about from the Indians in the Oklahoma Territory.

When Drew had realized that his grandfather was dead and not just sleeping in the coffin, he had lashed out at his uncle, thinking he was responsible.

"Why didn't you make Grandfather well?" Drew had screamed. "Why did you come here and kill him? You are nothing but a murdering Yankee and you better leave town fast or I'm going to have the police come and take you to jail." Drew then kicked Tyler as hard as he could.

Drew's mother had grabbed him and tried to calm him down by shaking him, but he wrenched away, ran out of the house, and out of the yard. He ran until he got to the city's docks where he slumped down beside a post and sobbed.

He didn't know how long he had been there when Uncle Tyler found him.

His uncle was the last person Drew had wanted to see. Why did he, of all people, come after him? Drew pummeled Tyler with his fists, but the run from Charles Street and the sobbing had zapped his strength. Tyler had gently but firmly grabbed Drew's hands and soothingly talked to his nephew.

"Trace, Trace," his uncle said softly, calling the youngster by the nickname the family used to distinguish him from his father and grandfather who had the same name.

"Could I share with you that I ran to this exact place to cry when my grandfather died? I spent several hours here, wondering why God was so mean that he had to let someone I loved so much die."

"But, Trace, there is a time for everyone's life to end. It was my grandfather's time. Today was your grandfather's - and my father's - time."

"I don't have any magic cures. In spite of all I know about medicine, and things that can help with illnesses and pain, there was nothing I - or anyone else - could do. Even if your grandfather had not died today, he would never have been the same as he was before he got sick. And, though it is hard for us to say good-bye, it is better than watching him suffer for a long time and grow weaker and weaker. "

Drew and Tyler had formed a common bond that day on the docks.

During the two weeks before Tyler returned to the Indian Territory, the attachment between uncle and nephew became stronger. They became more than uncle and nephew; they became comrades. Tyler played pitch and catch with Drew and took him to several of the Orioles games.

Instead of the relationship fading because of the distance between them, a great friendship developed and flourished. Drew wrote long letters telling Uncle Tyler about everything that he did and telling him of his deepest thoughts. He shared things with him he couldn't share with his parents, Flora, his Negro mammy, or his peers. Uncle Tyler always responded with words of wisdom and encouragement.

Since his grandfather's death, Drew had seen Uncle Tyler three more times, once at the funeral of his grandmother; once at the funeral of another relative, and once at his high school graduation. Drew had been so pleased that he was there just for him and was admittedly disappointed that Uncle Tyler had not made it to his college graduation.

A hand on his shoulder and the sound of a familiar voice ended Drew's thoughts. He turned around and jumped up to embrace the man he had been thinking of, a man who was the identical image of his father.

Like his twin brother, Tyler's once-flaming red hair was turning gray. Only the few who knew both men well would have been able to distinguish the difference in the two. Tyler, who had spent most of his life outdoors, looked more robust than Drew's father, who had spent most of his adult life indoors. Tyler's hair also was longer than was fashionable in Baltimore's conservative circles.

"I wanted to surprise you at your graduation, but I had all kinds of delays, which I will tell you about later. How does it feel to be a college graduate and a member of the Chesapeake Club?"

Before Drew had time to answer, his father spoke to his brother as he, too, embraced him.

"How did you get past Franklin?"

"I really don't know. I wondered if he would let a Yankee in, but I guess he thought I was you - or maybe it was because of this..."

Tyler reached into his coat pocket and brought out a card identical to the one that Drew had received shortly before. The date on it was June 9, 1855.

"I guess once a member, always a member!"

Taking time to survey his surroundings and study the club he had not been in for thirty-five years, Tyler remarked, "Doesn't this place ever change? It looks just like it did when Father brought us here after our graduation from Hopkins. I do remember that you could get a great meal here, though. Do they still serve? I am as hungry as a bear."

With that said, he signaled for a waiter to come over and was in the middle of his food order when one of the young graduates announced excitedly, "Come to the window and look! One of those fancy French horseless carriages is parked out front. Come see!"

Within minutes almost every man in the room was gathered at the windows looking down on the magnificent machine.

"What is it?"

"I know that it's a horseless carriage, but it's much fancier than any I've ever seen."

"Who owns it?"

"It's the first in Baltimore."

"We are as modern as New York, Boston, and Washington."

"Okay men, confess! Who bought this thing? I guess our wives will make us get one, too."

"Not me! My horse, Daisy, has a personality of her own. That contraption can't compare with my horse!"

Each man had his own opinion. It was the younger men who persuaded their fathers and the other older men to go down to look more closely at the automobile.

"Come on, Uncle Tyler and Father. Don't you want to see it?"

"Not particularly," both of the men said at the same time.

"I have never seen a group of men act so childish," Drew's father said, "especially these men, the leaders of our city!"

"You go on and look," said Uncle Tyler to Drew. "I really want to put my teeth into a good steak."

Drew left his elders and bounded down the steps. He pushed his way through the crowd so that he could get a closer look. His eyes sparkled as he looked at the brown exterior that glistened in the late afternoon sun. The interior of the doors, the seats, and the front were all made of tan leather. The thick carpet on the floor was a deeper shade of brown than that of the exterior of the car.

"Who owns this horseless carriage?" everyone seemed to be asking.

No one in the crowd admitted ownership.

It was evident that each new member of the Chesapeake Club was hoping that this was a graduation present for himself. Drew looked up to see his uncle and father standing beside him.

"They didn't have any steak, but that's okay. I'll just go to your house and eat some of Flora's cooking. It's better anyway."

To everyone's amazement, especially Drew's, Uncle Tyler reached into the automobile and brought out a turn crank. No one said a word as Uncle

Tyler walked to the front and placed the crank into the shaft. With two turns, the engine sputtered and took hold.

"Climb in and let's go home," said Tyler, turning toward his brother at the same time. "Or does Drew have to go through more ritual?"

"No. You two can go on. I'll drive my old out-of-date horse-drawn carriage home. You two just go on!"

Drew laughed as he realized his father was jealous!

Tyler slipped into a duster and handed one to Drew, along with a pair of goggles, both necessary to keep the dust of the road off their clothes and out of their eyes.

Tyler and Drew climbed into the car as the men around them cheered, in spite of the fact that the green-eyed monster had attacked most of them, especially those Drew's age. The green-eyed monster was Flora's favorite term for jealously. She would love to see so many under the spell, Drew thought.

Drew held on to the door as he traveled down the cobblestone streets. Only on a train had he moved so fast, but being in a small horseless carriage was far different than in a big train. The trees and bushes were streaks of green and brown blurs as they passed them.

People stopped and stared at the first automobile they'd ever seen on the streets of Baltimore. Horses reared up on their back legs, almost upsetting the carriages and wagons they were pulling. Although Drew couldn't hear them, he could see that the dogs were howling.

In no time at all Tyler had stopped in front of the palatial home both men had grown up in. Drew felt like he was still in motion for a few minutes. Getting his bearings, he got out of the carriage and opened the massive iron gate that had been forged by his great-great-grandfather Carr.

Getting back in the auto, Drew asked, "Is this why you were late? You didn't drive this all of the way from Oklahoma did you?"

"No, I made arrangements to pick this up in New York two weeks ago. When I arrived at the depot, they were just unloading it from the ship. I had to go through hours of paper work before they would release it to me. Then, I missed the train that I was supposed to take. I guess I'm lucky that I arrived when I did, but I'm sorry that I missed your graduation. Would it help if I told you that this is your graduation present from me?"

"Uncle Tyler. This is really too much! I think that you would get more use of it in Oklahoma than I would."

"That would be true, if I were going to continue to be in Oklahoma, but I'm not going back. I've called the Indian Territory - rather the reservations - home for the last 30 years, but now it's time to move on. I'm planning to go to Cuba when I leave here."

"Cuba? Why Cuba? Aren't they in the middle of a revolution there?"

"Yes, their fight for their independence from Spain has taken a toll on all of the citizens. Clara is down there and wants me to come. I've worked with her several times since the war and, as you know, we've always corresponded on a regular basis."

"She says there's a desperate need for doctors in Cuba and she has been begging me for some time now to go down and work with her and the American Red Cross she has started. I've decided to go. You know me, I live for excitement."

The two excitedly exchanged other parts of their lives, and finally, when there was a lull, Drew turned serious.

"Uncle Tyler, will you help me with something very important? I need support when I approach Mother and Father. I've been offered a chance to catch for the Orioles. I don't think that I can stand six more years of school."

Drew could tell by the expression on his uncle's face that he didn't approve of his plans.

"Drew, don't think of this automobile as a bribe, but I did get it for you to travel back and forth to Yale. I think the world needs good, qualified doctors. There are far too many quacks out there, with little or no training who are treating - and killing - people."

"I thought you would be all for me setting out on my own. It's not like I don't have a job. I will have a dream job! I'm just following your example."

"Sometimes I wonder if you are my brother's son."

Drew looked at his uncle with a puzzled look.

"Just kidding! But you are more like me than like him. I remember that I was eager to spread my wings when I graduated from Johns Hopkins with my B.A. but, thank God, my father persuaded me to go on and to get my medical degree."

"Think about your decision, Drew. The automobile is yours, regardless."

"Now let's go in and surprise your mother and Flora. Remember, I was starving more than an hour ago. Race you to the house!"

Chapter 3

YALE MEDICAL SCHOOL
New Haven, Connecticut
March 1898

Drew sat in the hard straight back chair in front of his desk. His mind was everywhere but on his studies. While his mind wandered, he threw his baseball high into the air and caught it with his glove.

He had not pursued becoming a professional baseball player after his conversation with his Uncle Tyler on the day of his graduation from Johns Hopkins. He settled for attending games when he was able to work them into his schedule and playing whenever he could get a group of medical students together.

His associates, both students and professors, teased Drew about being so good and often called him 'The Glove,' in admiration of the way he was able to scoop up almost any ball that came his way. The few who knew of the job offer with the Orioles were amazed that he had passed up the opportunity.

Instead of following his own dreams, he had followed in the footsteps of his grandfather, father, and uncle. After three years at Yale Medical School, he could have passed any state test and become a doctor without attending another class. The temptation to do that was always with him.

He looked around the room and felt the walls closing in on him. The space was basic college dormitory and was almost identical to the one he had lived in for four years at Johns Hopkins. There were two beds, two dressers, two desks, two wardrobes, and one washstand with a mirror. Above the desks, two bookshelves were crammed with the many textbooks he and his roommate studied almost every waking hour they were not in class.

His eyes stopped as they fell on the black leather bag on his bed. It was the highest quality medical bag money could buy.

"Thomas Drew Duncan, III" was engraved on the shiny brass nameplate. His father had presented the bag to him on Christmas.

"You'll need this bag starting this term. Look, there's a spot for 'M.D.' when you earn your degree."

His father's look of pride had haunted Drew since he had returned to school. So much was happening in the world and he wanted to be a part of it. Continuing with his classes seemed a waste of time.

He rose from his chair, walked over to his wall and read the clippings he had tacked up from *Harpers Weekly, Leslies, The Black and White, The New York World, The New York Journal*, and several regional papers which gave detailed accounts of the activities in Cuba and Washington. The events of each passing day were bringing the United States closer and closer to war with Spain. The editorial pages were full of the debate whether or not the United States should become involved.

The most recent clippings told of the February 15 explosion on *The USS Maine*. The ship had sunk, killing 266 American men. Although investigations were not conclusive, it was widely believed that the Spanish set off the bombs that sunk the ship. Almost everyone in the United States was ready to go to war.

Drew turned to look out of the window. Everything was covered with a thick blanket of wet snow, and more was coming down as a blizzard raged. It was unusual to have so much snow in this part of Connecticut.

He watched as his roommate, Jim, fought the wind, trying to make some headway across the Memorial Quadrangle and wondered how snow could look so beautiful, yet be so miserable when you had to get out in it. He was glad he was inside, and sat down at his desk to reread the letter he had received from Uncle Tyler that morning.

Havana, Cuba
20 February 1898

Dear Trace,

I know that you have read a lot in the papers about what has happened this past week here in Havana but now you can hear about it from an eyewitness.

For the first time in weeks I thought that I was going to enjoy a late dinner at my favorite restaurant on the harbor. I hadn't been able to eat there in weeks because of the rioting that had been going on all over Havana. The rioting had died down, though, when 'The Maine' anchored in the Harbor and I felt it was safe enough to go out there.

The waiter had just sat down a big plate of black beans and rice when I heard the worst explosion of my life.

I looked in the direction of the sound and saw red, orange, and yellow bursts of flame against the night sky. I was acutely aware that 'The Maine' was anchored in that vicinity. At that time I didn't know what had happened but only imagined that it must have been a bomb exploding.

The horrible sounds of the blast were only the beginning of many frightening sounds that night. As

16

people realized 'The Maine' had been blown up, men ran from everywhere, grabbing anything that could float to begin a very disorganized rescue effort.

I found an empty dinghy and rowed out to the sinking ship. You can't imagine how fast that huge ship went down. I was able to get six survivors into my craft. There wasn't room for any more. They say that eighty-six men have survived, although many of that number still barely cling to life as I write.

Clara and I had been out to the ship for a visit just last week. Actually, she had taken me there to introduce me to the medical unit and to the officers. We thought we would be working with them, not having some of them as patients!

I have been writing to you for so long about the torturing, the killings, and the mutilations of the Cuban Insurrectionists by the Spanish. Our hospitals have long been busy with the sick and the wounded rebels.

Since General Weyler was relieved of his command and sent back to Spain, we have been faced with even greater challenges. Men, women, and children of the rural areas were imprisoned so they wouldn't aid the Insurrectionists. We had never been in the camps before. Now we have found most of the people starving to death. The conditions in which they have to live are deplorable. I hear that close to one half million people have died. I am sick that we can't do much for them. I do hope that in time they will let us in or let the people go back to their homes.

The men who are fighting are so tired. If the Cubans are to win their independence from Spain, the United States MUST become involved. I know my brother and many others accuse Pulitzer and Hearst of grossly exaggerating the situation in order to sell their newspapers - yellow journalism I think it's being called. Maybe they have exaggerated, but the stories and pictures haven't told half of the horrible situation.

I've had contact with Frederick Remington, Hearst's reporter, on numerous occasions. His sketches of the melee are accurate in every detail.

I can only pray that the reports coming out of Cuba will make people mad enough to demand action from the government.

By the way, I received a letter from your father the day

before the bombing accusing me of being in cahoots with the Hawks to get a war started. Now, I trust he is singing another tune. But, then he might even blame Hearst and others for the bombing!

I must sign off now and return to my duties. Study hard and find a cure for malaria!

Affectionately,
Uncle Tyler

The letter had made it completely impossible for him to concentrate on his studies. He went to bed earlier than usual but tossed and turned all night just as he had done for the past month.

When he got up early the next morning, the sky was still dark. Snow was falling as fast as it had been the night before. He decided that it was time to put an end to his restlessness.

He quickly shaved and dressed. Jim didn't stir as he left their room. He ran down the dark, quiet hall, and out into the Connecticut blizzard. The fierce wind and the sub zero temperature did not hamper his determination to get to the Dean's office. At exactly two minutes before eight, Drew was standing in front of the door that read:

David Tully, MD
Dean, School of Medicine

Dean Tully had been Drew's professor, academic advisor, and mentor for the past three years. The professor had served as a medic during the War Between the States and had even worked in some of the hospitals with Uncle Tyler. Dean Tully had finished his schooling after the war and had said many times that serving in war time had made him a better doctor and a better teacher. Drew knew that Dean Tully would be the best person to talk to about his plans.

Tully, a short pudgy man in his late fifties, came through the door of the administration building precisely at eight. Brushing the snow off his overcoat, he grumbled, "There should be a law. No human being should have to come out in weather like this. It's insane!"

Drew, who had been sitting on a wooden bench on the other side of the hall from the office, called out to the dean as he was still stomping the snow off his shoes.

"Duncan! What brings you out so early? Classes don't start until nine. If I could, I would still be in bed. Why aren't you?"

"I really need to talk to someone. Can you spare a few minutes?"

The dean led Drew into his office. Bookshelves around the room contained the usual medical books that lined the shelves of most doctors and professors of medicine. However, one prominent wall proudly displayed a collection of pictures and war mementos from Dean Tully's service as a medic for the Union Army. For the next 45 minutes the dean and his favorite student discussed the situation in Cuba and Drew's eagerness to become part of the conflict.

"I've decided to join the Red Cross and work beside my uncle in Cuba," said Drew. "They need all the medical help they can get. You know I have more knowledge than a lot of practicing doctors. I could finish school when I get home, like you did after the War Between the States."

"Things were a little different 35 years ago, my boy. That war was an internal war. Most everyone felt it was his duty to serve in some way. We were out to save the United States."

"Then you know exactly how I feel."

"Yes, but we aren't at war yet. When and if we are it will be an entirely different situation. We will be there not only to help the Cubans, but to gain new territories."

"It is just a matter of time and you know it. Look at the headlines of *The Sun*."

He turned the paper towards the dean.

The large, bold headline screamed for attention.

Congress Passes $50,000,000 for Military

"You know there will be a call up for volunteers any day now," said Drew.

Dean Tully nodded, and then broached a subject both of them knew had to be addressed.

"What's your father going to say about your plans? I can't imagine that he will be happy."

Drew laughed.

"If you think that the explosion in the Havana Harbor was loud, you haven't heard anything yet! Father is the dove of all doves. He thinks the United States should take care of what she has and leave the rest of the world alone. There is absolutely no reason to expand beyond the existing borders."

Finally, Dean Tully said, "Duncan, I've been around a long time. I know when young men are determined to do things their own way. I have seen that determination end the relationship between a young man and his parents. Consider your father's opinions. If you go through with your plan without his consent, you might break with him forever. Fathers sometimes are unforgiving when their plans get altered."

Dean Tully paused, knowing Drew was not going to be dissuaded from his mission.

"I want you to promise me you will finish medical school after the war.

You are one of the best students that I have ever had. Don't get the idea that you can be a doctor by just passing state tests."

"It can be done."

"Yes, it can be done, but you have four more years of study and training. Those years are critical in your career as a doctor. You'll get a lot of experiences in the war, most of which, by the Grace of God, you will never use again. Remember the knowledge and modern procedures you'll only learn in a medical school. There are people practicing medicine who are using antiquated techniques simply because they didn't finish, or even go to medical school."

"I do plan to come back to get my M.D., but I am determined to do this, sir, in spite of the consequences with my father," Drew said.

"Why don't you consider this? Wait until there is a declaration of war. Then you could enlist as a medical officer. If you join the Red Cross now you will forfeit all the work you have done in the past two months. If you delay leaving school, you could make arrangements with your professors to give you an accelerated program. In fact, I'll help you make those arrangements. Think about it, Duncan. Consider your family."

Their conversation came to a close. Drew thanked the Dean for his time.

As he turned to leave, Dean Tully asked, "Say, what are your plans for that horseless carriage?" A hopeful expression came over his face as he continued. "I can buy it from you. Then you'll have the money that you will need to finance your schooling when you return."

Drew was more than willing to strike a deal. After the first road trip to school, Drew had traveled by train, which proved to be a much more reliable and faster mode of transportation than the automobile.

The two shook hands just as the 9 o'clock bell rang.

David Tully knew he had only been a sounding board for Drew's predetermined plan. He could only pray that one of his finest students would not be lost while he was on the mission to which he clearly had received a call.

That afternoon Drew met with the rest of his professors to discuss his plans with them. Some tried to discourage him, but in the end all agreed to give him the class work, labs, and practicums for the rest of the term so he could be ready to take his finals as quickly as possible after McKinley declared war.

That night Drew penned a letter to his father.

Chapter 4

GOODBYE TO HOME
May 1898

Drew received a response quicker than he had expected. His father's searing response was in the form of a telegram that was delivered to Drew in his anatomy lab.

NO MORE MONEY IF YOU DO
MOTHER CRYING

A letter followed several days later.

Baltimore, Maryland
March 11, 1898

Dear Trace,

Why in the Hell do you want to do such a thing? I know that you think that your Uncle Tyler continues to have a wonderful and exciting life, but the life that I have in Baltimore is very full and satisfying. I am offering you that kind of life. I have seen the horrors of war. I can still feel, taste, and smell all of the destruction and slaughter that I witnessed. I don't want that for you, son.

How many of your friends have a medical practice waiting for them when they finish school? Your life is set. Don't waste a minute of it. Forget this nonsense.

You are our only child. We don't want to lose you in this senseless, political war! Many a medic has never returned home.

Your mother and Flora have not stopped crying since your letter of intention came. Think of them - You are their life!

With love and hope,
Father

McKinley sent his war message to Congress on April 21, demanding the independence of Cuba. Drew finished his exams at midnight three days later as Congress made the declaration official. Although the semester was condensed, all of his marks were in the 90th percentile.

The next day Drew signed papers to join the U. S. Army Medical Corps in Hartford and was given a date to arrive at the New York Induction Center.

Dr. Tully bought Drew's horseless carriage and stored Drew's books and personal belongings in the attic of his house. Drew put the money from the sale of the carriage in the First National Bank of Hartford. It would be enough for one more year of school. He would worry about the cost of the other three years at a later time.

His father was still against his decision to leave school and had sent a letter almost every day telling him not to go or he would be cut off from him. Drew wondered if his father would change his mind once he saw that he was on his way. He remembered the grudge his father and grandfather had held against Uncle Tyler for over twenty years. Whatever the consequences, he had made his decision.

On Thursday, April 29, Drew was on a train heading south - south to war and to adventure.

In New York, the excitement of the war was everywhere.

Shouts of "Cuba Libra!" were followed by "Remember *The Maine*!"

Men from all walks of life were coming together as soldiers for their country - farmers, clerks, merchants, school teachers, cowmen, students. They all crowded into the passenger cars heading south.

The atmosphere was electrifying and Drew was right in the middle of all of the excitement. This was the right place to be. This war was for his generation, just as the War Between the States was for his father, and the War of 1812 had been for his great-grandfather.

The train full of a strange mixture of men with a common cause pulled out of Grand Central Station. On the wooden platform of the station, not minding the cinders that covered them as the great steam engine belched and chugged, the crowd waved tiny American flags and cheered. Drew sat by the window and stared at the countryside as it flew by. All across the landscape he saw men and women waving flags at the passing train.

Children sat on fences and waved handkerchiefs to honor the soldiers who passed their way. The train stopped in every town, village, and crossroad for more men. At each place, it looked as if the entire population had turned out to cheer their loved ones who were joining the war effort. Bands played and people cheered. Drew didn't see a protester in sight.

Was his father alone in his protesting?

Drew felt somewhat sorry for himself as he saw parents hugging their sons as they got onto the train. There was standing room only until the train reached Baltimore.

Drew realized for the first time the meaning of being an American. Arriving at his hometown station he realized that this was his day of independence. It was the day he had been waiting for all of his life.

His euphoria was somewhat diminished, however, as the train pulled out of the Baltimore station. He thought of his home, only a few blocks away. How could he be so close and not go home?

From the train's window, he could see the tall sycamore trees that lined Charles Street where his family home was located. Briefly he thought about the mansion that his great grandfather had built to reflect the fortune he had made in the shipbuilding industry. His thoughts included the ships that were carved in the mahogany mantles in all sixteen rooms as well as those that adorned the iron gate of the brick wall that surrounded the two-acre grounds. For another minuscule second he thought about his bedroom on the third floor where he could see over the trees and rooftops to the bay.

What made his memories linger, though, was when he thought of the basement kitchen that was by far his favorite room. It was in the kitchen where he had spent most of his time growing up.

He smiled at the remembrances.

He pictured Flora standing in the door with her huge chocolate arms stretched out, ready to enfold him. The tears would fall from her big round brown eyes and roll across her chubby cheeks as she said his name over and over. It was the same scenario each time he came home from school.

He remembered how Flora had comforted him his entire life. He loved it when she put her big arms around him. Her smooth dark brown skin was so soft it reminded him of the chocolate bonbons at the candy store or, better yet, hot cocoa that she would fix for him on cold winter mornings.

Flora and her kitchen had not changed any over the course of his life.

A pot of coffee and a pot of cinnamon water were always on the top of the black cast iron stove. Something was always baking in the ovens. Just thinking of those smells, plus imagining chicken frying, made Drew's stomach rumble.

The kitchen was also where Flora washed clothes in a huge pot in the fireplace and where she ironed. A combination of boiling water with lye soap, starch, coffee, cinnamon, and the aromas of the foods prepared by Flora's hands were, as far as Drew was concerned, the best smells in the world.

He couldn't imagine his home without Flora. She was as much a member of his family as were his parents - for she had been the one he had been with the most.

Most nights as a boy, he ended the evening in the kitchen talking to Flora. She always had a tall glass of milk and a big slice of chocolate sour cream pound cake, still warm from the oven, waiting for him. There was nothing in the world better than Flora's sour cream pound cakes.

As soon as he finished his cake, she would hand Drew a wet cloth to wash his hands, take away his empty plate, and then put her treasured Bible in his hands.

"Read ter me," she would command. "I's loves it w'en yous read."

From a very early age, Drew could read very well - and he thought that Flora couldn't read at all - but when he made a mistake, Flora could tell. She could correct him or pronounce a word that he didn't know without even looking at the words. As he read to her, Flora would sit down in a chair and stitch together pieces of his old clothes for a quilt - a remembrance quilt, she called it.

After the reading would come the bath, if Flora deemed he needed one.

Under her watchful eye he would be forced to sit in the large tin bathtub in front of the kitchen stove and wash his body with the lye soap according to her directions. Even now, every time he took a bath he could hear Flora's booming voice, "Scrub behin' dem ears!"

Every bath night would be the same. Drew would declare, "When I grow up I'm going to live in the Indian Territory with Uncle Tyler. People out there don't bathe but twice a year!"

"Don'tja plan on me ever goin' ter sees yo! 'Long as yo'r under dis roof wit' me, yo'll be clean nos matter ho' many times a day it takes!"

He had been twelve when his father had finally put in indoor bathrooms. He had been delighted that he no longer had to pump the water at the sink and carry it to the tub and that Flora no longer had to pour the scalding hot water from the stove.

Drew was aroused from his memories as he heard the conductor announce that the train would be stopping for a one-hour dinner break in Washington. He was very much at home in Washington's Union Station for he had spent his youth riding the train between Baltimore and Washington to shop, explore the museums, and attend the theater.

The station was full of the hustle and bustle of the excitement of war. Men from all over the country had gathered in the nation's capital to join the fighting. Middle-aged men who had fought each other over thirty-five years before in the War Between the States were now uniting to fight against Spain.

Just as Drew stepped down from the train he thought he heard his name. He turned his head even though he knew his imagination was playing tricks on him, but from down the platform Drew could see his mother and Flora running and screaming his name. Tears swelled in his eyes as he hugged the two women.

"What in the world are you doing here? How did you know when I would be here?"

He knew that there were many trains coming through heading south.

"Your father has the right connections," Drew's mother said with a smile.

She did not say that they had met every train that had come through for the past twelve hours. Drew looked up from his mother's embrace to see his father standing behind her. He, too, embraced his son. This wasn't typical of his father. Drew couldn't remember when they had ever shown so much emotion for each other.

"Times a wastin', child!" Flora's voice boomed. "I's fix all yo favorite foods. Better find somewher' ter eats dem 'for de whistle blows for yo hav' ter goes 'gin."

Drew, with his mother on one side and his father on the other, linked arms and inched through the madness trying to find a place where they could all sit and eat together. Flora followed behind with a picnic hamper full of food.

Just outside the front door of the station they found a grassy hill. Drew helped Flora spread the old and white checked gingham tablecloth that had been used for family outings for years. They sat down among the commotion around them and ate the dinner Flora had prepared. The fried chicken, as usual, was better than any he had ever eaten and the biscuits, although cold, were a treat with honey poured over them.

Then, Drew asked the question Flora had known he would, "Just where is my sour cream pound cake?"

"Right' jeer, Honey," she said as her dark eyes twinkled.

Flora watched in pride as Drew devoured two pieces of her cake. Then he washed it down with the lemonade that they had brought. If they could have brought milk she would have seen her boy's face really light up!

"Flora, do you know where I'm going?"

"Yes sir! You's goin' ter Cuba."

"I'll be in Florida first."

"Florida?"

Flora had a strange look on her face.

"What's wrong?" Drew asked, thinking that he had upset her in some way.

"My mama said that where she be wi' my daddy jus' 'for I's wuz born."

"Tell me more," Drew implored.

His father, however, interrupted their exchange.

"Son, I'm afraid that will have to wait. It's time to get you back to the train."

The four were solemn as they walked back to the platform. As they approached the train, his mother gave Drew a parcel wrapped in brown paper and tied with twine.

"I found this book in the Lighthouse Bookstore," she whispered. "It's about places in Florida. It's by that Yankee woman whom your father says started the last war. The cover says she spends her winters just south of Jacksonville. I thought you might like to read about where you are going."

Drew kissed his mother and whispered his thanks to her. He then hugged his father for the second time that day, but he was still afraid to make eye contact with him. Just before Drew turned to jump on the train, he gave a big squeezing hug to Flora. Flora smiled because she knew that Drew respected his parents, but she was the one he really loved.

"Wait! Mr. Trace, wait!"

Although few called him Trace anymore, Drew knew he would always have that name around Flora.

He stopped only to be shoved and pushed by all of the other returning men. Flora was able to push through the men and hand Drew a bag.

"Dat's fer later."

He smiled at her, knowing she had just given him more chicken and sour cream pound cake. He made his way through the car and returned to his same seat. The car wasn't as crowded as it had been before the stop.

There were no men standing up but there were three men in seats that had been meant for two.

As the train began to move, Drew looked out of the window to try to find his family in the mass of humanity that crowded the platforms. He finally found them just in time to exchange waves as the train began rolling out of the station. All three were waving little American flags just like everyone else. The time together had gone so fast that the dissention between he and his father had not been discussed. Drew and his father found each other's eyes for a brief second. It was enough to reassure Drew that even though his father was totally against this war and his determination to be a part of it, their relationship was not going to be altered as his father had predicted.

Dark came too soon. Drew would have loved to see the countryside as they passed through. He had never been south of Washington into Virginia. His family had traveled north and east. They had made the grand tour of Europe but his father had refused to go south. He knew he was traveling through battlefields where his father, Uncle Tyler, and Dean Tully had used their medical skills. He pictured the guns, the smoke, and the blood of that war over thirty years ago. His body trembled with excitement now because he knew that he would be in the same kind of action in a matter of a few days.

About ten o'clock, he opened the bag Flora had given him. He found just what he had expected: biscuits, fried chicken, and sour cream pound cake. When the men got a whiff of the aroma from his sack, he became an instant friend to everyone. Drew ended up with a drumstick and three bites of cake.

In the dim light from the lantern on the wall behind him, Drew then began to read the book his mother had given him - *Palmetto Leaves* by Harriet Beecher Stowe.

Chapter 5

FLORIDA, THE FIRST TIME
May 1898

Sleep was impossible that night. It was not only the excitement and the noise, it was also the smoke and embers from the engine and the putrid fumes from the cigars of the men inside the car. Worst of all it was the foul odor of the men who were long over-due for baths.

Drew's nostrils could not adjust to the stench. His eyes burned and he fought back tears. The stale air hung low in the over-crowded car and the rankness grew worse with every passing mile. The men most likely had not bathed since the past summer and now were wearing the woolen uniforms they had been issued when they were inducted.

Drew hadn't thought about the change in spring weather from the north to the south when he had proudly put on his blue uniform. Now with the heat, every thread of the woolen fabric cut into his skin. He and his comrades scratched in misery. Surely they would be given new uniforms when they reached Florida.

The train rumbled through the Carolinas as dawn broke on Friday, April 30. Because of heavy rain, it was hard to see the mountains that were on the right side of the train. The rain smelled wonderful and cooled the air somewhat. Drew was a fraction more comfortable because the wool of his jacket wasn't quite as prickly.

As the train lumbered southward, the rain continued. Sometimes the rain was only a drizzle; sometimes it was a thunderstorm with gale force winds. In spite of closed windows and pulled shades, the wooden passenger car as well as its passengers absorbed the dampness.

The heavy rains did not stop more men from getting on the train. Regiments from different states added cars to the train as it rambled south. Drew wondered if all of the other cars were just as packed as the one in which he rode. With all the stops, it was a slow trip. The rain finally stopped about three in the morning. The air once again hung low in the car.

The humidity grabbed at his throat. It was almost impossible to breathe. He had never experienced anything like this before. Most of the men, including Drew, coughed all night with the kind of cough that comes from down deep in the lungs.

Saturday's dawn produced a beautiful glow in the eastern sky and some of the wretchedness of the night before vanished as he watched the early morning rays of the sun play hide and seek through the tall symmetrical Georgia pines.

He was awed at the heights of the virgin pines and how much of the countryside was covered by them. As the sun rose to the tops of the trees, the sky turned to a bright blue. The fluffy white clouds in the sky seemed closer than any he had ever seen. It was much easier to breathe, but now it was unbearably hot.

He had just become accustomed to seeing all of the pines, when the landscape suddenly changed. Giant oaks and other hardwoods replaced the pine forests and on almost every tree long gray strings hung from the branches. The way they hung in clumps reminded him of the beards of some of the men on the train. His initial reaction was that the trees had some type of disease and the growth was the result. He asked the conductor if the entire forest was dying.

"No sur," answered the conductor with a deep southern accent, "That stuff's Spanish moss an' it don't hurt trees atall. It jus' grows an' grows, an' grows. Why, that's one of tha things that makes tha south, tha south."

Drew was relieved to know the trees weren't dying, but he was curious about this thing called Spanish moss. He would remember to ask someone else about the fascinating phenomena as soon as he could.

The rivers also seemed to be getting wider and wider and then the rivers gave way to vast expanses of open water with tall, brown grass growing in it. The wind rippled through the grass, causing it to move as though it were dancing to a waltz.

Drew now understood the descriptions about the coasts of South Carolina and Georgia that he had read in Sidney Lanier's *Marshes of Glyn*. Lanier's descriptions had been quite eloquent trying to convince his readers of the beauty of the salt marshes. When Drew had been required to memorize Lanier's words he had been in awe of the descriptive phrases, but only now could he really appreciate the author's meaning:

"... A league and a league of marsh-grass, waist-high, broad in the blade.
Green, and all of a height, and unflecked with a light or a shade,
Stretch leisurely off, in a pleasant plain..."

The terrain was again different from anything he had ever seen. He didn't recognize half the birds he saw. Several deer spooked by the train darted off into the marshes. The train came almost to a crawl as it approached Savannah. From his window, Drew saw wildlife he had only read about. Alligators and flocks of pelicans were the most unusual. He watched hundreds of tiny crabs scamper in and out of the mud.

Savannah was the breakfast stop. It was necessary for all aboard to detrain to partake of the meal served to the soldiers by local women. The meal was quite a contrast to the Spartan meals they had been served earlier on the trip. Eggs, grits, sausage, slices of ham, biscuits, butter, cane syrup, and coffee were dished up in abundance. This was Drew's first experience with grits.

A tall, lanky auburn-haired boy who couldn't have been over seventeen, told him to add some butter, salt, and pepper to the white corn cereal to improve the flavor. With that addition, he found the taste almost pleasing. The taste of the sweet, thick cane syrup was also new for him. He thought he might like it in time, but at the moment, he would rather have the maple syrup that he had grown up with.

As he ate, he watched the other men. He could tell by the way they approached their meal, which ones had been with him all the way from New York and which ones were recent arrivals. The newest recruits ate everything without hesitation. Most of the New Yorkers were reserved about the new tastes they were encountering. Luckily, they could fill up on the eggs and ham that tasted the same here as at home.

An hour later they were on the last leg of their journey to Jacksonville. Shortly after the train crossed the St. Mary's River, it stopped at a crossroads called Yulee where several cars were switched to another train. The regiments in those cars would be going to a camp in Fernandina, ten miles to the east, to await deployment to Cuba.

Drew knew little about Jacksonville, other than it was a tourist town and many people from the north came during the winter months to escape the harsh northern winters.

As the train pulled into the train yard in Jacksonville, he could see from his window that there was as much activity here as there had been in New York and Washington. It didn't take too long to find out why: The three-year-old red brick terminal was built to meet the new interest in Florida. It was reputed to be the largest in the world and was now the gateway for soldiers from all over who were converging on the city.

Most of the cars on his train would go on to the National Headquarters in Tampa. Still others would go to Lakeland and Key West. There was also some talk of a camp opening in Jacksonville and at the end of the train line near the small town of Miami. Indeed, it seemed that camps were all over Florida.

This southernmost state was a perfect place to drill and prepare for going to Cuba because the tropical climate was not unlike that of the island so close to Florida's southern tip. It also was easy to transport troops on the fairly extensive railroad network that ran down both coasts.

When the train's steam whistle blew the signal that it was coming into the station, Drew grabbed his Army issued bedroll, simultaneously with his black medical bag, and gathered with the other soldiers in the aisle. All were ready to disembark as soon as the train came to a stop.

As soon as his feet touched the Florida soil he saw a placard with "Lt.

Thomas Duncan" painted in bold, black letters. He immediately went over to the private who held the sign. The two exchanged salutes, a few words, and were quickly on their way.

They stopped only once, to allow Drew the opportunity to buy a paper.

He had heard the shouts of the paperboy a block before they got to him.

"Dewey takes Manila! Dewey takes Manila!" the lad shouted over and over again.

Drew's escort took him to a small hotel across the street from the station where the private produced a key and saluted once again.

"Here is the key to your room, Sir. I've been ordered to advise you to clean up, rest, eat, and then report to duty at the terminal at 1600 hours. There's a new uniform for you on the bed. Do you have any questions?"

"Just double checking, 1600 is 4 p.m., right?"

"Yes, Sir."

Drew took his roll and bag upstairs to his room, which he found beautifully decorated with wallpaper that was bright green with white palm trees. The white wicker furniture gave a vacation feel to the room. On the bed lay two pairs of white cotton pants and two white shirts. He looked for a wardrobe to hang up his clothes but saw none. Instead, he found a door that revealed a small closet, permanently built into the room.

Behind a second door he found a bathroom, which was another nice surprise. When he saw a door directly across from the one in which he was standing, he realized he would share the bath with the next room. Drew was delighted to have such deluxe accommodations for he had anticipated he would share a bath with the entire floor, not just one other room.

He quickly slid the bolt on the door to the other room and stripped off his woolen uniform while the tub filled with hot water. As he slipped into the steaming water, he thought of the men he had been with the past two days. He wondered if they had been required to take a bath! And he prayed they also got a change of clothes!

The next thing Drew was aware of was that the hot water had turned cold and that his skin was water-soaked and wrinkled to a prune-like texture. The warm bath had relaxed him so that he had fallen asleep in the tub. He jumped out of the tub and ran to the dresser to check the time on his pocket watch. It would be a disaster if he were late to his first assignment.

"Thank God!" he exclaimed.

Drew had just enough time to shave, get dressed, eat, and get back to the terminal.

A short time later, Drew bounded down the stairs in his new uniform, anxious to see what the next phase of life in the military would be like.

He followed the sound of voices and the aroma of food.

A large group of men were helping themselves from a table laden with food. He filled a plate for himself with large portions of country fried steak smothered in white gravy, mashed potatoes, field peas, turnip greens, steaming ears of yellow corn, sliced tomatoes and cucumbers, and biscuits. A large pitcher of water and hot coffee were available as beverages.

As he looked for a place to sit, a tall husky man about his own age asked him to have a seat and introduced himself as Lt. Doug Butterfield.

"Welcome to Florida," Butterfield said. "Don't get spoiled with this hotel's accommodations. The camps are living hells. We're lucky that we can stay here a few days. I'm setting up a training camp not far from here. Tampa is the embarkation point and most all of the troops have been sent there but it is way over crowded. Camp Cuba Libre' will be ready to open there in a couple of weeks, giving the Tampa camp some relief."

After eating his meal and exchanging more small talk with Lt. Butterfield, Drew excused himself and went across the street to the train terminal. He found the Medical Corps easily and saluted a captain who was seated behind a desk.

"Lt. Duncan reporting for duty, Sir!"

"Lt. Duncan! Boy, am I glad to see you! You can dismiss the formality as long as you are here. We're too busy for that." Extending his hand he introduced himself as Lou Sparks.

"Every man who passes through this station has to get a physical," said Sparks, "just in case one wasn't given when he enlisted. Did you get one when you enlisted in New York?"

"No. I just filled out paperwork."

"Well, the Army wants to correct slip-ups like yours. The same thing has happened all over. Only if a soldier has proof of an examination will he be able to pass through this terminal without one. You need to undress and see first hand just what you will be putting all of the soldiers through."

Drew plunged into his assignment giving physicals. For the first time, Drew worked with women who were Red Cross volunteers. They helped with the paperwork and nursed any of the men who needed their assistance. Negro women assisted with the Negro men, who were segregated from the others.

Many times, even after a long day of work, Drew found that he couldn't fall asleep, even though every fiber of his body ached. During those times he would walk or ride on a streetcar to explore the city. Not far to the east of the train terminal were wharfs that reminded him of Baltimore. There were also multitudes of fine stores on Bay Street where one could buy anything. Every store, he discovered, carried alligator teeth. 'A Souvenir of Florida' proclaimed the signs over the boxes containing the teeth.

One day as he walked into Malloy's Haberdashery, Drew heard an explosion at the back of the store, which opened up to the St. John's River. He ran to see Mr. Malloy lowering a double-barreled-shotgun.

"Got me another one!"

"What?"

"A gator, of course!"

"You just shoot alligators for the fun of it?"

"Yes siree bobtail! I love it. Want to try? We have thousands, if not millions, here in the St. Johns. Besides where do you think all those souvenir teeth come from? Someone will find the dead gator later and get the teeth."

Drew found the activity disgusting, especially when he saw the red trails of blood coming from the alligators' gaping sides.

Drew turned to leave Mr. Malloy with his sport and almost ran into a large, rugged-looking individual whose dark wrinkled skin showed he had spent a great deal of time out in the sun. The man, who stood several inches taller than Drew, extended his hand. With dancing eyes and a big grin from under his walrus mustache, the stranger introduced himself.

"Broward's my name, but most folks just call me Sheriff," the large man bellowed.

Something about Broward's speech and mannerisms was charismatic. His presence overpowered the room. Drew imagined the sheriff's personality captivated most people.

"Going to Cuba? I've made the run a number times myself," he laughed, winking at the same time. "I'm the captain of *The Three Friends.*"

Drew let the new arrival assume he knew the significance of *The Three Friends.*

He listened intently to the conversation that followed between Broward and the store's proprietor.

"When did you get back from Washington, Sheriff?" asked Malloy.

"A few days ago. They dismissed the case of treason against me. Seems as if I am not an enemy of the people any more since we are now at war with the Spaniards. Now no one cares that I helped the Cuban rebels. It sure feels good not being an outlaw any more."

"Sheriff, you were never an outlaw around here. Hell, all of us would have taken men and guns - I mean, stuff - to the Cuban rebels if we had a chance or the means like you did. Those Cubans in the cigar plant do a bunch of business in this town. When Marti' was here getting support for the Cubans, he came in here and bought a hat. He had a beautiful young Cuban girl with him..."

Drew stopped listening to the conversation when he glanced at the wall clock and saw the time.

"Please excuse me, gentlemen. I need to get back to the station. It was nice to meet you, Sheriff."

As Drew was leaving, he heard Malloy ask the sheriff, "I'm assuming you will be running again now that you won't be going to prison?'

A far busier section of the city, not far from Bay Street and Malloy's haberdashery, was LaVilla.

Enlisted men as well as officers found their way to the local brothels that thrived from their business. The district was close enough to the terminal for the men to have horizontal refreshments in the few hours they spent in Jacksonville before boarding the train that would take them to their camps.

Once Drew took the wrong turn on his way back to the terminal from Bay Street and ended up in the middle of the area. Women of all ages, sizes, and colors were on the verandas laughing and talking. Two, painted and scantily dressed, turned their attention to Drew as he walked by.

"Come on in, Baby," they teased. "It's fun inside."

"You'll never find better for your dollar."

Another voice called, "Baby, I's can give you wha' yous want fer two bits."

Drew tried not to make eye-contact with the women but it was hard to focus on just where he was and how to get back to the station. He finally got his bearings after at least twenty solicitations. As he rounded the corner of Davis Street heading south to Bay, he heard, "You don't know what you're missing."

He hadn't gone too much farther when he met Lt. Butterfield, who gave him a knowing look with his dancing crystal blue eyes. Drew just smiled.

Not too many nights later, however, Drew did have occasion to visit the inside of one of the brothels. He was eating a late dinner when a young private came screaming into the hotel.

"Is there a doctor in here? We need someone desperately!"

"What's the trouble?" asked Drew.

"There's a fight going on at Miss Alma's Place. They have knives and there's blood all over the place. I think they're going to kill each other! Please come quick!"

Drew and Jim, another medic, grabbed their medical bags and followed the private to the heart of the red light district. Girls gave them the usual solicitations as they ran by. When they reached the brothel, Miss Alma, the proprietor, met them at the front door.

She led them up a narrow staircase to the upper floor. Drew found himself admiring the woman, who, although well past middle age, was beautiful. A hint of perfume, impeccable make-up, and beautiful, fashionable clothes like she wore would command the attention of most men, even outside her place of business, Drew thought.

Miss Alma stopped at the doorway of a dimly lit room.

"This is just awful, just awful. I hate it when this happens. Johnny's lying there by the window and Bill is... Where's Bill? He was here when I went down stairs."

"Has someone called the police, Ma'am?"

"Yes, but they take their sweet time about coming down here - except when they're horny."

She sent a seductive glance at Drew that relayed a message he chose to ignore.

Jim entered the room first and rushed over to the man lying on the floor by the bed. He took the man's pulse and confirmed that he was dead. There was little surprise at the pronouncement - the inert form had a big butcher's knife stuck into the middle section of his back.

Drew asked the people standing in the hall, "Where's the other person? Is he still in the house?"

No one responded.

Drew walked on into the bedroom. The scene was the most gruesome sight he had ever seen. Blood covered everything. There obviously had been a horrendous fight before the stabbing. Chairs were broken, the mirror over the dresser was smashed and the lace curtains were ripped from their rods and the blood stained material lay in piles on the floor. Anything and everything that was breakable was broken. There was a trail of blood that led through the door in which they were standing.

"Did anyone see this?" Drew yelled as he ran down the hall following a path of blood. Jim ran behind him. The trail led to the back stairs and down to the alley and was easy to follow with the help of the moonlit sky.

"Look!" yelled Drew and Jim simultaneously as they spotted the prostrate figure of a man lying in a pool of blood under a big oak tree. Apparently the other victim had done a nice carving on this man's head and chest before he was stabbed.

"This man is dead too," Drew said after feeling for his pulse

"I don't know how he made it this far. He has no left ear and his throat has been sliced in several places. It is amazing that he even had enough strength to stab the other guy."

"Maybe he didn't," Jim commented.

"Do you think that a third party was involved?"

"It looks like that to me."

"No one followed us. I find that hard to believe," commented a perplexed Drew.

Back at the brothel Drew and Jim were greeted as if nothing had happened.

Jim asked, "Have the police shown up?"

"It could be hours," said Miss Alma knowingly, as if she had expert knowledge.

"Hours! We need to get back to the terminal. It's past time for our duty to begin."

"You can't leave 'til the police come," said Miss Alma as she brought the medics two huge pieces of chocolate cake that she insisted they eat. "Come on, fellas. You act like someone died," she giggled. "Joe, play us some music.

We don't have to sit around all gloomy. You know Bill and Johnny would be singing and dancing by now. Play for the boys, Joe!"

An elderly Negro man, dressed in elegant clothes ten years out of date, sat down at an old upright piano and started playing popular Ragtime tunes.

Miss Alma then turned to Jim and Drew, "It might be hours before you can go. Why don't you two have a little fun? You can have any girl you want. It's on the house!"

Drew saw her signal the unoccupied girls across the room with her eyes. Two of the most beautiful girls Drew had ever seen came over and sat in the men's laps. The two buxom, black-haired beauties playfully took the cake from the men and began feeding them with their fingers.

Another time both Drew and Jim might have enjoyed their company, but tonight they were in no mood for sex or even games. They were sick at what they had witnessed and sicker still at the attitudes of the occupants of the house. Knowing they were late to their duty added anxiety.

Drew was relieved when two policemen arrived a few minutes later.

"What has happened here now, Miss Alma?" the short roly-poly officer said with a rich base voice.

"Well, Pete, Johnny and Bill got into it again over Lillie. But this time they killed each other. Johnny is upstairs in Lillie's room. Bill's down under the hanging oak in the alley."

"Killed? Are you sure they are dead?"

"Of course I'm sure. These soldiers are doctors and they said that they're dead."

"Well, I see you got more than you bargained for when you came here for your fun," the officer said sarcastically to Drew and Jim.

"No Sir, we..." said Drew trying to explain. But the policeman had turned his attention to Miss Alma.

"You know this is going to close you down, don't you? The people of this city can turn their heads only so much."

"Now Pete, you know this ain't my fault or the fault of my girls. I run a clean, respectful place here. Besides Sam won't let you shut me down."

"Sam might be the richest man in town and your number one customer, but I think things have gone a little too far this time. Let me use your phone."

After the policemen had returned from his call, Drew asked if he and Jim could leave.

"No sir, all witnesses are to stay put."

"But sir, we were called in after it happened to see if we could do anything. We only confirmed what was apparent when we arrived. Both men were dead."

"Well, you still can't go. You doctors will have to sign the death certificates."

"We aren't doctors. We are just medics."

"Grrrrrrrrrrrrrrr. I will be glad when all this Army mess is over and I will know who is who and what is what around here again. Alma, call Dr. Powell to come over here, pronto!"

As the officer turned to walk up the stairs to check out Johnny and the damage, Drew pleaded again.

"We really need to get back to our duty."

"Go. But leave your names with Alma so we can get in touch with you if there's a need."

Drew and Jim wrote down their names on a pad Miss Alma produced. On the way out Drew looked at the occupants and the visitors of Miss Alma's. They were talking, laughing and singing to the music Joe played. Drew wondered how many of them knew just what had happened in that upstairs room.

The two medics walked briskly back to the terminal. Both were absorbed in their own thoughts about what they had just witnessed and made the journey in silence.

Drew was concerned about the shift that they had almost completely missed and knew Jim was thinking similar thoughts. What kind of trouble would they be in? Luckily only a few had arrived that day to be processed. It was necessary for only one medic to be on duty for the next shift, so Drew took the first half and Jim took the last.

Not long after the experience at Miss Alma's, Drew found other sections of Jacksonville more to his liking.

One afternoon walk found him at the corner of Beaver and Davis where there was a large mattress factory where he was intrigued to find that the Spanish moss he had so recently learned about was used to stuff mattresses.

He watched as workers gathered moss that had been drying in the sun, listening with interest to a conversation.

"I heard that we're goin' to stuff the seats that go in those new fangled horseless carriages," he overheard one of the workers say.

"I hope we don't stop making mattresses. How many people can afford to get one of them contraptions?"

"I don't know, but I do know that the seat will be comfortable. I can't imagine sleeping on anything else but a moss mattress."

In the next few weeks, from different sources, Drew learned that the moss was in the same botanical family as the pineapple and that some Southerners boiled it to make an herbal tea. Others used it for various home remedies, including drawing out the poison from a spider bite and stopping bleeding. This was an amazing, versatile plant.

One Sunday when given a rare afternoon off from his medical duties, he and Lt. Butterfield toured the city in Butterfield's buggy. They enjoyed lunch with Dr. and Mrs. Benjamin Para whose meal was as exquisite as their home on Riverside Avenue, referred to by the locals as "The Row." Dr. Para, a leading physician in the city, and his wife, like so many of the city's wealthy citizens, opened their homes to the young officers who were temporarily assigned to their city.

Later that afternoon Drew and Butterfield visited the camp that Butterfield was making ready for the overflow from Tampa. Located north of the city near the Fernandina Railroad in a new community known as Springfield, the homes were not as pretentious as the ones in Riverside but were comfortable and equally cared for.

Drew and Butterfield had their evening meal at Jacksonville's largest, and by far the most expensive, hotel, the St. James.

"I didn't know if you had time to walk this far on those treks you take during your breaks."

Drew interrupted Butterfield. "Only once for a quick glance."

"This is where all the high-ranking officers stay when they are here," said Butterfield, "but I brought you here for a reason other than to gawk at the big shots. Look out of that window. Do you see what they are building down in the park? That's a statue to honor the Rebs," Butterfield said. "They're planning to unveil it in June. It will be ironic if they invite all the soldiers that will be here. Some of them will be Yanks."

"I hope that thirty-three years has mended the wounds of most," Drew said. "It took twenty years for my family to come to some kind of peace when divided loyalties tore it apart. Just look at all of the former Confederate officers who are ready to lead us into battle in Cuba for a common goal. I think someone timed the unveiling ceremony well. Then again, we could all be in Cuba by that time and the ceremony can just be for the citizens of this city."

As Drew and Butterfield left the hotel they walked over to a man in the park who was sketching at an easel. They silently admired the charcoal sketch of the St. James Hotel but didn't say anything until the artist looked up. Lt. Butterfield introduced himself and Drew.

"Frederick Remington," the artist mumbled as he returned to his work without saying another word.

Both of them recognized the name of the artist. Remington was in the employee of Randolph Hearst whose newspapers had published many of the sketches Remington had made of the war in Cuba. His drawings had given subsistence to the news articles and editorials demanding that the United States aid the Cubans in their fight for freedom.

Drew's work continued around the clock and he began to wonder if and when he would ever get out of the Jacksonville train station. He thought he would waste away if he didn't have more to do than deal with the constant parade of men lined up for inoculations. Thousands of men had been processed and had gone on to the training camps further south. What was the hold up for him? He was ready to move out! He knew the killings and travesties in Cuba had become more heinous since the sinking of *The Maine*. He wondered when the invasion would come and he wondered if he would stay in Jacksonville until then or if he, too, would go to a training camp?

Orders finally arrived on May 23 for Drew to report to Tampa. He dreaded another train ride! Had he only been in Jacksonville for three weeks? It had seemed like a lifetime.

The Flying Cracker was the high-speed train that made daily runs between Jacksonville and Tampa. Making the trip in seven and a half hours, including a fifty-minute lunch stop, the train was a far cry from the crowded car on which he had come from New York.

He shared a private car with three other low-ranking officers and Frederick Remington, who recognized him. Remington explained that he was on his way to the Army's Headquarters in Tampa. He would remain there and sketch the generals and other key players while they planned their strategies. He had been ordered to ride in the flotilla that was to leave from Tampa.

The rest of the men exchanged only a few words, for they were all in deep thought or reading the newspapers that were in the car for their convenience. Drew's attention, however, was drawn outside and to the countryside they were passing through. The flat piney woods near Jacksonville gave way to open prairies of palms and palmettos.

Giant palm trees stood in clusters; others, by themselves. They rose straight and tall against the sky. There were also stands of massive live oak trees like he had first seen from the train to Jacksonville. The trees were again canopied with flowing Spanish moss.

As the train moved through the countryside, Drew admired the big cumulus clouds set against the sapphire sky. He had never seen clouds - or sky - as beautiful. He wanted to reach out and touch them. For a moment, he felt it was within his power.

He didn't see much wildlife other than the thousands of birds that at times darkened the sunny skies. Scrawny cattle and hogs roamed the prairies. He saw no fences other than wooden ones around the homesteads he passed. Corn and other vegetables were already being harvested. In Maryland and Connecticut the crops were barely in the ground.

The houses were different from any he had ever seen. Some were one-room log cabins. Others looked as if two cabins had been attached to each other with an open hall down the middle without any doors. He could look straight through to the back yards. Each house sat a few feet off of the ground and had high pitched, shingled roofs. Most had a porch all the way across the front or down the side. The yards around the houses were barren of grass.

Drew waved to scrawny, barefooted children. From their places along the tracks, they returned his wave.

Three hours out of Jacksonville the train began to slow down. He couldn't believe it was lunchtime already. At the small Silver Springs station house, the conductor directed the passengers to a boarding house not far from the station. They walked down a hill along a dusty, sandy road to Brown's Boarding House. Gusts of cool air rising from the nearby river made walking in the hot noonday sun almost bearable.

The noon meal was laid out on long tables around which all were seated. Once again Drew was amazed at the amount and the variety of food that was quickly passed from one end of the table to the other.

Choices this time were dishes of corn, field peas, greens, potatoes, tomatoes, and carrots, all fresh from a nearby garden. Fried fish, chicken, pork chops, and huge slices of ham were also passed on heaping platters. Hot biscuits, which the servers referred to as cathead biscuits, were brought out regularly. Most of the hungry soldiers ate at least three, spreading each with fresh butter, honey or cane syrup. To help wash down the meal, fresh milk and lemonade were also served.

Clear, cool water could be ladled from large galvanized buckets that were set up on separate tables. Dessert was blackberry cobbler.

Drew had enjoyed his meals in Jacksonville, but this was Heaven.

He finished his meal quickly and decided it would be to his advantage to walk awhile and let some of the large meal settle and to stretch his legs a bit before returning to the train. He was hoping he might see the springs mentioned in *Palmetto Leaves.*

He headed toward the river. As he approached, he saw a paddleboat coming around the bend. The railroad depot was unique, he realized, in the fact that it was not only a railroad station but a point of embarkation for boats. A few steps further and he was viewing one of the most magnificent sights of his lifetime, a beautiful body of crystal-clear water. He knew he was looking at the springs he had read and heard about.

At first glance, the body of water seemed to be a lake with a river flowing into it. On further examination, the river was flowing from the lake! The sparkling water was so transparent he could see the fish swimming as clearly as if they were in a fish tank. He was enthralled with the varieties and the different depths at which he could see schools of fish swimming together.

Several types of water birds were in the tall cypress and palm trees that lined the banks. Some of the birds were small and white; some were gray stork-like creatures; some, after plummeting into the water, raised only their heads and looked like snakes standing vertically to the water. Further down the riverbank he saw movement and splashing. His mouth dropped as he realized he was watching dozens of alligators sunning themselves as well as swimming along the shore.

"Hi there, young feller," yelled a man who was fishing at the dock.

Glad to hear the friendly greeting, Drew walked down the bank toward the man.

"They call me old Pete round jeer," said the crusty-skinned old man. "You on your way to Tamper?"

The man stopped briefly before continuing. There was an obvious catch in his throat.

"My son headed that away. He were in tha Navy an' he were so proud that he was goin' to Cuber."

After a brief pause, he whispered, "He went down on *The Maine.*"

Drew's heart went out to the old man.

"I'm truly sorry about your son, sir. I wish that it hadn't taken the death of so many of our boys to get us involved. My uncle is a doctor with the Red Cross in Cuba. He's been writing me for three years about the killings and beatings of the Cubans at the hands of the Spanish."

"Are you on your way jere?" the father asked, as his voice became stronger and more resolute. "If'n you is, I wantja go an' kill all those Spanish sons of bitches fer my son."

Drew didn't mention the fact that he was in the Medical Corps and would not be fighting. At the first opportunity, Drew changed the subject.

"Can you tell me about this lake and river? The river seems to start right here."

"I'll tell you what I know an' I know as much as anybody in these here parts. I've lived here in tha scrub all my life. This ain't a lake. It's tha head of tha Silver Run. It begins right over yonder."

He pointed to the river where the alligators lined the shore, then continued.

"See them pearly white bubbles? There be a spring down there eighty feet. It's called tha Silver 'cause of them white bubbles an' tha tiny bits of limestone an' shell that's in tha water. We jest call it tha 'Big Boil'. Never stops flowing. They say that fifty million gallons of water flows out of there a day. Tha spring forms the Silver Run, which runs into tha Oklawaha. Why, you could get on a boat jer an' go see tha Queen of England without even steppin' on dry land! Yes sir!"

"All winter long steamboats come down every day all of tha way from Palatka an' Jacksonville," he continued, "but this time of year, only a couple of boats come a week. We git thousands of people a year a'coming to see this here spring! I thought all of you Yankees already knew about our little corner of tha world."

The old man pointed to several odd shaped boats tied up at another dock.

"See them boats over there? I built them. Betcha never been on one like them. They have glass in tha bottom. You can go out in tha water an' see tha springs an' tha fish. It's a good-looking sight. Wanna go? I can get someone to take you."

"I'd love to but I have a train to catch. I'll be back someday, though! Hey, that alligator is huge!"

Drew pointed to a monster reptile not ten feet away from where they were standing.

"Aren't you afraid he will attack you?"

"Naw. He ain't never bothered us. We figure he's our friend an' protector - unless you feed him, of course. Figure he's a good twelve footer. Thar's plenty of people who would love his hide".

"Who would ever want to feed one of those things," asked Drew. "And why would it hurt anything if you did?"

"They git use' to humans feedin' them an' they grow accustomed to it. Then one day someone will come along without no food an' that gator will eat'm fer lunch."

Drew couldn't take his eyes off the huge reptile or two slick-skinned otters chasing each other in and out of the crystal clear water within a few feet of the alligator.

"Ya see, that old bull gator ain't gonna hurt nobody, but that one over there is another matter - if'n ya get close to er."

Drew's eyes followed in the direction of the pointed finger of his new acquaintance.

"That little gal over there is guarding her nest. She ain't somethin' you wanta fool with."

A fascinated Drew enjoyed the spectacular scene until he heard someone calling his name from the direction of the boarding house announcing that the train was getting ready to leave. They were also calling out to Remington.

Drew began running back toward the train and was joined by Remington, sketchpad in hand. Drew had been so focused on the wonder of what he saw he hadn't noticed Remington.

Both were panting as they ran to catch the train that was already moving slowly along the tracks.

By the time they settled in their seats the engine started pouring on more steam and began to move rapidly through the wilds of Florida.

"Did you go down by the river?" Drew asked the captain as he sat down in his seat.

"No, what was special about that river? I figure a river is a river. We found a billiard table and spent our time playing. We were wondering where you went off to."

Drew watched as Remington completed a sketch he had started while they were stopped at Silver Springs. He had captured the entire magnificent picture, the springs, the river, the animals, and the birds.

Like so many others, Drew had thought of Florida as a mosquito-infested, no man's land. He was beginning to see it in an entirely different light.

Sally Settle

Chapter 6

TAMPA
May 1898

The train pulled into Tampa just before dusk. Drew quickly sensed that things were going to be much different from Jacksonville. How right his first impression was!

He found the Medical Corps desk at the Tampa Terminal manned by a private. The private found Drew's name on his list and directed him to a wagon that would take him to the camp at the eastern edge of the city. He was barely able to squeeze onto the loaded wagon as it began to pull away.

Drew could smell the stench of the encampment before he could see anything. Soon thousands of tents came into sight. The tents of each regiment were together, but each regiment was some distance from the other.

The camp had been set up quickly to accommodate the thousands of recruits that had been sent to Tampa. It was constructed on very low swampland and water stood throughout the camp. Mud was ankle deep between the pools of water and the smell was horrendous.

Drew walked by gravely ill men stretched out everywhere, many of whom were crying out in delirium, probably suffering from swamp vapors - malaria. With one look, he knew he would probably stay here for a long time. Would he ever see action in Cuba?

He was shown to his sleeping tent close to the larger hospital tent that served all of the regiments. It was barely big enough for one, but he would share it with another medic. On a raised wooden platform were rolls of woolen blankets and small cots. There was no place to put clothes except to keep them in the Army bedrolls.

Drew found out later that only officers had cots. The enlisted men slept on the ground or on wooden planks on the ground, if they were lucky. When he was introduced to his commanding officer he extended his hand to shake it. Because of the informality in Jacksonville, he had forgotten Army protocol.

"Soldier, I expect a salute when you stand before me. Is that clear?"

"Yes, Sir!"

"You will have the rest of the night off. Report at 0500 hours to the hospital. Is that understood?"

"Yes, Sir!"

"Dismissed," barked his new commander.

Before returning to his quarters, Drew wandered through the camp to get his bearings. He found sick men everywhere, both in tents and out on the open ground. When he located the latrine he found it was only a ditch dug out of the sand. The odor was horrendous. Drew vomited.

Near the fly-infested latrine, Drew passed men bathing in cold water they caught in buckets as it came to them down long troughs. They were "showering" by pouring the water over themselves from the buckets.

"God knows where that water came from," thought Drew. "No wonder all of these men are sick."

Drew's stomach was queasy, whether from hunger or sickness, he did not know. It had been over eight hours since he had eaten in Silver Springs, so he sought out the chow tent.

However, he decided he wasn't hungry enough to stand in the long line and started back to his tent.

"Lieutenant!"

Drew turned to see a pale skinned lieutenant with sandy brown hair and an impish grin.

"I really don't think you want to eat what they serve us, but if you do, follow me."

Drew followed his fellow officer to the front of the line.

"Rank does have some privileges," the young man laughed, "but you might not agree with me when you taste this food. At least we don't have to stand in line! You will almost get used to it after you have been here for a while. Dinner is better than the rest of the meals. You can't see what you're eating."

With one taste of the meat, Drew spit it out. "This is rotten!"

"Yep!"

Drew ate the hash brown potatoes but left the meat. He thought back to Lt. Butterfield and his predictions about camp food. Surely, not even Butterfield would dream that rotten meat would be served.

Drew and his new companion, Tom, talked for the next two hours. Tom was from Kentucky. He had just graduated from Asbury, a small Methodist college near Lexington. His parents wanted him to be a minister, but he was still trying to decide his calling. He had found his way to the Army and was serving in the infantry. He joked that he was trying to train the recruits in something that he knew nothing about.

Just as Drew settled into his bed and was about to write in his journal, he heard a bugle blow *Taps*. He knew that he was really in the army when he had to go to sleep and rise to the sounds of a bugle. He closed his eyes and saw his nice warm cozy dorm room. He could still be there! Had he made the right choice? Right or not, it was too late to change course now.

The late May weather in Tampa was miserable. The air was still and the sun was bright. The temperature reached into the 90s in the afternoons and almost every day huge thunderheads rolled across the sky dumping out torrents of rain in massive electrical storms. After the rains stopped, the air was steamy, sultry, and muggy. The water stood even deeper in the already saturated ground.

The enlisted men still wore the woolen suits that had been issued when they joined. The clothing, the heat that the men were not accustomed to, and the impatience of most wondering when they would be shipped out to Cuba, made for short fuses and many fights.

The Medical Corps worked around the clock as they did in Jacksonville. Here the weather, the bugs, and the diseases were the enemies. The food was the worst garbage that anyone ever tried to eat.

In addition to the wounds resulting from the fights, thousands of men suffered from food poisoning and dysentery. Fevers, pneumonia, influenza, bronchitis, and worst of all, malaria, was rampant. Hundreds of men died without ever setting foot in Cuba.

Drew's on-the-job training was better than he would have ever had in a hospital setting in Baltimore or New Haven. A doctor would never have been required to empty bedpans and clean up all the vomit that he did. He was certainly getting hands on experience!

He was glad to have the help of the women nurses of the Red Cross but he felt sorry for them having to live in such substandard conditions. Four big burly privates were assigned to guard the nurses' tents night and day.

During Drew's short breaks, he wrote letters to his father and Dean Tully about the conditions of the camp.

One improvement finally came when the enlisted men where issued cotton 'campaign' shirts to wear. The cotton clothing was much more suitable for the hot climate, but they were still required to wear their woolies at formal drills.

Lye was brought in for the latrines and that improved the smell of the camp a thousand fold. Water still had to be boiled before it was drinkable.

There was nothing one could do about the bugs that came out at night. The only comfort from them was to stay close to a fire or a lantern. The light drew some bugs and the smoke from the fire kept the biting ones away. The extra heat generated by the fire, though, was not appreciated in the hot, humid night air.

In the daytime the sand gnats were more of a problem than any of the nocturnal bugs. They were everywhere; biting, swarming around eyes, and, invariably, getting sucked into their mouths. They also had to contend with the stinging of yellow flies and horse flies. The Florida insects did not endear the tropics to anyone.

Troops began training schedules and the volunteers learned how to handle horses, sabers, revolvers, and carbines. Drew watched as the troops shaped up and matured right before his eyes.

Gradually sanitation improved and, consequently, the men's sicknesses decreased Even so, as one man recovered, his bed was quickly taken by another who had been on the outside.

Little by little those outside were gone and the medical corps began working one eight-hour shift a day.

At last Drew had time to take in his surroundings. The days continued to be miserable but the nights were almost pleasant.

The stars were brilliant, seemingly so close that one could reach out and touch the twinkling lights. The sounds of the night included frogs, crickets, and owls, each species serenading in unique harmony.

There were some sounds that Drew did not recognize. No one else seemed to know them either. Some South Carolinians told him that the loud bellows they heard both day and night were the mating calls of the bull gators from the nearby swamps.

Drew felt ignorant for the first time in his life. He knew nothing about a lot of the birds, animals, and night sounds that he heard. There were no books to refer to and most of the men either did not know or didn't care to share. But, even with the heat and the misery, Drew was intrigued with this wild territory of Florida.

He promised himself that one day, under different circumstances, he would come back and investigate the area in depth.

The camp was too removed from downtown Tampa to visit the city even when the workload got lighter; however, he was able to go to the Cuban section, Ybor City, on occasion. The trips were always at night, with other soldiers, and for the purpose of drinking and women, both of which Drew couldn't get enough of.

The morning after one of the diversions to La Hacienda de Cuba Libre', Drew woke up with a smile on his face. He had met three interesting men and he couldn't stop thinking about the conversation of the inland sea and the wonders of interior Florida. His smile faded when he walked into the new mess tent only to hear of the happenings during the night at another encampment not far away.

"Hear those niggers did some real cutting last night. Blood was everywhere, they say."

"Yeah, leave it to the niggers. There won't be any left to fight the Spaniards. They'll kill each other first."

"They should be sent back to Africa where they came from."

"I don't understand why they are here anyway. Are they expecting us to fight with them?"

"I ain't fighting 'side of any nigger. They can't expect me to."

"Nope, I hear that they will be sent ahead of us. They'll git kilt; then we'll follow and kill the dirty Spaniards."

Drew had no idea what the talk was all about but he understood the hatred in the voices of the men. The attitudes made him mad, but there was nothing he could do because he knew very few people who thought of the Negro as being equal to the white man. Cruel jokes and comments putting the Negro race down were constant in his circle of friends, too, even though most of them, like himself, had been raised by Negro women. There seemed to be a time in life when the proverbial line was drawn in the sand and the women who raised them went from being a nurturing mother figure to servant.

He couldn't understand why so many people put the race down. What had been so different about the way he had been raised for him not to have the same racial hatred?

He sighed as he sat down with a group of officers.

"What happened over at the Negro camp last night?"

"There was quite a ruckus but it could have been a lot worse, I hear. Some of them saw a white soldier fire at a Negro child. She didn't get hurt but the firing of the gun incensed them. They became extremely angry and things got out of control. I hear that about thirty were hurt real bad."

"Did some of our doctors or medics go over there to help with the wounded?" Drew asked, wondering why he had not been called.

"Are you kidding? That was no place a white man should be."

"That would have been a real blood bath," said a captain who had been silent. "I want to take my chances fighting for our country, not niggers."

As the sick became well and returned to their regiments, Drew's duties became routine. His main duty now was to check on those still sick in bed. Many of these now were the men who had visited the women who had set up businesses near the camp and in Ybor and, consequently, had to be treated for gonorrhea and syphilis. Sometimes his job was just to check the stock of Cuban Rum that had been confiscated and then stockpiled in the tent for medicinal reasons.

Drew's boredom grew with each passing day.

On a hot, sultry afternoon as Drew left the medical tent, he heard the voice of Captain Evans call his name.

His voice resounded across the camp.

Drew walked over and saluted.

"I don't know who you are or what you have done but I have orders for you to report to Headquarters."

The tone of his voice was that of a very suspicious man.

"There will be a taxi here to pick you up at 1800 hours."

"Yes sir," Drew saluted. "Do you have my orders?"

Drew thought a paper would accompany the oral order.

"No papers. Just report to the Tampa Bay Hotel".

"Yes sir."

Drew saluted again. He took out his watch and knew he only had an hour to clean up and get dressed. As he poured cold water over his body, he wondered why he would be called to the Fifth Army Corps Headquarters. Only the top brass assembled there. They came out to the camp whenever they thought it was necessary and that wasn't very often.

He knew no one who had gone to Headquarters. Was he about to get orders to move out? Why would he have to go to Headquarters just to get his orders?

He wore his blue woolen suit for the first time since arriving in Jacksonville. Although it was hot and scratchy in the heat, there was not a wrinkle to be found.

His boots were spit polished. He tried his best to stay out of the mud all of the way to the edge of the camp where the horse-drawn open taxi was waiting.

The taxi headed west into the city turning onto Seventh Avenue. Even though they had gone only a short distance, it was as if Drew had been transported by a magic carpet to a foreign land. Seeing Ybor City by day was far different than the late evening and night, the times he had been there before. He hadn't noticed or cared about the things he was seeing now. He and his fellow soldiers only had their minds on La Hacienda and what was within. Drew noticed for the first time that most of the street names, the restaurant names, and the shop names were in Spanish.

There were a few shops with what appeared to have German words with Spanish underneath. Drew wondered why there were Germans in a Spanish neighborhood. Balconies overhung the sidewalks in true Spanish style. Every so often a side gate would be open and he could see patios behind the shops and houses. Brilliant colored flowers bloomed everywhere. In the beds planted near to the sidewalks, flowering vines ran up the buildings, and flowers bloomed in pots on the balconies.

The streets were jammed with people. Soldiers out-numbered the civilians four to one. Shouting, laughing, and music seemed to pour out from every open door.

As the taxi passed La Hacienda, his eyes locked with Salieta's. He waved and blew her a kiss. A puzzled expression crossed her face and then she ran after the carriage yelling for it to stop.

"Stop! Por favor!"

Drew tapped the driver and motioned for him to stop.

As soon as the carriage came to a stop, Salieta jumped in and began smothering Drew with kisses. He pushed her away, afraid that his uniform would get dirty and wrinkled. Drew finally stilled the excited girl.

"Salieta, I've been called to headquarters. I don't know why, but you need to get out of the carriage so we can be on our way."

She refused to leave.

48

"Take me! Take me! You will never come back," she cried. "You'll be just like José'. You'll go and never come back."

Salieta had boasted one night of meeting Jose' Marti' when he came to Tampa to get support for the Cuban Revolution. She told of how all the cigar workers gave ten percent of their wages to fight the Spanish. All were in hopes of someday returning to their homeland.

She had met Marti' when he had visited the Hacienda. She was proud that the "George Washington of Cuba" had picked her to be his constant companion during his visit. She had accompanied him to Jacksonville where he rallied the Cuban patriots.

She admitted she had fallen in love with Marti', who promised to take her home to Cuba when the war was over. When he was killed in an early battle, she had wanted to kill herself.

Salieta sobbed and her grip around Drew's neck became tighter and tighter. Drew, with the aid of the driver, was able to carry Salieta into La Hacienda.

"I'll come and tell you all about it tomorrow night. The next time I go, I promise to take you," Drew lied. "Be good and we'll have a date tomorrow."

He gave her one long deep kiss and then ran out the door. Three men constrained Salieta and Drew could hear her screams for several blocks.

As the taxi proceeded through the streets, Drew could smell the aroma of strong coffee and the odor of cigars. If he closed his eyes he might think that he was back in Baltimore in his father's stuffy Chesapeake Club. Most of the cigars that his father and his friends smoked were hand rolled only a short distance from where he was riding. In fact he could see the factories.

The horse-drawn taxi made its way slowly through the city. Over the tops of the buildings in the business district Drew could see the Moorish domes and minarets of the Tampa Bay Hotel. This hotel, Henry Plant's masterpiece, had been taken over by the United States Army to be the main headquarters for the entire war effort. Henry Plant himself had convinced the government to use Tampa because it was the closest port city to Havana with a railroad terminus.

As the taxi crossed the Hillsborough River, Drew encountered the most beautiful building that he had ever seen. It was as if the visual images one got from reading *The Arabian Nights* had come to life right from the pages of the book. The red brick building was huge and seemed to have no end. No wonder people came in droves to Florida from all over the world, if this was the elegance that awaited them.

Drew tried to pay the driver when he stopped the taxi but the driver told him his bill had been paid in full and he was to check in with the sergeant at the front door.

After exchanging salutes, the sergeant opened the door for Drew.

The inside of the hotel was more elegant than the outside. Massive furniture and statues lined the walls. Immense mirrors and paintings were encased in gold gilded frames. Banners and tapestries also hung on the walls. Drew had been in enough wealthy homes to know that the elegant furniture had come from all over the world.

Drew and his escort moved down a palatial hall where beveled glass doors opened into a large private dining room. A shimmering crystal chandelier hung over a banquet table set with 30 place settings of eloquent china, sparkling goblets, and silver.

What a difference there was between the camp and here! Drew wondered what would happen if any of these people were to spend just one night at the camp.

He was relieved when he saw that every officer in the room was wearing a wool uniform. He had worried about his uniform being wrong but it was the only clean one he possessed.

Before introductions were made, Drew surveyed the room and recognized several prominent faces.

The first to answer Drew's salute was Lt. Colonel Theodore Roosevelt, the former assistant Secretary of the Navy.

Roosevelt introduced Drew to General William Shafter, who commanded all of the Army forces. General Shafter seemed more than anxious to introduce him to William Jennings Bryan. After Shafter reminded Drew that Jennings was known as the 'champion of the little people', he turned to talk to others, leaving Drew alone with the orator. Drew recognized Bryan from the dinner at the St. James Hotel in Jacksonville.

It didn't take Drew long to realize why Shafter had broken away so quickly after the introduction. Bryan talked and talked without really saying anything. Drew's mind wandered as he pretended to listen to the man drone on and on. He again wondered why he had been called to be with this assembly of people.

He was glad when Frederick Remington walked over and introduced two fellow reporters.

"Sirs, I would like to introduce Stephen Crane and Richard Harding Davis, fellow reporters."

Bryan retorted, "I believe we have met many times. It looks like your bosses finally got the war you drummed up, now didn't they?"

Bryan turned abruptly and walked away.

"I can't believe I got rid of that man so easily, but I must remember to use the same tactics next time," said Remington. The four men laughed.

"Stephen and Richard, I would like to introduce Dr. Drew Duncan. We rode on the train together from Jacksonville. He should be a newspaperman. I watched him on the train; he observes everything. Nothing escapes his attention."

Drew shook the hands of both reporters.

Crane commented, "That's the mark, my boy, observation - eyes and ears. That is why I'm here - to observe."

As Drew shook hands with Crane, he realized where he had seen him before. He had been at Miss Alma's the night of the shootings. It was obvious to Drew that Crane did not recognize him.

"How long were you in Jacksonville?" asked Crane. "That's my home. I had to leave my bride and I am not too happy, but one must pay the bills. I wish this damn war would get started. It's boring just sitting and waiting."

Drew felt the anger build up inside at this man who was complaining while living in luxury. He also wondered why he had been at the bordello when he was newly married. Remington, realizing Crane had rubbed Drew the wrong way, cut in.

"I was out at the camp east of town yesterday and watched the men drill. They are looking rather splendid."

"They've come a long way," replied Drew. "The living conditions out at what we call Camp Hell are what the name implies, although it is much better than it was when I got there. We still have to contend with the heat, rain, and bugs, but the food that is served isn't rotten these days. You reporters need to go out there. You wouldn't be bored. There are more stories out there than your publisher could ever imagine."

He related to them more of the living conditions, the sicknesses and deaths, the riots in the Negro camp, stories from Ybor, the adventures of the cowmen, and stories of the common soldier.

"You have missed your calling Doc," said Remington. "You've made it plain that you are as good of a listener as you are an observer - the attributes of a good journalist. If you ever want a job with Hearst, I'll be proud to sign a letter of recommendation."

"You can say that, Remington," said Crane. "You do most of your work with pen and charcoal. I would be afraid of even mentioning the doctor's name to Pulitzer for fear of my job!"

"Here, here," uttered Davis. "Remember, I am Mr. Hearst's numero uno. I don't need any competition."

"You flatter me," replied Drew. "I guess that is why you have the jobs you do. I do want to make something clear though. I am just a medic. I haven't finished medical school."

"That's what you said in Jacksonville," Crane remembered.

"But," continued Drew, "I have no idea why I, a medic, was summoned here to headquarters. These guys are the ones running the show. I don't understand..."

Before anyone one had a chance to respond, Drew felt a tap on his shoulder and turned to see a small elderly lady who seemed very out of place in a room full of powerful men and fashionable women dressed in the latest styles and fancy hats with bird plumes of every hue. She was the picture of the ideal grandmother.

"You must be Trace Duncan," she greeted.

"Yes ma'am," he answered politely as he wondered who this lady was who knew him by his nickname. He thought about all of the older women he knew and quickly deduced she was Uncle Tyler's famous friend, Clara Barton, the 'Angel of Mercy.'

Within seconds she confirmed his guess. "I'm Clara Barton and I bring you greetings from your Uncle Tyler."

Introductions were made all around. The newspaper men who all knew of Barton and her work were as surprised as Drew when Miss Barton asked if she and Drew might talk privately. When they were at a distance from the others, Miss Barton continued.

"I'm so pleased to finally meet you, Trace. I've heard about you from Tyler since the day you were born."

After a brief pause, the diminutive lady said, "I guess you were surprised when you were ordered here. Forgive me, but when Tyler mentioned in his last letter that you were quartered in Tampa, I felt it was a very good opportunity to meet you, at last."

"I'm pleased to meet you, too," Tyler responded warmly. "Uncle Tyler thinks the world of you."

"The feeling is mutual, I can assure you. We have been best friends for a very long time. Let's sit down and talk until we are called to dinner, shall we?"

Miss Barton held out her arm for Drew, but instead of allowing him to lead her, she pulled him to a back table.

"Maybe no one else will sit here. We will be able to really talk."

When they were seated, Drew asked, "but you said something about a letter. Isn't Uncle Tyler in Cuba?"

"Yes, he's still there. I was evacuated and am working in Key West with the wounded from *The Maine*. I'm also working with the new Women's Corps of Nurses. Finally, powers to be have listened and I am now able to train women as nurses instead of aides to the men."

Miss Barton was eager to talk to Drew.

"I've made arrangements for you to go to Cuba when the transports leave from here."

Drew listened expectantly. He hoped she didn't sense his exuberance. Miss Barton continued to talk.

"I had Tyler get your school records for me. I hope that you don't mind. I knew from him that you were always at the top of your class, but I wanted to make sure in case he had exaggerated too much. You have enough knowledge that comes from textbooks to know what do in any hospital situation. You have also shown yourself to be a leader and that's what I was looking for. We need someone who is in the Army to coordinate the Red Cross efforts with the Army's. I know that you are the man for that job. And, it is yours if you want it."

"I would be honored. If you think..."

"I don't think. I know you will do a good job."

"I wish that I could go with you to Cuba," continued Miss Barton, "but I must get back to Key West as quickly as possible. I will leave on a transport tomorrow, but I don't know when you will leave."

"We will be working in the hospital that has been set up there. We're waiting to take the *State of Texas* to Cuba for a hospital ship. It seems logical for us to have a ship in Cuba rather than to send the wounded to Key West. But I am only a woman, what do I know?"

"But what a woman you are!"

Miss Barton smiled as they were called to dinner.

"This is a nice hotel, isn't it?" With more than a mischievous grin, she added, "I'm sure the wives of most of the dignitaries and the reporters are glad the government is picking up the tab. Plant, too, for that matter. Not too many people have been able to afford the $75 a night rooms since the panic of '95."

Clara continued, "I was sure that you would accept my offer, so arrangements have been made for you to stay here until they decide to move out. Your things have been brought to room 305. There you will find papers describing your duties and responsibilities. I have also had some books about Cuba sent up that I think you might enjoy, as well as a Spanish dictionary so you can brush up on your language skills. I know that you've had four years of Latin, Spanish, and French, but interpreting and responding to a foreign language first hand is always a challenge at first."

"You seem to know me better than I do myself."

As they walked back toward the dining table, Drew marveled at her skill of manipulation and the admiration others in the room had for her.

The waiters, formally dressed in tuxedos, served the food. The five-course meal was so delectable that Drew thought he was dreaming. Then he worried about his digestive tract. He had eaten repugnant food for almost a month. How would this meal set?

After dinner, the finest of Scotch whiskey was served. As Drew enjoyed the mellowness with each sip, he appreciated his good fortune. This was definitely not the cheap rum laced with codeine that his fellow soldiers had fondly named 'Cuba Libre.'

As soon as dinner was over, Miss Barton excused herself.

"It's getting late and I have an early boat," she said as she rose, quickly embracing Drew before departing.

The rest of the evening Drew talked with the men in the room. Crane sought Drew out and Drew was able to get over his initial reaction to the writer and enjoy a long conversation. They talked about Jacksonville and

Crane's shipwreck. They also talked about his experiences in Greece and the book he was writing about the civil war.

Not knowing how the subject came up, the two started discussing baseball and their love of the sport.

"Did you know that they say Doubleday invented the game when he was here in Florida during the earliest Seminole War?" Crane quizzed Drew.

"I got interested in his life when I was doing research for *The Red Badge of Courage.* I don't know how much fighting he did because he was a surveyor and made maps of south Florida, including the Everglades."

"Interesting how researching a topic can lead to more and more things," commented Drew. "I seem to be hearing more and more about the Everglades. It seems as if I am being drawn into them."

He went on to tell Crane about the cowmen and their stories.

They talked for the next several hours and before they parted company, they agreed to meet the next morning and toss a few balls.

Drew found that his room was a small corner room. It had all one might need - a bed, dresser, desk and chair. All were made of exquisite mahogany. When hanging his uniform in the closet, he found several khaki uniforms to replace his formal whites.

Although the room was impressive, Drew was far more interested in the adjoining bath. As he was soaking in his first hot bath in almost a month he reflected on his day. When he had left camp less than seven hours before, he never dreamed he would spend that night in such luxurious accommodations. He wondered if he would have to return to Camp Hell before going to Cuba. He also had a twinge of guilt when he thought of Tom and the others still out in the heat, the insects, and the mud. He also felt guilty for lying to Salieta. He knew that when he said he would be back, he never would. He wondered what would become of her?

The next morning, he swam fifty laps in the hotel's pool and luxuriated in the refreshing water. After breakfast he tried to read in the lobby and then out on one of the verandas, but everyone tried to engage him in conversations about what the government's next course of action should be. It seemed as if everyone had his own discourse on the Navy and the Marines already being in Cuba. Everyone was ready for the Army to follow.

The noise that Roosevelt and his men made during their training exercises on the hotel's lawn made it impossible to even think. Drew finally found solitude on the banks of the Hillsborough River in a cluster of palm trees where he found Crane writing in his journals. They worked the day away, each in his own way, taking occasional breaks to toss the baseball that was always in Drew's possession.

At dinner the next evening, Drew sat with Remington, who disclosed that he had been in the southern interior of Florida sketching the Florida cow hunters. Drew wanted to know if Remington's observations were the same as the men he had met.

"Doc, the cowmen I saw were a sorry bunch. They were unkempt and bedraggled. They rode skinny little horses and chased cattle so emaciated and puny that it would take four just to get a good size steak! They carry whips that they crack over the heads of the cattle to drive them and to get them out of the bushes. Their saddles are all left over from the war and are so no-count they have to tie their guns onto them. They also have the most disgusting, skinny, mongrel dogs tagging along with them that you've ever seen."

Although Drew was disappointed about the description of the cowmen, he was anxious to hear about other observations Remington had.

"Did you see the big lake?" Drew asked, hoping for someone with as sharp an eye as Remington had to be able to describe it in detail.

Again, Remington disappointed Drew.

"I didn't see a lake, large or small," he said.

Remington also said he had not seen any unusual wildlife.

Their discussion ended with an announcement by General Shafter that the men from Headquarters and the Tampa camps would leave for Cuba the next day.

All conversation turned to Cuba and what was ahead.

Drew could hardly contain his excitement. He was finally on his way to war.

Sally Settle

Chapter 7

CUBA
Summer 1898

Drew was assigned to accompany the 1st Volunteer Calvary under the command of Colonel Leonard Wood. He wondered if his assignment under the former physician to President McKinley was planned or just a coincidence.

The next morning, he and several others took the private rail car provided by the Tampa Bay Hotel to the Port of Tampa.

At the port they found utter chaos. The entire area was snarled with soldiers and supplies. Eight transports were waiting at the docks ready to load. Thirty-four others were anchored in the bay waiting their turn to moor. No one could board until Wood and his second in command, Theodore Roosevelt, arrived.

The sun grew hotter and hotter. Drew's only consolation was that he was wearing a uniform made of khaki. Thousands of others waiting under the squelching Florida June sun were dressed in woolen uniforms.

Vendors with lemonade and water were doing a booming business, as were the fancy ladies who had moved their business as close to the port as they could. The strip of land out to the port was named, "Last Chance Street."

La Hacienda de Cuba Libre' Numero Dos was the closest bordello to the docks. Drew saw Salieta scanning the crowd. Their eyes met just as a customer took her arm to go into the tent.

When Wood's Volunteers arrived an hour and a half later, Drew asked one of the privates about their tardiness.

"We couldn't get through on the track because of all the congestion," he explained. "Can you believe there's only one track in and out? Colonel Roosevelt was furious. After waiting for so long, he got right on the tracks and forced a train that was heading north to stop. Then we got on the train and the engineers backed the whole damn train nine miles back to port. It was insane!"

Drew watched in astonishment as Roosevelt arrogantly led his men past the New York regiments onto *The Yucatan*, the first transport in line, completely disregarding the fact that the New Yorkers had been assigned to the ship; his troops had not been.

Roosevelt, who had resigned his position as assistant secretary of the Navy in order to be directly involved in the action, took complete charge and refused to get off. Wood, the senior officer on paper, was relegated to taking orders from Roosevelt.

Shortly, the New York troops also boarded *The Yucatan.*

With the extra number of men, the ship was extremely over-crowded. Drew was in the middle of it all, watching Roosevelt, whom he viewed as a spoiled rich boy, and Wood, not much better.

Men were packed like sardines on the small vessel.

Both Wood and Roosevelt insisted their personal mounts be loaded with them. All the other horses were loaded on a separate craft.

Drew wished he had been allowed to ride on the other craft, too. The company of horses would have been much better than the group known as the Rough Riders, a combination of cowmen and spoiled brats from the east who were there for the excitement of war and a diversion from their rich lifestyle.

Tugboats whistled and the huge anchors of the transports were hauled in as they began to move out. Thousands of men hung off the railings as the ships began their journey. A band on the pier was playing the latest and most popular tunes, ones Drew hadn't heard since Miss Alma's in Jacksonville. He sang with the other men as the music played, *"There'll Be a Hot Time in the Old Town Tonight", "Won't You Come Home, Bill Bailey,"* and *"Ta-ra-ra-boom-de-ay."*

The ships were almost out of Tampa Harbor when they were ordered to turn around. Someone reported seeing a Spanish fleet in the waters between Tampa and Cuba. None of the transports were equipped for battle, so it was decided to wait until the Navy had checked out the sighting. The troops remained in Tampa for another week.

Drew's transport, along with forty-one others from Tampa, arrived off Santiago on June 21. They joined others already off Cuba's shores, bringing the total to 153 vessels. General W. Rufus Shafter commanded the 16,000 soldiers who were ready to rescue Cuba from Spain.

Unloading began at sunrise the next morning. Drew witnessed the same chaos he had seen in Tampa. Since the transports were too large to go into the shallow waters, long lines of smaller boats lined up to carry the men and equipment to shore. There were not nearly enough to handle such a vast number of men, horses, and supplies. Each regiment scrambled to get into the small boats. Because the surf was rough, the smaller boats were unable to make it all the way to shore. Men jumped in the water and struggled to carry their heavy supplies. When some of the boats capsized, two Negro soldiers drowned. Overloaded horses drowned trying to swim to land after they were pushed overboard. The landing went on through the night and into the next day. It was said by many that if the Spanish had put up any kind of fight, the Americans would have been slaughtered.

Cuban insurrectionists greeted the American arrivals with open arms. The American 'Yanquias' were greeted with shouts of "Viva Cuba Libre'!" and "Viva los Americanos!"

The Cubans were glad help had finally come. The Americans were glad to finally be in Cuba. Excitement filled the air as Americans met the men face to face who had been fighting for their freedom so valiantly; the Cubans had visions of the American Revolution's Minutemen. Both Cubans and Americans could hardly wait to fight next to each other.

It didn't take long, however, for the illusions to wane. The Americans soon resented sharing rations, tobacco, and clothing with dirty, unkempt jungle fighters.

The insurrectionists felt the hostility of the men from the north.

Nevertheless, an American regiment and Cuban rebels banded together to capture the town of Simony without a single casualty. Drew headed a team of Red Cross volunteers who went with the few Army doctors to the battle. They bandaged a few wounds and set some broken arms.

On the morning of June 24, the Army under the command of 'Fighting Joe' Wheeler, a Confederate cavalry leader, cut its way through the thick jungle toward the crossroads of Las Guasimas, under fire from well-hidden Spanish soldiers.

The Americans crawled inch by inch. Negro and white men were side by side. Colonel Roosevelt led the Rough Riders, most of whom walked because their horses had not arrived. Two other regiments forced the Spaniards to retreat. Wheeler jumped up and down, waving his sword and shouting, "Give 'em Hell, lads! We've got the damn Yankees on the run!"

Drew was attending a fallen soldier about ten feet from the general. He couldn't believe what he was hearing. The old man had his wars mixed up!

"How are we ever expected to win if we have people in command that are so old they don't even know where they are?" he thought.

As the day continued and the new Gatlin Gun fired off bullets continuously, the Medical Corps and the Red Cross worked side by side. Drew bandaged the wounded and set splints. The wounded were then loaded on wagons to go for further treatment in the field hospital. When the battle was over, 16 men were dead and 52 were wounded. At the end of the day, Drew made his way to the makeshift hospital. He worked all night and the following day. The lines of battle moved on but Drew remained with the sick and dying.

A few days after the Battle of Las Guasimas, Drew received orders to report to the Red Cross relief ship, *The State of Texas*. He was happy that Miss Barton was able to bring the ship to Cuba's shores but he wondered why she had summoned him? As Drew walked up the ship's gangplank, his vision was blurred from the sun in his eyes, however, when a familiar voice rang out, he didn't need to see clearly.

"Uncle Tyler!" Drew ran up the ramp and onto the deck. After the two embraced, Drew asked, "How did you know where to find me?"

"I know all," he replied in a mischievous voice. Tyler led his nephew over to two deck chairs where he poured two cups of strong, bitter Cuban coffee.

"Where is Miss Barton? I thought she was in charge of this ship."

"When she's here, she is in charge, but when she's away, I'm the boss. Clara's in Key West where she's also in charge of the hospital ship, *City of Key West*. Prisoners of war are sent there to be checked out before they are sent on to prison camps in Atlanta. She told me you had a pleasant conversation in Tampa."

"She was great. I can see why you two are such good friends. But Uncle Tyler, she's old. Should she be in a place like this?"

"She wouldn't be any other place. She has cared for soldiers and people in need for so long now, she would probably die if she didn't think she could help any more," said Tyler. "But let's get to the reason I called you here."

Tyler continued, "I badly need someone here to work with me. I have some wonderful nurses but I need someone with more knowledge than they have. We are desperate for doctors and medics. The few of us who are here, work around the clock. We need medical relief or we will become the patients ourselves."

As the two men walked side by side on the deck, Tyler continued.

"The most seriously wounded are sent here to this ship. We also have soldiers and Cubans who are suffering from ugly wounds and from tropical diseases."

"I need you to be my assistant. You will continue to be a liaison between the Army and the Red Cross, but instead of being in the field, you will be headquartered here."

"One of your primary duties will be to distribute relief supplies to the Army; however your medical knowledge is also needed on the ship."

"I won't be on the front lines anymore?"

"No. You will only leave the ship to go to the hospitals."

"Come tour the ship. You'll see how much you are needed. here."

Drew saw for himself that men being treated here were far worse than those in the field hospitals.

"I'm still needed on the front lines, Uncle Tyler."

"Think about that, Drew. How long were you out front and how long were you in the hospital? Where did you do the most good?"

Drew realized that he patched and provided a temporary solution on the lines, but the work had happened in the hospital.

General Shafter and Colonel Wood had already cleared the way on transfer orders.

Tyler told Drew another medic had already been assigned to take over

Drew's former position and with little time to think about where he had been, he was soon immersed with medical supplies both on and off the ship.

The communication center on the ship received messages throughout each day on the battles, skirmishes, stalemates, and, finally, the treaties. The ten-year revolution ended in less than two months with the aid of the Americans in Cuba. General Toral of Spain surrendered the City of Santiago to General Shafter on July 17.

Celebrations were held all over the island. The war with Spain was not over but Cuba was free. The *State of Texas* led a flotilla of American ships into Havana Harbor. The Red Cross ship was allowed to go first because the American Government and the U.S. Army wanted to show the Red Cross how much their help had meant during the war.

As the ship steamed forward, Miss Barton, Tyler, Drew, and the other members of both the Army and the Red Cross medical teams, together with the patients who were able to make it out of their beds, stood together on the decks.

It was a great day to be an American. Miss Barton led everyone in the singing of *America.* Being on deck of *The State of Texas,* surrounded by other American ships in Havana Harbor, was the most glorious feeling Drew had ever known.

He thought back to the disorganized troops he saw when he first arrived in Tampa. He remembered the deplorable conditions they had to live in. He also remembered the haphazard departure from Tampa and the day they disembarked in Cuba. Both had been chaotic nightmares. He thought it was a miracle that they were celebrating victory only a few weeks later.

Transports began leaving immediately, taking home American soldiers. Others left Cuba to be part of the invasion of Puerto Rico on August 1. Some, including Drew, stayed behind to help with clean-up efforts and to care for the two thousand soldiers who had contracted yellow fever and were quarantined at the hospital in Siboney.

Drew watched and talked to Dr. Walter Reed and several Cuban doctors who were doing research on the cause of yellow fever. Their premise was that the dreaded illness was caused by mosquito bites and not by the widely accepted theory, breathing vapors from swamps.

There were scars of war all over the tropical island and everywhere people were starving. The American government and the American people sent food and supplies. Drew again found himself in charge of the distribution.

Although the Armistice was signed in Washington on August 12, the Peace Treaty wasn't signed in Cuba until December 12. There was again much jubilation and celebration throughout the country. Because of this war, America was now a world power. She had shown her strength to the people of the world. The war had ushered in a new era.

Drew heard someone say this had been 'America's Splendid Little War.' He didn't know then how many times he would hear that phrase over the course of his lifetime.

Two thousand Americans died during the war. Only 385 had died as a result of battle. The rest died from diseases or accidents.

Drew's discharge papers came the middle of December. He would have just enough time to be home by Christmas and resume classes in January. He wrote Dean Tully that he would be back for the winter term and to his parents to tell them he would be home for Christmas dinner and Flora's gingerbread.

Tyler begged for Drew to stay until after the first of the year.

"You have seen two big celebrations, but the biggest is yet to come. Can you imagine what it will be like when the flag of the United States is raised in January?"

Part of Drew did want to stay but he knew that he wanted to be in Connecticut for the first day of the new term.

He received his discharge papers on December 21 and boarded a steamer to Miami in the late afternoon the next day.

Chapter 8

MIAMI
Christmas 1898

Drew's ship arrived in Biscayne Bay early on the afternoon of December 24. Being the only passenger, he had to wait for all the cargo to be loaded onto smaller vessels that waited in the shallow bay. Only the orange and red streaks from the setting sun were visible when he stepped ashore.

The minute he set foot on the U. S. mainland, he could feel a coldness from the people he passed. They greeted each other with season's greetings but when they saw him they either turned the other way or glared right through him. He had never experienced such distain.

What a difference from the fanfare that marked his departure from Tampa!

He shrugged off their attitudes and focused his attention on this small Florida fishing village. His eyes scanned the one and two story wooden buildings that lined the dirt streets. He was looking for a clothing store or a general store to buy some Christmas presents for his parents. He wanted to be prepared for Christmas when he stepped off the train in Baltimore - hopefully in two days - if he made the right train connections.

A Christmas/New Year Celebration in Baltimore!

It was then that he observed that these buildings were decorated for Christmas and that people were scurrying about with bundles. How could anyone observe Christmas in this temperature? He had celebrated Christmas sometimes without snow, but never without cold weather. The temperature at that moment could not have been under 75! Drew crossed the street to Burdines, the largest general store on the block. A banner over the door advertised, "Open for Business."

The new store was full of shoppers so he found the perfect gifts without the help of a clerk. They didn't seem too interested in helping him - in fact they seemed to be watching him with a good deal of suspicion. He thought about going to a different shop but suspected that it would be the same everywhere - for what reason he did not know. He looked down at his uniform. It was incredibly filthy. He knew that the two others in his roll were in no better shape. Then he thought about the men on the first train down from New York and the way they smelled.

"Maybe that's it. Maybe I stink. Have I gotten so used to it that it doesn't bother me?"

At that moment he decided he would buy himself some new clothes. He hadn't spent much money since he left school. He had his Army wages; some of the money from the sale of his car; money his mother had sneaked into the book in Washington; and Uncle Tyler's Christmas and birthday money. He quickly calculated in his head, counting the price of everything he bought. He knew he had more than enough for presents. If he was fugal when buying clothes, he should just have enough for the train, a night's lodging in a modest place, and meals.

When he finished shopping he had three white shirts, one striped shirt, a detachable collar and cuffs, a vest, and two pairs of trousers that a clerk reluctantly agreed to hem. He also bought underwear, socks, shoes, and a new straw hat.

As he paid his bill, a man with sparkling brown eyes behind the cash resister smiled.

"You must be just coming home from Cuba. If you are interested, our local photographer, P.J. Coates, took a lot of pictures down there. His studio is right down the street and he's put quite a few pictures of the war in the window."

"Thanks. And thanks for your smile. It's the first I've seen directed toward me since I arrived in Miami about an hour ago."

Drew continued his lament.

"People have been turning their heads as they have seen me walk by or they have looked at me with hate in their eyes. In this store I have been followed like they think I am going to rob the shelves. What in the world is going on? I thought everyone was friendly to everyone else at Christmas."

"It's the uniform."

He pretended he wasn't wise to the fact that his uniform was filthy and that he reeked of body odors.

"The uniform? What is wrong with my uniform? Bands played and people cheered when we left for Cuba. What is wrong with my uniform?"

"Were you at Camp Miami?"

"No, I was in Jacksonville and Tampa."

"Well, sir, the men who were in Miami, well, they weren't the best of the lot. They did a lot of fighting and carousing and..."

"I think that happened in all of the camps. The men were on short fuses and were anxious to get to Cuba," Drew interrupted.

Shoppers in the store joined the conversation.

"Well, they did a lot more here than have a few fights," said a little gray-haired lady who reminded Drew of Miss Barton.

"The decent folk were afraid to go outside. Soldiers would come into town and rob us blind. We were even quarantined for a time because of yellow fever at the camp. That shut down the whole town. We were more than glad to see the camp close."

Drew knew what an impact it was for a town to be shut down because of a yellow fever quarantine. Yet he knew that all southern coastal cities faced the outbreak of the fever every summer.

"For the past six months soldiers have been coming back and spending some time here before they catch the train back North or wherever they came from. Most of them don't have money to get a room after they visit the houses down on Ladies Street," said a large muscular man wearing railroad overalls.

"They end up sleeping anywhere they can roll out their mat. Some have even begged us for food. People aren't too friendly because they don't want to take chances. It is too bad for the decent men who fought in 'That Splendid Little War'. I hope you can understand why we are skittish."

The clerk added, "The best I can do is offer to sell a change of clothes but most can't afford one. They just have to endure the attitude of the people before they get a chance to board the next train out of here. I'm glad that you were able to buy clothes because there won't be a train out until the day after tomorrow. You do know that tomorrow is Christmas and the trains don't run?"

When Drew heard of the delay, his heart sunk. He would just have to make the most out of a bad situation. He knew his family would celebrate Christmas when he arrived, even if it was New Year's Day.

Drew's clothes were ready is less than half an hour.

The men in the store smiled their approval when he walked out of the door dressed in the latest fashion.

He hadn't taken but a few steps down the boardwalk when he turned and went back into Burdines.

"Can you recommend a place I can find a good bed without having to pay too much money?"

"Miss Nellie's is right down the street. You had to have passed it when you came up from the docks. I hope that she has a room. She stays full this time of the year with Yankees who can't afford those fancy new hotels.

Drew was now anxious to find a place to sleep and eat, and he thanked the clerk for his help, moving quickly to the door. He paused, though, just before leaving, and turned to everyone in the store.

"Merry Christmas," he shouted gleefully.

As he walked down the street this time, he received more smiles than he had earlier. However, the Army roll he still carried told others he was fresh off the boat and they turned their heads. At least now he knew why.

Drew found Miss Nellie's Boarding House nestled between the business district and Biscayne Bay. It was in the shadow of a large hotel by the Miami River that ran into town from the bay. Miss Nellie's was a two-story wooden structure. It was quite primitive by Baltimore and New York standards. The fanciest part about the structure was the intricate gingerbread molding that adorned the gables and porches.

He walked up the steps onto a large veranda that surrounded the house on three sides. Rockers, which lined the veranda, rocked by themselves due to the strong breeze blowing in from the bay.

He put down his bedroll, his medical bag, and his packages and twisted the bell on the double front doors. A few minutes later the door was opened by a short, full figured, middle-aged woman whose auburn hair had streaks of gray running through it.

Drew took off his hat and introduced himself.

"I'm Lt..uh,..Drew Duncan, Ma'am. I didn't see a sign in your window. Is there a chance that you might have a room available for two nights?"

"I'm Nellie Bradley and you are so lucky, Honey," drawled the owner in a thick southern accent, "A guest who had the room decided to go home yesterday. I forgot to put the vacancy sign in the window. I'm sorry, but it is the most expensive room that I have."

Drew's heart sank. Would he be spending the next two nights on the ground? Afraid to hear the answer he asked, "How much is the room?"

"Three dollars a night plus one more for bath privileges."

A grateful Drew handed the woman eight dollars for two nights. He still had enough money for train fare and food. Then he remembered that if he wore his uniform on the train, his ticket would be free. He breathed a little better knowing he wouldn't be flat broke when he arrived home.

"Your room is #1 up the stairs and all the way to the front."

Drew followed the plump jovial woman into the front room of her house. She took a key from the desk and handed it to him. Drew noticed a telephone hanging on the wall.

"May I use the telephone to call my family and tell them where I am and when I expect to get home?"

"This is Christmas Eve so there's no service until the day after tomorrow. You're most welcome to use the phone then," she said.

Disappointed and wishing he were back in civilization where trains ran and there was telephone service every day, he posed another question, "Do you have a wash board I could use?"

Nellie's eyes noted surprise but she said, "There's a board hanging on the wall on the back porch. You can hang your clothes on the line out back."

"Thanks," said Drew. "I appreciate your help."

"Dinner is at six. Don't be late. It's our Christmas meal. I think you will be pleased. From the reports I get from those coming from Cuba, your food wasn't the best down there."

"It was even worse in the Florida camps."

"Well, I hope I can change your mind about the meals we serve in Florida!" Nellie said with a smile. "Oh, my Goodness, we have to stop talking or I won't be able to set the table like I want and you'll have to come to my table dirty. Now scoot!"

She shook her head as she watched Drew walk out the back door.

"I wonder if that boy knows what to do with a scrub board," she thought to herself.

Drew walked down the hall that led to the back-screened door that opened onto a large screened porch. Stairs facing backward from the house led to the next floor. On the side of the stairs he found the small scrub board and carried it up the stairs, juggling it with the rest of his possessions.

The stairs led to a large sitting area where people were reading and talking. They all greeted him with warm hellos.

Drew easily found his room, a sleeping porch that stretched the width of the house. The half a dozen or so windows were open, letting in the late afternoon breeze from the bay.

"This must be the coolest room in the house," thought Drew.

Furnishings in the room were sparse. It housed an iron bed, a chest of drawers, a desk with a chair, and a washstand

Drew found the bathroom next to his room.

"I am never going to take small things like hot baths for granted ever again," he thought, as he lowered himself into the cool water, dreaming of the hot water in the bathroom at his home in Baltimore.

When he got out of the tub he put one of his uniforms into the water.

"I've watched Flora do this a million times. I also saw the enlisted men do it. How hard can it be?"

While the clothes soaked, he dried himself, shaved, and brushed his teeth. Next, he turned to do a task he had never done. He lathered his shirt with the Octagon Soap and scrubbed it along the board like he had seen the others do. He put the shirt back into the soapy water and scrubbed his pants.

"Nothing to it!" he praised himself. He let the water out of the tub and squeezed his clothes until he couldn't do it anymore. The water was still dripping profusely and it was soapy! What was he going to do? He hadn't noticed what anyone had done after the scrubbing part.

There was a knock on the door and Miss Nellie's voice asked softly if he was about finished.

Realizing how long he had been taking up space in the bathroom, he quickly pulled on his pants and grabbed his clean clothes, including the dripping wet ones.

He opened the door to face Miss Nellie who had not stopped thinking about the young man washing his own clothes and had come to check on his progress. When she saw the soapy water running all over the bathroom floor, she laughed.

"Son, let me help you with those clothes. I have time before dinner."

She took the wet clothes out of his arms and took them back to the tub.

"Go get dressed. I'll finish these and hang them out for you…Can you iron?"

She chuckled when she saw the young man's embarrassed smile as he charged through the sitting room carrying his new clothes - his WET new clothes.

When he got to his room he took off his wet pants and hung them over the chair. Then he hung his shirt over the iron post. Luckily his collar and cuffs didn't get wet. He attached them to another shirt and put on the other new pair of pants.

He then hurried downstairs to dinner, but found he was early so he wandered into an enormous front room off the entrance hall.

Windows extended from floor to ceiling. The curtains, made of a sheer blue fabric, billowed in the winds blowing from the bay. In the center of the room was an old piano around which chairs and sofas were grouped. The Christmas tree reached to the ceiling and was adorned with candles waiting to be lit. The tree looked strange to him. What was it? It just didn't look like a Christmas tree.

It took him a few minutes to figure out why it looked so wrong. It was not a fir tree like he was accustomed to, but a pine. He guessed it would do, but he would much rather have a fir tree standing in front of him. For the first time he had a tinge of homesickness. His thoughts were interrupted by Miss Nellie's tap on the shoulder.

"Dinner is ready. Are you?"

Drew was invited to join the other sixteen guests seated at the massive round oak table. Dinner was served on fine bone china with sterling silverware and crystal goblets. Drew hadn't realized he would be sitting down to a feast. He had always eaten his Christmas meal at noon on Christmas day.

Turtle soup was the first thing served.

"That turtle was swimming in Biscayne Bay this morning," said Miss Nellie, "and the deer is that fresh too, thanks to Mr. Cooper."

She gave a smile to a man who was sitting next to Drew. The meal included cornbread stuffing, sweet potato casserole, stewed apples, and ambrosia salad made from fruit trees that surrounded the house, green beans, and corn.

The biscuits were fluffy and crisp just like Flora's and almost as good. The gathering around the table was like a big family: warm, friendly, and welcoming to the new guest.

As plates were filled, Miss Nellie announced that it was customary for the newest guest to tell about himself. She told Drew the other guests would do likewise. Drew told them his home was in Baltimore and that he had been in his third year of medical school when he had enlisted to go to Cuba. He skipped all the things about the war that were vivid in his mind but he did add that he was on his way back to complete his studies. His experiences in

Cuba had established the fact that he did want to be a doctor for the rest of his life.

Five of the men sitting at the table said that they were also passing through on their way home from Cuba. Two had suffered head wounds at the Battle of San Juan Hill. The other three, recovering from yellow fever, had been with the last wave of soldiers to leave at the end of August. All five had decided to stay in south Florida and were working at various jobs around the town.

"I'm surprised you want to stay here," said Drew. "I got a very cold reception when I arrived. What was yours like?"

The two with head wounds said that they, like Drew, were met with disdain.

The three recovering from the fever said that they had met a photographer from Miami on their transport back to Miami. All had talked at that time about their futures and the photographer urged them to stay in Miami for the winter. The photographer's family met them at the docks and brought them straight to Miss Nellie's.

"Do you think the rest of the country will treat us in such a harsh way?" asked Drew.

Adam Coker, a delicate looking man from Boston who was using Miami as his base while he went into the Everglades to paint wildlife, spoke up.

"Miami is small. When the misfits of society infiltrated here, people got a bad taste in their mouths. They can't see the whole picture."

He continued, "America is very pleased with what has happened in Cuba. We gained new territories - not only Cuba, but Puerto Rico, and the Philippines as well. That was a big accomplishment! Cuba is the gateway to Latin America and the Philippine Islands are a stepping-stone to China and the Far East. Don't you know you have helped America become a world power? Europe is losing its hold in the Americas and Spain has lost everything. This war has ushered us into a new age!"

The rest at the table agreed with Adam and introductions continued.

Another Bostonian was Dave Cooper. Dave reminded Drew of the cow hunters he had met in Tampa. His accent and mannerisms were different, but he had the same coarse skin. He had also come to hunt in the Everglades but brought a gun instead of a paintbrush. During the winter, he bought skins and pelts from the Seminoles. In the spring he hunted native birds so he could profit from America's current insatiable desire for the beautiful plumes being used to adorn women's hats.

Coker and Cooper obviously loathed one another.

Mr. and Mrs. Wilson were from Detroit. This was their third winter with Miss Nellie.

Mrs. Wilson said, "I can't take those harsh winters anymore. Before we started coming, I was sick every winter. I wanted to get as far south as the railroad would take us. We don't have enough money to stay in those fancy places in Jacksonville or St. Augustine. This is just perfect."

Miss Nellie smiled from across the table as the compliment on her establishment was given.

Next to be introduced was Miss Mabel Burt from Cincinnati. She was in her late teens and was to be the teacher for the new school that was to open in January.

"I arrived three days ago," she smiled wanly. "Christmas is strange without snow, isn't it?"

The young girl choked back her tears. It was obvious to everyone that she was very homesick.

"Miss Burt," said a rather large man sitting next to her, patting her on the back, "It's going to be just fine. I'm Reverend Jonathan Winthrop and I'm chairman of the school board. When you meet your students you'll see how much you are needed. You'll come to love this place and the people, although we are not many. You'll begin to remember those Ohio winters and shudder at the very thought of snow."

Turning to the others, he said, "God sent me here three years ago from Cleveland. I can tell you right now, I am a blessed man!"

Drew responded. "I was captivated by Florida last summer when we were preparing to go to Cuba. I liked it despite the heat and the bugs. But tell me this, how can you really get in the Christmas spirit without snow or cold weather?"

"Son," said Rev. Winthrop, "Christmas is in your heart. It can be celebrated anywhere. Besides, do you think that our Lord was born on a cold snowy evening in Bethlehem? This weather and the palm trees are more like it would have been on that first Christmas."

Others at the table were members of Miss Nellie's family.

Drew continued to eat his meal. He loved every mouthful of it. He thought that only Flora was capable of cooking such a fine dinner. Flora! How good it would be to see her and his parents and home.

Suddenly he had a sickness that no medicine could cure. Maybe it was because his pace had slowed down and he could think. Maybe it was because this was his first Christmas away from home. He knew that being at home with his family was the only thing that could cure his misery.

After the meal, Nellie, her family, and guests retired to the front room where desserts of pecan and prickly pear pie, orange cake, and traditional fruitcake were served by two teen-aged Negro girls.

The atmosphere in the front room was radiant. The windows, which were on three sides of the big room, had been closed and the candles on the tree had been lit. The room glowed in candlelight.

Soon, everyone was gathered around the old piano while Nellie's fingers plucked out music from the yellowed ivory keys. The tone that resounded from the back was as mellow as any Drew had ever heard. She played all the familiar carols and led the singing. The entire group sang with gusto. Even the gruff old hunter sang. His deep bass voice delighted everyone.

With music in the air, the glow of the candles on the tree, the memory of a wonderful dinner, and the smiles on everyone's faces, Drew knew the preacher had been right. The joy of Christmas is in the heart and can be celebrated everywhere. Even in the 75-degree temperature. Christmas Eve, 1898, would be long remembered.

An extra bonus was that he enjoyed one of the best night's sleep he had ever had. He had often slept this way in his parents' old feather bed as a child but didn't remember it being as soft and comfortable as the one in room #1. The cool breezes that came in from the bay made it cool enough to sleep under the multicolored quilt. He might have to go hungry all the way home but he couldn't have asked for a more wonderful room. The luxurious room in the Tampa Bay Hotel wasn't anything compared to the one he found in this small boarding house in Miami.

The sun was high in the morning sky when Drew awoke on Christmas morning to the squawking of sea gulls. The open windows and the fresh air enthralled him.

He was soon out exploring the area close to the boarding house.

Within a few blocks of Miss Nellie's was Biscayne Bay where he had arrived by transport only the day before. Now he had time to appreciate its clear, blue waters. The view was breathtaking. Speckled across the bay were numerous boats, some fishing and others sailing. Sailing! On Christmas Day! Unbelievable! What a story to tell his friends.

He prepared to check out prospects of finding a way to sail and soon found a dock where there were small sailboats for hire. Finding the rental was only two dollars for the day, but realizing at once he had brought no money with him, he headed back to Miss Nellie's.

Once in his room, he remembered his money situation. Did he have enough money to even rent a boat? He had never been in a situation like this before. He dumped all his coins on the bed, wishing he had been more frugal with the clothes that he had bought. He had only ten dollars. It could be enough to go sailing and get home if he could get a free train ride but he wasn't sure of the free ride.

He sighed and put the coins back into his pocket. He decided that he would explore on foot - and be content to watch others sail.

He had his hand on the door when he heard a light knock.

"Lt. Duncan, are you awake?" drawled Miss Nellie in almost a whisper.

He opened the door and startled the bewildered innkeeper.

"Merry Christmas!" Drew greeted her cheerfully. "I was just about to come downstairs for the second time this morning. I've already been out enjoying the magnificent day."

"Merry Christmas to you, too," smiled Miss Nellie. "Your uniform is drying on the line and I'll have it ironed before the day is out. By the way, are you missing any money?"

Drew didn't really know. He was about to say something when Miss Nellie took a twenty-dollar gold piece out of her apron pocket.

"I found this in your pants."

Drew was so elated that he threw his arms around Miss Nellie and kissed her.

"Oh! I'm sorry. I just got so excited."

Drew took the coin, ran down the stairs, across the back porch, and down the hall.

Miss Nellie managed to convey to him that fresh cinnamon bread was being served for breakfast just about the time his nostrils were getting a whiff of the aroma. He stopped long enough to grab two pieces of the sweet bread from the sideboard.

Drew was greatly relieved that the sailboat was still docked and had not been rented. He paid the man and took command of the eight-foot wooden craft with its white sail blowing out in the breeze.

The cloudless, pale blue sky was a perfect backdrop for a day of sailing with the wind at about 15 knots. The day could not have been better.

Drew sailed across Biscayne Bay and headed to a little island about five miles across the water. He didn't land, but continued to sail south. He was skimming across sparkling water that was almost as clear as the water he had seen at Silver Springs.

Once again he enjoyed watching the multitudes of fish swimming around the boat. Three porpoises, close enough that he could see their eyes, leaped in and out of the water chasing a school of mullet. He hadn't sailed too far when he saw more sea turtles than he could count. Their gigantic size was unbelievable. Miss Nellie had said the previous night that their soup was from one turtle. She probably had enough left over to feed her guests the rest of the week!

Each boat that Drew passed shouted holiday greetings. How things had changed in less than twenty-four hours!

He continued to sail to a red brick lighthouse on the southern tip of the island. From there he turned in a westward direction and sailed back across the bay. As Drew looked at the shoreline, he saw hundreds of coconut trees and immediately thought of Miss Nellie's story at dinner the night before. He knew he was looking at the oldest settled part of south Florida, Cocoanut Grove.

Miss Nellie said the coconut trees were not native to Florida, but the large stand of trees that lined the bay had not been planted. Their seeds had just been washed on shore, probably from a shipwrecked vessel.

Most of the houses were built from salvaged wood. For a time the settlers scavenged sea wreaked ships for a living, but since lighthouses had been put up in strategic locations to guide the ships around the treacherous barriers and reefs, there was no more to scavenge.

Miss Nellie also told another story, which Drew found hard to believe, until he realized he could check it out from his boat. Spying the platform she had described, he set sail toward the structure.

In the middle of the salty waters of Biscayne Bay, according to Miss Nellie, was a spring that flowed with fresh water.

As he approached, he saw a man on another boat filling buckets with water.

"Is that sweet water you are getting?" Drew yelled.

"The freshest and sweetest you'll find anywhere," the man replied. "Come see for yourself."

Drew drifted closer. He saw the spring bubbling up through the salty water; then cupped his hand for a drink. He would not have believed it had he not seen - and tasted - the fresh water himself.

Miss Nellie had also told the group there was a traditional celebration every Christmas night at Cocoanut Grove's Peacock Inn. Everyone, both the crackers and the swells, in the Biscayne area were welcome to come. Not many from the new Miami hotels attended, although the invitation was extended. Miss Nellie always went and encouraged her guests to do likewise. She said that Christmas might not be Christmas without snow for them, but a Christmas without going to the party at the Peacock was not Christmas to her.

Drew had asked what crackers and swells were. Miss Nellie explained that crackers had grown up in the area and swells were like the swell of the water, they came in with the tide.

As Drew approached the shoreline, the houses as well as the green and colorful plant life fascinated him. Drew guided his craft north and moved leisurely through the water.

A massive brick home that was facing the water caught his eye. Four Corinthian columns graced the two and a half story house. A lush green lawn came right to the edge of the water. Dozens of palm trees, fruit trees, and flowers enhanced the grounds of the mansion. This house looked very out of place in the tropics. It would have blended in with the houses on Charles Street in Baltimore except for the lawn. None of his Baltimore neighbors' lawns could even compare with the beauty of this one.

"Wouldn't my neighbors marvel at this green lawn in December and all of the flowers that are in bloom?" Drew mused.

Drew continued his sail until he saw a large hotel and knew he had found the Peacock Inn of Miss Nellie's stories. He also thought about food for the first time. He tied his boat up to the hotel's dock and hopped out. He looked around the hotel grounds as he walked through the paths leading up to the hotel. Brunch was being served under a large yellow and white-stripped canopy and people were eating at tables distributed throughout the gardens that surrounded the hotel.

Drew asked a waiter if he could eat, although he wasn't staying at the hotel. The tall-distinguished gray-headed Negro dressed in a bright red jacket, said, "Go ahead, sir. It's Christmas. If anyone asks you, you jus' tell 'em Old Johnny said it wuz his Christmas present to you."

Drew thanked the kindly old man and fixed himself a plate of fresh fruit, eggs, potatoes, and bacon. He sat down at an empty table and was soon served coffee and orange juice by his new waiter friend. As he ate, he took note of his surroundings. Big clay pots of brilliant red poinsettias lined the walkways and verandas. Blooming flowers intertwined with palm trees that were around the lawn's circumference. Everything he saw was like a wonderland. He wondered if he had fallen through a hole like Alice. Everything seemed so unreal for Christmas Day.

Drew's attention then focused on the people around him. They were dressed in their finest clothes. When he saw the ladies with their broad brimmed hats decorated with plumes of every description and color, he was reminded of Dave Cooper and one of his reasons for coming to Florida. Drew became self-conscience of his dress-the striped shirt and straw hat. They weren't appropriate for this place. His casual attire was fit for sailing, not dining in these surroundings. Johnny must have thought he was a bum and was looking for a handout. He got up ready to bolt back to his boat before too many people noticed. As he stood, he heard his name.

"Trace! Trace! Is that really you? Oh my baby!"

He turned to see his mother running up to him with tears flowing down her cheeks. As the two embraced, Drew asked, "Mother, what it the world? Why are you in Cocoanut Grove of all places?"

Mrs. Duncan couldn't get any words out, she just sobbed. He stood there helplessly waiting for her to get herself under control so that his question could be answered. In the meantime he wondered why his mother was in this place so far from home. As Drew held his mother close, he saw his father hurrying towards them.

"You did get our letter! I was afraid it wouldn't get to you before you left Cuba. Thank God that it did. I would have hated to have missed you."

"I didn't get any letter, Father. Seeing you is pure luck. This is a total shock for me. I spent last night in a boarding house in Miami. I couldn't get a train out so I decided to explore. When I saw this hotel I remembered that I only had a piece of sweet bread for breakfast and that I was hungry. I docked my sailboat and came to find something to eat. What are you doing here?"

Drew looked around searching.

"Where's Flora?"

"I'll explain later why we are here," his father said. "Flora stayed in Baltimore to take care of the house. She will have Christmas off this year."

"But who will she spend it with? We are her family."

Drew's voice sounded more like a ten-year-old child rather than a soldier home from the war.

"She has her church friends. She said that a family had invited her over for Christmas dinner. I think she was excited that she didn't have to cook."

"Still, she should be here with us."

Drew was almost pouting.

"Drew, where would she stay? I didn't know the conditions of the servants quarters here or if she would have to stay in the Negro part of town. She's where she can take care of the house and go about her routine without having to be subjected to shame."

"Oh, I know you are right. She has gone everywhere with us though. Remember she even sailed with us when we went to Ireland and when we made the Grand Tour."

Drew continued his lament, "I've been around a lot of men who think of the Negro as dirt under their feet. The whole time they talked their filthy talk, I thought of Flora. I know if people knew each other better, there wouldn't be this stupid hatred."

Drew's father didn't think of the races being equal as his son did. He wondered what happened. Had the boy been left with Flora too much? He had grown up with Flora and Flora's mother had been his mammy, but he still believed in the Negroes staying in their place.

"Okay. Enough of our philosophizing. Why in the world are you here? Did you come to meet me and accompany me home? It would have been tragic if we had missed each other."

"Your mother hasn't been feeling well for a long while. She's been seeing Ned White for two years for respiratory problems. He advised us to come to a warmer climate for the winter. I left the practice with Bob until the first of April."

Dr. Duncan led them over to the big white rocking chairs on the veranda so that they could relax as they talked and discussed the past seven months.

"I have written to you about most of the things I have experienced since I saw you last. You can only guess how working with Uncle Tyler made me feel. Miss Barton is such a remarkable women. She's everyone's grandmother and that is the way she makes you feel when you are around her. I have never seen anyone with as much energy. She keeps everyone around her hopping!"

"Father, I am so glad that I joined the Army and got to experience emergency medicine first hand. I do know that I want to finish school and get my degree. I've already written Dean Tully to set up my schedule for next term."

Dr. Duncan grimaced at that point of the conversation but didn't say anything. Drew didn't notice. He excitedly went on to tell about his experiences when he landed in Miami. They talked non-stop until mid-afternoon.

The conversation slowed only when it was announced that an early Christmas dinner would be served at four.

"Did we skip lunch, dear?" asked Dr. Duncan.

"No, remember that we ate brunch at ten."

"Well, I ate at ten, an ungodly time for a man to have to wait to eat his breakfast. I am starved!"

"I'll excuse myself and take the boat back," Drew said remembering his lack of formal clothes.

"Nonsense, you'll eat with us and then return your boat. You did say that you rented it for the day?"

"I'm not very hungry and I'm not dressed properly to eat here. I'm totally out of place here."

"Your father has a clean dress coat in the room. We'll get that and you'll be fine."

She left the men and went into the hotel to get the coat for Drew.

"Father, is there really something wrong with Mother? She seems perfectly fine to me."

"We will talk later when we have more time but I can tell you this, she is a very sick lady."

Drew saw tears swell up in his father's blue eyes. He hadn't seen those since his grandmother died.

The buffet was one of the nicest Drew had ever seen. The table was laden with traditional Christmas foods in crystal bowls and silver platters and trays. Old Johnny was carving the standing rib roast. Drew smiled at him as he carved a piece of the almost rare meat for him.

"Thanks, Johnny!"

Drew laughed when he saw the puzzled look on the man's face.

"Johnny, these are my parents, Dr. and Mrs. Drew Duncan. They're staying here. I'm their guest tonight."

Johnny seemed pleased that Drew wasn't freeloading another meal. One meal was okay but two he would have had to report. Drew picked at his meal, which made his mother very nervous.

"Son, have you picked up jungle fever or something. I have never seen you pick at your food."

"Mother, I have had more food in the past twenty-four hours than I did during the past seven months! The meal last night was enough for a week and I had a big plate here for brunch."

After another futile effort to eat more, Drew announced, "I need to go and return the boat. There will be a big celebration here tonight so I'll be coming back with others from the boarding house. You are planning to go aren't you? Miss Nellie says the celebration here makes Christmas in the bay area special."

"Here? I haven't heard of anything happening here tonight. Maybe the celebration is somewhere else."

"I agree with your mother, son. There would be a notice up if there were a party here. I haven't seen anything."

"This is the Peacock Inn, isn't it?"

"No. This is the Palmetto."

Another wonderful irony, thought Drew, as he realized if he had not mixed up hotels, he would have never crossed paths with his parents.

"Why don't you go to be with Trace this evening?" proposed Mrs. Duncan. "I'll stay in the room and read. You two need to be together...and talk," she added in a whisper.

Soon the plan was finalized for father and son to spend the rest of the afternoon and evening together. Dr. Duncan kissed his wife goodbye.

"Don't worry about me, Mother. I don't think your son can get me into much trouble."

Drew hugged his mother, as he also kissed her. He promised to visit early the next day. Dr. Duncan smiled as he sat down in the sailboat.

"It's been years since I've sailed. I don't think I have since that day we went out on the Chesapeake."

"Oh, the day you were going to let me be the captain. I still remember Mother's protesting. You said no little rain storm would keep you from being with your son."

"I didn't know when we would get another chance and we almost didn't. I still don't know how we made it back to the yacht club. That wasn't a rain storm, it was a hurricane!"

"That was eleven years ago and I can still see Mother's face when we walked in the door."

"How about Flora's? Has it really been eleven years?"

Dr. Duncan was quiet for a time as they sailed north on the bay.

Then he said, "Trace, I have loved your mother since the day I first saw her. Now I am afraid I'm about to lose her. Since I'm eight years older, I always thought I would be the first to go. I've been preparing her for that time for years. If she had stayed in Baltimore over the winter, she wouldn't have lasted until spring."

"What exactly is wrong?"

"She didn't want you to know, but she had influenza three winters ago. It was easy to hide from you since you were at school. Now, for the past two winters she has had pneumonia. She almost didn't make it through last winter. I almost called you to come home, but she rallied right before I sent the telegram. Her lungs have become weaker and weaker. She has a hard time doing anything. She had just regained most of her strength back last spring when she insisted that we meet your train. She wasn't going to send her son off to war without even a kiss. That excursion was almost too much. She stayed in bed for the entire summer."

Drew grimaced. His father read his mind.

"She enjoyed the time with you in Washington so much. I think the thought of it kept her going through the summer months. She has a lot of guilt about handing you over to Flora to raise. You have to understand, that's the way she was raised. She was taught that a lady of means should be philanthropic and do anything and everything to make her community a better place. Children could be raised by someone else. I don't think it dawned on her until you were in college that she hadn't been a good mother."

Dr. Duncan did not give Drew a chance to respond.

"I have to be with her but I worry about my practice. I just can't relax. Maybe I can find a doctor down here who needs some help."

"You haven't relaxed your entire life, Father. It's a good time to start. Relish these days with Mother. You can read, sail, fish, visit with people, or play cards. She would love to watch you play lawn bowling or tennis. Think of the possibilities!"

"All that seems frivolous, a pure waste of time, to me! I still want to help people and to contribute."

"With all of these hotels up and down the coasts of Florida and a lot of the guests coming for their health, surely they need a doctor in residence in the winter. Why don't you check into that?"

"That is a grand idea. I knew that I had a son with a good head on his shoulders."

Drew smiled at the compliment.

"One more thing, Drew. I would feel more comfortable if you would go home and assist Bob. He just can't work his load and mine too during the winter months. We tried to find some one but couldn't."

"I would love to do that Father, but I do want to get my degree. It would be a little hard to help and go to school at the same time."

"You can do just that!"

"How is that possible? I can't work in Baltimore and be in school in New Haven."

"I talked to the new Dean of Admissions at the medical school at Johns Hopkins. They'll give you credit for all your work at Yale plus some for your service in Cuba. They'll also work with your schedule so you can assist Bob. Then, they'll credit that work to some of your required practicums. I'll return in the spring and you can go to school full time during the summer terms. I know what it means to have a degree from Yale. I have one. But Johns Hopkins is getting a fine reputation, too. Think about it for awhile, son, and please don't be upset at me for hoping this will be acceptable to you."

Drew's father paused to let Drew absorb his proposal, and then added, "One more thing. You can live at home. Flora will be there to cook for you; to take care of you. You know that she has really missed you during the past three years. I think she considers you to be her blood child."

Drew threw back his head and laughed. "You knew the mention of Flora's name would do the trick, Old Man!"

That was the first time Drew had addressed his father in such a casual way.

"I'll write Dean Tully tomorrow to transfer my grades. I'll also send money to ship my things back home. When does school start?"

It pained Drew that he wouldn't be under the guidance of his mentor during the rest of his school years, but he also knew that they had established a lifelong friendship and that the Dean would always be as close as a letter away. If things really got rough, he could call him on the telephone.

"May I stay down here with you and mother for a couple more weeks, or does Bob need me back as soon as possible?"

"Two weeks will be wonderful, especially for your mother. You can move your things over here tonight."

"I have my room paid for through tonight. I can't leave that bed empty. I might even stay at Miss Nellie's and come visit you everyday!"

"Must be a wonderful bed, Son."

Drew and his father returned the sailboat and walked up to Miss Nellie's. The family wagon was about to pull out when they reached the drive. They hopped aboard. There was just enough room for two more.

The sandy road they traveled wound through a paradise of tropical vegetation. Several varieties of palm trees peeked out from around ferns and colorful foliage that reminded Drew of the tropical forests in Cuba. Occasionally, Miss Nellie's driver reigned in the horses so the group could enjoy a look across the bay to the lighthouse.

The tropical balmy evening could not have been any more perfect.

At the Peacock Inn, Drew and his father met Charles and Aunt Bella Peacock. Aunt Bella, known fondly as the "Mother of Cocoanut Grove," knew more about the area and its people than anyone else. The couple had been friends of Miss Nellie's since they arrived from England in 1875.

Soon afterward they arrived, the Peacocks established a starch mill. The starch was made from the native coontie plant that grew on the pine ridge between the coast and the Everglades.

The Peacock, Drew realized, was far less elegant than the Palmetto where his parents were staying, but it had a charm all its own. It almost appeared that the inn had been built in three stages. One small house was where the cooking was done but it adjoined two other, larger homes. The largest structure, two stories with an attic, had an open porch that extended the length of the house on both the first and second floor.

Mrs. Peacock presided over the gala Christmas function like a mother hen. She made sure everyone had plenty of her famous turtle soup. The Duncans found themselves surrounded by people from all walks of life. Gathered together were a mixture of merchants, fishermen, farmers, and hunters. Absent from the crowd, though, were the guests from the Palmetto. Miss Bella said that she always invited them, but Dr. Duncan was the first to come.

Drew felt overdressed in his father's coat. This was the second time that day that his clothes made him uncomfortable. Then he thought about the day before when the uniform was really out of place. He took the coat off and felt a lot more comfortable in his shirtsleeves, which also seemed to be a more acceptable form of dress with this crowd.

Dr. Duncan seemed to forget his worries that night. Drew didn't remember if he had ever seen his father laugh, sing, and enjoy himself so much. It was also the very first time Drew had seen his father interact with people outside Baltimore society. He was like a different person; he was more like Uncle Tyler.

Again the tables were laden with food, much of it brought in large baskets by the ladies in attendance. Miss Nellie had brought three big basketsful in their wagon. The night ended with carols and fireworks. Again the spirit of Christmas was very present.

All of his life -up until April- Drew had been surrounded with the bluebloods of Baltimore. His classmates at Yale all came from old money and the children of the nouveau rich industrialists. Here, in the Army, and with the Red Cross, he mixed with the everyday common people, the crackers, as they called themselves. He felt more alive than he had ever been.

Chapter 9

INTO THE EVERGLADES
The day after Christmas, 1898

The first people Drew saw at the boarding house were Dave and Adam, who were smoking cigars on the veranda. The two seemed to be enjoying each other's company despite the fact they both had a hatred of each other's work. Drew felt comfortable stopping to talk awhile before heading up to bed.

"I was hoping that I would see you tonight," said Drew. "I wanted to talk to you about the Everglades. When I was in Tampa I met two men who seemed to have first hand knowledge. Since you two also seem to know a lot, I want to know how much of what they said was true or just talk."

"I don't know what they told you, but we have secured a boat to take us to the 'Glades tomorrow and we have room for two more people. Do you want to come see for yourself? We would love to have you - but aren't you catching a train north tomorrow?" Adam asked.

"No! My plans have changed and I'll be here for the next two weeks."

Drew suddenly realized, though, that Dave and Adam were planning their outing together. Drew knew their missions were entirely different.

"You two are going in the same boat?"

"Yes," laughed Dave. "I know that is a shock to you, young chap, but the next two days are just for scouting purposes. Then I'll go back without Adam."

"I'm going to go and stay for a while. I'll capture animals and scenes with my camera, make notes, and then go home and paint. It seems to be a better choice than staying out there for weeks and weeks.

"Any chance my father could be included as another passenger?" asked Drew.

"Your father? I thought you said last night that you were on your way home from Cuba. You seemed terribly homesick to me."

"I didn't know it showed. Well, today I ran into my parents when I was out exploring. They had written to me that they would be in Miami for the winter but I never received the letter."

Dave said, "There's room for one more...That is, well...How is his health?"

"My father's health is fine. My mother is the one who is sick."

"In that case, I see no reason for him not to go with us."

"Wait right here," said Drew as he went to the telephone to place a call to his father at the Palmetto.

When he picked up the phone and realized there was no operator at the end of the line, he remembered that Miss Nellie had reminded him that no phone service was available on Christmas.

Miss Nellie was coming out of the kitchen as Drew put the receiver back on the stand.

"I need to get a note to my father a quickly as possible."

"Write it and I will get our runner, Mason, to deliver it for you."

Drew penned a quick note to his father:

Father,

We have a chance to go out into the Everglades tomorrow with two of the men from the boarding house. We will be gone two days. Pack a change of clothes and meet us at the Palmetto dock tomorrow just after sun up. Be there!

Drew

By the time Drew had finished the note, Mason, a Negro boy of ten, whose smile was as big as his thin face, was there to take it to Dr. Duncan.

Drew returned to the veranda to ask questions about the mysterious place and verify things that had been said in the Tampa conversation. Adam told Drew what he knew of the ecological system of south Florida.

"There's nothing in the whole world like the Everglades. Most people think of the area as a wasteland. I can think of no better place for a wildlife artist.

"Not to mention a plume hunter and trapper," agreed Dave.

Adam grimaced before he continued, "There's a big lake one hundred miles to the northwest of us called the Okeechobee. That's the Seminole word for 'big water.' The crackers call it an inland sea because it's so big."

"A river called the Kissimmee, meandering in from the north, feeds it. The land slopes down gradually about two inches per mile to the tip of Florida and when that big lake gets full it just spills out all over the land south of it. That is the Everglades. It covers 2,700 square miles. The Seminoles call this 'Pa-hai-okee', which means 'grassy water'."

"Tall grasses grow all over the region," Adam continued. "In the winter the grasses die and fall on the drying ground to rot. Over centuries, the rotting matter has formed a rich black muck that is from four to twelve feet deep depending on where you are."

"Yep! El Dorado, Black Gold," chimed in Dave. "They're going to drain the land and sell it to farmers who can get rich from having three crops a year. I have friends who can't wait to come."

"Like I said," continued Adam, many people consider the land a swampy wasteland. At the same time, that swamp has created some of the richest soil in the world. The thought now is to drain it and farm it. They started draining and dredging the lake area and then they will move on south. The whole draining project will be funded by a National Swamp Act passed by the government a few years ago."

"Have you ever seen the lake?" asked Drew. "Is it possible to get there from here?"

"No, I've never seen the lake. I would imagine the Seminoles have paths from here to the lake, but I don't know. Anything is possible, I guess. It would probably be easier to get to it coming from the west or north. Hamilton Disston, who was a big sugar cane grower up on the Kissimmee, dredged a canal so that a boat can go from the Gulf, through the Caloosahatchee, into the Okeechobee, and on into the Kissimmee."

"I met a man who worked on one of those dredges," said Drew.

"I plan to take that trip in the spring," Dave announced. "They say there are more plumes on the lake than down here," he added, carefully avoiding Adam's scowl.

Drew said he would love to see the lake as it was described to him but right now he was more interested in tomorrow's trip than he was in some future possibility. He asked a few more questions about how they were going and with whom.

"With a half-breed Seminole Indian," Dave piped in before Adam could respond. "His name's Gopher. For the past ten years he's been escorting white hunters and map makers into the wilds."

"Gopher was raised on Key Hammock, southeast of the Big Cypress, by his mother's people," added Adam. "He began to explore the region around the hammock with his grandfather when he was very young and now knows the grassy waters of southern Florida as well as any man alive."

"His people were very suspicious when he started bringing the white men into their last retreat," said Adam. "And with good reason!"

"After the white man began to take their land away, some of the Creek and the Cherokee escaped and settled in north and central Florida. The runaways were known as Seminoles.

They were great farmers and were content to live the life of their forefathers but in a different location. Then the whites wanted their Florida land."

"Two Seminole Wars pushed them farther and farther south. Many of the Indians surrendered and were sent west to be with the Indians of all the Nations in Oklahoma and Alabama. Every promise to the Seminole was broken. One of their bravest leaders, Osceola, was imprisoned under false pretenses and soon died."

"The third and final war - The Billy Bowlegs War - was the most costly Indian war the United States has even been engaged in - in terms of both lives and money. It cost more than all the western wars rolled up into one. Soldiers followed the Seminoles into the 'Glades. Many of the older Indians fought the whites in this swampy land. That hasn't been but forty years ago. There are tales of how the Seminoles set traps for the soldiers and then let the gators do their handiwork."

Adam continued, "The soldiers gave up fighting the Seminoles when the War Between the States started and they had to go back up north. The Seminoles who remained in the 'Glades were few but they were very proud. They have never yet signed a peace treaty with the United States."

"Early on, though, the Seminoles welcomed a lot of escaped slaves and outlaws. It seems they felt that all who were runaways had something in common with themselves - all of them had no where else to run."

"Although most of the Seminoles continue to be distrustful of the white man and look on him as an intruder, they have begrudgingly begun to work with white settlers. A few white families have now settled on the edge of the 'Glades and built trading posts."

Adam was enjoying sharing his knowledge with Drew, who hung on every word.

"Some Seminoles venture as far as Miami and trade animal skins; gator hides and teeth; and feathers and plumes of large birds for ammunition, beads, tobacco, kettles, thread, and axes."

"They particularly like the wy-ho-mee - the white man's liquor - and would trade just about anything they have to get that firewater!" interjected Dave, who was always ready to bring out the negative.

Adam continued his history lesson.

"White ladies at the trading post have learned to use the starch of the palm-like coontie plant in their puddings, cakes and breads. In fact, they like it so well that they have learned to make the starch themselves."

"There were a few accidents before they learned how to make it, though," Dave interrupted. "If the coontie root is cut in the wrong place, it produces a lethal toxin. More than one white person died before they learned the Indian's method of processing the plant."

Adam jumped back in, "Now there's a big processing plant - owned by your new friend Charles Peacock, who was your host at the party tonight."

Adam continued with Gopher's story.

"Gopher's family finally accepted the idea of Gopher's bringing the white man to their village - only because they realized that more goods could be obtained with the white man's money than by finding things to trade to him."

Gradually, knowing they needed to be up early, the men's conversation drew to a close.

The next morning, as the sun was coming up over the water, Gopher poled his boat up the Miami River to the dock at Miss Nellie's Boarding House.

Gopher was owner and captain of the *Rose Egret*, an 18-foot long, two-foot wide wooden skiff he had built specifically for transport. The craft had a flat bottom and a pointed bow that allowed it to cut through the dense sawgrass and glide through shallow water. When in deep water, Gopher sat in the middle and paddled. When he was in the shallows, he stood on a platform near the back where he used a pole to push the boat. When he was alone, he much preferred to travel in his two-person cypress canoe, because it was both easier to handle and faster.

Gopher stood six feet tall and on his head he wore a six-inch high red turban, which made him look that much taller. Only the bangs of his straight ebony hair could be seen. Intense blue eyes sparkled against his golden, amber skin. He wore a shirt, a vest, and a knee length skirt made of calico. The skirt was held up with a buckskin belt from which a hunting knife hung. Around his neck were several brightly colored neckerchiefs. On his legs he wore buckskins to protect himself from the cutting edges of the saw grass. Soft leather moccasins covered his feet.

As Gopher paddled up next to the dock he looked over the three men waiting for him.

"On the dock were guns, cameras, bags for clothes, and more. The youngest man in the group held tightly to a black leather bag.

The three passengers - and their luggage - soon filled most of the space on the boat.

The dock attendant, who was also the interpreter between Gopher's limited knowledge of English and the passengers' non-existent knowledge of the Seminole tongue, directed Gopher to go to the big hotel down the bay.

Another man was going with them.

Gopher looked at the load that he already had and knew he had barely enough room for one more man.

Not long afterwards, as Gopher pulled up to the dock of the big hotel, he analyzed his next passenger. He was an old white man who appeared too frail to be heading out to the world of his people. He worried that the trip would be cut short, which would mean there would be less money.

Gopher frowned as the old man got into the boat. He had two bags with him. One was a leather bag that looked the same as the one the young man already had.

"No!" Gopher shouted pointing.

In his broken English he explained that there was no room for two more pieces of luggage. Dr. Duncan saw that his son was carrying his medical bag so he gave his own to his valet to carry back to the hotel.

Gopher relaxed and moved to the space in the middle of the boat that had been left for him. He picked up a paddle to move through the deep water.

Adam took another paddle to help maneuver the vessel.

The craft and its passengers turned west into the Miami River. It was going to be a cloudless day and Gopher was glad to have the sun at his back.

The *Rose Egret* passed several groups of Seminoles in their hand-made canoes. Each canoe was filled to capacity with pelts and hides to be traded in Miami. Drew waved at the brightly clad men and women but his greeting was not returned.

Gopher was apprehensive as he approached the ridge that was a barrier between the salt water and the fresh water of the Pa-hai-okee.

The unique formation, a natural dam, created a six-foot difference in water levels. Gopher was glad that Adam had been with him before. White men usually balked when they reached this point because they had to disembark and drag the boat against the swiftly flowing current. Gopher was very surprised when none of the men, including the old one, complained about the task.

As they cleared the rapids, Gopher carefully made his way to the back of the skiff. He stood on the platform and skillfully used the six-foot long pole to push through the now shallow water.

As the river turned into just a little stream, Drew saw before him a vast expanse of brown grass, stretching out in front to the western horizon. It was an extraordinary sight. Drew immediately knew why the place had received its name. This glade was like an ocean of brown grass waving softly, which reached to the horizon in every direction. Sometimes the grass was taller than a man's head, at other times it was short. Scattered through the grass were clumps of high ground on which grew trees, lacy ferns, and other shrubs. These, he was to learn, were called hammocks.

Drew could identify very few of the trees. He knew the pine, the palm, the oak, and the cypress. On the cypress and oak hung the gray Spanish moss. Additionally, there were plants that looked like orchids.

He saw birds of every description - big birds; small birds; white birds; black birds; gray birds; pink birds - all beautiful.

How could Dave want to kill these beautiful creatures? Drew couldn't decide which bird was the more beautiful, the pink flamingos or the roseate spoonbills.

Magnificent bald eagles soared overhead. There were also sleek, long-necked black birds with wingspans of almost four feet that circled overhead Several of the species were in the water with only their head showing. The long necks that remained out of the water looked like great black snakes standing upright.

Tiny parakeets, bright colors of every hue, darted in and out of the trees. Their shrill chirping seemed to be the loudest sound around. It was as if the smallest of the birds had the loudest voice.

Alligators, ducks, and turtles could be seen in the grass as the boat passed. Fish jumped often beside the boat.

Gopher stopped poling when he saw a mother black bear and her two cubs close to them in the grass. The group watched silently. Dozens of brown osprey with their massive wingspan, swooped down from high up in the sky to catch fish. After what seemed a very long time, but, in reality was only about 15 minutes, the bears ambled away. Only then did Gopher begin to push the canoe forward.

The boat continued its westward path throughout the morning as frightened white ibis, blue herons, and egrets saw the boat and left the water. Often it was hard to see the blue of the sky. Drew remembered how the men in Tampa had told them about the sky turning white as in a snow blizzard. That, he thought, was a very good description.

The sky also turned black as hundred of birds blocked out the sun's rays just as they had said.

As the boat went deeper and deeper into the mysterious region, Drew and his companions enjoyed eating the sandwiches Miss Nellie had prepared for them, made from leftover meat from the night before. She had also included oranges picked that morning from her yard.

Gopher pulled his boat up to the shore of Pine Hammock in mid-afternoon. Other vessels that lined the shore were not like the one they were in. They appeared to have been made from the trunk of a single tree. Drew estimated that the sharp bowed craft were about twenty-five feet in length.

Adam saw Drew eyeing the canoes.

"Those dugouts are what the Seminoles use to get around in these waters. Every Seminole male makes his own canoe when he is a boy, usually under the direction of his grandfather. The craft, made of cypress, will last him a lifetime."

Gopher made camp early so the men could get their bearings and enjoy their surroundings for the next few hours before sunset. He led them to where they would sleep for the night, pointing to an opened-sided hut which had a high pitched roof made of palmetto fronds and bear grass. Four dwarf cypress poles supported the roof. The floor was a platform made of split planks of palmetto logs that were several feet off the ground.

"You sleep," said Gopher, pointing to hammocks that were hanging from the hut's rafters.

Drew put his bags on the platform and began to look around. There were other dwellings around the perimeter of the camp just like the one they were in.

"Are the mosquitoes going to eat us alive tonight?" Drew asked Adam. "I've been very surprised that with all this water around us, I've not noticed any during the day. Is that because it's December? I know this isn't a place to be in the summer......"

Adam interrupted, "One of the reasons the Seminoles have been able to live so deep in The Everglades is that there are few mosquitoes here, in spite of the water. There's a fish that actually eats most of the mosquito larvae, and, because the water is constantly moving and not stagnant, most mosquitoes don't have a chance to mature. That's another wonder of this place."

"Adam, how are you so knowledgeable about everything you see here? I have never felt so ignorant in my life."

"This is my tenth year coming here. I have been here in all the seasons - winter, spring, summer, and fall. They say the only seasons that are really here, though, are the wet season and the dry season; but I do see subtle differences all during the year that others sometimes don't see."

"I spend a month taking pictures and making notes in my notebook. Then I go back home and paint for the next twelve months. I find it more comfortable that way. My wife likes it better, too."

"By the way, I think that you're very much like me."

"How's that?" Drew laughed. "I can't paint or draw anything."

"No, but you are an observer. So am I. I take everything in around me. When I don't know about something, I ask. I read books to find answers when no one knows."

"Another artist told me the same thing only a few months ago. I have sometimes been accused of staring, but I'm just curious. I want to know everything. I'm very intrigued with the 'Glades."

"Well," said Adam, "shall we begin our exploration and your education? This hut is a sleeping chickee."

He was quick to explain the practical aspects of the dwelling.

"The thatched roof is a good camouflage which also repeals rain and reflects sunlight. The rising hot air can escape through the roof. The platform is high not only to keep it dry and protect its occupants from animals, but it's also high for air circulation".

Drew inquired about the chickees that were away from the camp.

"What are those for? I don't see any activity around them."

"That is where the babies are born. The mother and baby are kept apart from the others for awhile - I did know how long, but the time escapes me right now."

Drew understood the purpose and wondered what the mortality rate was with newborns when they were kept separated.

"I rather like the idea," commented Drew.

Pointing, Adam continued.

"See the fires by each of the sleeping chickees? They're for protection from bugs and from wild animals. The chickee in the middle of the camp is for cooking. As you can see, that one is built directly on the ground, with no platform. The cooking chickee is also always on the highest point of the camp, though you might not be able to tell it."

"You might notice this, too. The logs of the fire are placed in a circle, like spokes around a wagon wheel. As the logs next to the fire burn, the spokes are pushed inward. Unlike the campfires of the white man, the fire of the Seminole is kept small."

"What's in that big pot?" Drew asked pointing to a huge kettle over the fire.

"That's sofkee. It's a gruel that can be made out of most anything, but most of the time it's made from corn or pumpkin. A squaw is there all the time. When anyone is hungry, no matter the time of day, they can go and get a ladle of sofkee. The squaw standing beside her is pounding corn with the cypress log."

"Is there a special meaning to that pole?" asked Drew as he nodded toward the tall straight pole that towered above the chickees, yet stood alone.

"That pole marks the very center of the community. There are ceremonies at various times of the year that take place near it. That's all I know 'cause those ceremonies are just for the Indians and closed to us outsiders."

There was suddenly a lot of commotion as four wild boars charged through the camp. Chickens clucked and flew in all directions as they scurried out of their paths. Children squealed and climbed quickly onto the nearest chickee platform. Drew and Adam took their lead from the others who were getting away from the wild animals and likewise moved to a safe haven behind a clump of palmettos.

When the boars had disappeared, Drew and Adam continued their walk cautiously. A group of naked little boys chased a litter of playful puppies. They nodded to the Indians as they walked through the camp; occasionally, someone acknowledged their presence with a similar gesture. Drew noticed that most of the men of the camp wore bright red turbans wrapped around their heads, similar to the one Gopher wore. Others, mostly young boys, wore no turbans. They wore their straight black hair pulled back into a braid and cut short on both sides. Their clothes were made of many bright colors and the handiwork was extremely intricate. Across the colorful fabrics of the shirts and the knee-length skirts were sewn pieces of contrasting fabrics. The patterns reminded Drew of some of the tropical sunsets he had seen.

The girls were clothed in plain calico dresses but the women wore the same bright clothing with the radiant designs as the men. The women's' patterned skirts were long enough to cover their bare feet. A long sleeved solid colored cape trimmed with multicolored designs draped from the shoulders to the waist.

"Adam, those patterns in their clothes, do they mean anything? They look like sunsets."

"That is exactly what I thought! Do you remember seeing snails on the trees as we passed?"

"Yes, trunks were covered."

"Those are Liguus tree snails. In the spring and summer their colors are blazing with many different brilliant colors. The Seminoles patterned their clothes after the snail. Also, notice the different designs. They mean a variety of things, such as lightening, snakes, and the snail's path."

"Okay, now, why do the women wear so many of those beads?" Drew asked Adam. "It has to be something important because they have to be very uncomfortable, not to mention miserably hot!"

"I've heard several explanations. The one that most people agree on is that each strand stands for an important event in their lives. Others say there is a strand for each year of life. Still others say the beads are a sign of wealth."

"Why don't we just ask Gopher, instead of guessing and supposing?"

"You'll find the Seminole will tell you only what he wants you to know. They're very tight-lipped about their rituals, ceremonies, and the like. And, you will find that most of them speak only limited English."

"I love exploring this new frontier," Drew remarked. "But I feel as if I am invading a place where I don't belong and am not welcomed."

"Just enjoy yourself, Drew. Gopher and the rest are making money off us. How many chances will you get to see this again? I've often felt as you do, but the scenes I paint immortalize it. People who will never get the opportunity, or will not come because of the elements, will get to enjoy it, too. I only wish something could be done about people like Dave. Even he is better than some who come and just kill the animals for the fun of it and leave them where they lay. They don't do it for profit, or the meat or hides, just fun."

"That's contemptible," retorted Drew. "I watched a man just killing alligators in Jacksonville. He was thrilled just to be able to stand in the back of his store shooting."

"See all of the hides?" Adam asked as he pointed to hides drying in the sun everywhere. "Those animals weren't slaughtered just for the hides. Every part was used. Those hides will be for clothing, as well as for trading."

The two continued their walk. By each of the sleeping chickees, corn, green beans, tomatoes, pumpkins, sweet potatoes, and other vegetables grew. There were also patches of sugar cane, banana trees, guava trees, and lime trees and other varieties of food producing plants.

Drew's attention was drawn to the bundles of drying herbs on many of the chickees. He knew some herbal medicine, but desired to know much more.

Going closer to a bundle, Drew asked, "Adam, do you suppose that anyone would share what they use each herb for? My uncle used herbs during his time in Oklahoma. I have his notes. My desire is to learn enough to use in my practice. I dream of writing a book some day."

"Doc, I don't think you'll learn much about their herbal medicines. They believe the herbs are sacred and have been given to them by Breathmaker. They guard them jealously."

"They also have many annual celebrations, the biggest in the late spring that is known as the Green Corn Dance. Outsiders are not invited to attend any of the celebrations but I do know that it is a time when those who have committed a crime are punished and young boys, twelve years old, receive their names. I think that is also the time when the herbal pouches are replaced."

Walking further, they saw a young teen-age boy and an older man, chiseling out the middle of a twenty-foot long cypress log. Children were sitting on the ground hitting the log with sticks.

"They are making one of the dugouts that we saw earlier," said Adam. "It is nearing the end of a very long process."

"When the right cypress tree has been selected, people gather round and sing until it's felled. When the tree is bare of all limbs and leaves, it's put into a mud bank where it remains for 18 months. When the log is unearthed, there is great feasting. What you see being done here happens after the log is dried out. While the men are hollowing out the dugout, the children are getting it to the right thickness."

They were so intent on watching the canoe rituals that Gopher startled them.

"Sam in canoe. You go?"

"Oh, yes! We'd love to go!" said Adam.

"Where is my father?" asked Drew, as he hesitated.

Just then Drew saw his father following Dave and another Indian with cane poles.

"Always loved to fish, Son. Never really got the chance. Come with us?"

"No, I'm going with Adam out in a dugout. Have fun. Dave says bass and bream are known to hang around the cypress stumps and there are more cypress knees here than anyplace I've ever been, so the fishing should be extremely good. I'll see you when we get back."

"We'll have fish for dinner!"

The doctor laughed as he ran to catch up.

"Tell Sam to wait while I go get my camera!" yelled Adam as he ran to the chickee for his camera and notepad.

Drew walked to the waiting boat.

Sam was about the same age as Gopher. The two men's features were almost identical, including their blue eyes. They were about the same height, making it pretty obvious the two were brothers, if not twins.

No one spoke as Sam poled silently over watery trails cut through the sawgrass by earlier boats. He occasionally pulled his long pole out of the water, exposing a triangular bracket about one-half inch from the bottom. This simple device kept the end of the pole from sinking into the mud.

Adam was waiting for the perfect shot in the soft afternoon light and Drew was absorbing everything he saw. They continued to pass the same kinds of birds they had seen earlier, as well as alligators, deer, and turtles.

The canoe stopped many times for Adam to take pictures. Every time the "explosion" of the flash went off, the birds and other creatures were frightened away.

Just as Sam turned the dugout around to head back, they came close to the shore of a tiny hammock. In a tree branch hanging low over the water, close enough to touch, lay a large tawny brown panther. He looked royal and majestic as a king, lying there on his throne.

Adam seemed as much in awe of the creature as Drew, and was poised to take a picture when Sam shouted, "NO!"

It was not until that moment that Drew realized the potential danger they might have been in if the flash of the camera had startled the panther and he attacked. As it was, Sam poled faster because his voice had made the panther aware of their presence. Disappointed that he couldn't take the picture, Adam wrote as fast as he could every detail of the animal so he would be able to remember details when he attempted to draw him.

As the three made their way back to camp, the sun was setting. Drew soaked in the beauty and Adam hurriedly took pictures and recorded the colors in his notebook.

From the canoe, in every direction, they could see the horizon. It was as if they were at the center of the universe. The sky was sapphire blue except in the west where the sun was setting. Streaks of reds, pinks, and oranges stretched across the sky. Clouds that had appeared late in the day were like ribbons streaming down from a Maypole.

Nightfall descended quickly after the sun had set. As darkness surrounded them, they could see the village campfires twinkling in the distance.

The evening meal was ready when they arrived back at camp. The men ate while the women and children waited. Each ate from the sofkee spoon that was passed around. The corn gruel was the consistency of oatmeal and tasted much like the grits he had been eating ever since he had first set foot in Florida.

In addition to the sofkee, the men feasted on deer, wild boar, and bear meat. A plate of fried bream that had been caught by Dr. Duncan and Dave was also passed around. In addition there were sweet potatoes, beans, tomatoes, corn, and cabbage.

The bread that was served was shaped like a biscuit but the color was orange. It was made from pumpkin and was sweet. It was even sweeter when eaten with some of the bees' honey that was available in abundance. Eating this bread was the most delightful part of the meal.

After they finished eating, first the men and then the women gathered together near the pole to sing and dance. There was a lot of laughter as the old men told their stories.

Although Drew didn't understand the Seminole language, he could guess what some of the stories might be by watching their body language.

He lay awake that night long after the others were asleep. He reflected on the day's events and the animals and foliage he had seen.

This land of Florida was wonderful. In this wild, remote place he felt a sense of home but he didn't understand why.

Sally Settle

Chapter 10

THE LONE CYPRESS
Christmas 1915

In the fall of 1899, Drew's father became the staff physician at Flagler's Royal Palm Hotel during the winter season. In addition to his salary, he was given a suite of rooms for his residence. It was an ideal arrangement for him and his ailing wife. When she died in July of 1904, he continued to make the annual migration to Miami.

The older he got, the more the doctor hated the cold weather, though he would never admit that to his son. Instead, he professed that he, like his wife, had been advised to be in Florida in the winter for his health. He couldn't admit he just liked being in Miami.

Since his first visit he had seen the village become a small town and then a small city. More and more people seemed to arrive every day. People were moving there because of their health or to make new starts in life. A lot were there, however, just to turn a fast buck.

As Christmas approached, Dr. Duncan was looking forward to the arrival of his son on the morning train. Although Drew had been in Florida with him last year, he had missed their annual Florida Christmas reunion the two years before that.

Dr. Bob had requested time off over Christmas in 1912 and Drew thought that only fair, since he had been away for so many years and left his partner with the practice. Subsequently, he made a quick trip down in February but did not get to stay as long as usual.

Just after Thanksgiving in 1913, Drew had fallen from a horse and cracked a rib. He was just too uncomfortable to make the long trip south, especially knowing that once he got there he would not be able to make his yearly trek into the Everglades.

Last year, to make up for the two Christmas visits he missed, Drew had spent an extra long time with Gopher.

This year, he looked forward to a more routine visit - and possibly being able to finally get up to Lake Okeechobee. The 61-mile long New River Canal had been finished a few years earlier from Ft. Lauderdale to the lake and it could be an interesting trip.

As the train sped down Florida's east coast closer and closer to Miami,

Drew's heart beat faster in anticipation of the upcoming week. He planned to repeat the schedule that had now become his way to celebrate Christmas. He and his father would enjoy the parties at both Nellie's and at Cocoanut Grove. The next day he would be off to explore the 'Glades with Gopher.

New Year's Day he would be back with his father, having their now annual discussion of the pros and cons of leaving the well-established family clinic and beginning a new one in the wilds of Florida - although Miami could no longer be considered wild.

Following his graduation from medical school, Drew had become a partner in the family's Baltimore clinic, but for several years, Drew had wanted to sell their share of the practice and set up offices in Miami. The elder Duncan always resisted, however.

His family had been doctoring the people of Baltimore for the past eighty years and he wasn't ready to break that tradition. But every year, Drew became more insistent. Every year it was harder and harder for the elder Dr. Duncan to fight his son's desires and reasons.

This year would be different. First, Drew had extended his vacation until January 6. Second, he had made a New Year's resolution that he would buy property in Miami.

He had been in correspondence with several realtors who all advised that now was the time to buy. They foresaw a land boom on the horizon and prices were going to escalate. They predicted that a fortune could be made in real estate in the near future. If he and his father were ever going to make the move, they needed to do it now, before the anticipated land boom.

As the train slowed for its approach to Ft. Lauderdale, Drew knew he was only a few miles away from the 'Glades. His thoughts turned to his adventures with Gopher who had taken him deeper and deeper into the wilderness every year.

He couldn't believe how fast the years had flown.

The week Drew sat aside to be with Gopher in the 'Glades was the best in the entire year. Gopher and Drew were from entirely different worlds but they had established a steadfast bond as a result of the time they had spent together. It was a friendship both of them found hard to explain to others.

Gopher taught Drew how to spear fish and gig frogs. Drew watched as Gopher hunted gators. Drew learned how to measure the length of a gator by estimating the space between the eyes. If the space between the eyes was ten inches, then the gator was ten feet long; fifteen inches, fifteen feet.

After ten years of getting up his courage, Drew finally joined in a hunt. The three-day excursion was one memory he tried to erase. Over one hundred alligators were killed each night. The red glow from the animal's eyes haunted him when he remembered that as soon as the hunters saw the eyes shining in the dark they would quickly drop a noose around their long snout, just before fatally spearing the huge reptile. The smell from the slaughtered carcasses still lingered in his nostrils. The hunt was the only Everglade's experience he did not care to repeat.

Drew also learned how to find herbs and how to use the bark, leaves, flowers, and roots of the plants and trees for medicinal purposes.

The names of the trees and flowers that were so foreign to him on his first trip were now as familiar as the sycamores that had lined the street of his Baltimore home.

One of Florida's most unique trees, the cabbage palm, was used by the Indians in almost every aspect of their lives. They used the tree for building their shelters, for arrows, and for ornamental wear.

Every year he slept on a comfortable bed of cabbage palm fronds on top of pine needles.

He learned the portions of the tree that were used to eat. The heart of the tree actually tasted like cabbage and was delicious raw or boiled. The berries could be ground into pulp to create a concoction that had a taste similar to peanut butter. The berries could also be made into syrup.

It was fitting that the Seminoles called the cabbage palm "the Tree of Life."

Gopher had taken Drew all the way across the 'Glades several times. It was in the estuaries on the western side of the 'Glades where Drew saw Florida crocodiles. They were so much like the alligator that Gopher had to explain the difference.

"Look at snout. Long in crock. Short and wide in gator."

One year as they had paddled into Chokoloskee at sundown, Drew had marveled at the rookeries of thousands of birds. Flocks a mile long flew into the trees. When all had roosted, it looked as if a sheet had been put over the trees, as one might place over stored furniture. When the tide was out, hundreds of pink spoonbills fed on the mud banks.

Another year the annual excursion was to Flamingo, at the very tip of Florida. The spectacle had been virtually the same.

Each year there had been a noticeable decrease in the numbers of birds due to the slaughter of thousands for their plumes, which were sold to the fashion industry. The high price paid for the plumes made the birds expendable.

In an effort to stop the mass butchering, laws were passed making the killing of birds illegal. The Audubon Society hired game wardens, but that made little difference. The hunters killed the men as well as the birds.

It wasn't until 1910 when New York passed laws making it illegal to make hats with plumes that the mass killings ended.

Even now, poachers shot the beautiful birds and smuggled their feathers to Cuba where they were then shipped on to the European market.

Another place Gopher took Drew was an area referred to as the Big Cypress, where a forest of virgin cypress trees covered acres and acres of land. A railroad ran to a big lumbering operation to harvest the centuries old trees, prized for their beautiful hard wood.

"Cut trees. Swamp die," Gopher said. "Four chiefs grow old, go to meet Breathmaker while trees grow."

Drew knew his friend was right, though it did look as if there were enough trees to last a lifetime.

Adam had accompanied Gopher and Drew several times. There was a constant exchange of letters between the two men as they shared discoveries and trips and sustained their friendship. Many of Adam's paintings were now in Drew's collection. The favorite, in the place of honor above the fireplace in his office, was the sunset they had enjoyed together on Drew's first trip into the Everglades. Over the fireplace in his bedroom hung the picture of the majestic panther that Adam had painted from memory.

The walls in both his house and his office were also covered with artifacts that Drew collected from his annual pilgrimages. Every book that Drew found written about Florida, from the landing of the Conquistadors to the present, found its way to a shelf in his home or office library. Drew enjoyed leafing through Audubon's *Ornithological Biography* and *Habits of Birds* in which Audubon had painted and described many of the birds that Drew saw each time he went into the 'Glades. Drew also read William Batram's *Travels* about the natural life of Florida.

He devoured Lanier's work, *Florida: Its Scenery and History.* He loved this author's beautiful descriptions, especially of the Oklawaha River. Drew had now traveled twice down that river and thought Lanier's portrayal was as accurate as any could be of such an exquisite place.

One book, written in 1889, was entitled *Florida of Today: A Guide for Tourists and Settlers.* Its author, James Wood Davidson, had explored the Okeechobee by traveling up the Caloosahatchee, the trip Drew had dreamed of making since he heard about the lake. In his book, Davidson gave the area south of the lake along the connecting canal the ultimate compliment: "If I were a younger man, I would live here."

Drew read every book he could find written by a resident of Cocoanut Grove, Kirk Munroe. The author intended for his reading audience to be young boys but Drew was fascinated with his characters and locations. He especially liked *Canoemates, a Book for Young Boys.* The book about the Florida reef and the 'Glades, had prompted Drew to seek the author out one year when he was visiting in Miami. Since that time, they had corresponded regularly and always enjoyed personal time together at the annual Christmas party at the Peacock Inn, and later at the Christmas parties at The 'Barnacle', the Munroe's home.

Drew followed the politics of Florida with great interest.

A leader in Florida politics was Sheriff Napoleon Bonaparte Broward, whom Drew had met briefly at a haberdashery in Jacksonville where he was bragging about how he had just escaped jail for gun-running.

Broward's magnetic personality propelled him to run for governor — and win - on a platform to drain the Everglades so that farmers would have the richest soil in the world to grow their crops.

"No greater scheme for the benefit of the whole state has ever been devised," one Miami newspaper had written. Additionally, the writer had noted, "An empire, now a wilderness, is to be brought into cultivation and thousands of families will find homes and farms where now is nothing but a vast waste."

During Broward's administration work was begun on five major canals as well as many smaller ones. As a result, the area just south of Lake Okeechobee opened for inhabitation and cultivation.

The canal work and the drainage were not without detractors. The railroads, in particular, were opposed. Many claimed the project would drain the state coffers.

Broward's knowledge of drainage and his popularity with the people also propelled him into national politics. Once an admiring Ocala audience had listened to him talk from 11 a.m. to 2:30 p.m., in spite of threatening rain.

Drew's friends and patients joked that Drew knew more about the southern tip of Florida than about medicine, although he was the best doctor they had ever encountered.

The jokes about Florida were never ending. Land speculators and promoters sold land unseen to farmers. When the purchaser arrived, he usually found it not drained, but under several feet of water. The scandals disturbed Drew but they did not deter his dreams. He was interested in establishing a practice in Miami. He would then be able to explore the 'Glades. He had no interest in buying the drained land.

The first thing that caught Drew's eye when he arrived at the Royal Palm this year was an announcement board in the rotunda of the hotel.

BLACK GOLD FOR SALE
SEE FOR YOURSELF
THE NEW MUCK LANDS OF THE OKEECHOBEE
BOAT LEAVING DECEMBER 26
SEE JAMES MOORE
ROOM 478 FOR DETAILS

Drew could hardly wait to see if there was room for him on the boat Perhaps, this was the year he could finally see the big lake.
He hurried to his father's office.

Almost before they could embrace, Drew asked his father what he knew about this boat trip to the Okeechobee and Mr. Moore in Room 478.

"I knew you wouldn't miss that sign! I knew the promoters of that muck land would be over here to get some of the dollars that are flowing into Miami. Mr. Moore has a speedboat to take potential buyers to a town he has started on the southwestern corner of that big lake. I booked your passage for your Christmas present. The trip lasts for three days. I hope that it doesn't interfere too much with your plans with Gopher, but I knew how you have always wanted to see that big lake. Here's your chance."

"Gopher knows how badly I have wanted to see the lake. He'll understand, I hope. You're going, too, aren't you?"

"No, son, I'm not feeling too well."

"What's wrong?"

"Only a little cold."

"Do you feel up to going to the parties in Cocoanut Grove tomorrow night?"

"Drew, we have been going to those parties for the past seventeen years. A little cold won't keep me away!"

"Speaking of that cold, let me check you."

"It's really nothing, son."

"Sit down!"

Drew examined his father and found him to have a deep chest cold.

"You need to take it easy and rest. You don't want this to turn into something bad. You know you aren't as young as you used to be! But I think that some of Miss Nellie's victuals will fix you right up."

There was a knock at the office door as Gopher walked through without waiting for someone to ask him to enter.

Drew and Gopher grabbed each other's elbows in the traditional Seminole greeting, and then hugged each other in the manner of the white man. This had been their greeting for many years. To them it signified both of their cultures coming together and becoming as one.

"Father told me you be here today. I brought you present."

Drew opened his present. It was the most beautiful jacket he had ever seen. He knew that Seminole women were making these now to sell to the tourists. It was made of red cotton with patches of yellows and oranges much like the colors he saw on the Seminoles every time he came to Florida.

"What a wonderful gift, Gopher. I don't think I have ever seen anything so beautiful. I'll wear it as often as I can and my friends will call me Dr. Florida more than they do now!"

"And, I have something for you in my bag," said Drew as he opened his suitcase for Gopher's gift. Gopher smiled when he saw the present. He knew immediately what it was. Drew always brought caramels in a tin box. The caramels always had the same delicious taste; the pictures of northern snow scenes changed each year. In addition to the caramels, Drew had stowed a Case knife into the tin. Gopher's blue eyes danced with excitement as he took the knife out of its velvet pouch. He turned the knife over and over, obviously pleased with the special gift.

"You be ready to go in two days?"

"Gopher, do you mind if we wait a few days? I have a chance to see the Okeechobee!"

"Hump! Drain Okeechobee, no Pa-hai-okee! Now no fast water. No clear bubbling waters. Salt in Pa-hai-okee. You go to Okeechobee. I see you later. Come back in five days."

Gopher turned and left abruptly. Drew was left standing facing the office door, not knowing what to think. He didn't comprehend what Gopher had just said but he didn't have much time to think about it. It was time to get ready for the Christmas celebrations at Miss Nellie's and at The Barnacle.

The day after Christmas, Drew walked to the Royal Palm dock with James Moore, a short man who was impeccably dressed. He talked nonstop and reminded Drew of a snake oil salesman. His small dark eyes looked smaller because of his overly bushy eyebrows and large handlebar mustache.

Five men joined Drew and Moore to travel north in Moore's speedboat, the *O.U. VIM*. The others were potential buyers of Moore's land. Drew cared nothing about the buying and selling because he knew that it was just another land scheme. Drew just wanted to see the lake where the Pai-ho-kee originated.

Moore's boat was impressive. The *O.U. VIM's* varnished mahogany decks were buffed to a mirror-like finish and moved across the water at some thirty-five miles per hour. The boat cruised up the inland waterway to Ft. Lauderdale. The fast boat would have the visitors in Moore's new town by dark.

At North New River, five huge, gray sea cows swam so close to the boat that it was easy to see their small flippers and gigantic flat tails. The only resemblance to a cow was the size of the animals.

As the spectators looked at the almost hairless creatures that sailors of old supposedly had taken to be mermaids, and laughed at how it had ever been possible for such an ugly beast gaining such a reputation, there was a discernible bump. The *VIM* had, apparently, hit one of the sea cows.

Moore said it was a common occurrence for a boat to run over one of the slow moving animals but that they usually survived.

"Not much of a loss if one does die," he said. "There are too many of them anyway. It's hard to imagine a sailor being drunk enough to ever think one of those things was a woman."

Laughing hard at the image, one man noted the sailors must have been more blind than drunk.

The laughter continued as the boat turned into the New River Canal and headed northward towards the Okeechobee.

Drew attempted to tell the men that they were passing through the Everglades but they were not at all interested. Only Drew seemed to marvel at the birds that circled and swirled in the vast blue sky overhead.

"I don't know what you see here, Doc," said one man. "All I see is miles and miles and miles of nothing."

Obviously, it wasn't the wildlife or the unique country that these men had come for; it was an opportunity to turn a profit from the Black Gold they had heard about.

Drew was in awe when the party boat left the North New River Canal and entered the big lake. Although he had long anticipated visiting the inland sea, he had not visualized the enormous expanse of fresh water that now lay before him. He could see nothing but blue water dotted with grass and little islands as he looked to the north and to the west. He could barely tell where the sky met the water on the horizon. The mysterious lake he had heard about, read about, and dreamed about for sixteen years, lay out in front of him.

As he gazed out on the silent waters, five flocks of white curlews flew overhead. Their constant changing formations looked like white ribbons waving against the blue sky.

The boat slowed to make its way through flags, bonnets, and high grass in the water. Dense forests lined the lake's southern shore. A few fishing villages were interspersed between great expanses of forest.

Drew wondered if the people who lived there could be happy so isolated from everything. He also wondered what these people must be thinking as the *VIM* whizzed by them. Were they aware that the men in this boat and others like them were coming to change their lives forever?

It was almost dusk as Moore turned the boat southwest at a rather large marshy island with thousands of birds that were roosting in trees. Turtles covered the shore in such abundance that even Drew's fellow passengers took note. Moore identified the place as Observation Island, but said that many of the locals called it Bird Island, for obvious reasons. Birds, in the shadows of the early evening skies, seemed to be on every tree branch and bush as well as on the shoreline. Drew was delighted that the *VIM* had slowed down when making the turn. He was able to name all of the birds he saw.

As they sped away, Drew looked back at the island. It was so white with the plumage of birds that it appeared that a Christmas snowfall had covered everything.

Great egrets and wood storks with their long legs towered above the other birds. The snowy egret and the white ibis also added to the effect. Interspersed with the white birds, other species offered a kaleidoscopic of colorful splashes. Blue was contributed by blue herons; pink by the roseate spoonbills and flamingos; green by green-backed herons and mallard ducks; black by anhingas and the American coot; and browns by limpkins.

A flat-topped cypress tree on the horizon became the next focal point as the boat headed straight for it. The tree was unique in the fact that it was not draped with moss nor was it among a cluster - or dome - of trees, as were most cypress trees. Standing alone like a sentinel watching over the nearby land, the tree became more imposing and magnificent as the *VIM* drew closer to where it stood.

Drew was preparing to ask questions about the location of the tree and whether it had any particular significance when Moore cut the motor. As they approached he began talking.

"That tree there is referred to by most people around here as the Lone Cypress," said Moore. "As most of you have already observed, it can be seen from far out into the lake. For centuries, it has marked the entrance to this canal-first for the Indians, then soldiers and fishermen. Now, it's our landmark."

"This canal leads to two small lakes and the Caloosahatchee River three miles south," Moore related. "The Caloosahatchee goes on out to the Gulf of Mexico."

"About twenty-five years ago a man named Disston was responsible for the dredging that ties this town to the lake and to the Gulf. Now, a large boat can go from the Kissimmee, through the Okeechobee, down this canal to Lake Hicpochee, into the Caloosahatchee and on into the Gulf of Mexico. People had been talking about draining the 'Glades since 1850 when Federal monies were given to states to reclaim swamp lands.

"It is too bad that Disston lost his shirt. But he did have a good plan. And, because of his vision and work, my town can be reached by boat as well as by road. It won't be long, I can assure you, boys, that the train will be here, too."

Moore stopped briefly to make sure he had everyone's attention. Then he waved his hand to encompass the Lone Cypress and the solid ground beyond it.

"Welcome to my town, gentlemen. Moore Haven."

That was the first time Drew had heard the town's name. What kind of man was this to name the town after himself? Wasn't that an honor that usually went to the more famous? Drew immediately decided he did not particularly care for Moore's character.

The *VIM* docked in the shadow of the Lone Cypress. Across from the docks was a long single wooden building that contained Moore's real estate office, a bank, and a post office. The sun was sinking fast in the west behind the buildings so Drew was unable to tell anything else of the new frontier town.

Moore had made arrangements with the owners of the Glades Hotel to house all his prospective buyers. The hotel was one of few businesses in town he did not have an interest in or own outright. As he walked with the men to their accommodations, a block from where they had docked, he was quick to tell them his new hotel was on the drawing board.

"Sorry for this rustic place. I know you are accustomed to those on the coast. I can assure you the hotel that I am going to start in a few months will be equal to or better than any you have ever slept in."

Drew felt at home the minute he walked into the hotel. Everything in the front room looked so familiar. He didn't have to think very long. He realized this was just a bigger version of Miss Nellie's. The walls were from the same tongue and groove lumber, the light fixtures were very similar, and the furnishings were almost identical. The Christmas tree standing in the corner also duplicated the ones he had seen at Miss Nellie's every year since '98. He was waiting to hear Miss Nellie's soft southern voice at anytime.

The man who showed Drew to his room on the second floor talked as much as Miss Nellie but his story was much different.

"Lookin' to buy here?" asked the tall, slender young man with red curly hair. His Irish brogue was as thick as Nellie's was southern. "I am Patrick Dunican. Me and the missus landed here from New York and we love it. Some things take a little getting used to. But more about that later. The bath's at the end of the hall. Take your bath and then come down to dinner. My wife, she's the best cook this side of Dublin."

Drew was more than exhausted when he got to his room and decided to take a brief nap before heading down to dinner. He drifted off to sleep with the luscious smells of fried fish and chicken filling his nostrils.

The next thing Drew knew, the early rays of the morning sun were coming into his room.

Anxious to see as much as possible, he went to the window where Royal Poinciana trees formed a beautiful canopy over the road. He knew they would be ablaze with brilliant orange flowers in the early summer months.

The canal was lined with mango bushes; moon vines whose white blossoms had not yet closed; and morning glories that were beginning to open to greet the day. Tall trees with twisted trucks also grew along the edges of the canal. Underneath the trees were soaring, leathery ferns. Glistening spider webs, wet with the morning dew, blanketed the ground and the ferns. Hundreds of gorgeous painted buntings with scarlet bodies, bright blue heads, and brownish wings darted in and out of the trees' glossy green leaves.

Drew watched boats being loaded at the docks where the *VIM* was still moored. The primary cargo seemed to be potatoes and a procession of wagons waited to unload.

In the midst of all the beauty came a strong, overpowering earthy odor. It was unlike anything he had ever smelled and was so intense it burned his nostrils.

Needing to escape the odor as well as to prepare for the day, he went down the hall, took a quick bath, and headed out for breakfast feeling refreshed.

The table in the dining room was laden with the foods he had grown accustomed to in the small hotels and boarding houses of Florida but in spite of that, he instinctively asked the young redheaded girl who was waiting tables, "What are you serving today? No matter, though, I could eat a horse. I missed dinner last night."

"We did miss ye," said the young woman with a thick Irish brogue. "You weren't t'only one. Two more didn't come down. 'Tis quite common wit' folk Mr. Moore brings in."

"Are you Patrick's wife?"

"Aye, I am Joan Dunican."

Drew extended his hand to her.

"I am Drew Duncan, the American form of Dunican. My father's family was from County Cork. I want to talk later. One question though, do you like it here?"

Joan didn't answer, but asked if he was ready to place his order. Drew then realized there were others in the room and Joan was the only server. He ordered, than apologized for taking up her time.

"Sure, 'tis alright. We will talk later after you have been shown the sights."

As she turned to walk away she said with tears in her eyes, "'Tis not home. I miss me family. Talk to me Patrick about his family from Crosshaven, County Cork."

After breakfast, James Moore led Drew and his group around the new town. The main thoroughfare of Moore Haven ran parallel and adjacent to the canal. Moore was very proud of the asphalt marl on the streets. The mixture of shells and tar proved to be a good pavement. The roadways were lined with brilliant colored trees, shrubs, and flowers that gave an Eden-like appearance.

New construction was everywhere. Business houses were being built near the canal and homes were being built down the avenues. The town wasn't just for the speculators. People, hundreds of people, were making it their home.

By the time the men had walked a few blocks, all were coughing or holding their handkerchiefs over their noses trying not to breathe the air that was filled with the strong odor Drew had smelled since he first awoke that morning.

"Mr. Moore, what is that horrendous smell?" one of the buyers demanded to know.

"The muck's on fire," said Mr. Moore. "The smell takes a bit of getting used to. Soon you don't even notice it, believe me."

"What do you mean by the muck is on fire?" questioned Drew.

Others in the party reacted in similar fashion.

"You mean this dirt burns? The Black Gold that drew us here?"

"Hump" grunted one man. "I can't see investing in land that burns. What will be left after it burns? Sand?"

"This always comes up. I guess I should tell people about the muck lands before we leave Miami. I've gotten so used to the smell that I don't notice it and I forget all about it until someone mentions it. I'll tell you all about the land when we get to my office."

"Another potential buyer said, "I don't know how one gets used to that! You better have some good explanations! I agree with Mr. Clemons. I can't see investing!""

Twenty minutes later they were sitting in Moore's office with walls that were lined with maps and plats of land of the town and its surrounding area.

"Well," Moore commenced, "I guess I'll begin by telling you all about the muck land you are now sitting on. This is land that has been reclaimed from the Everglades. The muck is what's left when water is drained from the Okeechobee and the 'Glades."

"Eons ago all of this land was at the bottom of the ocean. The muck is another name for peat that has built up over thousands and thousands of years over the limestone and shell. The muck is our gold. The land around this section of the lake is far richer than the land to the south and to the east. The richness and depth of our soil can be divided into three categories or sections."

Taking a long pointer, Moore pointed to different areas of the largest map.

"Here, in the southwest corner, around Moore Haven, is the richest and thickest muck. Throughout this area," he pointed out, "are custard apple trees. The birds feed on the fruit of the tree and deposit their waste, which over the centuries has helped to create the soil that is as deep as twenty feet."

"South of the custard apples are willow elders. Birds feed on them, too, and the soil is also rich, but the muck isn't as deep."

"Beyond the willow elders," continued Moore, "is sawgrass. That's what you saw a lot of as we were coming up here yesterday. Nothing feeds on the sawgrass, but the decaying grass itself makes the soil rich."

"All the soil is far richer than the Mississippi Delta. It will produce three good crops a year and with the help of the University of Florida people, farmers are getting the best quality of vegetables in the country. Just a few years ago things grew in great quantity but the quality was - how should I say? - well, the caliber was not at all good."

"Those college boys up in Gainesville discovered how to put nitrogen and other nutrients into the soil and now tons of celery, potatoes, lettuce, and other produce are shipped out of here every year," Moore bragged. "Soon, the railroad will build a track here to get in on the shipments that now have to go across the lake or down the Caloosahatchee by boat."

"What about that damn smell and the fire?' asked one of the visitors as Moore paused for a breath. "If we bought property, what is to ensure us that

106

everything we build won't get burned up."

"I'm getting to that," Moore interjected. "When something sets the muck on fire, it is just like Irish peat. It will burn for days and days. I want to assure you the town is in no danger of burning from a muck fire. We keep everything wet, especially in the dry season. We also have the very best fire engine available and we're working on getting a well trained fire department together."

"But you haven't explained just how the fires start."

"There are two main causes," Moore explained, "lightning and man. Lightning needs no explanation. Gator hunters set fires to snuff out gators and cow hunters set fires to keep their cattle out of the sawgrass. Most fires are hard to locate because they burn mostly under the ground, but just in case one does come close to town, remember that we have a deluxe modern fire engine!"

Moore was a smooth talker.

"You will be only the fourth owners of this land. Back in '84 a man named John Henderson surveyed the swamp and the overflowed lands the state sold to Disston. He was given 98,000 acres here on the southwest side of the Okeechobee as payment. His heirs sold the property to me. I in turn will sell it to you. Just think, men. How many other places in this great nation of ours, can one buy such virgin land?"

By the time Moore was through with the accolades of the territory and the prominent people who already had purchased land, the prospective buyers relaxed their concern about the danger of the fires.

They were all dazzled by the names Moore rattled off. As he gave a name, he pointed to land holdings on the map. The list of people who owned land in and around this new "Chicago of the South" was impressive.

Judge Alton B. Parker, who had run for President against Roosevelt, had bought five thousand acres. William Jennings Bryan, well-known orator and three-time Presidential candidate, whom Drew had met briefly in Tampa, had bought two lots in town and forty acres west of town. Florida's governor, Sidney Catts, had purchased three hundred and twenty-five acres on which he was planning to retire. Bankers, lawyers, stockbrokers, and people from all walks of life were buying land as fast as they could. Salesmen were promoting the town to farmers in the Midwest. They were buying land sight unseen and were coming by the droves to set up small truck farms.

By the end of the day every man who had come on the *VIM* bought property, including Drew.

Drew, the sensible doctor.

The Drew who had come just to see the Okeechobee.

The Drew who had a strong established practice in Baltimore.

The Drew who had dreamed of living in Miami for seventeen years.

THAT Drew was first in line to buy property in this land of Black Gold.

THAT Drew bought two city lots and forty acres south of town on the large canal.

Chapter 11

THE LONG TRIP NORTH
January 1916

On January 5, 1916, Drew sat in the dark compartment of the northbound train out of Miami. He was in the process of berating and reprimanding himself for the complete loss of his senses a few days earlier. What had possessed him to buy that property in Moore Haven? He had thought that he was wise enough not to be suckered by that fast-talking salesman, James Moore. Drew's father called him a fool and Gopher called him a name in Micosukee that he would not translate. After which he said, "Thought you loved the Pa-hoi-kee. Why you going to be its killer?"

Gopher wouldn't explain why he thought the drainage would kill the 'Glades and Drew had been reassured by civil engineers both in Moore Haven and in Miami that the drainage would do more good than harm.

For the past decade Drew had dreamed of setting up a practice in Miami. The town had mushroomed in size since the war and it was now a small city. Just two weeks before he had dreamed all the way from Baltimore about how life would be practicing medicine full time in Miami, having time to spend in the 'Glades with Gopher, and attending cultural events with the wonderful person to whom he had become betrothed this past year.

How could he have invested so much money without consulting her - and in a place he had never mentioned to her before?

Soon his thoughts turned from his present situation to the past sixteen years since he had first fallen in love with Florida. There had been few moments when he hadn't dreamed of it and the life he could live there.

He had started classes at Johns Hopkins in January of '99. When he wasn't in class he assisted Dr. Jack at his father's clinic. His formal education had been very slow. When he finally received his medical degree in June of 1906, he was the oldest graduate in his class. He was also the one with the most practical experience.

He had received a standing ovation when he crossed the stage to receive his diploma. He was recognized that day for his work in Cuba as well as for his work with the Red Cross during the Baltimore Fire of 1904.

That fire - that horrible fire! It was a miracle that no one was killed. All of downtown Baltimore was destroyed on that February day.

Drew had smelled smoke from the fire that began several blocks away from the clinic. As he became aware of more smoke and intensifying screams of terror, he stuffed his black bag with extra bandages, salves, and ointments, grabbed it on the run and dashed towards the fire. He ran to the warehouses on the docks. Flying sparks, whipped by the strong winter winds coming off the Chesapeake, were jumping across the roofs.

Men were working desperately to fight the flames before they engulfed the entire town. Drew immediately began to help with the water brigade, but as the night had worn on his medical skills were needed more than his fire-fighting ability. There were burns to treat, cuts to bandage and stitch, and broken bones to set. Additionally, numerous men had to be treated for smoke inhalation.

Drew worked along with Dr. Jack, fellow classmates, his professors from school, doctors that he had known all of his life, and others who were new to the community. The fire burned all that night. By the next morning the city lay in waste and ruin. The Duncan Medical Clinic established by his grandfather was one of the thirteen hundred plus buildings that were lost. Luckily the wind died down before it reached the residential area.

Drew and Dr. Jack set up a makeshift clinic in the downstairs of the Duncan's home on Charles Street. By July, a new, more modern clinic had been built at the original location.

Drew had been instrumental in getting the Red Cross to help with the fire's aftermath as well as the city's clean up and reconstruction. The Red Cross personnel were the only outsiders the people of Baltimore would allow to come in. For a second time, Drew worked with the Red Cross and Uncle Tyler.

Tyler had come from the Texas coast where he had been since the Hurricane of 1900. The hurricane had devastated Galveston and had been called the greatest natural disaster ever to hit the United States.

The speed of the train slowed and Drew pulled his shade to see where they were. He could see that they were approaching the Jacksonville Terminal.

Downtown Jacksonville, too, had lain in havoc after a terrible fire in 1901. Out of the ashes had risen a modern city just like he had seen happen in Baltimore. Was there a lesson to be learned here? Drew was always looking for life's lessons in everything.

He pulled his blind and again drifted back into his deep thoughts.

Shortly after his graduation from medical school, Drew took his black doctor's bag down to have the 'M.D." engraved in the space that had been waiting for eight years to be filled.

One of the clerks asked him if he wanted a new bag. The one he had seemed to be a little worn to be the property of a newly graduated doctor. Drew laughed and said that his bag had served him well and would likely do for some time yet. It had already been through war and fire. It had been there to assist in the pains and joys of birth as well as the pains and agonies of death. He intended to keep the bag until it or he fell apart!

Life had been good to Drew. He had been born into a wealthy family and he had been given anything a person could ask for. School had been easy. Everyone, even the professionals, admired his athletic ability. He was an equal partner in a well-established medical practice. Every year he went deep into the Everglades, an adventure that was personally fulfilling and exciting. He had experienced war, although his involvement had not been as horrible as the war years his father had experienced.

The one thing that gave him trouble was his love life. Sex wasn't the problem. That was easy to find. None of his relationships were the type that lasted. He always had an escort to the society functions of school and the social activities of Baltimore. None of the companions ever held the same interests he did or they were wrapped up in themselves - shallow, silly girls who quickly bored him. Girls seemed to be attracted to him so he was confident that when he decided he wanted to get married, he would have no trouble finding a girl who would be willing to be his wife.

When Drew became a full partner in the family's practice, at the age of 31, he decided it was time to look for a wife. He thought this would be an easy process. When he started looking, eligible girls seemed to have vanished. None of the girls who had just yesterday been flirting with him were around. Every girl he knew was married. He had attended most all their weddings but didn't realize that available girls in Baltimore in his age group were becoming fewer and fewer. Finally, Janette came into his life.

Janette Boyee had walked into his office one day with a terrible head cold and running a fever of 102 degrees. Although her long blonde hair was not combed and she looked as if she had slept in her dress, there was something about her that reminded him of a fragile, china doll.

Drew gave her some cold and cough syrup and told her to drink plenty of liquids. He wrote down the dosage he had prescribed in his Physician's Record Book and smiled as he thought of her drinking the liquid that was 75 per cent whisky. Drew wanted to find out more about this Janette Boyee.

He knew that his best source would be Flora. She seemed to know about every one in the city, no matter the segment of society. But, at dinner that night, Drew didn't have a chance to ask about the beautiful new girl in town. Flora was so excited, she brought up Janette's name first.

"I's at de market today an' Charlie Mae was there. Yous knows Charlie Mae. She works for Mr. Gant, de banker? Anyways, he's gots a niece visitin' all of jere way up here from Savannah, Ga. Charlie Mae say she's a charmer an' a beauty. Charlie Mae says she's got a terrible cough an' been runnin' a high temperature. Why don'tja git over dere an' doctor her, Dr. Trace?"

Flora had a twinkle in her eye thinking that there was a possible bride for her boy right in the neighborhood.

Drew laughed.

"We've already met. She came into the office today, probably about the time you and Charlie Mae were doing your gossiping."

"We's don't gossip! She jest knows dat I'm on tah lookout for yous a wife. I still gots time ta raise a third set of Duncans if'ns yous gits busy."

"Oh, that's your motive? Not really concerned about me, but you just want more children."

"Dr. Trace, I..."

Drew interrupted. "Thanks, Flora, I really did want to know where she lived."

He let a few days pass and then went to Mr. Gant's house to check on Janette's progress.

Drew's heart stopped when he saw Janette. She and her aunt were sitting in twin white wicker rockers on the front veranda sharing a story from the latest issue of *Collier's* magazine. The sunlight sparkled as it reflected on Janette's golden hair, which was hanging loose and fell just below her shoulders. When she saw Drew walk up the walkway, she stood up and came toward him.

In her thick Georgia accent she declared, "You must be tha best doctor on tha face of this entire earth! I have never been cured of a summer cold so fast."

She then threw her arms around Drew's neck and kissed him full in the mouth.

"Janette Boyee, what has come over you, girl? A southern lady doesn't do that!" Mrs. Gant reprimanded.

She kept her hands on her hips as Janette led Drew up the front steps. Janette kept talking nonstop. Drew found that no words came from his mouth. He had never had that problem. Before he left to go to the clinic, Janette had asked him to be her escort to the box supper that night at the Presbyterian Church.

"Thank you, Miss Boyee. It would be my pleasure."

As Drew left he could hear the young fair-haired lady get another scolding from her aunt.

The next few months were like a whirlwind. It could be compared to any of the romantic novelettes in *Collier's*. The couple attended every social in town. Most Saturdays they sailed out into the Chesapeake. On Sundays they attended church and concerts in the park or took long rides out into the country. Sometimes they took the family's old surrey and sometimes they drove in Drew's new Oldsmobile.

Drew knew that Janette was the girl he was going to marry, although she wasn't the least bit interested in his work. She even seemed a little jealous of it. Whenever Drew had a medical emergency she pouted and cried. She never understood when he missed their dates altogether because of his work. She sulked until he took her in his arms and kissed away the tears. He even gave up going to see the Orioles play and he dropped off the local team because she abhorred the game.

Drew's love for Janette was blind. Just when he thought that love had passed him by, Janette had arrived to fill the deep void. He knew that in time she would understand his work and his love for baseball but for now he would cater to her. When the two were alone they laughed and laughed. They could also talk for hours on end about both silly things and world events.

As a graduate of Agnes Scott College, Janette was as smart as she was beautiful. Whenever Drew was alone he could just close his eyes and picture her the first day she had kissed him on the walk in front of her uncle's house or in the meadow where they had their first picnic. She had been surrounded by black-eyed Susans. Her hair and skin had glowed that day as the golden flowers framed her exquisite features. It was a picture that he could recall in every detail even now.

After what he considered a proper courting period, Drew decided the time for proposing marriage was opportune.

One fall morning he took extra care in shaving and combing his hair. He dabbed on a few extra drops of tonic water. Then, he carefully placed a small box containing his mother's diamond ring in the front pocket of his coat. He was almost out of the door when Flora called to him.

"Dr. Drew. Where'd yous think you's goin'? I's given you breakfas' every day of your life when yous has been in this house. Why do yous thinks today's any different? What's wrong wit' you? What's tha' smug look on your face?"

"Flora, I'm really not hungry."

He took out the ring to show Flora.

"Dat's yo'r mama's ring! W'atsa...You's gonna give yo' mama's ring ter dat girl? Yo's sur'? She's no's good 'nough fer yo'."

"Flora! I thought you liked Janette. Mother said that you didn't think she was good enough for Father at first. You see how that worked out. Just give Janette time. You will love her as much as I do, and besides, how can I have those babies for you if I don't get married?"

"I's je't gots a bad feelin' 'bou' jer."

"Don't be silly," Drew replied as he grabbed a piece of bacon and quickly drank a glass of juice before heading out the door. He could hear Flora sobbing until he reached the front gate.

The cool crisp autumn air refreshed Drew. As he walked the three blocks to the grand home of Janette's uncle, he whistled and jumped into every pile of leaves that he saw. He felt as though he was a kid again. His neighbors stared at him as he landed into their freshly raked piles. A few smiled as he greeted them. They knew of his relationship with the lovely golden blonde from Savannah and they seemed to know what his mission was today.

As he rounded the corner of Mr. Gant's front lawn, he saw a strange man on the veranda with Janette. He had a muscular build, was somewhat taller than Drew, and appeared to be about the same age. As Drew walked closer and mounted the steps, he gazed into the man's stone cold gray eyes. Janette's voice sounded strange as she introduced him to Ben Garmon of Savannah.

Drew sat down and made small talk but was having a hard time with the way things were going. Why, of all days, did Janette have a friend come to see her? He was anxious to ask her to marry him.

After what Drew thought must have been hours, Ben stood up and said, "Enough of this damn small talk. I've come to take Janette back home where she belongs. She's been in Baltimore long enough!"

Drew was stunned. Who was this man who thought he could just waltz into their lives and take Janette away with him? Janette began to cry uncontrollably. As Drew went toward her to take her into his arms, a fist came out of nowhere and struck him on his right jaw, causing him to fall to the floor of the veranda. Drew pulled himself up from the floor, still not comprehending what had happened. He raised his fist to strike Ben when Janette yelled for them to stop. Drew staggered over to the chair he had been sitting in while Janette went inside to get a wet cloth.

"What in the hell was that for? Who are you?"

Ben didn't respond to the question but retorted, "You no good ingrate! You have been dating my fiancée. Where I come from a gentleman doesn't date someone who has been spoken for. We can solve this the gentlemen's way. Name your weapon, Sur."

"Name my weapon? For what? What do you mean, fiancée? Janette is in love with me, not you. I have come to ask her to marry me."

The men were about to start fighting again when Janette came back with the wet cloth. Before anyone could say a word, one of the neighborhood boys came running up the path.

"Dr. Drew Dr. Drew! I been sent to fetch ya. Muz Smith's baby is a'comin'. They say to tell you to hurry!"

Drew knew he had to hurry because he knew Laura Smith's babies always came fast once the contractions started.

"I have to go. We'll discuss all of this when I get back!"

Janette yelled as Drew went down the walk. "You never stick around when something is important. You always leave me."

He could hear her sobbing and turned to see her fall into Ben's arms.

Janette left that day to go back to Savannah.

Drew never got any explanation about why she had led him on or any of the other whys that he needed to be answered. He did hear through Flora's grapevine that the Gants had gone to Savannah to attend her wedding the next December.

Drew got up and walked to the dining car. He had just ordered coffee when the train pulled into the Savannah station. Drew stared out his window into the cold black darkness of the winter's night. Ever so often he could see a snowflake land and melt on the glass.

Drew's mind drifted back to another snowy night two years before. He had been invited to a party at Miss Ida Gilman's. Miss Ida was the sister of his major professor at Johns Hopkins and she had been a close friend of his mother's. The only reason for one to miss one of Miss Ida's social gatherings was to be dead.

Drew hoped there would be an emergency and he could escape the boring affair. He would have preferred to spend his time in his library reading but he ended up at the party, which progressed just as Drew had expected.

The large house that was built for entertaining was packed with most of Baltimore's top social class and a few who were hoping to arrive at that status. Drew made small talk with the women and talked politics with the men. A few inquired about his latest adventure in Florida as well as the health of his father.

The group gathered in the ballroom where the walls were adorned with paintings of such masters as Rembrandt and Monet. Crystal chandeliers lit the room. The lights had only recently been changed from gas to electric. Potted palms and expensive velvet chairs filled the room along with an exquisite Steinway baby grand piano.

The entertainment included orators, singers, violinists, and pianists. Drew hoped that his hostess didn't see him shifting in his seat. He even had to catch himself from nodding off to sleep.

When a shrill soprano belted out the popular song, *Listen to the Mockingbird,* Drew's dozing was over. He shuddered at the piercing sounds and let his mind drift to the beautiful natural sounds of the mockingbird.

Drew was so bored that when he looked at his program and saw there was only one more performer he said to himself, "Thank God!"

However, when he received several looks of disdain from people around him, he realized he had expressed his relief out loud. At that, he straightened up and prepared to endure as politely as he could.

From the moment the young lady struck the first note on the piano, however, Drew was mesmerized. Others before her had presented classical pieces, but when this woman played Beethoven, the music came alive. When she finished, Drew and the entire audience rose to their feet with tremendous applause.

The group had begun to disperse when the young lady started to play some familiar and popular ragtime tunes that were not listed as part of the program - and were a definite change from the earlier decorum of the evening.

Miss Ida's face turned ashen. Others appeared somewhat stunned, but many seemed amused and applauded the new energy that the music brought to the room. Soon a group was gathered around the piano singing as the girl played. Drew was drawn toward the piano himself when he heard the melody of *The Miami Waltz.* Before he got there, however, Miss Ida pulled him to the side, calling him by the name of his childhood.

"Trace, what am I going to do? That girl has turned my ballroom into some kind of sideshow at the circus or a honky tonk. Oh, what will I do? I can't imagine that all those people over there around her like THAT kind of music."

"Calm down, Miss Ida. I think it was a lovely way to end the evening."

He hoped he hadn't said the word, 'boring' out loud.

"Trace! I thought you would agree with me! What would your mother say?"

She turned abruptly and started the same conversation with friends who were leaving. Drew laughed out loud when he recalled that night, the first time he met Mary Elizabeth, his future wife.

The spunk and spontaneity that was so evident at the recital was manifest in everything Mary Elizabeth did. Everyone seemed to love being around her - but no one more than Drew. Her emerald eyes had a special sparkle and seemed to twinkle and dance even more when she looked at him.

At five foot nine inches, she was taller than any girl Drew had ever known but he liked the fact that they stood eye to eye when they talked, walked, danced, and kissed.

By far, Mary Elizabeth's most endearing trait was that she was interested in everything that he did. She asked questions about his practice and was never jealous of the time he needed for his patients. She was even a good ball player. Drew had waited a long time, but he had found the right person to share his life and his bed. As he crawled into his berth that night, he wondered how she would react to the news of his new investment.

Chapter 12

MARY ELIZABETH McRAE
Rosemont, Maryland
January 1916

Mary Elizabeth McRae was preparing to return to her teaching position at the Peabody Institute in Baltimore. She had spent her Christmas vacation with her parents and her family on the horse farm where she had grown up in the Shenandoah Valley near Rosemont, Maryland.

She loved coming back to the farm to ride. Prize ribbons still hung in her bedroom from all of the competitions she had won as a child.

For the first eight years of their schooling, Mary Elizabeth and her brothers attended a one-room schoolhouse that was a mile from the farm. Sarah Robinson, the teacher, had for many years boarded with the families of her students, including the McRaes.

While she lived with them, Miss Robinson recognized a talent in Mary Elizabeth for the piano that only a few possess. Because Miss Robinson was a very accomplished violinist, she and Mary Elizabeth often practiced together and gave performances for the family on Sunday afternoons. Soon these performances reached out into the community whenever there was a social gathering as well as every Sunday in church. Little by little music became more important to Mary Elizabeth than horses.

After grammar school, the McRaes sent their sons to a secondary boarding school in Brunswick, fifty miles away; Mary Elizabeth attended a convent school in Frederick.

The sisters of the convent encouraged her musical abilities as much as Miss Robinson had earlier. The April before graduation, Mother Iris made arrangements for a good friend, Grace Hawkins, from The Peabody Institute of Music in Baltimore, to come hear Mary Elizabeth play. Grace was so impressed with Mary Elizabeth's performance that she offered her a scholarship on the spot.

Although Mary Elizabeth's faith had deepened in her years at the convent and had drawn her toward serving the church as a nun, Mother Iris recognized that it was the feeling of security that Mary Elizabeth wanted more than being a nun. She encouraged her to take the scholarship. The convent would always welcome her back if she felt God wanted her there.

At the Peabody Institute, Mary Elizabeth excelled beyond the expectations of her parents, her teachers, and herself. The more she explored the world of music, the deeper she was drawn to it. Music was her favorite companion. She was often called upon to entertain at gatherings and she played at wedding after wedding.

Her brothers married.

Her friends married.

On the day her childhood friend, Ruth, was married, Mary Elizabeth wondered about this thing that everyone was getting into? Why did they seem so happy?

Love was something she had read about in books and had played songs about, but what was it? She hadn't allowed herself to think about it before. After all she still intended to be a nun.

The night Mary Elizabeth returned home from Ruth's wedding, she gazed at herself in her dresser mirror. She had always hated mirrors and didn't like to see what she perceived as an ugly woman staring back at her.

She summoned all of her bravery and gave herself a long self-examination. She was taller than any of her friends but had never seen that as much of a disadvantage. Both of her sisters-in-law were at least six inches shorter than her brothers, but her friend Ruth stood an inch taller than her new husband.

Mary Elizabeth loosened the braid that she always wore and watched as her thick brown hair fell down below her waist.

Mary Elizabeth never liked the looks of her face. She had been forever kidded about her freckles. Looking carefully now at the face she had avoided for so long, she realized all of her freckles, except the ones across the bridge of her nose, were gone. Her complexion was now smooth and creamy. Was it too pale? Had she sat inside in front of a piano for too long? She studied her other features.

Her nose was too pugged, her cheeks too pudgy, and her deep dimples too deep. She hated the deep crevice in her chin; a distinguishing family mark shared by her father and brothers. As she analyzed her features one by one, her green eyes sparkled as she realized that she wasn't the mousy looking girl she had always thought of herself as being.

She completely disrobed and stood in front of the highboy mirror. She had never dared to stare at her naked body as she now did. She took a long slow look, starting with her face, and then down past her short neck to her hourglass-shaped body. She looked at her torso from the front and from the side. Her legs were long and sleek, her stomach was flat, her buttocks were firm, and her breasts were full.

As she pulled on her gown to go down the hall to the bath, she felt confident that she was a woman who would be desired by men. As she sat down in the tub of hot water she became acutely aware of the same sensation she had earlier in the day. Were these desires and longings coming from within her body normal? She dared not ask a soul. She then came to her senses. What had she just done? She was going to be a nun. She had made that decision years before. But yet she liked the feelings that became more alive as she let her hands explore her own body. She wondered if nuns ever felt this way. Surely not.

That night of self-examination was a turning point in Mary Elizabeth's life. She started going out with friends and learned a variety of new music and popular songs. She could easily pick up new songs and play by ear. She learned the ragtime tunes that were all the rage. She began to date a variety of men who took her out to dinner, to the theater, concerts, and to socials. Soon, she was convinced she did not want to be a nun.

Many courted her as her popularity soared, but she ended the relationships if the proposal of marriage came up. She was waiting for a certain Prince Charming. Telling her friends that she would know when her special man arrived in her life, she laughed at their advice to "settle for less" because she was fast coming to the age that she would be a spinster, and there would be less and less opportunity for a ring.

On May 20, 1905, Mary Elizabeth graduated with top honors from Peabody. At the reception held in honor of the graduates and their families, she was surprised when the Dean asked her to stay and teach. She quickly accepted the offer because she knew of no place she would rather be than in Baltimore and at Peabody.

For the next nine years Mary Elizabeth taught music and played with the Baltimore Symphony. She was asked by the socialites of Baltimore to play for them. She usually chose music to fit the surroundings, whether classical or contemporary.

One cold winter night in 1914, she substituted for a sick friend at the home of Miss Ida Gilman at Johns Hopkins. She was last on the program, and, as she waited, she began to study the expressions and body language of the people in the audience. She was amused when she saw a rather handsome middle-aged man trying to keep himself from falling asleep.

He kept checking his watch, turning as if he were expecting someone, checking his program, and sighing. He repeated these things at least a dozen times. She reluctantly went to the piano when it was her turn. She was having a much better time watching the man.

After what she thought was a fair rendition of a sampling from each of Beethoven's famous concertos, Mary Elizabeth received a standing ovation. The audience wanted more.

She wondered what type of music the man whom she had been watching would like. She bet it would be popular music. She played several ragtime tunes and waltzes and was just finishing the second playing of *The Miami Waltz* when Miss Gilman asked her to stop because the hour was late. She could tell she had provoked Miss Gilman's ire even before she escorted her to the next room.

"How dare you make my house into some kind of honky tonk! I will make

119

sure that you will never play for the well bred people in this city again!"

Mary Elizabeth wondered if Miss Gilman knew that she would be playing with the symphony the next night in a private concert for the governor?

Quietly, Mary Elizabeth prepared to leave but in the front hall, the man whom she had watched during the concert, was waiting for her.

"Excuse me. Miss Lindsey? I read your name on the program. I'm Drew Duncan."

Drew extended his hand to the musician.

"No, my name is Mary Elizabeth McRae. Miss Lindsey couldn't come tonight and asked me to perform in her place."

"Well, Miss McRae, I loved your playing of Beethoven, but I was thrilled when you snubbed protocol and played my favorite music. *The Miami Waltz* is my favorite song."

"Thank you kindly, Sir. I don't know what came over me. I had watched you and several other guests who seemed to be very bored. I guess I wanted to wake you up and I think I did more than that."

"What do you mean?"

"I really upset Miss Gilman. She informed me that I would never play for her or her friends again. I guess I deserve that."

Tears came to Mary Elizabeth's eyes as she was talking to Drew. To her surprise he put his arm around her and assured her everything would be all right.

The most handsome man that Mary Elizabeth had ever met, drove her home in his Oldsmobile that night. Two nights later Drew and Mary Elizabeth went out to dinner and to the theater.

That was the beginning of a new life for them both. Whenever they were not working or sleeping, they were together. There was a ten-year difference in their ages but age didn't seem to matter.

Mary Elizabeth smiled as she looked at the diamond that glistened from her left hand. It was hard to realize two years had passed since that snowy night at Miss Ida Gillman's, the night she met her Prince Charming.

Chapter 13

FINAL GOODBYES
May 1916

The following article appeared in the May 10, 1916 edition of the *Baltimore Sun*:

> **Dr. Thomas Drew Duncan, III, well known physician of this city, and Miss Mary Elizabeth McRae, beloved teacher at the Peabody Institute of Music and pianist for the Baltimore Symphony, have announced plans to be married.**
>
> **The nuptials will take place at the Rosemont Methodist Episcopal Church, Rosemont, on Saturday, June 24 at 5 o'clock in the afternoon.**

In the same edition of the paper and in the days and weeks to follow, the society page was full of parties given in the couple's honor.

On the night of June 9, Flora cleaned up the dinner she had fixed for Drew and his father. Drew left right after dinner to attend another wedding function and shortly thereafter his father went upstairs to his room to read. Flora starched and rolled up both of the doctors' shirts to be ironed the next morning. Before leaving for the night she went upstairs to tell Dr. Duncan good night. As she climbed the long stairs a strange sensation came over her. She knocked softly on the door.

"Dr. Drew, is deres anythin' yous wants me ter do 'fore I's leave?"

There was no response. Since the door was slightly open, Flora peeked in the room. The doctor had fallen asleep while reading. She walked over to his bed and removed the book and his glasses as she had done many times before.

As she walked back across the room to leave, she again felt an odd sensation. She told herself she was a crazy old woman and that there must be a draft. She went over to the window to make sure it was closed. Then, before she realized what she was doing, she was feeling for the doctor's pulse on his neck, as she had seen him do so many times before with his patients. She felt nothing, but really didn't know what she was feeling for. She shook her beloved old employer and friend trying to wake him up, but he did not move. Only when his arm fell limp from the bed did she understand that he was dead. She picked up the telephone on his bedside table.

"Miz Maybelle, please git me Dr. Trace, I's means Dr. Duncan a' Mister Rollin's."

Drew answered the phone laughing.

"Hello, Hello."

He could only hear sobs at the other end of the line. A faint voice finally choked out the words,

"Dr. Trace."

"Flora?"

"What's wrong?"

"It be Dr. Drew, Dr. Trace. He be dead."

Flora hung up the receiver and sobbed. She had helped her mother and old Dr. Duncan deliver Dr. Drew and his twin brother in this very room, in this very bed. She had grown up with him and had protected him like a little brother. She had been with him through the good times and the bad. Now he was gone. Flora sat down in the old rocking chair at the foot of the bed and sobbed and sobbed.

Except for the addition of the telephone and the electric lights, the room hadn't changed any since the day she first cleaned it. She had made the bed six times a week ever since she was ten. How many thousand of times had she polished its cherry wood?

Flora's earliest memories were right in this room. She couldn't have been over five years old. She knew that her mother had been taken away from a plantation before she was born. Flora's name, according to her mother, was chosen as a beautiful reminder of the happy times she had enjoyed in that place - Florida.

Flora's first job was to bring the first Dr. Duncan's wife water and pat her head with wet compresses when she was confined to bed before her twins were born. When the boys were born, Flora was their companion and protector. She had devoted her life to taking care of the Duncans and their house.

The only thing she did outside of her work for the Duncans was to attend the African Methodist Episcopal Church where she had taught a Sunday School class and sung in the choir for over fifty years.

Flora was still sobbing and rocking when Drew rushed into the room. He checked his father's pulse just as Flora had done, then, together, as tears flowed from both, Drew and Flora cleaned and prepared Dr. Duncan to be laid out.

While Drew called people on the telephone, Flora went into the kitchen to prepare food for the hundreds of people she knew would be coming.

The article that appeared on the front page of *The Evening Sun* the next afternoon surprised Baltimore citizens:

Doctor Drew Duncan Dies Suddenly

The citizens of Baltimore will be saddened to hear of the death last night of Dr. Thomas Drew Duncan, Jr.

His healing hands have touched most Baltimore citizens.

Dr. Duncan was 77 years old. His wife, Mary, preceded him in death in 1904.

One son, Dr. Drew Duncan, III, of this city and a twin brother, Dr. Tyler Duncan of Havana, Cuba, survive him.

Dr. Duncan had practiced medicine in this city with Duncan, Duncan, and Watson for the past fifty years. In recent years he was the winter physician at the Royal Palm Hotel in Miami, Florida. Dr. Duncan was a physician for the Confederate States of America during the War Between the States.

He was a member of the CSA Veterans, St. Stephen's Episcopal Church, and the Chesapeake Club where he held all offices.

He was also a past Worshipful Master of Baltimore Masonic Lodge #102.

Services will be held at St. Stephen's Episcopal Church on June 12 at 10:00 a.m.

The mayor and two former governors were among the pallbearers. The high Episcopal service was lead by the Bishop. Dr. Thomas Drew Duncan, Jr. was laid to rest in the family plot in the Westminster Burying Ground next to his wife.

Flora tried to work through her grief by cooking. She cooked into the wee hours of the morning. She said she was getting ready for the wedding. She was going to take food to Rosemont when they went because she wasn't sure how those country white people cooked. Drew knew she wasn't going home but sleeping in an old soft rocking chair that she kept in the corner of the kitchen.

Finally Drew persuaded Flora to go home. He insisted that she had prepared enough food. There wouldn't be room in the Oldsmobile if she fixed any more. She reluctantly left but not before laughing and commenting to Drew.

"I's bet I's be ta darkest member o' tha wedding party."

Drew insisted that she would sit in his family's section since she was the only family member he had left except for Uncle Tyler, who was too sick to make the trip.

Drew went to work the day after the funeral, wanting to keep his mind occupied. When he left for his office, Flora had not yet arrived, which was rather unusual, but Drew felt that she really needed to take a day off for a change. Sleep would be a good thing for her and she had really been doing too much. After all, she was older than his father.

After getting in late that night, he left the house at three the next morning to deliver a baby, then went directly to the clinic where he had two waiting rooms full of patients. When he arrived home that night, exhausted, he realized Flora hadn't come to work that day either. He couldn't recall that she had ever missed two days of work. They were to leave for Rosemont the following day. Flora always worked a whole day before a trip getting his clothes ready. Drew began to shudder when he realized something terrible must have happened to keep Flora away from her job. He immediately knew he needed to go find her.

There was no telephone at Flora's house so Drew drove over to the Negro section of Baltimore. Over and over again he had asked Flora to come live at the Duncan house.

When the Duncan's carriage house was converted to a garage for the automobiles, an apartment just for Flora had been added. However, she still would not move to the Duncan property on a permanent basis. She had insisted that she wanted to be near her people.

Drew never understood what she meant by that statement. She was his second mother and he loved her as much as he had loved his own mother. He couldn't understand why she didn't want to live in his house. It would have been so convenient for her.

He knocked at the door of her simple wooden house. When there was no answer, he opened the door and went into the front room. He found a kerosene lamp near the door and lit it. The glow of the light illuminated the room. He could see that everything was in perfect order, as only Flora would have it.

Drew called out Flora's name and heard a muffled sound coming from the next room. He walked into the dark room with only the light coming from the lamp in the front room, where he saw Flora lying in bed. She was under the quilt he had seen her working on so many times. He quickly crossed the room to the bedside of his beloved friend.

Flora opened her big brown eyes and said,

"Dr. Trace, I's know' dats yo's come."

She reached out with the once-strong hand that had fed, bathed, spanked, and cared for Drew for forty years.

"I's holdin' on fer yo'. De a'gels huz com's buts I's sen' dem awa' tell'n dem I's ha' to see yo' jes' one mo' tim'. I's loves yo', boy, as much a' if'n I's giv'n birth ter yo'. You be's goo' ter Muz Mary. I's smile dow' from Heave' a' yo' chilluns. Hug me one mo' tim' 'cause I's sees sweet, sweet Jesus acomin' wi' his angels."

She squeezed Drew's hand.

"I's loves yo', Dr. Trace."

Drew felt Flora's grip let go as he embraced her for the last time.

Drew was devastated. With Flora's death, the world of his youth had drawn to a close. Grief overwhelmed him. The deaths of two loved ones in less than a week traumatized him. His family was all gone. How could he face that big house without the others?

Drew made the arrangements for Flora's funeral. Mary Elizabeth went with him to his second funeral that week. In contrast to his father's funeral, this one was very informal. The choir sang several of Flora's favorite spirituals - ones she had taught to Drew as a child. Drew and her many church friends eulogized her. Drew was surprised how many people - teachers, nurses, lawyers, doctors, and others gave thanks to God for Flora's paying for part or all of their education.

She was laid to rest under a spreading oak tree. The simple headstone of Flora's mother nearby read: "Anna, Freed Slave.

The following article appeared under NOTICES in the June 17 edition of *The Sun:*

Flora Greene
Negro female,
Buried, Lot 28,
Greenbrier Cemetery

In that same edition, on the Society Page, was a prominently displayed announcement:

DUE TO THE DEATHS OF LOVED ONES,
THE WEDDING
OF
DR. DREW DUNCAN
AND
MISS MARY ELIZABETH McRAE,
ORIGINALLY SET FOR JUNE 24,
HAS BEEN POSTPONED UNTIL FALL.

Drew spent much of July and August settling his father's affairs. He also sold Flora's house, which a note in her Bible indicated was to be his.

He used the money from the sale to buy marble headstones for both Flora and her mother. Flora's was adorned with a beautiful angel whose outstretched arms reminded him of the always-welcoming arms with which she had always embraced him.

With the rest of the house money, Flora's savings, and one of his father's accounts, Drew set up a scholarship fund for deserving students from Flora's church.

The only personal items that Drew kept were Flora's Bible that he had read from so often and the quilt she had made from his old clothes.

Chapter 14

HONEYMOON
South Florida
September 1916

On September 10, Drew stood in front of the altar in Rosemont's Methodist Episcopal Church waiting for Mary Elizabeth to come through the front door. The flickering lights of a hundred candles bounced off the stained glass windows. The church was full of Mary Elizabeth's family, their neighbors, and friends from Baltimore.

There were no Duncan family members on the groom's side of the church, but standing beside Drew was his uncle. At the age of 77, Tyler Duncan looked at least twenty years younger. He could have passed for Drew's older brother.

As Drew waited at the front of the church, Mary Elizabeth entered at the vestibule, silhouetted by the rays of the setting sun coming through the open door. Mary Elizabeth and Drew's eyes locked, as Mary Elizabeth seemed to float down the aisle towards him. The congregation couldn't remember when they had seen a lovelier bride. They had long since given up hope of seeing Mary Elizabeth marry and here she was, more beautiful and radiant than any bride they could remember.

Drew was overwhelmed with his good fortune. Vows were exchanged in a blur. The next thing he remembered was the minister asking for the ring. Drew placed his mother's wedding ring on Mary Elizabeth's finger and she placed a matching gold band on his.

The reception was held in the McRae's back yard. Lanterns hung from the trees, giving just enough light to the waning day to illuminate the tables where a picnic style dinner was served.

The couple cut their cake under a cascade of falling red, orange, and yellow leaves. The Rosemont Barbershop Quartet and local fiddlers and pickers provided the music.

The crowd was having such a wonderful time that they would have missed the bride and groom's departure if Stephen hadn't caught sight of them.

The guests postponed their merriment to throw rice at the couple as they were getting into their Oldsmobile. Mary Elizabeth tossed her bouquet, never knowing who caught it. They drove down her parents' winding drive followed by strings of boots and shoes.

Drew had made arrangements to take his wife to a country inn just southwest of Brunswick on the Potomac River for their wedding night. It wasn't far from the farm, yet was a world away. He gave no hint of where they would spend their first night because he knew how Mary Elizabeth's brothers and their friends liked to pull pranks. He knew that the men would arrive later for a chivaree — if they had any idea where they were.

When Drew was much younger, he had followed friends after their weddings and had been party to the noisemaking outside the bridal chamber. What seemed like fun ten years before, now sounded outrageous. He wanted to be far away from such frivolity on his wedding night.

He had seen the lights of several trucks as he rounded a corner two miles from the farm. He ducked his car behind a clump of trees until they passed; waited until they came back by half an hour later, and, at last, headed to the inn.

At the bedroom door, Drew swooped Mary Elizabeth up in his arms and carried her into the room laughing. The bedspread was already turned down. There was a rose on the pillow. A fresh arrangement of fall flowers on the washstand brought the smells of the outside into the room.

The proprietor had lit a lamp by the bed and a fire in the fireplace, which gave a romantic aura to the room.

Mary Elizabeth went into the bathroom to change. Her mother had made a beautiful white silk gown for her to wear on this special night. She sprayed on some of the sweet smelling French perfume that her friend, Mae, had given to her. She took the pins out of her hair and shook it loose. She ran a brush through it for about twenty strokes, not the two hundred she usually did every night. She took a long deep breath, said a little prayer, and went out to become a wife to her wonderful new husband.

The light of the fireplace cast shadows on the wall of the two eagerly making love until the fire became embers.

The newlyweds left the inn after eating lunch and arrived in Baltimore in time to leave the car at the Charles Street house and catch a taxi to the train station. By 9 p.m., they were southward bound to Florida.

Two days later Dr. and Mrs. Drew Duncan, III, stepped off their honeymoon special into the September sunshine of Palm Beach. They had left an autumn world of golds and reds to come to a place alive with the greens of summer.

They were taken to Palm Beach's Royal Poinciana Hotel in a carriage that was pulled by a Negro man on a bicycle. The vehicle, Drew said, was called an Afromobile, one of the trademarks of the hotel.

Mary Elizabeth could see why her husband was in love with this lush land. She herself loved the way the fronds of the palm trees fanned out and gracefully fell from the top of each tree and then fell towards the ground. She was also enchanted by all the flowering plants that surrounded the hotel.

As they stood in front of the columned entrance to the four-story hotel, Mary Elizabeth was amazed at its size.

Drew explained to her that the hotel was one of the many that the railroad tycoon, Flagler, had built along the East Coast of Florida. The one here in Palm Beach, proclaimed to be the largest wooden structure in the world, was built specifically to accommodate the rich and famous that Flagler's railroad was bringing to Florida on a continuous basis each winter.

Once inside the edifice, its disarray astounded them. Boxes were piled to the ceiling in the hallways, painters were on tall ladders with drop cloths covering the floors to catch the dropped paint, and coverings were on most pieces of furniture. Everything indicated that the hotel was not open. The hotel clerk behind the reception desk seemed to read his mind.

"You are Dr. Duncan, I presume."

"Yes, but I don't understand what is going on here. I have brought my wife here for our honeymoon and it looks as if you are not even open."

"I'm so sorry if you were under the impression that we were in full operation during the fall. This is the time of year that we get the hotel ready for the high season, which begins the week after Christmas. Except for the repair work, though, this is an excellent time to be here. It's especially nice if you enjoy good food. The chefs want to try out everything they've learned over the summer and the fall crowd gets to taste a lot of special dishes.

Drew was leery of the situation but, because of the death of his father, he had decided to stay in Palm Beach rather than Miami, as they had at first planned.

He had been to the Poinciana several times on his way home from Miami and thought it would be a treat to stay there with Mary Elizabeth a few days before continuing on. 'The Season' never crossed his mind. He had always visited after Christmas with his college friends and their families. The hotel always seemed to be bursting at its seams with famous and wealthy people the weeks following Christmas.

Deciding to make the most of the situation and hoping that his honeymoon would not be spoiled by the fact that they had arrived before the high season, Drew asked the clerk to show them to their rooms, but he also told him if the accommodations were not satisfactory they would go on to the Royal Palm in Miami.

"Very good, sir. Here is your key. Adam will be your attendant as long as you stay with us."

Drew and Mary Elizabeth turned to see a young black man in his late teens already carrying their luggage.

"Thank you', Sur. Can I's do anythin' els' fer yo' en de missus?"

Adam's smile was ear to ear when Drew tipped him after he turned on the lights, put the bags down, and opened the windows. A moment after Adam left, as Mary Elizabeth and Drew started to embrace, the bellboy was back. "'scuse me. I's...Well, I's...I's new here...I's jes wanted ya ta know tha even though de rich folks...'scuse me 'gain...Leas wa's w'ats I's tryin' ter say...Der's go'n ter be a bas'ball gam' dis 'fternoon.....We's practic'n...Mos' us comes down fro' de Negro League ter work in de hotel. We's gits paid en we's can play ball in fronts of peoples all year...'scuse me agi'n....but I's kinda suspec' you'd likes ter know."

Adam closed the door, realizing that he wasn't supposed to talk that much to guests.

Mary Elizabeth was amazed at the conversation she had just heard. She knew of Drew's passion for baseball but had no idea why the subject had just come up between the Negro boy and Drew.

"My dear husband," chided Mary Elizabeth, "is there a secret look or something that all baseball players and baseball fanatics have so you know each other as soon as you meet?"

"Don't know. Maybe. I thought there was something about that boy I liked."

At a buffet lunch, in a grove of royal palms, the Duncans found that they weren't the only guests. About fifty others enjoyed the meal. When the hotel's chefs appeared, they were greeted with tremendous applause.

After lunch, Mary Elizabeth and Drew went for a swim in the hotel's pool. Neither had seen a man sit down at the water's edge and dangle his feet into the water. They looked up only when he spoke.

"I say, Glove, old chap, is that you?"

Drew looked up to the side of the pool.

"Cornelius! You son of a gun! What are you doing here?"

Drew pulled Mary Elizabeth over to the side.

"Cornelius, I'd like you to meet my bride, Mary Elizabeth. Mary, this is an old chum of mine, Cornelius Vanderbilt."

"You want to play a round of golf? It's a perfect day."

"I'm so sorry, but I'm on my honeymoon. I'm surprised to see you here since it isn't 'The Season'."

"I go where I want and when. I'm thrilled with the golf course here and like to play it right after it has been refurbished in the fall. Now's the best time to come. I want to know the lay of the land before others arrive. Who decrees the proper time to come here anyway? Probably my mother!"

Cornelius stood up and turned to Mary Elizabeth. Taking off his hat and half bowing he said, "So pleased to meet you, Ma'm. I'm so glad that the old chap was caught. Most of our friends are on their second or third wife."

As Cornelius picked up his golf club bag and slung it over his shoulder he asked, "Will you please join me for dinner? I think I'll be easy to find. When my parents and their friends are here, hundreds are served in the dining room. We're now being served in a smaller room, but the food is superb. Are you sure you won't play a round, Glove?"

He smiled as he walked towards the golf course.

"Was that a real Vanderbilt?" asked Mary Elizabeth.

"Of course he is real," Drew teased.

"You know what I mean. Is he one of THE Vanderbilts?"

"Yes."

"I can't believe you know him - and apparently you know him well!"

Drew diverted his bride's awe of his famous friend by grabbing her and dunking her several times. The two played together in the pool for the next hour before retreating to their spacious room that overlooked beautiful Lake Worth.

The beauty of the scenery was soon forgotten as the newlyweds found their own wonderland.

Later, Drew was drawn to some familiar sounds outside the window and wasn't surprised to see a group playing baseball.

He was ready to go down before Mary Elizabeth knew what was happening.

"Darling, I love you, you know that. Why don't you rest here while I go down and watch the game. I won't be long. I promise."

Mary Elizabeth hadn't had a full night's rest since their wedding. She readily agreed.

When she woke up at four to find her husband not in the room, she dressed and went down to the game, where there was plenty of noise and cheering.

She couldn't find Drew in the crowd of spectators, which should have been easy, since most were Negro hotel staff, watching an all Negro baseball team. She watched as a runner rounded third base on his way home. His foot was almost on home plate when the catcher, in an instant, caught a ball thrown from the outfield, touched home plate, and then the player.

"OUT!" the umpire yelled.

The crowd went wild. The team in the field ran to the catcher and one of the bigger players put him on his shoulder. They had won the game 5 to 4. The catcher up in the air was Drew, 'The Glove'!

That night at dinner the newlyweds ate with Cornelius and his friends. All of them were sons, nephews, or cousins of people who made headlines every day. Drew seemed to know them all.

Drew and Mary Elizabeth spent the next two days exploring Palm Beach, going for walks along the beach, swimming, playing ball, and inspecting Colonel Bradley's famous casino near the hotel which wasn't yet opened. They spent a lot of time talking with Drew's friends. But the majority of their time was spent exploring one another.

The night before Drew was to take her to the town of his dreams, Mary Elizabeth tossed and turned. She was impressed with everything she saw in Palm Beach. She was more impressed with the weather, the beach, Lake Worth, the birds and animals, and the plants than she was with the newly built grand homes and other structures in various stages of construction.

During the past two years she had realized that Drew's Baltimore friends were some of the wealthiest and most influential in the city. She felt a little uncomfortable socializing with them instead of entertaining them, but she loved Drew so very much that she knew she could adapt to his world. She never dreamed his circle of friends included the Vanderbilts. Probably he would introduce her next to someone with the last name of Rockefeller! She felt very uncomfortable in this society, but if this were Drew's life, it would be hers, too. She was sure that she could learn to act the part of the high society's doctor's wife.

What about this new town, Moore Haven? Was it another Palm Beach? Drew said that national figures like Alton Parker, William Jennings Bryan, and the Florida governor already had extensive holdings there. She pictured in her mind the same type of houses that lined the Palm Beach streets.

She had read all of Drew's books about Florida, as well as articles about the state that had appeared in popular magazines like *The Ladies' Home Journal* and *Goodey's*. She just had to learn as much as possible about the place her husband loved so much.

Drew, in all his excitement, had painted many different versions in her mind about what she was going to see. One day he would tell her about the untamed Everglades they would cross and in the next breath he would tell her of the city that was rising in the middle of all of the wilds.

No wonder, on the night before they were to actually leave to go into the Everglades, she dreamed of women in mink coats being chased into a swamp by alligators and bears!

The next afternoon Drew and Mary Elizabeth boarded a bus to go down the East Coast to Ft. Lauderdale. For part of the way, the drive followed close to the beach. Mary Elizabeth watched bathers as they swam and played in the aqua blue waters of the Atlantic.

Until this trip, the largest body of water Mary Elizabeth had seen was the Chesapeake. She had seen white caps and waves on its waters but nothing like what she saw when watching the waters of the Atlantic. The roll of the waves awed her as they became long swells, reaching their peaks, and rolling over like waterfalls.

At seven that evening they boarded *The Queen of the Glades* that would take them to the interior of south Florida. Drew was disappointed that his bride would make her first trip into the Pa-hoi-kee at night.

They stayed out on deck for a long time. Drew wanted Mary Elizabeth to hear the sounds, even though they couldn't see anything. In their hands were palm fronds they had been given when they boarded. Both thought the fronds were a welcoming tradition of some type until the mosquitoes attacked. After realizing the frond was their defense against the biting insects, they fanned madly and continued to enjoy the night air.

"Listen to the way all the animals try to outdo one another. Don't they remind you somewhat of an orchestra with dozens of instruments?"

Mary Elizabeth could feel her husband's excitement. She was interested in all that Drew pointed out, but couldn't understand why he didn't tell her about the hundreds of red lights she saw reflecting the lights of the boat. He changed the subject when she asked about them.

Both Drew and Mary Elizabeth were not quite sure if they liked their cabin bed or not. Even honeymooners needed more than a one-person bed for a good night's sleep.

They were up and out of bed at dawn both because of the sleeping situation and because Drew didn't want Mary Elizabeth to miss anything.

They were eating breakfast as *The Queen* entered the Okeechobee. Mary Elizabeth let out a squeal of delight that tickled Drew. The water was as smooth as glass, as far as one could see, and seemed to touch the sky at the horizon.

Thousands of ducks were resting on the water on their long flight from the north before flying further south for the winter. A cloud of black birds rose off the water in flocks as the boat drew near. They squawked, loudly protesting the boat's intrusion. Other birds swam in front of the boat, seeming to show the captain the way.

Then Mary Elizabeth caught sight of her first alligator. She thought at first it was a floating log. Then she saw its eyes, still visible and out of the water when the rest of the body was submerged. They were the same distance apart as the lights she had seen the night before. She suddenly realized what the lights were.

"Drew, those lights last night, they were the eyes of alligators? Am I right?"

"Yes, my dear. I didn't know how you would react seeing so many at once. I was hoping that you would enjoy all the beauty and sounds of the night. I didn't want to ruin the evening, but I am surprised you didn't hear the others talking."

Mary Elizabeth laughed nervously.

"Do you think an old tomboy like me would be bothered by a few hundred alligators? My goodness, if you had told me what they were, I would have tried to catch a few!"

The boat traveled west from South Bay, to Ritta Island, to Ritta, and then to Sandy Point. It stopped at each of the settlements to let off passengers, supplies, and mail. The doctor stood on the deck with his arm around his bride's waist as they waved to the residents who gathered near the docks awaiting goods and news from friends and family.

From Sandy Point the boat continued on a westward trek until it reached Observation Island. The turtles, the birds, and other animals of the island captivated Mary Elizabeth. When she felt Drew's grip tighten as the boat turned south, Mary Elizabeth turned her attention to the scenery in front of the boat. She could sense her husband's rush of adrenaline and she knew Moore Haven wasn't far ahead.

"Look straight ahead!" Drew exclaimed.

All that Mary Elizabeth could see was a flat-topped tree standing alone in the water.

"Look!" he said again as he pointed. "That's the Lone Cypress!"

Mary Elizabeth realized the tree was the one that Drew had talked about that marked the entrance to the large canal. The tree had come to symbolize the town that was built in its shadow.

As *The Queen* docked just below the newly constructed locks, Drew pointed out the different buildings he saw in town. New construction was everywhere. Buildings that had been under construction in December now were open for business.

Mary Elizabeth loved what she saw. The only structures were one and two stories. She appreciated the way every two-story building seemed to have a porch overhanging the sidewalk below. The town looked like it could have been in any of the pictures she had seen of towns on the western frontier.

It was mid afternoon on September 18 when The Duncans descended from *The Queen*. Storm clouds were moving in fast from the west as Drew and Mary Elizabeth gathered up their luggage from where it had been unloaded onto the dock. With a group of their fellow passengers, they walked quickly to the hotel in the next block.

A plump, middle-aged woman met them at the front door.

As she lifted the latch out of the hook and opened the screen door the woman said, "Come in! It looks as if you made it just in the nick of time. We are about to have a gully washer."

"I'm Mrs. Edwards. My husband and I've only been here a month but I have gotten used to these rain storms."

"Aren't the Dunicans still here?" inquired Drew.

"The Dunicans? Oh, you mean the young couple that ran the place a while back. I don't know where they are but they might have gone back to New York. I hear the wife was very homesick. They were gone before we arrived. Must have been nice folks because I'm asked about them all of the time."

"That's too bad. I thought I had found a family connection.

As Drew signed their names into the guest book, Mrs. Edwards handed them the key to their room on the second floor.

"You are in room 24. There are extra towels on the bed."

Drew thanked her and turned to leave.

"You might need this."

Mrs. Edwards handed him a whiskey bottle filled with amber liquid. Drew waved the bottle aside.

"No, Ma'am, I don't drink."

The stout woman gave a belly laugh.

"You might if you don't take this. This ain't whiskey. It's Walker's Devilment. We use it to keep the mosquitoes away! You take this strap and dip it into this liquid."

She demonstrated with a little piece of cloth about the size of a lamp wick

Drew had failed to notice at first.

"Then you blow on the liquid," she continued.

"That should kill the mosquitoes in the room. Do that anytime they get bad. You know we are still in the rainy season and sometimes those pesky things can be as thick as molasses. Also, there's mosquito netting that you can pull around the bed."

Drew watched his wife's reaction to Mrs. Edwards' advice. He smiled when she didn't seem to notice. As they climbed the stairs, Mrs. Edwards yelled across the room,

"Supper will be at six."

As Drew continued to climb the stairs he thought about the amber liquid he was carrying and realized he had never been in Florida during the rainy season. He had only read about the significant changes the wet season brought to the area. He understood how the water level, the mosquitoes, the plants, the animals, and now the humans were all affected by the wet season of the summer and fall. It was a different world from the dry season of the winter and spring. Thank goodness he came now so he could experience the wet season first hand.

The rain started falling heavily on the tin roof just as the couple entered their room. Drew put his arms around his wife and embraced her.

"I want to thank you again for coming with me to see what else I fell in love with, instead of taking the European holiday we had planned. I know that this is a world away from everything and everyone you know and love. It just means so much to me that you wanted to see my investment instead of calling me a crazy fool."

"Drew Duncan! I have known you for almost three years. I have never known you to do anything foolish. I'll love what you love and go where you go. You know we couldn't go to Europe because of the war. So far, this has been a wonderful alternative.

Drew held Mary Elizabeth even tighter, smiling at his bride as he said, "Yes, just look at this room. We have electricity! And something called Walker's Devilment. Could there be anything nicer?"

Drew didn't wait for an answer. He knew the room at the Royal Poinciana was a palace compared to this.

"This room has everything. Why we could live right here! See, here is a desk that I can write my memoir's of the first week of the greatest marriage in history and there is a rocking chair where you can just rock your life away."

"Very funny. Come look at this view."

Drew joined Mary Elizabeth at the window. The rain was still coming down in sheets, but from their open window through the wire mesh screen, they could see the landscape of the hotel's lawn and the banks of the canal. The royal palms and oaks which lined the lawn were bowing and swaying in the heavy wind; leaves from the poincianas carpeted the street; the yellow

135

and pink hibiscus had closed their petals because of the lack of sunlight; and rain bounced off the multi-colored leaves of the croton hedges beneath them. The rich, luscious greens of thousands of ferns confirmed that this was truly a topical paradise.

"I love this view, even through this downpour."

When Drew and Mary Elizabeth went down to dinner, there were about twenty others in the cypress-paneled dining room. They recognized three from *The Queen.* The specialty of the house was catfish. With the fish came fried potatoes, grits, hushpuppies, and cole slaw. The fish, grits, and hushpuppies were new to Mary Elizabeth but she immediately liked the tastes that seemed to be made for one another and enjoyed seconds of every dish.

After dinner the guests retired to the lobby where there were enough overstuffed couches and chairs for everyone to sit and be comfortable. Mary Elizabeth was intrigued with the menagerie of local animals that some taxidermist had ensured were lifelike.

A variety of fish adorned one section of the wall. Three deer heads, a full-sized bear, and a panther poised to jump gave a realistic view of what the area's wildlife was like.

The skin of a rattlesnake and the hide of a ten-foot alligator, however, made Mary Elizabeth cringe. Curiosity overcame repulsion, though, and she reached out to see what the now-harmless creatures felt like. Drew thought she had passed one more test that would make her life in Florida more acceptable.

Before the evening was over everyone had become acquainted with the other guests. Some were in town to buy property. Others were staying in the hotel while their homes were being built. Still others were town residents who had come for dinner and stayed to socialize.

The rain continued through the night. The intensity of the rain could be measured as it hit the tin roof overhead.

The couple woke the next morning eager to explore but still heard the steady beat of the rain.

"I have never been in a storm which has lasted this long!" said Drew.

He smiled at his wife. "You know what it means when you can't go outdoors."

"And what have you been doing when it rains for the last forty-one years?"

"I could only dream; but now I'm ready to make up for lost time!"

The rain continued all day. Most of the guests talked, read, and played cards and board games. Drew paced the floor like an expectant father. He was ready to show his wife the town and where he wanted to build a house. He hoped she would still want to live here even if they had to live in an ark half of the year.

The rain slacked up in the late afternoon. An elderly white-haired man with rubber boots, a raincoat, and big umbrella came into the hotel. In his left hand he was carrying a black doctor's bag. Several people greeted him at once.

"Good afternoon, Doc!"

The old man mumbled as he took off his wet over garments.

"Where's Vera?"

The doctor left the room without another word and went into the kitchen. One of the guests who was staying at the hotel while his house was being built, turned to Drew.

"That's Dr. Martin. He is our only doctor and I don't know how long we can keep him. He treats everyone on this side of the lake. Sometimes he might be in Ritta. Then he might be in Lakeport or out with the cowmen. He really needs help. There is a limit to what one man can do."

"Say, aren't you a doctor? Are you moving here or are you one of those land speculators?"

"I am a doctor and I hope I can move here but it won't be for a while."

"We sure need you. And when the train gets here even more people will be coming. We'll be quite a city in just a few years."

"You mentioned a train. Is one coming?"

"All the big landowners talk about it. Moore had big plans."

"What do you mean, had? He is the one who sold my land to me last December."

"Mr. Moore sold his company to some guy from up north back in the spring. He brought in two Northerners as partners and then they had a squabble. Now a Mr. Horwitz and a Mr. O'Brien have formed the Desoto Stock Farms Company."

"But what does that have to do with the railroad?"

"I was getting to that. Mr. Horwitz's brother-in-law is vice president of the Atlantic Coast Line - and he is a business partner of J.P. Morgan's. So you see..."

"Let us hope. It will be a lot easier to get here by train."

Loud talking in the kitchen interrupted their conversation.

"Vera, you sit down!" boomed Dr. Martin. "You can't stand up like that with your rheumatism. I came all the way over here in a boat to see you. I knew you would be a fool and would continue to be on your feet during all of this rain. I know you're in pain."

"And who is going to run this place? You know the only help I have is Selma when Mr. Edwards is away. Things just don't happen by magic, you know. Selma can't do it all by herself."

"Get some more help. I know lots of women down in those tar paper shacks that would love the extra money."

"And how do I pay someone else and clear a profit?"

"Make a good profit and put yourself in a push chair. It's up to you. I have had my say."

"Stubborn old cuss!" Dr. Martin was saying under his breath as he came out of the kitchen.

He began to greet people as if he didn't know they had heard every word of his conversation with Mrs. Edwards.

Dr. Martin's eye's brightened as Drew introduced himself.

"When can you start? I needed you yesterday."

"I would love to start tomorrow but I still have a practice in Baltimore. I've bought some property here but am still debating a move. My wife and I are here on our honeymoon so she can help with my decision."

"Honeymoon? You brought your new wife here on your honeymoon? Son, you do have the muck in your shoes. If you chose Moore Haven for a honeymoon, you're hooked and you just don't know it yet."

"I must admit that I'm hooked and I can't figure out why. What is it about this place?"

"It's more than the land. It's the people. It's a new frontier. There's excitement in the air."

"But," the doctor continued, "I'm afraid I might have to leave soon because the load is too much for one man. I need to go where the pace is slower. But then again I hate to leave the town and the entire south lake area without any kind of medical help."

"If you do decide to come, your wife has to be behind you 100 percent. I don't know what your workload is in Baltimore but I do know there are many other doctors. Here you will be alone; unless, of course, I stay. You might be gone for days treating patients who can't get into town. I want you to know what you and your family will be getting into."

"Doc!"

Drew and Dr. Martin looked up to see a rain-soaked Negro boy.

"Doc, come quick! Mama's in trouble wit' de baby an' Miss Wanda she told me to come fetch ya. I's got a boat. Please come, Doc."

"Do you want to come with me?"

Drew was about to say yes when he remembered Mary Elizabeth.

"I wish I could, but remember I am on my honeymoon."

"Well then, you better stop talking to me. You don't want to get your wife's dander up already. There will be enough time for that."

It was only after Dr. Martin left with the boy that Drew realized Mary Elizabeth was not in the lobby. He leaped up the stairs to their room, but she was neither there nor in the bathroom.

"Where could she be?" Drew wondered.

As he began to panic he told himself she wouldn't leave the hotel in the rain. He went back down the stairs to find only men in the lobby. When he went into the dark dining room he could see a light coming from beneath the kitchen door. He opened it to find his wife washing dishes and another woman drying as Mrs. Edwards watched them, laughing and talking with her legs propped up on a kitchen chair.

That night, Mary Elizabeth was awakened from a deep sleep by the sound of a woman screaming. She, too, screamed, awakening Drew, who began to laugh as he listened.

"That's a wild cat," he told her.

Mary Elizabeth began to cry hysterically; not believing her husband could laugh at a woman in distress and call her names, too.

Drew reached for his wife when he realized she definitely did not follow what he had said.

"Darling, that sound is a wild animal - a panther. Its nighttime call sounds just like a woman screaming, as you've just heard. Listen closely and you can probably tell the difference."

He held her until she relaxed and she finally believed him. But, she also planned to check out his story with Mrs. Edwards in the morning - just in case.

The next morning the sun shone brightly into the newlywed's window. Drew leaped out of bed as soon as he woke up and saw the sun. His first thought was, "We'll finally get to leave this damn hotel. Another day inside and I will go stark raving mad."

After they finished breakfast they headed for the front door. Mrs. Edwards came scurrying from the kitchen.

"Do you really think you'll be going anywhere today? It's been raining for thirty-eight hours. Where do you think all of that water is?"

Drew opened the door and all he saw was a lake. His heart dropped.

"How long will it take for the water to drain off?"

"You should be able to get out tomorrow if there is no more rain. Maybe even this afternoon."

Drew couldn't believe it. So this was what the wet season meant. Mary Elizabeth found two books on the bookshelves behind the registration desk. She brought out a book of poetry by Carl Sandberg for Drew to read while she opened *Little Women,* a childhood favorite of hers. By two o'clock Drew could contain himself no longer.

"I'm getting out, even if it is in a boat!"

Mrs. Edwards met them at the front door with rubber hip boots.

"If you just have to go out, put these on. Have fun in the mud!"

"If you see snakes, and you probably will, just stand still and let them pass. That's a rule of the land down here."

Drew thanked Mrs. Edwards for her advice, but did not tell her that he had learned that lesson years ago from Gopher.

Drew took his wife by the arm and they went outside together. He was surprised to see how much the water had receded during the day. The streets, just a little higher than the adjacent land, now had only a few puddles; however, the streets were still muddy and not easy to navigate. The land around the streets was still covered with a lake of water, probably about two inches deep.

Drew and Mary Elizabeth followed the avenue that connected with the street in front of the hotel. Mary Elizabeth laughed when she saw the street sign.

"Avenue K? I suppose the one to the north is J and the one to the south is L."

"You catch on fast. I didn't realize you were so smart."

"Don't tell me they really are? Couldn't someone come up with something better like birds or flowers or even Presidents?"

"I think the alphabet is unique."

"You can tell men did all of this. The first thing I will do if we move here is get a petition started to give real names to the streets and avenues. I guess the streets are numbers."

"Right again, my dear."

Mary Elizabeth shuddered. The couple followed the road to a new section of houses that were being built.

"Why are the houses so far off of the ground?" Mary Elizabeth asked, as she saw they were on posts some five feet off the ground.

"For air circulation and because of high water. See the water standing under them now. The Indians do the same thing with their chickees."

A black indigo snake about five feet long crossed the road in front of them "Ohhhhhhh, a snake!" screamed Mary Elizabeth, getting closer to Drew for protection.

"Stand still. Always stand still and give them the right of way. You won't have any problem. I learned that from Gopher. It's a harmless indigo snake. Look at its beautiful color. When the sun is brighter, you can see the blue hue. It's just like indigo ink."

Drew continued, "We need to get a book on snakes so you will know the harmless from the poisonous."

"A snake is a snake."

"Honey, I told you we were coming to the Everglades and you have read all the books I have about the area. You knew there would be snakes."

"But this isn't the real Everglades. It isn't a swamp."

"The 'Glades aren't all swamp. What do you think this land would be like if it hadn't been reclaimed? We are standing in the Okeechobee basin and the northern part of the Glades."

Carefully the two went on. Mary Elizabeth was caught up in the construction of the houses that lined the avenue. The houses were bungalows, the same type being built throughout the country, but were adapted to south Florida weather with the windows and doors situated across the rooms from each other so there would be good air flow.

There seemed to be only two floor plans. The one-story houses were all the same size and built in a box shape with a screened-in porch across the front. On one side was a big room with the kitchen behind it. Off to the side were two smaller rooms with an even smaller room between them. They concluded that these were two bedrooms and a bath. The larger houses seemed to have more character with what appeared to be an attic bedroom. The ground floor was basically the same plan as the smaller houses.

Mary Elizabeth was startled when Drew said, "Here we are!"

She looked up to see an empty lot between two of the bigger houses. "Where are we?"

"This is the lot I bought last December. Do you like it?"

"But I thought you bought acres of land, not just a lot."

"The forty acres are south of town. This is the land I thought we would build on."

Mary Elizabeth tried to imagine a house and yard on the sticky black dirt, but she couldn't.

"Do you agree with me? This would be a perfect place to raise our family."

Turning away to hide the tears in her eyes, Mary Elizabeth almost choked as she said, "Yes, Drew. I love it."

The words were the ones she knew he wanted to hear, but not the ones her heart wanted to say. Seeing the emptiness of the muddy lot and trying to imagine what Drew visualized, she began to face the reality about coming here to this place so far away from her family and the life she had always known.

"I have the acreage south of town but it is so isolated. I thought this would be a better place to live because of the neighbors. I don't know how much I'll be away and I would feel better about you having people around." He pulled her close as he shared his dream.

Thankful he could not see her quivering face and the tears she was fighting to hold back, Mary Elizabeth could think only of wild animals and snakes. She could not imagine this place as her future home. She cringed inwardly at the thought.

Drew never noticed that she had not embraced his dream.

At last he suggested they tour the rest of the town.

They walked a block farther west. New home construction continued. They turned and made their way to Avenue J and followed it until they reached the business district. There the wooden boardwalks were high enough off of the ground not to have been submerged by the flooding. They walked down the boardwalk, glad to get out of the mud. Drew was ready to eat again so when they saw "Mae's Cafe" they went in and ordered Coca Colas and a piece of apple pie. When the waitress brought the orders, she introduced herself.

"Name's Mae. Are you two just visiting our new city or are you going to stay?"

"We have some land here and we are discussing moving here. What do you think?"

"I can't think of anything better. We came from Iowa a little over a year ago. I'm happy here but you have to learn to love the muck smell, water, heat, mosquitoes, snakes, and other varmints. My husband is farming a hundred acres south of town. He has just brought in his third crop of beans this year. You can't do that in Iowa. We started out living in a little tar shack like most of the other farmers, but we have already built a house. Say, are you farmers, too? No, you don't look the type but I've seen others come that weren't the farming type and they have done real good. What do you do?"

"I'm a doctor and my wife is a pianist."

"A doctor! Listen we really need a good doctor here."

She called to the other people in the cafe'.

"Listen, folks. I want you to meet this man. He's a doctor."

They all gathered around, introducing themselves, and wanting to know when Drew would be setting up shop.

By the time Drew and Mary Elizabeth left the cafe, the sun was getting low in the sky. They walked down the boardwalk in front of newly constructed businesses to the Lone Cypress at the end of the street.

"Look at those spikes that go all of the way up the tree," observed Drew.

Before Mary Elizabeth could say a word, Drew had pulled himself up to the first spike and was climbing the tree.

Dark was encroaching fast. If he wanted to see anything, he had to climb the tree as fast as he could. At the top of the tree, Drew was overwhelmed. To the west he could see the sun setting; to the north was the endless blue water of Lake Okeechobee; to the south the canal ran through twisted pond apples, willow elders, and ferns to a small lake. Surrounding the lake and beyond lay an endless sea of green saw grass. He had never seen it green before. At Christmas time, it was always brown.

As the darkness closed in, Drew promised himself he would come to this land and take care of its people. If he had to be the only doctor, he would. If this tree could stand alone and survive, so could he. He had the advantage of having Mary Elizabeth as a mate. She seemed to have fallen in love with this place, too.

"I don't believe you just did that," said Mary Elizabeth as Drew reached the ground. "I didn't know you were so impulsive."

"Mary, it was wonderful!"

He told her about what he had seen and how he felt.

"That will be my retreat whenever I feel overwhelmed by work and need to get away."

"Yes, and what will your patients think of having a doctor who roosts in the trees with the birds?"

"Not just any tree. Only the Lone Cypress."

The couple walked hand in hand to the hotel. Drew's heart was leaping and Mary Elizabeth was on the verge of tears.

After dinner (supper as the locals called it), the hotel guests enjoyed listening to Mary Elizabeth's playing on an old squeaky piano. They were delighted that she could play any song they requested. She played *Alexander's Ragtime Band* and *I Love a Piano*. She also played *The Miami Waltz* for her husband.

"Honey, if you can play that well, you must play with a band or something," commented Mrs. Edwards. Mary Elizabeth looked at her with her big green eyes. She didn't say anything, but Mrs. Edward's saw tears swell up in her eyes. Mary Elizabeth excused herself and ran up the stairs to her room.

"Oh, Doc. What did I say? I'm sorry I upset her."

Drew dashed after his wife but turned before he mounted the stairs.

"Yes, she does play for a band. It is called the Peabody Symphony Orchestra."

Everyone looked astonished. Mrs. Edwards broke the silence as soon as she knew that Drew was out of hearing range.

"Poor dear. You can tell the doctor wants to come here but I'm betting she doesn't and will come here only to please him. She definitely doesn't want to leave that other world behind. My husband and I came here to start all over again after we lost everything in Nebraska. Even Mr. Moore was looking to regain the fortune he lost when he lost his britches in Washington State. That couple, on the other hand, seems to have everything already. Why would they want to come to this wilderness far from any culture?"

"But Mrs. Edwards, we are about to get culture. The flickers are coming right here to Moore Haven."

Everyone laughed.

When Drew got to the room, Mary Elizabeth was coming out of the bathroom. It was apparent that she had just washed her face. She smiled at Drew and laughed, "I don't know what came over me."

Drew took his wife by the hand and said, "Mary, we came for you to see this place. If you don't want to come just say so and that will be the end of it. We can sell the land here and turn a good profit."

Mary Elizabeth had seen and felt Drew's excitement more than ever during their afternoon walk. She loved Drew and would go to the ends of the earth with him. She felt she was just about there, but she was determined to convince him she shared his enthusiasm. She hated that her emotions had betrayed her. Now she had to convince her husband she shared his joy.

"Drew, I want to be where you are happiest. When we have children, I can't be with the Symphony. People need you here. There aren't too many places left to pioneer. I know you have always wanted adventure. Let's build that house here and build a new life together here with our children."

The next day Drew and Mary Elizabeth walked into D.B. Donaldson's Contractor's Office to look at house plans.

"Folks, I have one set of plans. I can add an attic room if you want one, and a fireplace."

"Mr. Donaldson, if you can add an attic on to your plans, why can't you add a back room?" inquired Mary Elizabeth.

"Let me see what you have in mind."

While the contractor and his wife focused their attention on house plans, Drew went over to the office of the Desoto Stock Farms Company. He was astonished at what happened the moment he said he would like to sell his forty acres south of town. Drew had a buyer before he left the office. He had tripled his investment in ten months. Mr. O'Brien drew up the papers and Drew walked out of the office a much richer man.

"Look, Drew!" Mary Elizabeth cried as soon as Drew came through the door.

"Mr. Donaldson agreed to what I wanted. We took his basic plan, and added a fireplace and built in book cases in the living room; glass enclosed shelving between the living room and dining room; a window seat in an alcove in the dining room and a big back room where he had a porch. He even agreed to put stairs to the upstairs room coming down into the back room. Don't you love it? And Drew, if you approve, he can add a small wing with a bath, a bedroom, and an office off to the side of that room."

"Anything that would please my wife, he smiled. "But, Mr. Donaldson, I haven't seen any other houses with additions, have I?"

"Well, Doc, no one else tried after I gave the spiel of just the one basic plan."

"Are you sure? There will be women after us."

"I think we can handle them," he said as money signs replaced his blue eyes.

"What kind of siding will we have?" Drew questioned.

"You can choose. We have wood or shingles made from asbestos or cypress."

"Cypress."

"That will run much higher than the others."

Drew thought about the profit he had just made and said, "Give my wife exactly what she wants and give me cypress. Can you build a three car garage with cypress shingles too?"

"Three cars?" Mary Elizabeth and Mr. Donaldson exclaimed together.

"Yes, one for my car, one for the one you will have some day, and one for my boat."

Drew signed an agreement and a check so construction could begin as soon as possible. The couple had planned to take a steamer down the three-mile canal to Lake Hicpochee, to the Caloosahatchee River, and into the Gulf. From there they would travel north to Tampa where they would board a train to take them back to Baltimore. Instead they took the first steamer back to Palm Beach and caught the train to Baltimore.

Plans were made to sell the house on Charles Street and his partnership to

Dr. Watson. With the money from both sales he could set up a medical clinic and the new house in Moore Haven would be paid in full.

He estimated they would be in Moore Haven to live by the first of the summer, not knowing that world events would conspire to put those plans and dreams on hold.

Chapter 15

BALTIMORE
Fall and Winter, 1916

Drew and Mary Elizabeth arrived in Baltimore on September 26. As they stepped from the train they were almost blown off their feet by a strong, bitterly cold wind. The light dusters they were wearing were designed to give protection from the dust, not the cold. They hailed a taxi and snuggled under a blanket provided by the taxi driver. By the time they reached Charles Street, they were chilled to their bones.

As Drew was paying the driver, the frail old man said, "It looks like an early winter. I hope it won't be a long one."

Drew smiled when he thought this would be his last one in the snow.

They hurried from the taxi into the house. Drew didn't bother to find his keys because he had wired Marquita, his new housekeeper, of the date of their arrival. He turned the big brass doorknob, only to find the door locked.

When he rang and no one came, Drew grew impatient, as well as much colder, and rang the bell for the second time. When there was no response again, he found the spare key in the Boston fern planter, which should have been moved inside before the freeze and was definitely an item in the house that he'd not have to worry about disposing of. The neglect of the staff had taken care of that for him.

As Drew opened the door, Marquita came running. The young blonde, German immigrant approached the couple, and apologize

"Oh, Dr. Duncan, I would have hurried if I had known it was you."

Mary Elizabeth climbed the stairs because she didn't want to hear the reprimand she was sure Marquita was about to receive from her tired husband.

Mary Elizabeth heard Drew say after a lengthy time behind the closed doors of the library, "I'm going to join my wife upstairs. Would you please bring us some sandwiches and milk up to the master bedroom?"

When she heard Drew, Mary Elizabeth got up from the chair she was sitting in at the top of the stairs.

"Mary, I thought you would be taking a bath by now."

"Drew, I don't know where to go."

Drew laughed.

"I have already become so used to you that I can't remember when you weren't with me. Since I know every corner of this old house, I just took it for granted that you did, too!"

As they walked down the hall, Drew asked, "Was I as harsh to that girl as I think I was?"

"Yes, dear. I think the trip and excitement have taken a toll on you."

Drew opened the door to the master bedroom. "What a beautiful room, Drew!" Mary Elizabeth walked around the room admiring the old samplers and the pictures of several generations.

"In the morning you will have to tell me who are in these pictures. Right now I'm going to take a bath. Where is it?"

Drew opened the door to the room his father had created from half of the room next to the master bedroom. The other half had been made into the hall bathroom.

When Mary Elizabeth disappeared, Drew surveyed the room. He had few reservations about bringing his wife to the bed of his parents, but realized it was probably his last right of passage. Still cold, he leaned over to check the furnace grate. Heat was just beginning to come in and he once again realized how inept the housekeeper was.

When he awoke the next morning Drew wondered why he was in his father's bed. Mary Elizabeth stretched out her arm and he remembered everything. For the first time since their wedding night, he kissed her and hopped out of bed, ready to make life-changing plans.

On December 21, the papers were signed and an agreement made with the president of the Baltimore Bank and Trust to take possession of the house on January 10. The president was not only pleased to be buying one of the most prestigious homes in Baltimore, he also had negotiated with Drew for some of its fine furniture. Mary Elizabeth and Drew kept a few of the family's treasures, including the master bedroom furnishings, Flora's' kitchen table, and the shipmaster's desk made by Drew's great-grandfather.

Drew persuaded Dr. Watson, who held one-third interest in the clinic, to buy his father's third, which would make him the senior partner. Drew would keep a third both for financial reasons and to keep the family name on the clinic as he knew his father would want. Dr. Watson knew he couldn't handle the workload alone so he persuaded Drew to stay with him until the end of August when his son would graduate from medical school.

Drew had written to Mr. Donaldson to finish the blueprints for the house, but to put the construction on hold until the summer. Drew wanted to be there to watch each board put in place on his Florida home.

The following evening, Drew and Mary Elizabeth lit the candles on the tree in the parlor. Drew was somewhat sad, realizing it would be the last Christmas in this house that he and his family had called home for four generations. He was also happy to be sharing Christmas with his lovely wife, his first Christmas as a married man.

As they finished lighting the candles, Drew took in the grandeur of the room and reflected on the memories associated with every object. A fir, decorated with candles, had stood in the same corner for all of the Christmases of his life.

Mary Elizabeth disappeared into the kitchen, returning with a plate of gingerbread.

"I knew I smelled gingerbread!"

He took a bite.

"This is absolutely wonderful."

He continued, "Mary, I don't know how you did it, but your gingerbread is as good as Flora's."

"Why thank you, sir, that's a supreme compliment."

Mary Elizabeth paused, and then continued, "I do have a confession to make though, about my cooking ability. I had thought at one time I'd never tell you."

"Go on, you have me intrigued."

"Well, I got the idea last Christmas when I saw how you loved the gingerbread. I asked Flora to give me the recipe. She had nothing written down and could tell me none of the measurements."

"Well, this tastes just like hers. How did you get the recipe if she couldn't tell you?"

"I watched her make some and I wrote down what she did. Then she said that I must have all her other recipes just in case she wasn't around to cook for you. Then she laughed and said that she planned to be around to see our children's children."

"I spent many afternoons over here watching her prepare your favorite meals. I wrote down exactly her ingredients and the amounts. I timed her mixing, the baking, and the frying times."

"Frying? You mean you can fix chicken the way she did."

"Chicken, biscuits, sour cream pound cake, gravies, dumplings, and all of the others. Not only did I copy the recipes, I fixed them, too, with her watching everything I did. She wouldn't let it go out of her kitchen until it tasted just like hers - or to hear her tell it, "Purty close, it'll pass, I reckons.""

"I passed the test because you always gave her a compliment. The night you told her that chicken I had fried was the best she had ever made, I think I saw tears in her eyes."

Later that night, twenty of Drew's closest friends sat with Drew and Mary Elizabeth around the massive dining room table. The china, silver, and crystal would be packed away after the meal. As Drew stood at the head of the table carving the goose, he gave his farewell speech to his friends.

"All of you know how much I care for you. Some of you I've known since we ran hoops up and down Charles Street as boys."

He looked directly at Ernest Culpepper and said, "Ernest followed me everywhere. He even went to Yale with me although he became a lawyer instead of a doctor. Now look at him. He's a judge."

"Most people in Baltimore are wondering if I have taken leave of my senses. All of you know I've always wanted to wander and seek adventure. Most of you thought when I turned forty and got married that would remain a dream."

Drew inhaled deeply, looked at Mary Elizabeth, and continued his discourse.

"Well, I'm going to follow my dream. This is the last time you will be with me here in Baltimore."

"We'll leave this house tomorrow morning and Baltimore the first of August," Drew continued. "Mary and I are going to be pioneers in the reclaimed Everglades of Florida. Moore Haven, the town where we're going, is vibrant and growing. It will be a good size city by the 30s. I hope a few of you will come visit us - and perhaps even come with us and be a part of the adventure that is waiting," Drew concluded.

After a few comments about how he would be missed the conversation centered on the war in Europe. That was the last thing that Drew wanted to discuss. He tried to talk about the land opening up in south Florida and about the opportunities his friends would be missing if they didn't buy some acreage, but they didn't appear too interested, except when he shared that he had tripled his money in less than a year with the forty acres. Then the conversation went back to the war.

"We should have declared war on Germany when their U-Boats blew up the first merchant ship. It's a crime against mankind that we didn't get into war when they blew up the *Lusitania* last year. Something should have been done then and there. I agree with the person who called Wilson a 'human icicle'."

"Did anyone hear what has to be a rumor? They say the Germans sank the *Lusitania* as an act of war. They claim guns and ammunition were being carried in the cargo headed for the Allies."

"Well, I support Wilson. He says that he'll keep us out of the war and he has so far. He's been good for the country. I think that America is doing her duty already for the Allies. We are their breadbasket and their arsenal."

"I, for one, want to keep out of it. My grandfather is still living with me. He came to this country to get away from the constant wars in Europe. He thought America would be far enough away not to be bothered by their affairs."

"I agree."

"I think if America gets involved, we could put an end to the Huns fast. Look how our boys pushed Villa back into Mexico. And after ten years of the Cubans fighting the Spanish, we ended the war in less than two months. I say, let's go and end this thing now."

"Didn't we show the world we were strong in Cuba? We came out on top of a powerful European force."

"That was to protect our own backyard!"

"I say let them fight on foreign soil. I'll fight when the war gets to American soil."

"Don't you think we should fight BEFORE the war gets to our shore?"

The younger men at the party were anxious to get into the war. They wanted to go participate. Drew remembered another time twenty years before when he felt the same. He was glad he was past forty and wouldn't have to go if the nation did indeed get into the war that seemed to be knocking at America's front door.

The talk of the war stopped when Mary Elizabeth came back into the room and started playing Christmas carols. The crowd of friends gathered around the piano to sing. Snow began to fall and someone suggested that they made a good enough sound to sing to the neighbors. They all bundled up and went out to sing of joy and peace to their neighbors.

The next morning Mary Elizabeth and Drew left Marquita to clean up after the party, take down the tree, and pack up their personal things in the downstairs rooms. They left to spend Christmas on the farm in Rosemont.

Chapter 16

THE WAR TO END ALL WARS
1917

The week after Christmas, Drew and Mary Elizabeth settled into their rented home on Margaret Street. The red Georgian brick row house was large enough for entertaining, although parties were not on the newlyweds' agenda.

Whether he was at home or at work, Drew always had a notepad at his side ready to jot down plans and ideas for his new practice. Mary Elizabeth taught two classes a week at Peabody and continued to play with the Symphony.

All of Baltimore seemed to be crazed with the idea of war. German-Americans were the targets of hate throughout the city.

One day in March, as she rounded the corner of her house, Mary Elizabeth saw a crowd of men gathered around her neighbor's stoop. As she drew closer, she heard a young man ask a German immigrant girl about four years old if she wanted the American flag or the doll he was holding. When the little girl reached out for the doll, the crowd went into a frenzy.

"Burn the house of the Huns."

"See how disloyal the Germans are."

The little girl didn't know what all of the yelling was about and started crying for her mama.

Mary Elizabeth pushed through the angry mob and took the little girl in her arms.

"Don't you realize that this is just a little girl?" she screamed. "Which would your little one choose?"

After more yelling and the shouting of obscenities, the crowd began to disperse. Mary Elizabeth took one last glance at the looks of hatred on the faces of the people standing nearby before taking the bewildered little girl inside to her mother.

She wondered how often a scene similar to the one she had just witnessed would be repeated in a city that was full of German Americans.

It was late when Mary Elizabeth got home that evening. Drew was sitting at his desk with only his reading light on.

"I'm sorry I'm late, but you will never believe what happened on my way home, in this very block."

When she turned on another light, she realized something was very wrong. Drew, who held his head in his hands, had not looked up.

"What's wrong, my darling?'

She ran across the room to kiss him. He looked up at her with tear-filled eyes and handed her a letter. The letter was from Uncle Tyler dated the week before. Her anger boiled as she read the letter.

> *Havana, Cuba*
> *16 March 1917*
>
> *Dear Drew,*
> *I am writing to you on behalf of the Red Cross.*
> *There is another great need for our services. It is just*
> *a matter of time before the Americans will be at war in*
> *Europe.*
> *The Red Cross is already over there.*
> *I want to go but I am just too old. I know that my*
> *time is about to run out and I have recommended you*
> *to President Wilson to head the Red Cross operations*
> *in Europe. He has agreed.*
> *Please telegraph your answer.*
> *Give a kiss to your darling wife.*
>
> *With love,*
> *Tyler*

Mary Elizabeth was furious. She screamed in frustration, "Why you, Drew? Why you? Doesn't your uncle realize that you have just gotten married? Your commitment is to me now, not the Red Cross... you..."

Her voice trailed off as Drew handed her a telegram.

> **HABANA CUBA**
> **20 MARCH**
> **REGRET TO INFORM YOU THAT DR T DUNCAN**
> **PASSED AWAY THIS AM**
>
> **JOSE GARCIA MD**

A week later memorial services were held for Dr. Phillip Tyler Duncan, M.D. Since he had been buried in Cuba, only a few friends of the family and several from the National Headquarters of the American Red Cross were in attendance. A marker was put in place in Westminster Burial Ground next to the graves of other members of his family.

After the services, the members of the Red Cross came to the house for a dinner that had been prepared by family friends. Mary Elizabeth knew what the topic of the night's conversation would be. They hadn't discussed the job offer any further, although she knew it had been constantly on Drew's mind. She also knew it would be an enormous responsibility and that it was the last request of Uncle Tyler's. How would her husband respond if the offer?

It wasn't long before the conversation turned to the topic.

"Dr. Duncan, we know of your work with Miss Barton and your uncle in Cuba. Shortly before your uncle's death, he recommended to the President that you be appointed to head up Red Cross operations in Europe. We are hoping you have considered it. You know exactly what to do, although it's on a much bigger scale now, of course."

Mary Elizabeth, who was exercising her stance on women's rights by staying in the room with the men after the meal, held her breath.

"Thank you for your consideration. I got the request from Uncle Tyler minutes before the death telegram came. I've given the matter a great deal of thought over the past week. I'm afraid I have to decline your offer."

Mary Elizabeth let out her breath.

"Won't you please reconsider? You could probably end up being the head of the American Red Cross after the war."

"The head of the Red Cross!" Drew knew the job fell under the authority of the President. Politics was the last thing he ever wanted to get entangled in. Mary Elizabeth squirmed in her chair.

"Thank you very much for your confidence," said Drew humbly, "but the offer has come a year too late. I'm committed to my new wife and the new life we are planning in the Florida frontier."

The visitors proposed several alternatives to Drew, but each was gently rebuffed. At last, they knew Drew was not to be their candidate. As he walked them to the door, Drew thanked them once again for considering him for the post and commented, "I am sure you will find someone more qualified than I am. Good luck and thank you so much for coming to the service."

As each day faded into another, it seemed as if the United States was drawn closer and closer into the war in Europe. Drew and Elizabeth continued their lives as normally as possible. They made plans to place the furniture and the household goods in storage the first of August. Drew made arrangements for everything to be shipped by boxcar when the new house was completed. The shipment would first go by train to Sebring, which was the terminus for the train line. From Sebring, they would have someone haul their belongings the last sixty miles to Moore Haven.

Construction on the house was to start in mid-August, giving Drew enough time to be there to supervise each day's work. He already had a realtor scouting for a good place for his office. He had lists of equipment and supplies needed to set up a practice and he placed orders for everything to be there when he and Mary Elizabeth arrived.

Drew reluctantly traded in his Oldsmobile for a Model T Ford, a car higher off the ground and better suited for rough terrain than the Olds. He bought an extra set of wide tires that would go through the sand, mud, and even the deep water of south Florida.

Less than two months after Tyler's death, on May 2, war was declared against Germany. Signs of patriotism were everywhere. Young men flocked to sign up to go 'over there.' Walking down the bustling city streets, Drew felt the excitement in the air that reminded him of the atmosphere during the war with Spain.

Posters all over town were proclaiming the virtues of fighting the Huns. Men were beseeched to join the Army, Navy, and Marines. All were charged with the duty of buying war bonds, joining the Red Cross, and changing their diets so America's food could feed the soldiers.

"**Food Will Win the War,**" one poster reminded.

Another poster portrayed a young businessman looking through a window at an American soldier. Overhead was a big American flag. The poster practically screamed the words, "**On which side of the window are you?**"

Each time Drew passed the sign he had twinges of guilt for not accepting the offer of the Red Cross. He deliberated on the possibility of volunteering, but put his feelings aside because he had fulfilled his obligation twenty years ago.

On May 18, Congress ratified the Selective Service Act. All American males between the ages of twenty-one and thirty were required to register for active duty. June 15 was the official registration day. The day took on a holiday atmosphere. The patriotic occasion reminded Drew of a religious crusade. In banner headlines the next day *The Sun* proclaimed that ten million males had registered for the coming battles.

The article went on to say it would just be a matter of time before age requirements would be raised to men in their forties. The Allies especially needed those in medical fields. Doctors under fifty who had served in Mexico, the Spanish-American War, the Philippines, or China were urged to volunteer.

Drew and Mary Elizabeth debated for weeks whether Drew should volunteer or wait for the orders to come. He knew that it would be just a matter of time until he was called.

On August 1, Drew and Mary Elizabeth closed their rental house and put all their things in storage.

On August 2, Drew was once again inducted into the Army. The next day, Mary Elizabeth left Baltimore to stay with her parents in Rosemont and Drew left for New York to be shipped out to France.

Mary Elizabeth's face was wet with tears and her mind raced as she drove the Model T through the Maryland countryside to her parent's home. Less than a month before she thought that today she would be in the car with her husband on the road to Florida, not going back home to live with her parents!

She stopped the car as she turned into the long drive up to the farmhouse. She said a little prayer for her husband's safety and that she would be able to bear being treated like a ten-year-old.

As she rounded the last bend of the drive she noticed a newly erected flagpole directly in front of the house. Under Old Glory was a small white banner bearing three blue stars. She knew exactly what the stars meant, although no one had bothered telling her.

Her nieces, Susan and Frances, ran to open the car door when Mary Elizabeth stopped near the back porch.

The girls yelled, "Aunt Mary is here! Aunt Mary is here!"

Susan came running towards Mary Elizabeth while Frances ran to the porch and yelled through the open screen door once again, "Aunt Mary is here!"

Then she ran back and gave her aunt a hug. Before Mary Elizabeth could get out of her nieces' clutches her mother, father, sisters-in-law, and nieces were embracing and smothering her with kisses.

George McRae and his granddaughters took the luggage upstairs while the women gathered in the big farm kitchen. A big kettle of vegetable soup was on the black wood stove, filling the room with fragrant smells.

Handing a wet cloth to her daughter, Hattie said, "Go to the back porch and wash some of that road dust off, then come back and sit down and rest from your trip. Just talk to us while we finish dinner. We'll put you to work tomorrow."

Her daughters-in-law were busy setting the table and cleaning up scraps left from the freshly cut vegetables. As the cornbread baked, the conversation consisted of talk of the weather, the trip from Baltimore, the gardening and canning, but nothing of the war and the separations.

When the bread was out of the oven, Hattie called everyone to dinner while Cynthia poured fresh milk into the glasses.

"Mama, do you want me to ring the dinner bell for the boys?" Mary Elizabeth asked.

"No," was all that Hattie said.

As the family held hands, George McRae prayed, "Lord, thank you for the food that we are about to eat." He paused and then continued, "Please watch over the boys we have sent to fight the Hun. Please help me as I watch over the women and girls while my sons, their husbands and the girls' daddy, are away. Thank you, dear Lord. Amen."

Tears were in the eyes of everyone as they lifted their heads.

Mary Elizabeth spoke up. "No one let me know Stephen and George joined. Why didn't anyone let me know?"

Her distress heightened and so did the sound level of her voice.

"Why did they go, especially Stephen - he has children! They should have waited. They wouldn't have been called."

George spoke.

"They felt it was their duty. They're going to keep the Huns out of America and put an end to the nonsense of war. I wish to God that they would take me."

"I can't believe that you feel that way!" Mary Elizabeth cried.

"Drew felt he had to go because of the shortage of doctors. We discussed his involvement for months. I was and still am totally against our men going to fight someone else's battle. You should be in Baltimore. This war has made everyone crazy. Everyone is so suspicious they think everyone is a spy. Why, I had to protect a four-year-old German immigrant from a mob. America should have stayed out of this war because it isn't our concern. I think we could have supported the European Allies in many other ways. We didn't have to send our men."

"Drew and I sold Liberty Bonds and helped raise funds for the Red Cross. I quietly went along with all the propaganda dished out by that muckraker, George Creel. I trusted Wilson when he created the Public Information Committee, but under Creel's leadership the committee has control of the thinking of America. Can't anyone see that?" Mary Elizabeth continued, not believing no one stopped her.

Her voice rose an octave when she broached her passion.

"The Public Information Committee went too far when they banned German music. The symphony had to stop playing any compositions of Handel and Beethoven because they were German. I couldn't even teach the classics." Continuing, "Do you know what a hot dog is? It's the new name for the frankfurter, but of course we can't say 'frankfurter' anymore! And 'liberty cabbage,' that's 'sour.'..."

"Hold it there, young lady," roared her father. "We have sent three men from this family over there to make the world safe for democracy. We will win this war and there won't be any more. Your sons and their sons will never have to fight again! In this house we will support the war effort in any way we are asked. I respected your husband's wishes for you to come home and be with your family while he is away but if you are going to be negative you can go back to Baltimore and your German friends! If you want to stay under my roof, I'll not hear anything more about how wrong we were to join the war effort. Is that clear?"

His voice got louder and louder as he talked and his face turned a deep shade of crimson.

When Mary Elizabeth didn't respond to his question, he repeated it.

"Is that clear, Mary Elizabeth McRae...Duncan?"

"Yes, sir," she responded just like she was ten years old. She was too intimidated to say anything else, as were the others gathered around the table.

Finally, George McRae spoke again.

His voice was very quiet. "I just pray that this war doesn't come to this door like the one did when I was a boy. My two oldest brothers were killed and my papa spent two years in a Yankee prison. Then he came home and saw everything except this house burned to the ground. He was never the same after that."

After the dishes were washed and put away, Mary Elizabeth excused

158

herself and retreated to her room. Tears were just under the surface as she wrote a letter to Drew.

She had pledged to him when they parted that she would write every day. As she penned this first letter, she wondered how many more she would be writing before she saw her husband again.

She was about to blow out the light when there was a soft knock at the door. Her mother opened the door before she could respond. Hattie came over to the bed, picked up the brush on the bedside table, and brushed her daughter's hair just as she had done when she was a child.

"We are glad that you came home, Mary Elizabeth. Your father is upset about sending both of his sons and Drew to Europe. He feels guilty that he couldn't go instead of them."

Mary Elizabeth began crying and her mother held her in her arms as she sobbed.

Mary Elizabeth settled into life in the country. Her days were spent canning vegetables from the garden. People had been urged to plant home gardens so that farmers' vegetables could be sent to feed the fighting men as well as the women and children in the war-torn countries.

A garden was nothing new for the McRae's, but they called their garden a 'war garden' as did those who planted one for the first time at the urging of the government. The family signed pledge cards when they became members of the Food Administration. Joining millions across the nation who pledged conservation and constraints on the food they served to their families. In doing so, they felt they were part of the war effort.

On the inside of the kitchen's pantry door was a poster that proclaimed food would win the war. Herbert Hoover, head of the United States Food Administration, had been responsible for this and other slogans that were being used to encourage citizens to think about the war effort throughout each day and make sacrifices for the war effort..

The chart read:

Food Will Win the War
Feed a Fighter
Eat Only What you Need
Waste Nothing

Monday........Wheatless and Heatless
Tuesday.........Meatless
Wednesday.....Wheatless
Thursday........Porkless and Wheatless
Friday............Heatless
Saturday..........Porkless
Sunday...........Gasless

Every time someone opened the door, they laughed at the 'Hooverizing' poster.

Among the comments they made were, "We only need this list to remind us that we can't ride in Mary Elizabeth's car to church."

"Hoover must have grown up in the McRae house because he is telling children to clean their plates. That has always been a law in this house."

"The other Hooverisms declared throughout the nation in the name of freedom were laughed at, too, because no one had to tell the McRae's to conserve.

NO LIGHTS EXCEPT ON SUNDAY
(They didn't have electricity.)
MORE CORN BREAD
(Corn bread was a staple in the house.)
MORE FISH THAN MEAT
(Chicken for Sunday dinner was the only meat for the week.)
USE SYRUPS INSTEAD OF SUGAR
(Sugar was too expensive to buy.)

As the family cleaned out their attic and bookshelves to send reading materials to the soldiers, Mary Elizabeth was glad her books were in storage. And she didn't feel guilty about the fact.

Each Tuesday morning the Women's Missionary Society became the local unit of the Red Cross. They met in different homes to roll surgical bandages and learn first aid techniques. Every night the McRae women knitted socks to send. When they were canning peaches, they saved the pits to be made into charcoal for gas masks.

Susan and Frances, together with their classmates, signed a pledge card stating:

"At the table I'll not leave a scrap of food upon my plate. And I'll not eat between meals but for supper I'll wait."

The school sent 5,000 pounds of hickory nuts to Washington for the war effort. Susan and Frances picked up their share. The girls also spent part of each school day tending the school garden. They bought War Savings Stamps with half of the money they made selling eggs to Mr. Packard, the owner of the Crossroads General Store.

Mary Elizabeth replaced Mr. Gilbert as church pianist when he was drafted. She also gave piano lessons to her nieces and several other children from the surrounding farms. As much as she loved German music from Beethoven to the polkas, she did not play or teach them out of respect for her father.

Each evening she rode Buttercup down to the Crossroads General Store to post her daily letter and check to see if anything had come from Drew. Each night before bed she wrote of the day's events to her husband.

Summer turned into fall. Mary Elizabeth's days and weeks began to blend together. She was beginning to wonder if she would ever hear from Drew.

On September 18, the azure sky was cloudless and the air was crisp when she headed out for the store. Buttercup's hooves crushed through the leaves that were just beginning to fall.

She walked into the store and spoke to the old men who were gathered around the potbelly stove.. They smiled at her, but continued their conversation. It was not their usual conversation about the war. Mr. Packard was quoting from an article in *The Literary Magazine*.

"It says here she is feeding the nation with her potatoes," said Everett Packard.

Finally acknowledging Mary Elizabeth's presence, Everett turned and said, "Say, Mary Elizabeth, aren't you about to move to Florida? It seems that Florida has more than mosquitoes. Some town has elected a woman mayor. Don't that take the cake? That Moore Haven must be some strange town."

"Moore Haven! That's where we are moving after the war," said Mary Elizabeth excitedly as she asked to see the article that the men had been reading. She quickly scanned the article, "The Duchess of Moore Haven," which told how the town had incorporated and elected as their first mayor, Mrs. Marian Newall Horwitz O'Brien, the wife of the man to whom Drew had sold his property.

"May I borrow this?" asked Mary Elizabeth. "I want to read all about this woman. I'll bring it back tomorrow."

Everett handed Mary Elizabeth the magazine and the conversation continued between the men.

"Ain't no reason for men to elect a woman to run the affairs of a town. Women have no business in politics. The next thing you'll know women will be telling men when they can have their way with them. My woman ain't never going to vote!"

"Mary Elizabeth, does your daddy know what kinda place that city feller is moving you to?"

"Mr. Packard," Mary Elizabeth interjected - because she had no idea where the conversation was heading - "may I please get the mail and post my letter?"

"Of course. And, I think you have a copy of *The Literary Magazine* in your mail," Everett said as he went over to the post office in the back corner of the store.

Mary Elizabeth posted her letter to Drew as usual. Everett handed her an unusually large bundle of mail for the family that contained the copy of *The Literary Magazine* that had just been under discussion. At the bottom of the pile was a large brown envelope with a French postmark.

She finally had a letter from Drew! She couldn't contain her excitement.

She smiled at Everett and, at the same moment, the world started spinning.

The next thing that Mary Elizabeth knew she was looking up at wallpaper with big yellow flowers she had never seen before.

"Where am I?" Mary Elizabeth said, starting to get up.

"Just lay back, sweetheart," said Helen Packard as she applied a cool wet cloth to her forehead.

"You took a spill and we brought you back to our bed. Ben has gone to get Doc Williams."

"Dr. Williams? I'm okay. I don't need to see a doctor," Mary Elizabeth protested as she tried to get up.

But Mrs. Packard insisted that she lie in bed.

"No one faints for the fun of it. There has to be a reason."

"Yes, there is a reason, I just got my first letter from my husband in almost two months. That's reason enough."

"Maybe, but you are going to stay put just the same!"

Mary Elizabeth couldn't do anything with the woman watching every move that she made.

"Here, Honey, have some water."

Mary Elizabeth had just finished the water when her father rushed into the room followed by Dr. Williams.

"Daddy, I'm really okay. I got excited when I saw a letter from Drew, that's all."

"That's well and good, but the doctor is here and he's going to check you out. I've been noticing that you have been a little puny these days."

"Don't be silly, Daddy. I've been feeling fine."

George and Mrs. Packard left the room while Dr. Williams began his examination. He checked out her eyes, ears, and throat just like he had done when Mary Elizabeth was a child.

"Doctor, I think I know what is wrong. Give me a complete examination."

When the doctor was finished, he confirmed Mary Elizabeth's suspicions. "You're in the family way, my dear. I would guess you'll be a mother by the early spring."

Mary Elizabeth had thought she might be pregnant. She didn't want to think about it because she wanted Drew to be with her through her pregnancies and to be able to deliver his children into the world. Here she was pregnant and he was on the other side of the world! She could only hope that he would be home by spring.

"Are you ready to let the secret out? They're waiting on the other side of that door wanting to hear what is wrong with you. I can make up something if you want me to. It's up to you."

"Let's make something up. I want my husband to know first. At least I can write him before I tell. Besides, I think my mother should know before Mrs. Packard, Rosemont's town crier."

162

Mary Elizabeth got up slowly and she heard Dr. Williams lie to the others in the next room.

"She's coming down with a cold. I think the day's excitement and the impending cold made for a good combination for her to pass out. Other than that she's perfectly okay. But, I don't want her to ride that horse home."

The doctor gave Mary Elizabeth a wink as she came out the door.

Mary Elizabeth welcomed the seclusion of her bedroom when they returned home. Her hands trembled as she tore open the envelope. Inside she found four smaller ones. She carefully opened the one that was marked with a large #1.

20 August 1917

My Darling Mary Elizabeth,

I am writing to you only a few hours out from the shore of France. The crossing has been uneventful. I am sharing a stateroom with another doctor. He is a young lad from New York City just out of medical school. He reminds me of myself when I was on my way to Cuba.

He is so very anxious to work under the adverse conditions that we will soon face.

As I walk around the ship I have looked into all of the faces of the men - well, some are mere boys. You know how I love to read the faces of people. I have seen every emotion in the book.

These men are all trying to be brave but they are also anxious, scared, nervous, bored, and lonely. I can testify that I can tell the lonely ones because that is the group that I am in.

I miss you with all of my heart. Each moment that we are apart tears at my soul. I dream of the day we will be together again and in each other's arms.

With all my love,
Drew

Mary Elizabeth fought back her tears as she opened #2.

24 August 1917

My Darling Mary Elizabeth,

I wish I could hold you close to me at this moment. I need you so much. With each passing day that desire grows stronger and stronger.

I haven't heard from you yet, but I know that I will receive the letters that you promised any day now.

163

*I am working with the Red Cross. Don't you think
that is ironic? I am treating the French, English, and
Belgium soldiers.*

*General Pershing and the other Allied Generals
are having quite a political bout. I don't know when
the American troops will get in battle. All are so ready
in spirit. With all the training they are receiving, the
Germans won't know what hit them when they do
begin to fight.*

*You won't believe what we are facing. We work
until we drop and then are up again to do more. Some
nights we get no opportunity to go to bed, so we sleep
whenever we can.*

*It seems that I have been here forever. I feel as if
I jumped off a high dive and plunged into the deep
water the moment I arrived. I am in a hospital - if that
is what you want to call it. I don't think that I will ever
be on the front lines. The medics do the minor things
on the battlefield and bring those who need surgery
here to us.*

*We are getting much needed help from the Red
Cross nurses, as well as those who have joined the
Army. My Darling, how I wish you were the one at my
side.*

Must go as more wounded have just arrived.

All my love,
Drew

As Mary Elizabeth tore open #3 she prayed that Drew would have only
loving words for her. It was hard to read the descriptions of the atrocities of
war. She glanced down the pages and realized that he was sharing his life
with her as he always had done.

29 August 1917

Dearest Mary,

*I miss you so very much. If it hadn't been for this
war, we would be listening to the birds in Florida
instead of the hideous noises of war.*

*I can't believe Americans still are not fighting! It
reminds me of Tampa - drill, sit, and wait. This war is
so different from the war in Cuba.*

*Think of all the modern conveniences we didn't
have twenty years ago. Well, man has modernized
his capabilities to kill and to maim. We have to face*

*not only gun and knife wounds, but now have death
and injuries from bombs falling from aeroplanes.
They don't always hit their targets, so bombs fall
everywhere. Some are low flying planes they call
Fokeers. They fly close to the ground and shoot
everywhere with machine guns.*

*The Germans have been using their Zeppelin
blimps for a long time to bomb everything in sight. I'm
beginning to think the skies are more dangerous than
the ground.*

*The Gatling gun that was used some in Cuba is
widely used here. It is an automatic that can keep
firing and firing without stopping.*

*Giant machines called tanks can go anywhere,
over any terrain. They can plow down bushes, little
trees, and even walls. There is a huge gun on them
that can fire great distances.*

*The Germans have the biggest thing yet. I have
heard about it but pray that I never see it or the
damage it causes. 'Big Bertha' is what they call it and
they claim she is as long as a ten story building and
will fire shells up to eighty miles. I don't know if this is
an exaggeration, but it seems ludicrous to me.*

*By far the worst thing is the gas. Some of the gases
are invisible. Chlorine gas has a light green color and
is like a mixture of pineapple and pepper. Mustard
gas is brownish yellow and smells like perfumed soap,
garlic, and mustard all wrapped up in one. We all are
equipped with gas masks to protect us from fumes that
will suffocate, blister, and blind. The mask is heavy
and uncomfortable. The contraption is made out of
rubber and contains chemicals to purify the air you
breathe.*

*Anyone who is unprotected is a goner. Exposed
skin becomes blistered and quickly turns to oozing
sores. Gas in the eyes causes blindness. Some of the
blindness is temporary, but others will be blind for the
rest of their lives.*

*I get so mad when I think that a lot of the gas is
produced in the United States. People will do anything
to make money. Bet you hadn't read that in any paper!*

*I am glad I brought some of the herbs and
remedies I have learned from Gopher over the years. I
mixed some coontie flour with water to make a gruel.*

It is the only food the gas victims can keep down.

I wrote to Pershing and advised him of the effects of the coontie remedy. As a result, we have just received a big shipment in from Miami. Now every hospital will have a supply along with my prescription.

We are not only treating soldiers but innocent women and children. We are fighting diseases that are running rampant in the trenches. Everyone I come in contact with has lice. It is so bad that the 'delousing' agents we use are useless. We have lost hundreds to influenza.

There has never been the mass destruction of everything as it is here. I cringe to think this war is called a world war because the very thought of battles like these being in the United States and in Maryland scares me to death. I really can't understand the politics of war. It is beginning to scare me.

I am sorry I have gone on and on about things here. Maybe I have said too much. If so, I am sorry. I can't wait until I hear from you and news from home.
You are in my heart always,
Drew

PS. If you are helping make bandages, we all thank you from the bottom of our hearts. Our supplies have been very limited and have been of very poor quality. When we don't have soft cotton gauze we have to use white tissue paper. Bandages are in short supply, too, so we are grateful when the bandages arrive that have been made by women back home. Tell your friends to keep them rolling!

The letters frightened Mary Elizabeth. She loved the thought that Drew was thinking about her even when he was in the midst of so much blood and gore. She was also proud that he would render his medical services but she was angry that the United States had been rallied around a cause, sent loved ones to fight, and now their intervention was detained.

She needed Drew home. She needed him to deliver their baby!

She was almost too afraid to open #4.

1 September 1917

Dear Mary,

We are near our very first anniversary but thousands of miles away from each other. I never dreamed we would ever be apart.

I remember every detail of our first night. Oh, God! How I long for you!

How I wish I had never come here. I wish I had waited until they came to the front door to drag me here in chains.

I thought I had experienced 'war' in Cuba like my father had described to me - NO, I DIDN'T!"

Reading over my last letter, which I promise will go out with the mail today, I left out two of the things I will probably never forget besides the total disregard for human life.

1) The noise - I hope I still have my hearing when I return to you. Just think, I am not even on the front lines.

2) The smells - lingers in the air day and night. I won't even begin to tell you about the other horrific smells.

Remember all of us in your thoughts and prayers. The best part of my day is when I can close my eyes and think of you.

Love,
Drew

P.S. I guess I should have sent you poetry, but the words won't come.

Mary Elizabeth prayed the angels would surround Drew, protect him, and keep him safe. After she and reread the letters, she tied them in a purple ribbon, and placed them in the bottom drawer of the bureau.

The article about the Moore Haven mayor from *The Literary Digest* was in another envelope in the drawer; she took it out, momentarily. She had already read the article so many times she had almost memorized it, but whenever Drew mentioned Moore Haven in one of his letters, she seemed to be compelled to reassure herself that the town was someplace she could really live and be happy. She still had nagging doubts.

Finally, she picked up a pen, dipped it into the inkbottle, and began to write the news of the day.

The night of March 31, 1918, typified the old adage about March going out like a lion.

The rain pounded against Mary Elizabeth's windowpane with all of its fury. She lit a fire in the fireplace to remove the chill that the spring rain brought into the room. Every bone and muscle in her body ached. She had helped her mother all day with the spring house cleaning. Her mother had urged her to rest but all she wanted to do was clean. She had beaten the rugs from every room, ironed the living room and dining room curtains, and had swept and mopped all the downstairs floors. She would start on the upstairs in the morning and was glad they had decided to wait and wash the windows last. It was too bad the rain didn't automatically clean them.

She reread letter #53 and sat down at her desk to write to Drew. The baby was unusually active.

"I guess he/she is glad that I have sat down so we both can rest," she said as she patted her enormous stomach.

"Speaking of resting, I think I'll take a short nap before I write to Drew," she thought as she stretched out across the bed and closed her eyes.

A quilt was over Mary Elizabeth when she woke up. She realized she had slept much longer than she had planned because only hot coals remained in the fireplace. Her mother must have put the quilt on thinking that she would sleep through the night. The storm was still raging. The branches of the elm tree outside of her window creaked as the wind and the rain danced upon its branches. As Mary Elizabeth lit the lamp, her stomach made her acutely aware that she had missed her dinner.

She descended the stairs to find a dark house. It was much later than she had realized. She went into the kitchen and put her lamp down on the counter. The light gave the kitchen a soft warm glow. What did she want to eat? She remembered the apple pies that she helped her mother make the day before. As she opened the door to the pie safe she had a sharp pain through the middle of her back but it was over so quickly she thought she had imagined it. She found the pie and decided to finish what was left in the pie pan. She nibbled the crumbs, got a fork out of the kitchen drawer, and helped herself.

"Cold milk would be wonderful with this," she thought. She went to the icebox and took out a bottle of milk. As she lifted the bottle, the second pain hit. She screamed louder than she thought possible and she dropped the bottle, sending milk and glass everywhere.

Hattie and George came running into the kitchen when they heard the scream, followed by the sound of breaking glass. Hattie realized what was happening with one look.

"George, go and call Doc."

George grumbled, "Why do babies pick the worst nights to be born?"

As he reached for his raincoat and hat, he said, "Guess you were right earlier when you said that we should be ready 'cause of the way Mary Elizabeth cleaned today."

Hattie helped her daughter back up the stairs while George rode Buttercup to the crossroads to call Dr. Williams..

George had little trouble getting through the storm but when he reached the Packards, it took forever to wake them.

"Why are you out on a night like this one, George?" Everett asked as he opened the door. "Oh, the baby must be coming."

"I need to use the telephone to call Doc."

"Sure, but Doc isn't going to be friendly. Brace yourself!"

"Hello, Della, George McRae. Please ring Dr. Williams."

The doctor's phone rang and rang. When he finally picked up he grumbled.

"And who needs me on a night like this one?"

"Dr. Williams, George. It's Mary Elizabeth. She's ready."

"How far apart are the contractions?"

"She had three by the time I left. I would say they were about five minutes apart."

"I'm leaving right now."

"We'll be looking for you. Thanks," George said as he put down the receiver.

"He didn't cuss at all?"

"No."

"Strange."

Hattie helped her daughter out of her clothes and into an old nightgown before the next pain arrived. She had Mary Elizabeth sit in the chair while she put five layers of old sheets on the bed.

"The bed is ready for you, honey. Come get in."

"Ohhhhhhhh Motherrrrrrrrr! I have ruined the chair."

Water ran everywhere.

"That's just part of it. I'm glad that happened before you got into bed. Don't worry about it. How wet are you?"

"Wet!"

"Take off your nightgown and get into bed. Just pull the blanket up Mary, have you ever seen a baby being born before?"

"Nooooooooo!"

Another pain hit.

"Well, you're going to be baptized by fire tonight!"

"Just relax and I'll get some hot water and towels."

Two hours passed and the labor pains were getting closer and closer together.

"Where's that doctor?" thought Hattie. "George said that he was going to leave the minute they hung up. That was over two hours ago. It's only five miles to his house. He could have walked here by now!"

Mary Elizabeth screamed in pain.

Dr. Williams ran into the room at that moment. He had heard the scream from the kitchen where he had stopped to wash his hands. He was still drying them when he ran into the room.

"Lift up your knees. Help her, Hattie. Push, Mary, push!"

"Mama, what do I do? It hurts so bad. Drew, where is Drew? I want Drew!"

"Push one more time." Dr. Williams said as he pushed down on Mary Elizabeth's stomach.

"I can see the head. Push!"

The next moment the doctor was spanking the bloody baby on its bottom.

"You have a son."

He handed the baby to his mother and cut the cord.

Hattie took the baby and cleaned him up while Dr. Williams cleaned up Mary Elizabeth.

Hattie laid her first grandson in the cradle his mother had laid in and then closed the door while Mary Elizabeth and the baby slept.

"Doc, you did it again. But what took you so long?"

"The rain has washed the bridge away. I had to take my flivver home and saddle Nellie. She hasn't been ridden in a good while and didn't want to come out in the storm at all. I talked to her and we got an understanding by the time we got to the creek. She waltzed right through that rushing water like she was on a dry highway."

"Stay here until the rain quits. You can sleep on the couch or in the attic bedroom."

The April sun was shining into the bedroom when Mary Elizabeth woke up. She looked over at her new son in the cradle beside the bed and smiled. She was about to get up to pick him up when her mother came in the room.

"Mary Elizabeth! You can't get up! I have pillows to put behind you so that you can sit up. Then I'll give you the baby."

Mary Elizabeth didn't remember holding the baby when he was first born so when her mother handed him to her and he opened his eyes a feeling that can't be described came over her.

"Well hello, Thomas Drew Duncan, IV. I'm your mama."

The only thing that would make this moment any more perfect would be to have Drew there with them. She counted the baby's fingers and then unwrapped his blanket and counted his toes. She unpinned the diaper and checked him all over.

"Perfect!" she declared.

Hattie came into the room with a big breakfast tray for the new mother. From then on she was there to care for her daughter and her first grandson night and day.

Much to her dismay, Mary Elizabeth stayed in bed the entire month of April. All she had to do was feed her son and write letters to Drew.

Hattie allowed Mary Elizabeth to join in some of the household chores in the latter part of May. She felt happy that she could finally contribute again to the family even though her mother still babied her.

27 May 1918

My Dearest M.E. and Son,

 Finally, the Americans are officially fighting in this war!

 The American Expeditionary Forces led their first offensive today. I hope that nine months of training proves to be a quick end to this war. I guess Pershing decided to fight because if he waited too much longer, I am afraid he wouldn't have any soldiers left to fight his battles.

 Now we are battling the influenza. It is the worst I have ever seen. Men in good health yesterday are dead today. It is spreading like wildfire. We are losing hundreds everyday. A few survive, but only a few. It is heart-breaking not to be able to do anything for the victims.

 They complain of being weak, having aches in their muscles, backs, joints, and heads. Then the fever strikes resulting in reddish-brown splotches all over the face.

 Next comes the delirium, then death.

 I have it on good word that the flu is in the States. Honestly, I think it started there. I don't think there is any worry on your part because it seems to be just in the military camps. If, and I don't think it will, if anyone in the Rosemont area contracts the virus, don't leave home without a mask. I would advise not to leave home at all.

 As always, don't worry about me. I wear a mask and take other precautions. The good Lord knows what I have waiting for me - you, my son, and Florida.

 Speaking of Florida ... Did I tell you that someone I had met in Miami a few years ago was here at the hospital? A reporter from the "Miami Herald" visited the hospital. I am so very lucky to have had an uninterrupted lunch with her. I had met Mrs. Douglas (who, by the way, is the daughter of Stoneman, the "Herald's" owner) a few years ago at the Cocoanut Grove's Christmas party.

 We had talked then about our mutual love of the 'Glades. Our conversation seemed to continue just

171

*where it had ended. She invited us to visit her when we
are settled.*

*I have also encountered several of the flyboys who
trained in Florida. One was even stationed in Arcadia.
That's the county seat of Desoto County, the county
Moore Haven is in.*

*Give Thomas a kiss. Tell him that I am sure I will
be home for his first Christmas.*

Love,
Drew

"Please, God, protect my love from this terrible disease he has written about," Mary Elizabeth prayed. "I don't want to be selfish, but I do need him. I want him to be able to fulfill his dreams."

June was pleasantly cool. In addition to caring for the needs of Thomas, Mary Elizabeth's daily duties became the same as before the baby arrived. Every trip to Packard's store brought news of the influenza. Drew had been wrong; it was spreading to the general population. The large cities were in a panic. Most of the doctors were in Europe. They were depending on medical students and retired doctors to man the hospitals and clinics.

Everyone was praying for a vaccine to be found.

With every letter she received from Drew, Mary Elizabeth cringed more.

He told of the mud, the rats everywhere, the bombs, the blood and gore, the agonies, the influenza casualties, and all the other horrors the newspapers and magazines didn't carry. Everything they printed glorified the war effort and reinforced the duty of those on the home front.

Mary Elizabeth, like everyone else, was shocked when *Collier's* magazine came on the first of July showing a graphic picture of a wounded American soldier. He was being carried on a stretcher from a trench. Even though the picture was in black and white, the blood on the head bandage was sickening to the family. Drew had written so much about the atrocities but visualizing it in one's head was so much different than seeing pictures. The picture brought the war into the living rooms of Rosemont and the nation.

Chapter 17

THE WAR COMES HOME
July 4, 1918

The entire McRae clan was excited about the Fourth of July. The government was encouraging every community to show its patriotism by having the biggest and grandest celebration ever. The day began with a parade down Rosemont's Main Street. Leading the parade was the town's band comprised of old men, women, and children. Veterans of the Civil, Mexican and Spanish American Wars marched behind the band.

After the veterans came a band of Women Suffragettes, then decorated wagons and bicycles.

Spectators waved American flags and followed the parade down to the town's park bordering the creek. Residents from the surrounding farm community came with baskets and baskets of food that was spread out on long tables.

Boys played baseball and shot marbles while girls played hopscotch and jumped rope. Men played checkers and pitched horseshoes. Women exchanged the latest news, complained about the picture on the cover of *Colliers* while they arranged the food for everyone to eat.

The Reverend Wesley Scott blessed the food and the hands that prepared it. He also prayed for the men who were fighting the war to end all wars and that all of the soldiers be home by the next Fourth of July.

A barbershop quartet consisting of men in their sixties and seventies sang several songs after the meal. Everyone in attendance sang as the town band played patriotic songs.

The fireworks display was the most beautiful display the gathering had ever seen. They were so engrossed with the sparkling display in the summer sky they didn't see a messenger boy ride up on his bicycle and hand a telegram to George McRae. And no one noticed as the McRae family left the celebration early.

Mary Elizabeth took her nieces to her room so they could watch her put the baby to bed. This was a good night for them to help with the nightly ritual.

After they each kissed him good night, Mary Elizabeth laid him in the cradle and turned her heavy heart to the girls.

She wanted to protect her nieces from the sad news of the day for as long as she could.

"Now it's your turn," she smiled at the two. "You are much too dirty to get in my bed."

She took them down to the tub on the back porch. Knowing she needed to stay busy herself, she announced to the girls, who had long since bathed themselves, that she would bathe them tonight "to make sure we get all that dirt off."

She reached for the bar of Ivory Soap. First she soaped Frances all over and then she turned to Susan.

"Now you girls rinse that soap off by the time I count to ten. One...two...three... "

Each girl stepped out of the tub into a towel that their aunt was holding for them. She rubbed each down and gave each one of their grandfather's undershirts.

"Let's be very quiet when we go up the stairs, okay?"

"Why?"

"Grandpa isn't feeling well and besides you might wake up the baby."

As she tucked the girl's into bed they began to ask questions.

"Why are we sleeping at Grandma's tonight? Why are you putting us to bed? Where is Mama? Why did we have to leave the fireworks so early?"

The questions would have gone on and on but Mary Elizabeth whispered, "I promise that all of your questions will be answered in the morning. You need to be quiet now so you don't wake the baby."

Together they said their prayers, "Now I lay me down to sleep...God bless Mama, Grandma, Grandpa, Baby Drew, Aunt Mary, Uncle George, Uncle Drew and please God bless and keep our daddy safe and let him come home soon. Amen."

Mary Elizabeth hugged them and said, "Don't let the bed bugs bite!"

She then tickled them and pulled the sheet up to cover them. As she reached over to blow out the light, both saw tears in their aunt's eyes. They felt warm and secure in the big double bed, but they could sense that there was something terribly wrong.

Mary Elizabeth went downstairs and took the telegram from her father and read it for the first time. She wanted to be sure her father had read it right and she wanted to comprehend the words he had whispered in her ear earlier that evening.

DEPARTMENT OF WAR
WASHINGTON DC
WE REGRET TO INFORM YOU THAT PVT 1ST CLASS
WILLIAM STEPHEN MCRAE WAS KILLED IN ACTION
JUNE. BURIED WITH MILITARY HONORS.

The war had taken all of the young men that the McRae family knew to the other side of the world and Drew wrote daily of the death and destruction that he dealt with every day.

174

Until the moment they received the telegram, the war was "over there'. The family had sent three to war and now only two would come home.

Cries of hunger came from the baby just as Mary Elizabeth sat down to talk to the family. Before she retreated to her room she hugged and kissed her mother and father. She gave an extra long embrace to Cynthia and then ran up the stairs to grieve alone.

She picked up her son with his quilt and climbed the stairs to the attic bedroom where she and her brothers had played so often. She found an old rocker they used to play on. She sat down in the rocker and tried not to cry as she nursed for fear she would sour her milk. She sang softly to Thomas as she stroked his hair. Then, to keep from crying, she told him all about the uncle he would never meet.

The baby fell asleep and she laid him on the bed.

Mary Elizabeth prayed, "Dear Lord, thank you so very much for this beautiful son that you entrusted to me. Thank you, too, for his father. Please, Lord, watch over and protect both Drew and George. Please bring an end to the war so all of the men can come home. I pray that this is the last war we ever have to experience and that my brother's death was not in vain. I pray there will not be another war which will take my son away."

The news of Stephen's death spread quickly through the small community.

Friends arrived with food and condolences as early as breakfast the next morning and came almost constantly for the next two days.

A memorial service was held on July 7 and the tiny Methodist Church was overflowing with tears and friends. Many of the mourners also had sent their men to the same far away war. They knew to a person that Stephen could have been their own son or husband. In fact, they realized, the casualties of the war were not necessarily going to be limited to Stephen.

His death made the war very personal.

The service gave some closure to Stephen's life but the family wished that his body wasn't buried so far away. They erected a marker in the family cemetery on a hill overlooking the entire farm.

Mary Elizabeth continued to receive letters from Drew once or twice a week. She had learned what the time lapse would be between her letters and his answers and vice versa. She estimated that his condolence letter about Stephen would come sometime in mid August. She was surprised when she received a letter on July 20.

30 June 1918

My Dearest Darling,

I know you and your family will have received the word about Stephen long before this letter will arrive. I am sorry I can't be there and put my arms around you and be there for you as you have been there for me during my losses. I do hope that my letter will give you some comfort. I want you to know that I was by Stephen's side when he died and I attended his burial.

For the first time since I arrived in France, I was sent to the field hospital. I won't go into the details because at this time that is not important to you. Very few of the doughboys were brought back to the hospital, but Stephen was one of the few. I don't know why except for Divine Providence, because there was nothing I could do for him.

I won't lie, he was in pain, but I know he was glad that I was there at the end.

We did get to talk before he died and he told me to tell all of you that he loved all of you and said that you should not grieve for him. He hoped that what he and his fellow soldiers have done over here would make a better life for his family back home.

He said that I am to give Cynthia and the girls a kiss from him the minute that I see them.

Stephen was buried near the battlefield with 50 other soldiers who fell today. General Pershing spoke a few words.

I don't know if 'Black Jack' is in the habit of doing that, but he did today. There was a twenty-one-gun salute. As the men were lowered into the ground, several buglers played "Taps". I don't think one of us left the gravesites with dry eyes.

White crosses topped with a helmet were being placed at each grave when we left.

God, I wish the 'Good-bye Girls" - the telephone operators - who keep the generals informed, could connect us. I do want to comfort you.

With a heavy heart and much love,
Drew

Chapter 18

IT'S OVER
November 11, 1918

It wasn't the rooster that woke up the McRae family on the crisp Monday morning, but the sound of a long blast from a train engine. Every train engine that passed a road crossing would alert residents of its arrival by blowing its whistle twice. The whistle on the train lumbering through the valley was blowing nonstop. The sound echoed through the valley and echoed through the hills.

George McRae jumped out of bed, pulled on his overalls, and headed out the door to saddle Buttercup. He was determined to find out the reason for the strange train signal, even if he had to ride beyond Rosemont.

Just as George opened the back door a group of men from Rosemont's band rode up on horseback.

"George, The war is over! We just got word. Western Union is going crazy! We're out spreading the word and telling everybody to meet at the band shell just before eleven. We're going to celebrate big. Tell the wife to fix sandwiches and stuff."

Before George could say a word, the group was off to tell others the news.

Conversation around the breakfast table was nonstop. Hattie expressed her feelings.

"If just this family can produce the excitement that is in this room. I can only imagine what it will be when the whole valley gets together."

She wanted to say that her boys were coming home. The war wouldn't take the other two. She saw Cynthia on the edge of tears, so the thought wasn't spoken.

Hattie and her daughters-in-law talked about what they could take with them to spread for lunch. Mary Elizabeth was quiet. Her father noticed it first.

"Why are you so quiet, Mary Elizabeth, aren't you happy? This is the time to celebrate, not mourn."

"But, Daddy. Do you think it's safe? Safe for everyone to get together? The influenza..."

George cut his daughter short. "I know that you haven't left this farm since the first death in Rosemont three month ago. There were only eleven cases in the entire valley. Eight of those survived. I read yesterday that it had run its course for this year and someone has found a vaccine for us next year. Many in the cities were inoculated this year."

"I'm sure it is safe now, dear," added Hattie.

All the McRae family squeezed into Mary Elizabeth's Model T. George drove. Hattie was crammed in between her husband and Mary Elizabeth who was holding her baby. The girls were in the back seat squeezed between their mother and aunt, both of whom held picnic baskets.

They were all deep in thought when they passed the family's flagpole. The white banner that had contained three blue stars for fifteen months, now had an additional star. A gold star had been added after the death of Stephen.

Everyone from Rosemont and the surrounding valley gathered at the park. They walked, rode horses and mules, came in the family wagon or buggy, and many came in their Model T's. All were dressed in their Sunday best. Mary Elizabeth and her family were the only ones wearing black armbands bearing a gold cross.

The band shell was decorated with the banners from the Fourth of July. The band inside was playing patriotic music by the time the McRae's arrived at 10:30 a.m. At 11 a.m. the bells from the three churches and the school began pealing. The engines' whistles at the roundhouse blared their signals through the air. The whistle at the electric company bellowed its imposing sound that usually was reserved for 7 a.m., noon, and 5 p.m. For five minutes the fanfare resounded through the air. Firecrackers were set off. Men fired shotguns into the air. The people's cheering all but drowned out all the other noises.

The crowd only quieted down when Mayor Adams, standing on a platform inside the band shell got their attention by speaking through a megaphone.

"My fellow citizens, on Saturday, November 9, The Kaiser abdicated."

The crowd cheered for another five minutes. They hugged and kissed one another and threw hats into the air. The mayor again got the attention of the crowd.

"I am proud to say that my brother in New York City called me this morning as soon as the *Times* came out. This is what it said and I am quoting:

"Special to the *New York Times*
By *Edwin I. James*
with the American Army in France

November 11 - They stopped fighting at 11 o'clock this morning.
In a twinkling, four years of killing and massacre stopped as if God had swept His omnipotent finger across the scene of the world's carnage and had cried, 'Enough'.
People, the war to win all wars is over.
Our men will be coming home!!!"

178

The crowd went mad again but burst into song when the band started playing the new song by Irving Berlin, *God Bless America*. Most knew the song but when *Over There* was played the crowd sang it over and over again until the mayor called for Reverend Scott to bless the food.

Mary Elizabeth and her family sang all the way home. The sun was setting in the western sky as they came in view of the flag and banner. The singing stopped.

Happy as they all were for the war to be over and to know that George and Drew would be back with them soon, the gold star reminded them of what no one mentioned that day.

Stephen had given the supreme sacrifice to his country. He would never come home.

Sally Settle

Chapter 19

HOMECOMING
Christmas 1919

The first snow of the year was beginning to fall as George McRae, his granddaughters, and his son left to cut a Christmas tree in the nearby woods. Christmas 1919 was the one that they all had dreamed of for so long. Christmas the year before had been joyous because the war was over and everyone knew they would soon have their loved ones home.

There were two empty places, though, at the McRae home. One place, they knew for certain, would always be empty; the other, for Drew, whose status was still unknown.

George arrived home the middle of June. He appeared to have come home without any injuries whatsoever. The family soon learned differently. He jumped at any noise, lost his temper easily, stared off into space the majority of the time, and screamed every night in his sleep.

Mary Elizabeth moved around in a daze. She remembered the letter she received from Drew last Christmas Eve. The letter was the beginning of her worries.

12 November 1918

My Dearest

It is over! So they say, anyway. We are still hearing guns and seeing fire explosions on the night's horizon.

There have been no more men brought from the front since Yesterday morning. The sounds must be those of celebration.

Mary, I am so very tired. These past fourteen months have been Hell. I want to come home. I want to hold you in my arms and shut out the world and everything I have experienced. I put in a request to come home on the first transport but it was denied. I was told the Medical Corps would be the last to leave. I am going to try again. What does one old doctor matter? Don't they know they have taken the best out of me?

Kiss Thomas and tell him I love him.

Love,
Drew

The letter was the last she had received.

The first of March Mary Elizabeth started writing the Department of War, the Army, the Red Cross and various other agencies trying to locate Drew. All replied back that with the war ending there was great confusion and few were getting letters.

In May when her letters returned unopened, she started writing letters to congressmen, senators, the Vanderbilts, the Rockefellers - everyone with influence she knew or who knew Drew. Everyone responded but no one had the news she wanted.

Mary Elizabeth regretted insisting Drew not take the Red Cross position. That decision haunted her every day. If only he had been in charge, if only he hadn't been in the field hospitals, if only. She tried to pray but the prayers turned into agonizing cries. "God, you took my brother, please don't you dare take my husband! You know I can't live without him."

One day, Mary Elizabeth watched with horror as a messenger rode his bicycle toward the house. She dreaded opening the telegram he delivered.

24 JUNE 1919

CAPT. DREW DUNCAN, US ARMY MEDICAL CORPS – MISSING IN ACTION

Missing in Action, what did that mean? Was he alive somewhere? Was he dead? She still knew nothing. At least with Stephen, they knew where he was. Mary Elizabeth did not know whether to mourn or to be glad it wasn't as final as the news had been about Stephen. What would she do with the rest of her life if he didn't come home?

Finally, daily life returned to normal for everyone but Mary Elizabeth. She read and reread her love's letters. She became inspired to carry on in some fashion his dream. She would go to nursing school, go to Florida, and carry out Drew's plans to the best of her ability. She remained silent about her intentions, but made the resolution that she would be in nursing school before 1920 was over.

George helped his father set up the tree in the living room and then helped the women with the decorations. After George lit the candles, they sat and enjoyed the soft glow and the togetherness of family.

Soon, carolers appeared at the front door. Hearing the basses and tenors made Mary Elizabeth feel somewhat at peace.

The family and carolers ate gingerbread and drank eggnog while they gathered around the piano. Mary Elizabeth played as they sang carols interspersed with patriotic songs.

The entire McRae family slept in the same house that night so they could enjoy Christmas morning together.

On Christmas morning, after the presents were opened and everyone had a hearty breakfast, they bundled up in their warmest clothes, hitched the old wagon up to Buttercup, and sang *Jingle Bells* all the way to church.

Joy filled the air that morning. Not only was it Christmas but most of the families had been reunited. Others knew that their loved ones would come home any day. Stephen was the only one from the community who was not coming home, although most were certain Mary Elizabeth would never see her doctor husband again.

Many of the men in the church service were still recovering from wounds. Others would carry their injuries to their graves. Two had lost arms, one had a missing leg, one was blind because of the gas, and some, like George, brought home demons that lived inside them. The war had changed them all.

The Reverend Scott's message was short and to the point. He spoke of the words of Christmas — hope, peace, love, and recommitment.

As the congregation stood for the last hymn, only the Reverend Scott saw the back door of the tiny church open as a thin soldier walked in and stood in the light of the stained glass windows. When the congregation sang *Silent Night,* the soldier joined in the singing.

His strong tenor voice could be heard above all the rest singing, "...sleep in Heavenly peace."

When she heard the voice, Mary Elizabeth looked up. She knew her prayers had been answered.

The congregation had barely finished the last note when Mary Elizabeth slid off the organ bench, ran down the aisle, lifted her son from her mother's arms, and ran to embrace Drew at the back of the church.

The congregation did not hear the Reverend say the benediction because they were joining with the McRae family welcoming their son-in-law home.

No one questioned why he left the embrace of his wife and kissed Cynthia and her girls.

They knew that Drew was delivering the promised kisses from Stephen.

Chapter 20

A NEW LIFE BEGINS
January 1920

The war had taken a devastating toll on Drew. He had lost 60 of his usual 170 pounds. Pale from the lack of sun, poor nutrition, and a near fatal illness, he looked like living death. His hair had turned white and the weight loss had left him very wrinkled. He looked fifteen years older than his forty-four years.

He had fallen victim to the influenza during the last days of the war. He remembered the celebrations the day the artillery fire stopped. There had been all forms of jubilee but sometime during the merrymaking, the fever he had fought for a week intensified.

The next thing he remembered was waking up among strangers in a field hospital where he was told he was lucky to be alive.

Although still weak, he and dozens of other sick and wounded soldiers were ordered to be transported to an Army hospital on the outskirts of Paris, because the field hospital was closing.

The trip to Paris in the back of the transport was excruciating torture over practically non-existent roads. The suffering soldiers were tossed about until they screamed in pain. Wounds, still far from healed, were jolted open. Soldiers who had bravely accepted their wounds from the battlefield now died from pain and a loss of blood.

Drew, far from being over his bout with influenza, lost consciousness.

When the driver stopped to check on the men in the overcrowded truck, he pulled the bodies of the dead out to give more room to the living, throwing them carelessly in a heap by the side of the road. Because he was unconsciousness, the driver presumed Drew was dead also and put his body with the rest. A second truck would come by later and pick up the dead.

According to the story he heard later, when the truck stopped for the bodies, the driver saw young boys running away screaming about the dead men moving. When he investigated what was causing their terror, he found Drew, gasping for air and barely alive.

The driver took Drew to St. Jude's, a small institution that served as a hospital and an orphanage. Ten days later, when he regained consciousness, Drew had no dog tags, voice, or memory.

His recovery was slow. It was late spring before he could sit up. In June, the nuns started taking him out into the sunshine in a rolling chair. The first steps came in August. By the first of September he was helping the gardener.

The nuns realized Drew was American only when his speech returned the first of November. Two nuns took him to the American Army Headquarters in Paris in a car loaned to them by the town's butcher. Memory returned when former patients recognized him and called him by name.

On the first of December he was on a steamer home.

Drew wanted to resume the life he had left twenty-nine months earlier but he wasn't physically ready. He consented to wait a month before launching his long awaited plans.

As he regained his strength, he dictated letters to Mary Elizabeth for his bank in Baltimore, Dr. Martin, and supply companies. He wrote to the Gram Real Estate Company asking them to find him a suitable office and to Mr. Donaldson to start laying the foundation for the house. He poured over road maps he had ordered from the *Jacksonville Florida Times Union*. Drew's plans were to head south the first of February, although Mary Elizabeth didn't think he was ready to undertake such a journey. She prayed for a delay.

Her prayers were answered when a snow and ice storm hit that section of Maryland January 15. Snow stacked up ten feet in some areas. It was so cold that no one ventured out, even on horseback. There was no way an automobile could make it out of the valley. When the blizzard passed, the cold remained, turning the snow to ice.

Just as the ice began to turn to slush, another heavy snow. The pattern continued through February.

Thanks to an extra month inside, Drew grew more and more healthy. He was ready to leave and resented having to stay indoors in Maryland.

All through his recovery, he was adjusting to family life. Being closed in with the McRaes for so long wasn't easy for him. He was short-tempered with Mary Elizabeth and was agitated every time Thomas cried.

Mary Elizabeth and her parents tried to understand, but he was putting them through every test of endurance. George McRae worried that, like his father, and George, Jr., Drew would not make a full recovery from his war experiences.

Finally, as March approached, Drew made the decision that his family would leave the first of the month, regardless of the weather. With his decision, there was a radical change in his disposition.

The late winter sun was coming over the McRae's barn as Drew, Mary Elizabeth, and their son waved goodbye to her family. Tears of joy and the anguish of parting were in everyone's eyes as the Duncan family drove down the long winding drive.

The Duncans spent the first few days of their trip in Baltimore. Drew had the Model T checked over from bumper to bumper and bought a new set of tires.

He made arrangements for most of his funds to be transferred to the First Bank of Moore Haven. It was agreed the Baltimore Bank's stock office would handle his stocks and bonds instead of sending them to a new firm in Miami.

He confirmed with the storage company that the railroad now extended to Moore Haven so his household belongings could be shipped all of the way.

With each day that passed, and each farewell, Drew became more and more his old self.

On their last night in Baltimore, the banker who had bought the house on Charles Street, held an open house in honor of the Duncans. More than three hundred friends came by to say their good-byes to the man many had known for almost half a century. With every breath Drew tried to convince his friends to come south with them. The only responses were negative.

A few had family stories of an uncle or cousin who had ventured to Florida after the Seminole Wars and the War Between the States. Some had suffered from the freezes in the '80's and '90's and others had lost their hopes and dreams because of yellow fever.

Drew turned their concerns aside.

"We know the cause of yellow fever and we now have a cure for it. And there won't be any freezing temperatures where I'm going to go in Florida."

"I hear a man is dredging up the bay at Miami to create a fantasy island," said Douglas Hawkins, a fellow member of the Chesapeake Club.

"The dredge is apparently becoming the symbol of Florida. Land is being sold by the quart, not by the acre," he said.

"Maybe that's why you are drawn to Florida, Duncan. Those dredges are made right here in Baltimore by the company that bought your family's shipbuilding business."

Douglas continued, "For years we heard you talk of nothing but Miami. Now you are going into the swamp. Are you sure you are moving to dry land? I think I'll live the rest of my days here in Baltimore. Our great-grandparents civilized it a long time ago."

"I'm no pioneer, but I might visit you one day," said another friend. "You can take me fishing or hunting. It must be a sportsman's paradise."

"It is paradise. You will get muck in your shoes when you come down to visit and you won't want to leave," Drew responded.

Spring greeted the family as they traveled through Virginia and the Carolinas. The trip was amazingly smooth and Drew marveled at the good condition of the roads.

"Everyone seems to be heading south with us. I guess they know a good thing when they hear about it too," Mary Elizabeth commented.

"It does seem that everyone is on the move. Mr. Ford has made his car so affordable, that most families can own one. Many men were at bases in Florida during the war. They're now bringing their families down here to live. I do wish that I could have picked up and moved in '98. Why, I would be a native!"

"Look over there, Drew," Mary Elizabeth interrupted. "What are they? Those trucks look like they have little houses on them!"

"I think that is exactly what they are. People have been calling the people who drive them 'Tin Can Tourists.' People actually live in the backs of those trucks with their pans and the rest of their belongings. I've read they have beds, sinks, and stoves – a home on wheels."

"I would love to have made this trip in one of those trucks. We could have had hot meals instead of sandwiches. Thomas could have had a bed and we wouldn't have had to search and search for a hotel."

"This is a fine time to tell me, now that we are almost in Florida!"

In the late afternoon they parked in front of The Seminole Hotel in the heart of Jacksonville, "The Gateway to the Sunshine State."

Drew registered and carried their luggage to their room. Mary Elizabeth couldn't wait until she had a bath to rid herself of the road dust. Drew was too excited to rest.

"I'm going out to explore. I want to see if there is anything that I recognize after twenty-one years."

"How will you find anything from '98? I thought that Jacksonville burned to the ground since you were stationed here."

"I'll just walk and see. Why don't you put on a fancy dress and we will find a nice place to eat? We need to celebrate that we are finally in Florida."

"What about Thomas?"

"We'll take him too, silly."

As Mary Elizabeth looked down at her sleeping son, she said, "You go on and explore, then let's see how we all feel later. For now, all I want to do is bathe and sleep."

The city was teeming with people who were walking, driving about in Model T's, or jumping on and off the streetcars. While the streets were crowded, the numbers didn't compare at all to the amount of people who were there in '98. Of course, it wasn't host to thousands of soldiers either. There were still many fine hotels and buildings, although the ones he saw were less than twenty years old.

One building reminded him of one he had seen in Chicago that was designed by the great architect, Frank Lloyd Wright. He was curious enough about the similarity that he made a mental note to ask someone if Wright had been employed to design some of the buildings following the fire.

He tried to find buildings and landmarks he remembered. All were gone, but the names of the streets remained the same. He found Bay Street and started looking for its fine shops. There were some stores lining the street, but most of the buildings were now either warehouses or obvious houses of ill repute.

A new drawbridge for autos was being built and a new railroad bridge spanned the St. Johns River. He followed Bay Street west looking for the train terminal. He knew the big Jacksonville fire had not destroyed the terminal where he had spent so many hours working; however, a new, more impressive looking concrete building had been built to replace the old brick one. The new terminal was far busier than the streets outside.

Despite the enveloping darkness, he walked back past his hotel to St. James Park where he had first seen Remington sketching the statue of the Confederate soldier. The fancy hotel was gone but the statue was still in place.

Many were out enjoying the balmy spring evening. The flowers on the azalea bushes took on a mystical quality in the luminescence of the streetlights. Drew sat down to rest on a bench beside a distinguished, elderly man wearing the hat of a Confederate officer.

"I was here in '98," commented Drew. "Things have really changed. I think Jacksonville is much more beautiful now," he said.

The old soldier was grateful someone would talk to him and savored telling of his city's somewhat gloomy past.

"You know, twenty years ago this was a rip-roaring place. Then the soldiers left; a fire came and burnt down everything; and the trains came and took the winter tourists farther south. After the northern folks left, we became the motion picture capital of the world, but they filmed on Sunday and that perturbed most folks. Others complained of their drinking and immoral ways. They left us and went to California. Now, we have more shipyards than any other place in the south. Of course we've had our share of yellow fever and influenza epidemics but we're still the biggest town in the state. They say 100,000 people live here. Jacksonville is a good place to live, but most new people seem to be passing through. Are you stayin' or passin', young man?"

"Passin'. I am on my way to the Glades."

"Figures."

"See that statue there?" the old man asked, pointing to the bronze soldier. "I guess Jacksonville is as steadfast as that old soldier. It was unveiled in '98. Were you here?"

"No, just before. I saw it before the ceremony."

"I'll never forget the day. All the Yankee boys that were camped here waiting to go to Cuba attended the ceremony. Of course, we Rebs were the ones honored, but I remember seeing tears in everyone's eyes during the speeches. I think we all flinched some during the thirteen-gun salute."

Drew reluctantly told the old soldier good-bye; he was suddenly exhausted and anxious to get back to the hotel for some rest.

Only when he saw Mary Elizabeth, dressed up and dejected, did he realize he had promised to take her out to dinner. He lamely talked her into ordering room service.

He was asleep before dinner came. Mary Elizabeth cried softly, the tears running through the special makeup she had carefully applied so much earlier.

Drew slept fitfully, in spite of his fatigue. His restlessness had nothing to do with Mary Elizabeth's tears. He kept waking up, realizing he was now a permanent resident of Florida. It had taken him almost a lifetime to get here.

The next day, the family headed south on hard surfaced roads lined with tall pines and ancient, majestic oaks. Everywhere they looked, trees were covered with gray Spanish moss. Dogwoods were in full bloom, their white petals interspersed among trees of varying shades of green. White, purple, orange, and pink azaleas dotted the landscape also.

The farther south they traveled, the flatter the land became. Oaks gave way to more pines; then open prairies on which cattle grazed. The prairies were studded with oaks, pines, and palms.

Wildlife became more abundant.

As they neared Orlando, they smelled citrus blossoms.

"That is the most heavenly fragrance I have ever smelled, Drew," Mary Elizabeth commented.

"Just another confirmation that we are entering our own paradise." Drew smiled as he inhaled deeply several times to absorb the breathtaking aroma.

Late in the afternoon Drew found the Seminole, a small hotel on Lake Eola near the center of Orlando. The Duncans enjoyed walking around the small town before having dinner on the veranda of the hotel. They stayed at their table until Thomas became restless.

The next morning they were up early, hoping they could reach Moore Haven by nightfall. Just west of Orlando, the Duncans passed through hills that reminded them of Maryland's Piedmont. Well-established citrus groves were interspersed with new plantings.

"I haven't been in this part of the state," commented an impressed Drew. "Who would have thought there would be these gorgeous hills?"

Citrus trees were being planted everywhere. Little lakes were at the bottom of almost every hill.

"I wonder if a doctor is needed here," Drew mused.

"Wait just a minute. You fell in love with the 'Glades twenty years ago and dreamed of going there. Don't change your plans on me now."

"Just kidding."

The day turned out to be the most beautiful of their journey. Fluffy cumulus clouds against the clear blue sky caused both to comment that they had never seen a sky so beautiful. The clouds changed shapes constantly.

Mary Elizabeth was glad Drew had spent hours studying the maps before they left. He had written down every turn. She laughed when she first read they would have to turn left by an oak tree or right by Aunt Susan's Cafe. She wasn't laughing now. That was exactly what they had to do.

"How do most people do this? I can't see everyone studying over maps like you did."

"If they're going where we are, they do. Have you noticed many cars or tin can tourists since we left the Dixie Highway south of Haines City?"

"We haven't seen many people. Why was that road so well marked and had so many people?"

"The Dixie Highway is the one Carl Fisher and his friends built to bring people straight from Michigan and Illinois to Miami Beach. Where we are headed now, isn't a place most tourists know about – yet."

Just past three, the Duncans arrived in Sebring, a small town that had been settled next to beautiful, picturesque Lake Jackson. The road guide had advised motorists to stay overnight before proceeding south, even if they arrived in the early afternoon. The Duncans knew their guide had been correct so far, although they didn't see why they couldn't make it the last sixty miles before dark.

When he stopped at a store that had gas pumps, he asked the clerk his opinion.

"Book's right," said the young clerk. "Will take ya most tha day ta get there even if ya don't git stuck in tha sand. Do ya gotta shovel witcha?"

"No. Really think I need one?"

"Ya do if ya be wantin' to git ta wheres you wanna be. That sand's deep an' ya need a shovel ta dig out."

When Drew returned to the car, he carried a new short-handled, round-headed shovel.

Mary Elizabeth looked at Drew with curiosity as he put the shovel in the back.

A disgruntled Drew said, "Just look for any place with rooms. We do have to stay here. I sure hate to be so close and not go on."

"There, Drew. Over there!" Mary Elizabeth was pointing to a magnificent three-story building on the lakeshore.

As they pulled into the drive of the Kenilworth Lodge, they saw the stucco building was surrounded by charming gardens and a beautiful golf course. At least twenty rocking chairs were lined up side by side across the veranda where guests could obviously sit and look at the small beautiful lake.

The smell of orange blossoms greeted them as they left the car and went up the stairs into the huge lobby. Although a large fireplace was a prominent part of the lobby, it was unneeded on this day. The open windows across from one another provided cooling cross ventilation.

"Oh, Drew, this is a gorgeous place!" exclaimed Mary Elizabeth.

"It's grand," Drew agreed. "I wonder why the man back at the store didn't tell me about this place. He said to look for vacancy signs in front lawns because many people are now renting rooms out to passing tourists."

The hotel clerk looked up as Drew and his family approached his desk. He was friendly, but informed them the Kenilworth guests stayed for the winter or extended vacations.

"I can direct you back to some of the motor hotels or a guest house."

Dejected, Drew was about to leave, when he heard his name.

"Drew Duncan, is that you?"

Drew turned to see Professor John Gilman and his sister, Ida. Mary Elizabeth wanted to run, remembering the night Ida Gilman had wanted to end her career. Although both women exchanged pleasant greetings, neither was sincere.

"Professor! I heard you had come to Florida for the winter, but I just assumed..."

"I just didn't tell anyone where we were going in Florida. Most people thought we would be on the coast somewhere. Well, I wanted to be a hotel doctor like your dad. Since I had been a professor for so many years and not a practicing doctor, this was the only place that would even talk to me. I couldn't convince other places that, because of my teaching, I was more knowledgeable about current medical care and medicines than most."

"Were you afraid you would be badgered like me? My friends told me they could almost understand living on the coast in Palm Beach or Miami, but they think I have taken leave of my senses by living in the 'Glades."

Drew paused, "All kidding aside, this is a beautiful place. It's so peaceful."

"I have thought about you often. I even visited your Moore Haven. It seems to be turning into quite a little city. Too bad the roads aren't any better."

"How bad are they?" Drew asked. "They can't be any worse than the one we have been on since the paved road ended at Haines City. We've been on gravel since then. The guide book told us to spend the night in Sebring and the clerk back at Brown's talked me into buying a shovel."

The professor laughed. "You haven't seen anything yet. Just be glad you stopped for the night and that you do have a shovel. It's a full day's trip from here even if you leave early."

Thomas started crying.

"I guess we better go find a place for the night."

"You'll stay right here," insisted Gilman. If there isn't an extra bed, although I can't imagine that, you can stay in our suite."

Mary Elizabeth nudged her husband at that suggestion.

"We really can go to a place where they cater to us motorists," replied Drew.

"Nonsense."

Drew's professor left them and talked to the desk clerk. He then came back with a key.

"You're in room 224. We'll see you here for dinner at six."

They were on the road early the next morning. It was soon apparent the professor and the others had been right about the roads. At Lake Sterns, only ten miles south of Sebring, the gravel ended and gave way to sand. In some places sand was baked hard by the sun; in other places the Model T slipped and slid through deep mud; and in still others the sand was so deep it was impossible to get through without shoveling.

Often the washboard road was so rough that the fastest Drew dared drive was about 5 MPH. They were jostled and tossed, regardless of their speed.

The rough terrain made it extra hard on the family who had now been on the road for ten days. Little Thomas had been extremely well behaved all during the trip, but those last sixty miles of bouncing were too much. He was vocal most of the way.

His parents were completely exhausted when they saw the distant lights of Moore Haven in the dusk. The lights meant the end of their journey, but more importantly, now it meant a hot meal, a hot bath, and bed.

Knowing he was just minutes from ending the long journey, Drew drove a little faster. Mary Elizabeth was not pleased with the increased speed. She knew he was going to run off into the deep canal that ran along side the road. She held her son close to her, closed her eyes and prayed.

A few moments later what Mary Elizabeth had visualized almost happened. Drew stepped on the brakes, lost control of the car, and stopped within inches of the canal.

"What, the...Where did those cows come from?'

Mary Elizabeth opened her eyes to see several cows, just like the scrawny ones she had seen all day, grazing in the middle of the road.

"I have been warning you. I haven't seen a fence since we left Jacksonville!"

Drew backed the car to the road and proceeded with caution, driving in between the cows, who seemed to know they had the right of way.

Mary Elizabeth breathed a sigh of relief when the tires bounced onto the shell marl pavement at the city limits.

Drew drove straight to their building site and, through the enveloping darkness he could see that the pilings for the house were in place. He stopped the car and the family got out.

Mary Elizabeth looked only a few moments at the beginnings of her new home. She turned toward her husband and saw the most satisfied look she had ever seen on his face. He had planned and waited so long for this and now their new life was about to begin. As she had many times in the last few months, Mary Elizabeth told herself she could be happy anyplace as long as Drew was with her. Even in Moore Haven.

Knowing the time was right, Mary Elizabeth whispered in Drew's ear the secret she had kept to herself since they had left Maryland.

The Methodist Women were just finishing their meeting in the lobby of the Moore Haven Hotel when the tired party of three arrived. Drew recognized a few faces in the group but the majority of the women he did not know.

One of the new faces was that of a husky, large-framed older woman with yellowish white hair. She was obviously the leader of the group. She was what Mary Elizabeth's mother would call "handsome" rather than pretty.

The woman came over to Drew as he started to register.

"Hello, you must be our new doctor," her welcome exuding instantaneous affection.

"Yes, I'm Drew Duncan and this is my wife, Mary Elizabeth, and our son, Thomas," Drew said extending his hand to the woman's.

"We have been expecting you and are so delighted that you have arrived safe and sound. My name is Mollie Carter. My husband and I have a dairy farm south of town on property that I believe you once owned."

Drew smiled. "I wonder how much they paid for it?" he thought to himself.

Mollie went on.

"Our house is much too big for my husband, my son, and myself. We would love to have you and your family stay with us while your house is being built."

Drew couldn't believe this total stranger would offer her house to them. "Ma'am, that is so nice of you to offer, but we..."

Thomas, who had been confined much too long on this day's hard trip, had run head-long into a table that was just the right height to hit him in the forehead. He began crying at the top of his lungs, and no one could console him. One of the ladies scooped him up and headed for the kitchen, emerging a few minutes later with a happy little boy drinking a Coca Cola.

"We don't allow him to drink ..."

Drew cut off his wife's comment and said, "Thank you so much for looking after our son. I'm glad you knew what to do."

"Mary, please stay here with these fine women while I go to the car and get my bag."

"He just wants to check the baby," Mary Elizabeth explained. "He was in Europe during my pregnancy with Thomas and he is a little over protective. The baby I'm carrying now will be the first baby that he has delivered...that is...of his own."

194

Drew returned to see his wife sitting and laughing with the other women. Mollie again asked Drew to stay at her house.

"Dr. Duncan, do you really want your wife to live in a hotel for the next few months or at my house where I could look after her while you are working?"

Drew looked at his exhausted wife and son then back to Mollie.

"I'll take you up on the offer tonight. We will see about other arrangements tomorrow."

"Good. I told Charlie – that's my husband – I would find a way home," Mollie said as she squeezed into the already over-packed car. "Just follow this road and it will take you right to the farm."

The four bumped their way down the rough sandy road that ran parallel to the big canal. It was only a mile from the hotel but it seemed like ten. Drew saw that his wife was very uncomfortable and wished that he hadn't consented to staying with the Carters.

"Miss Mollie! How much farther is it? I don't know if we can take very much more of this bumping!" Drew yelled as they hit another bump and his head hit the roof.

"Just ahead to the right. See those palms? That's our house."

Drew turned into a semicircle drive along which royal palms had been planted. The young palms were almost as tall as a man's head.

"Thank goodness!" Drew said as he opened the door for Mollie and Thomas to get out. Mollie took the boy by his hand and led him into the house. Drew swooped Mary Elizabeth up in his arms to carry her up the steps.

"Good God Almighty."

"Drew Duncan!! Don't ever let me hear you take the Lord's name in vain again!"

"I wasn't, Sweetheart. I was praying."

"Right."

"Look at those steps!"

This house didn't stand the usual four feet off the ground like the ones in town. It was at least twelve feet up in the sky.

"I think that I will assist you, not carry you. If I started up those steps carrying you, I don't think either one of us would make it to the top. I would take you back to the hotel but I am afraid to take you back over that bumpy road."

Just when they made it to the porch, a tall thin man in his late sixties opened the door for them.

"I'm Charlie, Miss Mollie's husband. I'm sorry that I didn't help you up those steps, young man, but Miss Mollie had to shake me awake. I guess I had fallen asleep reading the *Saturday Evening Post*. We have the front bedroom ready for you. It's the first door to the left. I'll go down and get your things."

"Thanks, Charlie. We only need the bags in the back seat tonight."

"Mary Elizabeth, I want you to go to bed. I'll get some washcloths so you can get some of the dirt off."

Before he could get the words out of his mouth, Mollie knocked at the door with a bowl of warm water, some Lux soap, washcloths, and towels. Charlie was soon there to hand Drew their luggage.

Mary Elizabeth took off her dusty dress and allowed her husband to give her a sponge bath. She put on a gown from the bag and crawled into the bed. Thomas was already asleep in the big feather bed. Drew washed the dirt from his son's face, hands and feet. He didn't have the heart to wake him by changing his clothes.

"Did you all bathe from that same little bowl? We have a bathroom in the back. You can take a good hot bath if you want to. We are proud of our bath– or at least I am."

"Mollie!"

"Oh, Charlie, he's a doctor. Charlie won't use it. He still has a little house in the banana trees!"

Drew knew he was going to like this couple. They were about the same age as the McRaes and reminded him of his parents, too, when they were in their sixties, yet Mollie was different from either of their mothers. She had spunk. He could tell she usually got her way, but from the sparkle in their eyes when they looked at each other he knew they had a very special relationship.

Their 'tree house' reminded Drew of his in-law's. He would later find out that almost everyone referred to the house just that way: "the tree house."

It was the kind of home that says that you are home when you enter the front door.

Drew could only see the living room and dining room from where he was. Old furniture was mixed with new, including modern wicker. The walls were the same tongue and groove he had seen in so much of Florida. There was a double fireplace between the dining room and kitchen, which seemed to be the only source of heat for the house.

Charlie noticed Drew admiring his house, but he also remembered his reaction to the height it was off the ground.

"Let me explain a little about this house. I didn't build it, but I'm glad it's as high off the ground as it is. The water comes up occasionally, but I don't think I'll ever have to worry about it getting so deep here that we'd be on our roof. There was an open porch running along three sides of the house. I enclosed the back to make a bedroom, a bathroom, and a screened porch so Miss Mollie could work out there when it is real hot and the mosquitoes are bad. I also added a big cypress cistern to store rainwater so we don't have to have a well."

"Tomorrow," Charlie continued, "I'll show you up underneath the house. Since we don't have basements here like other parts of the country, it's nice to have a little space. A man can stand up under this house, as you might have guessed. After Miss Mollie thought the house was going to blow off the pilings when a little wind came up once, I anchored them."

"What do you mean?"

"I'll show you in the morning. I took two-by-fours and crossed them between each post. Now when a good wind blows the house doesn't shake. Since I have done that the house hasn't even creaked."

Charlie took the pipe he was smoking out of his mouth, shook out the tobacco and put more in from a Prince Albert can. "Do you want a smoke?"

"No, thanks. Tell me how you came to be here. Everyone has a story, don't they? I heard quite a few when we were here on our honeymoon in '17."

"Honeymoon here? Well, that does take the cake. Well, my story, short version, is: I am a retired civil engineer from West Virginia. I surveyed too many coal mines. My breather got bad."

"And you smoke?"

"Aw, Doc, a man has to have at least one vice. Anyway, our daughter got sick and we had to take her to a warmer climate in the winter. We went first to the Oklahoma Territory. Then the next year we came to Florida and settled in Clermont. We were very happy there. I even worked for the city surveying for a while. I had the most beautiful garden that you ever saw. The garden was on a small piece of black dirt– muck – that jutted out into a small lake. When they advertised the Black Gold of the Okeechobee bottomland, I came down with a friend to check it out. I sold my land up there in the hills of central Florida and bought my forty acres here."

Charlie paused to let the silence catch up with him.

"I know that you were the first to buy this land from Moore because I saw your name on the title. Don't ask for it back."

"I wouldn't think of it. The profit I made from this piece of property is building me a nice house. Go on, how many children do you have?"

Mollie, who had just come into the room wearing a house robe, spoke up.

"We have four sons. Frank is married with two girls in Oklahoma and he has a baby on the way. He is a civil engineer. Ed is our oldest and is an engineer also. He can't decide if he wants to live in Orlando or West Virginia. He has a boy and a girl. Paul just got married and manages a farm around the lake near South Bay. Daniel is our youngest and we pray that he will just grow up. He is thirteen."

"You mentioned a daughter."

"Yes, the warm winters weren't enough. We buried her four years ago in West Virginia. Mary was twenty."

Mollie's voice cracked. Drew could tell the emotions still ran high when Mary's name was mentioned.

"It's late and I don't want to keep you up any longer. I can tell you my history tomorrow."

He was about to excuse himself when in ran two teenage boys letting the screen door slam as they came in. One of the boys was tall and lanky, and closely resembled Charlie. The other was short and wiry.

"Daniel, Connally, shush! There are two people asleep in the front bedroom. You know better than to come in with all that noise at anytime."

"But, Mama," exclaimed her son, "we won our first ball game today. We beat those LaBelle wimps – 15-5 in LaBelle!"

"Daniel made two homers. One of them was a grand slam! You should have been there! He knocked in three runners! It was sure a good ride home!"

"Connally did a great job too. He came in twice and caught three fly balls."

"That's great, Son," smiled Charlie. "I'll be glad when you have another home game. I can't go anywhere out of town when I have cows to milk."

"Stop talking a minute. Daniel, Connally. I want you to meet our new doctor," said Mollie. "He and his family are from Baltimore and will be staying with us while their house is being built."

"I don't know about that, Miss Mollie," interrupted Drew.

"Baltimore!" Daniel exclaimed, avoiding looking at his mother's frown.

"Baltimore Orioles! Have you been to any of their games? Did you see the Babe play when he was there?"

"I watched the Babe, as you call him, play for a long, long time, even in grammar school. I have been going to the Orioles games practically all of my life. I was even drafted to play for them right out of college."

"You played in the Majors? Wow!"

"They were still part of the Minors then," Drew said, as he clarified another point to the boys to whom he had become an instant hero.

"I never got to play for the Orioles," Drew continued. "I decided to go to medical school instead…but I was a catcher all the way through college."

Drew smiled as the boys looked at him with envy in their eyes.

"Would you please help Coach Hall? He really could use some help."

"Boys! That will be enough!" exclaimed Mollie. "Dr. Duncan has come to serve the medical needs of our community, not to be your baseball coach!"

Drew responded, though, to the boys' question. "I will be glad to help you when I can. I'll be busy with my practice and my family, but I look forward to watching you play."

"Daniel, you have to get up early in the morning and milk before school, so scoot to bed. You did take a shower after the game, didn't you?"

"Connally, you better stay over tonight. It's too late for you to be out on that canal by yourself. Your mama will know where you are."

"I'll excuse myself, too," said Drew. "It's been a long day."

Drew was awakened the next morning by the smell of coffee and bacon. He looked over at Mary Elizabeth still sleeping. Thomas was looking at him and laughing. Drew picked him up before he could wake his mother.

He found clean clothes, his shaving mug, brush, razor, toothbrushes, and baking soda. With Thomas under one arm and the clothes and supplies in the other, Drew headed out to the bathroom. He saw that their big trunk and the rest of their luggage had been placed by the door to their room.

When the father and son reached the kitchen, Mollie greeted them.

"Breakfast is ready anytime you are."

She pointed the way to the bathroom.

"Go out this door and across the back porch. It is the first door that you come to on the right."

Drew put his son in a tub of warm water to play while he shaved and brushed his teeth. The little boy splashed and giggled as he played in the water. He was delighted when his daddy got into the tub with him.

As soon as they dressed, Drew and Thomas made their way back to the good smells coming from the kitchen. Drew put his son in a high chair and then sat down. The aroma of fresh-baked apple pies and fresh-brewed coffee intermingled. A churn with fresh buttermilk was on the floor and Mollie was molding butter in a decorative wooden form.

Charlie and Daniel had already eaten and were out milking when Drew sat down to eat.

Cold, fresh milk from the dairy, eggs from the Carter's chickens, and fresh squeezed orange juice from their trees were part of the breakfast that also included bacon, grits, and biscuits with homemade guava jelly. A block of the newly formed butter was also on the table beside a pewter pitcher filled with cane syrup. The pitcher sat in a bowl of water.

Mollie laughed when she saw Drew eyeing the pitcher with interest.

"That's to keep the ants from eating the syrup before Charlie does," she said.

Drew was hungrier than usual and then remembered he hadn't eaten anything since the afternoon before. Meanwhile Mollie was feeding Thomas. Drew didn't know who was enjoying the occasion more, his son or Mollie.

Drew had just finished his meal when Mary Elizabeth came running by with her hand over her mouth, headed toward the bathroom. Mollie had fixed her some dry toast and was pouring a cup of hot tea when she sat down. Before she could get two bites of bread down, Mary Elizabeth was back in the bathroom.

"I'll take you back to the bedroom where I don't think the bacon smell will bother you so much."

Just the word made her run again.

"Doc, I hope you don't mind me asking, but isn't she a little too far along to be this sick?"

"Not really, but I'm going to watch her closely. I still think the trip, plus the excitement, has triggered this. This is the first time she's been sick. She didn't even tell me about the baby until we were here because she didn't want to further delay our trip. The near miss of a wreck last night didn't help anything either. I almost hit cows right outside of town."

"That is a common occurrence. You've got to be careful of those range cattle. The cowmen have a lot of political pull. I don't know if we will ever have fences," Mollie said with a sigh. "I know you are in a big hurry to get started on this new life of yours so why don't you go and let me tend to Thomas and his mother? I promise I will be a good nurse."

Drew had mixed emotions about leaving his wife but he knew that there was nothing that he could do for her.

"I'll check in later," he said as he walked out of the door.

Drew decided to say goodbye to Charlie and Daniel before he left for town.

He walked around to the south side of the house where he saw the cross braces on the pilings of the house that Charlie had told him about the night before. Drew could have stretched his arms to their extremes and still not been able to touch the floor of the house, high over his head. Mollie's clothes washer was on a wooden platform.

"It's an open-air basement," he joked to himself as he headed to the dairy barn, hoping to find Charlie and Daniel.

There were no cows and no Charlie nor Daniel. The barn floor was wet from being washed down. It was the same in the room where the milk was bottled. Recently washed glass bottles were turned upside down on draining racks. Drew savored the smell of fresh milk mixed with water as he walked across the wet cement floor of the milk room.

He checked the time on his pocket watch. It was 7:30 a.m. Charlie and Daniel were already delivering milk.

On his way back to toward the house, he took a closer look at what was once his property. He had a sense of pride in what he saw, not because it had once belonged to him, but that he had sold it.

If he had retained the ownership the forty acres would still be full of elderberries and sawgrass.

Now most of the land was pasture except for about two acres which was shaping up to be a beautiful yard. A freshly tilled garden was filled with vegetables and fruit ready to be picked; a multitude of flowering bushes and trees dotted the yard; and a stand of banana trees was planted along the north edge of the yard.

A large chicken coop was on the south side of the yard.

Behind the house stood the biggest cistern he had ever seen except near hotels. Several outbuildings were painted the same pale yellow as the big house.

"It is a pleasant home," Drew thought as he approached his Model T.

The road from town that paralleled the canal went on past Charlie's house to other farms. The front lawn he was standing on actually continued on the other side of the road, toward the canal, and he walked across the road to get a better view.

Palm trees bent by the south Florida winds hung gracefully from the banks out into the water. An array of butterflies of different colors and sizes fluttered around flowering shrubs that also lined the shore. The sunlight glistened off the dew, making everything sparkle like diamonds, including the gigantic web of an enormous yellow and brown spider.

Purple morning glories were opening up while white moon vine flowers were closing. Five white wooden Adirondack lawn chairs on the bank welcomed visitors to sit down.

Drew knew immediately that a lot of activity went on here, for, in addition to a rowboat that was tied to the long wooden dock, a long rope hung from a large cypress tree at the edge of the canal. Drew pictured Daniel and his friends swinging out from the bank and dropping into the water. The sensation of falling into the dark water was very real.

Drew sat down on one of the lawn chairs. The sun that was still low in the eastern sky was partially hidden from view by the same type of big fluffy clouds they had fancied the day before. These, too, seemed to touch the horizon. Drew wished he was talented like his friend, Adam, and could paint a picture of the white cotton clouds against the royal blue sky.

The weather was cool and pleasant as he observed a great blue heron on the dock in front of him. He watched a succession of ripples fanning out from the center where a large bass had broken the surface a few minutes before.

A turtle crawled onto a log that was protruding out of the water and then proceeded to stretch out its long neck and draw it back into the shell again. Not only was the turtle interesting, but also its black neck with the yellow stripes was unique.

Birds called to each other from above him.

The wildlife was what brought him here and he could hardly believe he was finally going to enjoy sights like these every day, not just on a short vacation.

Extolling his good fortune, he pulled himself away, climbed into his car, and drove down the bumpy road to town.

At the construction site of his house, ten men were already working.

The next stop was a small restaurant on the busy waterfront just north of the Moore Haven Hotel near Gram's Real Estate Office.

"It's about time you made it!" yelled Charlie, who was at the table with a group of men. "Fellows, this is Dr. Drew Duncan, who's ready to start his doctoring right now. Is anybody ailing?"

They all laughed but no one volunteered to be Drew's first patient. One by one they introduced themselves. The last person he met was Fredrick Gram.

"Mr. Gram of Gram Real Estate?"

"The same."

"Do you have an office ready for me?"

"Yes, sir, that I have. Your equipment and boxes of supplies arrived yesterday by Railway Express. Let me finish my coffee and then we'll go see if the place is to your liking."

"Let's drive your car so you won't have to come back here."

Drew drove to Main Street, about half way down the block from the Lone Cypress. The realtor took Drew into the drugstore on the first floor.

"I want you to meet John Dowd, our new druggist. He took over when Dr. Martin left."

"Glad to meet you, but when did Dr. Martin leave? I just heard from him in January and he didn't say a word about leaving."

"He left about a month ago now."

"Am I the only doctor now?"

"Dr. Mitchell has an office at the end of the street but he's only here three days a week. He comes down from Sebring on the train. Folks will be real glad you are here."

"Please don't think me rude, but could I see my office? I have been looking forward to this day for the past twenty years."

"Here's the key. Take the stairs right outside the store. It is the same office that Dr. Martin had but he didn't leave anything there. I'll join you in a minute."

Drew found the stairs behind a set of double screened doors. He bounded up the rather wide stairway. At the top, spread throughout a large lobby, was his furniture, equipment, and boxes of supplies.

Several rooms opened up into the lobby, which Drew found were all inter-connected.

"Dr. Duncan."

Drew jumped as Mr. Gram walked into the room where he was.

"I didn't mean to startle you. Is this agreeable to you?"

"This is better than I hoped for."

"Are you comfortable with the contract I sent to you?"

"Yes, the lease is fair; however, I would prefer my own building in the future. I believe I will be more comfortable owning rather than leasing. Here's the check I had drafted for you before I left Baltimore. It should cover me for a year, but if any building becomes available that I can buy, even before this lease runs out, please let me know. Now, how do I go about finding some men to help me move in?"

"I would be glad to find you some workers. How many?"

"Three should do nicely."

Drew took off his tie, rolled up his sleeves, and began to set up his supply cabinets. After an hour, sweat was pouring out of every pore of his body. He went downstairs to Dowd's Drug Store for a cold Coca-Cola.

"You sure are hot, Doc," commented the druggist. "You can get some fans down at Heard's."

"What good would that do? I understand there is no electricity during the daytime."

Drew's voice trailed off as he noticed a fan swirling overhead.

"I thought lights were only on from sundown to midnight."

"Nope, that has changed with more people coming into town. Electricity now runs from 10 in the morning until 10 at night. I'll call and tell Bob to come turn your current on. You'll need a telephone, too. I'll take care of that."

"First let me call Mr. Gram. He might already have that under control."

Drew started to crank the telephone that hung on the wall next to the soda fountain counter.

"Doc," said Mr. Dowd, "There's no need in calling Gram. Here comes Bob now."

Just at that moment two middle-aged balding men walked into the store, one holding a telephone.

"Mr. Dowd, where is that new doctor? We went upstairs and he isn't there."

"I'm Dr. Duncan."

Drew extended his hand to the men. "Seth Porter," said the man with the telephone as he extended his hand to Drew. "This is my brother, Bob. He's here to check your lights and I guess you figured out what I'm here for."

Seth grinned as he held up the telephone. The men went back upstairs.

"Your lights are turned on. Let me see if you need any bulbs."

Bob walked around punching the pearl buttons on the walls. In the rooms where there were no switches, he pulled on the strings extending down from the light bulbs in the ceiling.

Drew decided which room would serve best as his office and then he had Seth install the telephone. As Seth began to work, Drew said. "I would rather have it in the lobby for my nurse, that is, when I get a nurse."

"You don't want one in here, too?"

"Oh!" Drew seemed surprised. "You can hook up two?"

"I would be glad to do just that."

"Can you install a phone out at the Carter's farm for me? It looks like I'm going to be staying there until my house is finished here in town."

"I wish I could, Doc, but there aren't any lines going out the River Road. I don't know when there will be any either. There aren't too many people out that way."

Bob came back where Drew and Seth were talking. "You are all set, Doc. All you need are ten light bulbs."

"Thanks. Send the bills to..."

"Just go to the post office. They already have a box for you."

Drew was saying goodbye to the two brothers, when three other men came up the stairs. Each was almost a carbon copy of the other – short, greasy hair, missing teeth, and smelling because of the lack of baths and consumption of liquor.

"Doc? Mr. Gram says you need hep movn' in. "Name's Mac. This here's Henry an' this here is Dooley."

"I sure do need help. The pay will be three dollars for the day. Is that acceptable?"

"Sure is. What do we do first?"

"You can start by turning over and unwrapping every piece of furniture and piece of equipment you see. If a box says, 'electrical', wait for me. I'm going down to Heard's to get some light bulbs and fans. Will two of you come with me?"

Heard's General Store was in the next block. The aroma of Arbuckle's newly ground coffee hit Drew in the face as he opened the big plate glass door. Shelves lining the walls were filled with a wide variety of merchandise, including food, bolts of cloth, sewing notions, shoes, clothing, toys, fishing tackle, and farm, home, and electrical supplies. Groceries were in the very back, in addition to feed, fertilizers, seeds, and building supplies. Fans were in with the groceries. He selected four for the small rooms and two for the lobby waiting room.

"How much do I owe you?" Drew asked the clerk who had not introduced himself.

"I'll just put it on your tab, Doc. I'm Lynn Newkirk. My wife is expecting our first baby. I'm nervous because she ain't seen a doctor yet. When can she come to see you?"

"Nice to meet you, Lynn, and thanks for the credit. I don't know how long it will take me to set up my office; a couple of days I would imagine, but if you have an emergency, just come up to the office anytime during the day. At night I will be at Carter's Dairy Farm. I almost forgot, may I have a dozen light bulbs?"

Mac, Dooley, and Henry set up the fans and arranged the furniture in the lobby.

"We're going to have to find another room for the Negro waiting room," noted Drew.

"Are you going to treat those niggers up here in the same place as us whites?" asked Henry.

Drew contained his anger the best he could.

"Doctors are bound by oath to treat all people, no matter what color. You can spread the word around town that I will treat any person who needs me – whether he is rich or poor, red, yellow, black or white – and please, don't ever use that word in my presence again," Drew said through clenched teeth.

"What did I say that got you so riled up? All I said was nig..."

"I know what you said."

"Since when is that a bad word? That's all I've ever heard. I meant no harm."

"They are Negroes or Coloreds."

The hired men didn't reply because they all needed the pay.

The end room off the lobby had a window and a door that opened to the back steps to the building.

"The nig – Negroes – could come up this way," said Henry. "That gives 'em their own entrance."

"Perfect!" Drew said; but he thought, "Life should not treat any one like this."

They worked through the morning and into the afternoon. At noon, Drew gave Henry money to go to the drugstore to buy sandwiches and Coca-Colas. By three o'clock all the equipment, supply cabinets, and other big items had been uncrated and put in place.

Drew paid the men and thanked them for their work. Henry wanted to stay to help load the supply cabinets but Drew told him he had to do it himself because he had a certain order for everything.

As the three men walked down the stairs, Mac commented, "I wonder how long the Klan will let that nigger lover stay in town?"

They decided they would say something at the next meeting.

Drew had emptied only one box when a young, slender, blonde-haired woman in her late thirties, appeared at the door of the room in which he was working.

"I am sorry, I'm not open yet. But if there is an emergency, I'll be glad to help."

"Oh no, Dr. Duncan, I'm not sick. My name is Anna Wright. I am a registered nurse. I worked for Dr. Martin until he left last month, so now I'm looking for a job. I was wondering if you needed a nurse. Please forgive me for my boldness, but I do want to work."

"Well, Nurse Wright, I will need a nurse, but I don't know how many days I'll need you. I have no idea how busy I will be."

"You'll be very busy, I can assure you."

"How much experience do you have?"

"I practiced three years before I got married and I worked for Dr. Martin for the past year. I was tops in my class at Charity. I have my diploma and my license right here if you want to see."

Anna handed the documents to Drew.

"Charity is a good school – and I see that you graduated with honors – congratulations. I trust it wasn't all work and no play, though, especially in a city like New Orleans," Drew smiled.

He stopped to further analyze the woman who might assist him. It didn't take long to decide that she may have come sooner than he was ready for a nurse, but it was certainly a blessing to know someone so qualified was available.

"You're hired. If you can start to work right now, we will discuss pay when we are through. I need help unloading these boxes. You do remember the correct medical order and what instruments go together as well as the bandages, gauze, and medicines?"

"That was first year."

"Good, let's get started."

By seven that night the clinic was operational. Drew could open the next day.

The two went down the stairs together. Drew locked the double glass doors behind them. "I'll see you by nine tomorrow. "

"How about eight? That will give me more than enough time to get here after the children get off to school."

Mollie warmed supper for Drew when he arrived home. He enjoyed the meal and after a long hot bath, had a long conversation with the Carters. He wished that Mary Elizabeth could have rubbed his back but she was in bed when he arrived home.

"Oh, and Doc, your bags have all been unpacked," said Mollie. "You will stay with us."

"Do you always get your way?"

"Yes," interjected Charlie. "It doesn't pay to fight her."

"We'll stay on one condition. I'll pay you the same as board would be at the hotel."

"Then you can leave. No one will pay me to sleep under my roof."

"Doc," began Charlie, after Mollie had left the room, "Mollie needs you as much as your wife and little boy need her. She has become used to having a brood to care for close to thirty-four years. She misses it. Until that house is finished, your family will have nothing to do while you're gone. It will take months. They can stay here and keep Mollie company. Your wife has been with her mother since Thomas was born and has grown accustomed to having a mother figure around. Daniel has always wanted to be a big brother and now he has a chance. That should be good for him as well as Thomas."

"You are right on all accounts and Mollie can help Mary get acquainted with the women in the community. But I want to pay you. Mollie need never know."

"But she would wonder where I got the extra money."

"I have the solution. You, Mollie, and Daniel can have free medical coverage the rest of your lives. That includes Daniel's family when he is grown."

The next morning Mary Elizabeth was awake when Drew woke up. She had already dressed Thomas and taken him to breakfast. When she turned and saw Drew's eyes open she fell back in bed.

"Oh, Drew yesterday was wonderful. I helped Miss Mollie and we are already good friends. I want to stay here. May we please?"

206

"Well," Drew paused, as if he wasn't sure.

"Please, Drew. The Carters are dears. They remind me of home. What would I do all day in the hotel? Please, Drew, I'm begging."

Drew looked at Mary Elizabeth and smiled, "Charlie and I discussed it last night. We have settled the details between us."

Then he scolded, "I heard what all you did yesterday. You can't do that. I don't want you to lose the baby. You were so tired I couldn't even wake you last night when I came home a little before eight. Promise me you will take it easy, at least for a few days until you get over the trip. I wish we had come down by train and bought a car here. There is a brand new Ford dealership here."

"Well we are here now. Tell me about yesterday. What did you get accomplished?"

Drew was recounting the activities of the day and talked until they heard the clock in the living room chime on the quarter hour. Drew took out his watch.

"It is 7:15. I need to get started toward the office if I am going to make it by eight."

He quickly dressed and ate, almost swallowing his breakfast whole. "I must get up a lot earlier from now on," he thought to himself.

Drew kissed Mary Elizabeth, his son, and Mollie goodbye as he raced out the door.

Driving out of the Carter's drive, he paused to look over the water at the rising sun.

"Tomorrow I will take time to come out and enjoy some of this beauty. I need to remind myself that this environment is the reason I came here. If I wanted to rush, I could have remained in Baltimore."

Drew parked in front of the drugstore. He was unlocking the heavy stairwell doors when he noticed Mrs. Wright standing by him waiting to go up the stairs. She was wearing a crisp white uniform and a cap with Charity's color stripes on it.

"Mrs. Wright."

"Call me, Anna."

"Miss Anna, we haven't discussed salary."

Just at that time the door opened and Sallie Newkirk, heavy with child, came up the stairs. Drew gave her the first physical of her pregnancy – as well as the first one of her life. She nervously clasped and unclasped her hands. Anna assured her that everything the doctor did was routine and that she was going to be fine. Anna left after the examination while Drew told Sallie that she probably had two more months until the baby came. He gave her instructions on diet and exercise. As he escorted her through the office door he told her to come back the next week.

"Miss Anna, please make an appointment for Mrs. Newkirk for next week and have her fill out an information card."

Then he looked up to see a room filled with patients. Each of them was already filling out cards. When Drew finished with the next patient, he checked the Negro waiting room. It was his policy to alternate between the waiting rooms. There was no one in the room.

None came that day or on the following days. Each week there were more and more patients. The doctor was also summoned on numerous house calls. Anna went with him to show the way. By the third week of practice, Drew was concerned about the lack of Negro patients.

"Where do the Negroes go when they need medical attention? Did they come to Dr. Martin or do they go to Dr. Mitchell? Who helps them deliver their babies?

"Wanda Jones is the Negro midwife. I do know that Wanda helps with all kinds of ailments. Dr. Martin only went out to clean up after fights or pronounce someone dead. Sometimes he delivered a baby. I don't know what Dr. Mitchell does. There is also a Voodoo medicine man out there in the Quarters. He came here with the bunch of Caribbeans. I had enough with Voodoo in New Orleans. That can be some powerful bad stuff."

"Hum...I have learned a lot from the Seminoles."

Knowing he had just arrived from Maryland, Anna gave him a questioning look

"Long story." Drew continued, "Maybe I can learn some Voodoo, too." Drew smiled. "Well, it's slowed down now. I think I'll go see Wanda. If anyone comes in, help the best way that you can. If they really need me, leave me directions to their house. If there is a real emergency, send them to Dr. Mitchell. Close the doors at five. Now, how do I get to Wanda's?"

Drew followed Anna's instructions and easily found Wanda's house. A trim middle aged woman with cream colored skin came to the screen door of her porch when she saw the white man get out of his car, she figured he had the wrong house. Shelia's house was the third one in the next block.

Wanda always had white men stopping at her house because it had the misfortune of being the third one in the first block as you came into Lakeview.

"If you're looking for Shelia, her house is down on the next block. It's the one with the red lacy curtains."

"I'm not looking for Shelia, I'm looking for Miss Wanda Jones."

The woman he was addressing had coal black hair, without a trace of gray. He thought it must be Wanda's daughter.

"I'm MRS. Jones but everyone calls me, Miss Wanda. What can I do for you today?"

Wanda was still at her door and Drew was at her front gate.

"I'm Drew Duncan, the new doctor in town. I hear that you're a mid-wife.

I was wondering if we could talk."

"Come up on the porch."

Wanda opened the screen wider.

"How may I help you, Dr. Duncan?"

Standing on the steps, Drew proceeded with his conversation.

"Mrs. Jones, I mean Miss Wanda. First of all I'm not here to take any of your patients away. I want to work with you. I know that you know everyone in the Quarters."

"We call our part of town Lakeview," interrupted Wanda.

"Please forgive me. I'm still new in town and I was just repeating...It won't happen again."

Drew continued, "If anyone is sick and you have done all that you can, send them to me or call me and I'll make house calls. I charge $1 for office calls and $2 for house calls. If anyone can't pay we can make other arrangements. If you need my assistance with any deliveries, I'll be more than glad to help you. My office is over Dowd's Drug Store. There are stairs that lead from the alley right into the waiting room."

He was embarrassed to have to say alley but he could put it no other way.

"Dr. Duncan, are you really saying that you'll help my people with every day aches and pains?"

"That's right. I am here to serve the needs of the entire community, not just the whites. An old friend told me years and years ago that 'We's all God's child'n.' I try to live by that philosophy."

"Well, then. Why don't you come in an' sit a spell."

She paused a moment as Drew settled into a sagging, cane-bottom chair on the un-screened front porch.

"The friend who told you, 'We's all God's child'n' – a Negro friend? Am I right?"

"Right you are."

Drew proceeded to tell about Flora and what she had meant to him. He knew that he looked at Negroes differently than most other whites but because of Flora he could not be any other way.

"You better watch it down here, Doc. The Klan's very active. They aren't going to take too kindly to the fact that you'll treat us black folk the same and that you'll come out here for anything but pleasure."

"If I have trouble with the Klan, I'll remind them that I'm the only full-time doctor they have here."

Drew couldn't help but think about the attitudes of the men who helped him set up his office. The Klan probably already had heard about him.

"Dr. Duncan, where're you come from?"

"Baltimore."

Wanda's eyes danced.

"I knew it! Your Flora was Flora Greene, right?"

"How in the world?"

Tears blocked her sight from his view.

"I'm from Baltimore, too. I went to Miss Flora's church all of my life. She taught me in Sunday School an' I don't think there was a week that went by that she didn't say to remember, 'We's all God's child'n.' I remember the way she could sing. She paid my tuition to nurse's school. Yes, she did."

"What? I didn't realize you were a nurse. Most midwifes aren't."

"There were many of us she touched through her teachings an' her gifts. My mother an' brother were at her funeral an' wrote me all abou' it an' you. The words you said were the words of a son, not an employer. Mama also said that you set up a scholarship fund in her memory."

Tears were in her eyes as she realized who she was talking to.

Wanda then laughed, "Mama tol' me she was shor' glad when that prissy girl went back to Savannah an' left you alone."

"Don't tell me! Charlie Mae..."

"Is my mama."

"Now tell me, how in the world did you get here?"

"It's a long story," said Wanda as she began to fill Drew in on her life.

Chapter 21

LIFE IN MOORE HAVEN
March 1920

Engraved invitations were received by both the Carters and the Duncans that read:

The Honorable Marian Horwitz O'Brien
former Mayor of Moore Haven
and
Dr. H. J. Mitchell
request the honor of your presence
at a reception
honoring
Dr. and Mrs. T. Drew Duncan, III
Saturday, March 20, 1920
7:00 P.M.
Moore Haven Hotel
River Road
Moore Haven, Florida

RSVP

When they arrived at the reception, Charlie introduced Drew and Mary Elizabeth to the former mayor, a beautiful blonde woman about the same age as Drew.

"Mr. Carter, the doctor and I don't need introductions. Why, we are old friends!"

Mary Elizabeth looked at her husband with disbelief. He had not said a word about knowing this liberated woman who had made headlines all over the country when she was elected as first woman mayor in the United States. She was flabbergasted as Mrs. O'Brien locked arms with Drew.

Drew was as bewildered by her statement as Mary Elizabeth. He didn't know any more about the woman than anyone else. He had read the same information as had Mary Elizabeth.

"I'm sorry, but if we have ever met, I don't remember," said the befuddled Drew.

"Think back. Yale, '98. Winter Frolics. Blind date. Ring a bell?"

"Oh, You're THAT Marian! Of course, I remember now."

"Are you always such a good liar? I remember I thought I was so lucky. For once in my life my blind date turned out to be a handsome med student. I secretly had our lives together mapped out, but your mind was a million miles away. I supposed you were thinking about your next cadaver."

"No, then I was thinking about going to Cuba."

"Cuba? Did you get there?"

"Yes, but tell me, do you like it here as much as you say in all that I have read. Are you really responsible for the railroad?"

"My late husband was a good friend of my present husband. They both invested in the South Florida Land Company after Moore sold out to Busch. They came down here together to manage their investments. After a while, they didn't see eye to eye with Busch and the way he ran things. They thought he wasn't being fair to his buyers. They pulled out their investments and formed the DeSoto Stock Farms Company."

"Before that project got underway, my first husband died. I came down to manage my property. John and I worked together and we fell in love. That's the story in a nutshell."

"How did you get the railroad in? When Mr. Moore had Alton Parker drive a golden stake down, everyone thought the railroad was on its way then. What did you do that Moore couldn't do?"

Marian smiled.

"Well, Mr. Moore only rounded up mere politicians like Parker and Bryan to publicize this place. You have to remember that my daddy is THE Pennsylvania Railroad and my brother is a partner of J.P. Morgan's. They get things done fast."

Drew laughed. "Once again, it's not what you know but who you know."

"It was in my case; but enough history. Now, let's meet some of your future patients."

The gracious former mayor whisked Drew away from Mary Elizabeth and the Carters. For the next half hour Drew shook hands with and was slapped on the back by every man in the crowd.

Baltimore society would have been comfortable with the gala affair. Among the fountains of citrus punch, some flavored with illegal beverages, were hors d'oeuvres of all descriptions and a variety of sweets and pastries that would put the Baltimore Bakery to shame.

Scores of the county's residents were both inside and outside the hotel ready to meet the new doctor and his wife.

Dr. Mitchell went to a podium on the stage.

"May I have your attention please? As you know, you are here to meet our new doctor. I must say I am the happiest man in this room. When Dr. Martin departed, it left the community in a medical crisis. Because of family obligations, I can only be here three days a week. Babies, accidents, and sickness just won't adjust to my schedule. So, we are extremely pleased that Dr. Duncan has chosen to set up practice here. Before I let him speak, I want to tell you his background. I have friends in Baltimore who were more than willing to forward information to me about our new doctor. I think you will be impressed with his credentials."

With that, he gave details about Drew that did indeed impress the guests.

A warm round of applause greeted the guest of honor as he went to the podium to address the crowd.

"I don't know what to add to what Dr. Mitchell has said. I would like to know the name of our mutual friend. You have been told some of my history but not what I consider the most important."

"I fell in love with South Florida in '98. I have visited almost every winter since then and dreamed of the day I could move here. Family obligations and the Great War postponed my dreams until now. I'm glad to finally be here. I want you to know that my door is always open, both to my office and to my home. That is, when we move in."

Drew paused and turned toward Mary Elizabeth.

"Now that you know something about me, I want you to meet my wife, Mary Elizabeth. She's a talented concert pianist and former teacher at Peabody Institute of Music."

When the crowd heard this, they urged her to perform a few numbers at the piano.

Mary Elizabeth remembered how out of tune it had been almost three years before and wondered if it had been tuned. One note and she knew it had not been touched. She wished she hadn't consented to play but continued to do so through the end of the pieces she had chosen. She knew she was embarrassing herself and her husband in front of all of these people.

However, when she got through with her medley of songs, the crowd clapped and cheered.

"That was the prettiest thing that I ever heard," someone said.

Mary Elizabeth thought the entire assemblage must be tone deaf.

Later, on the way home, Mary Elizabeth talked excitedly with Mollie about the party and the people she had met.

"I should have known that Drew knew the mayor," commented Mary Elizabeth, "Mollie, I have entertained many important people, but my husband here seems to be on a first-name basis with every famous person we meet, from the first woman mayor in the United States to the Vanderbilts."

"Mary, I didn't even remember that woman!"

The badgering went back and forth all of the way to the farm, as Drew drove on the side of the road near the canal where he had found the road to be the smoothest.

Only Charlie was quiet. He had his eye on the lights that had been following them since the hotel. When the others went inside, Charlie stayed outside to smoke his pipe.

As soon as the door closed, however, he walked down the steps and over to the corner of the yard where he had seen the lights go off.

When he reached the shadows of the massive oak at the north corner of his property, he was surrounded by a group of white-robed men.

"What do you want at my house? J.D., Bill, Al, and the rest of you hoodlums, don't you even dare think about burning a cross in my yard. I don't know why you think those robes will cover your identities!"

"We have no fight with you, Charlie. It's that fancy Yankee doctor of yourn."

"Yeh. He's courting tha niggers an' is goin' ta treat 'em in his office downtown. We don't like that!"

"Report is that he spent a whole afternoon cavorting with that nigger nurse."

Charlie retorted, "The doctor will be working with Wanda treating people in the Quarters. It's none of your business, but they are both from Baltimore and know a lot of the same people."

Known as a man of few words, Charlie launched into one the longest speeches he had ever made.

"What do you want, anyway? Every last one of you was at the reception drinking up that spiked punch. You heard Dr. Mitchell say that he can't serve our needs. What are you going to do when one of you is in a cutting on Saturday night or your child has a high temperature that you can't get down. I tell you what; you will likely die! Drew's a fine man – and by the way, he's not a Yankee. His father was a doctor for Lee himself!"

Charlie continued, "That man wants to be here. He's going to be busier than he even knows, serving this entire side of the lake. You know that there's no doctor, except for Doc Mitchell - and he is part time - from Palm Beach around to Okeechobee City. Now go away. Give the doctor a chance. If he feels it's his duty to serve all, no matter what color, so be it."

Then, bravely, he added, "If I hear tell of you harassing the doc again, I will personally see to it that every one of your wives is called. I'm sure no milk will be delivered to your doors in the morning either! Now excuse me, I hear Miss Mollie."

Charlie didn't start shaking until he reached his front porch. He sat down in a rocker and took out his pipe, watching as the trucks turned north.

"Enjoying the night air?" Drew asked as he walked onto the porch. "Mind if I join you?"

By 8:30 the following Monday morning, both of the waiting rooms were full. Drew worked until three without a break.

"Miss Anna, close the office at five. You know what to do if anyone else comes in. I'm going to get acquainted with the area."

"Where?"

"I don't know, but I thought that I would head west and take the roads and trails that I see."

"Do you have a map?"

"Not a good one."

"Give me a few minutes and I'll draw a rough map of the county and point out most of the roads and trails that I know about...by the way, do you have a shovel and some boards?"

"I have a shovel. Why do I need boards?"

"I'm glad that you didn't try to come here from Baltimore without at least a shovel for the sand and mud. Go down to Heard's and get two boards. Lynn will know just what you need."

Drew heeded Anna's words and stopped by Heard's.

Lynn brought out two long planks.

"Everyone who drives carries these with them."

As he took the planks to Drew's Model T, he said, "Let me see what kind of shovel you have."

Drew showed him and it was approved.

"Doc," said Lynn. "Be sure and put palmetto leaves down in sandy places."

Over the course of the next few weeks, on the slower afternoons and on Saturdays and Sundays, Drew drove to settlements in the outlying area.

On his first visit to Buckhead Ridge, he was introduced to Doc Anna Abner. Her office was in Okeechobee City and her circuit included Buckhead. Drew was relieved that one of the remote areas of the county was served by another doctor.

There was some variation in the houses that people lived in, but almost without exception, the houses were from two to four feet off the ground, had high-pitched roofs, and porches. Many were one-room wooden cabins or two room structures connected by an open breezeway – a dogtrot – typical of the north Florida homes he had seen on his first trip to Florida.

Shotgun houses were also prevalent, especially in Lakeview. These houses were one room wide with usually three to four rooms connected together. It was said one could stand with a shotgun and fire "clean through the house from the front door to the back door."

Tarpaper shacks and huts built of cane poles with cabbage-thatched roofs were more typical of lakeshore homes. Many fishermen lived on houseboats. Most, whether they were poor fishermen, farmers, merchants, or cow hunters, welcomed Drew into their homes. They were pleased to know that there was a doctor in the area.

Some, however, were hostile and cold. They did not cotton to his store-bought clothes or his talk. What would anyone who drove an automobile want with them anyways?

Robert Lee Taylor was typical of many of the Cracker homesteaders.

Robert's skin was brown and weathered, as were most whose daily lives required being out in the sun. At the age of fifty, he had no teeth. Numerous scars were visible on his slender frame. Robert Lee refused to acknowledge Drew as being a doctor.

"Ain't got no use for citified doctors. Ma an' Pa teached us how ta make potions an' cures from roots, barks, berries, an' such. We ain't needin' no outside hep."

Others wanted the doctor to stay off their property because they didn't want him to see their moonshine stills. However, other moonshiners welcomed him in and were proud to show him how they made their 'shine.

Drew made a regular route of going to general stores in each community to treat those who might be there. He would leave samples of medicines and tonics and instructions on how to use them and counted on word of mouth to spread the news of his medical practice.

It was at Beck's Store in Lakeport that he learned about the Raleigh Man who went door-to-door selling patent medicines. Drew explained that he had a better brand. He never knew he would have to become a salesman to practice medicine!

Drew's circuit reached as far east as Sandy Point. To get any further east he would have to board a boat, but to his surprise many people were willing to take boats to come see him. They came from as far away as Ritta and Ritta Island.

He was also successful in making friends with a number of cattlemen and their hired hands. Jake Summerlin's name was often mentioned. He asked among them if any knew a man named Hathaway, the cowman who, twenty-two years earlier, had implanted the dream of seeking this area of Florida. No one seemed to know him and Drew was left wondering if Hathaway ever got a piece of the black gold.

On the first Saturday night of the month, the day after payday, most of the cow hunters headed out to indulge in gambling, women, and moonshine. All seemed to know exactly where to go. It was as if Prohibition didn't exist in south Florida.

Early one Sunday morning, after being up most of the night patching up the wounds of several cowmen, Drew was having a bite to eat at Mae's.

A rider came up on horseback at a gallop, jumped from his horse and ran in asking if anyone knew where the doc lived. He said he had a man out at Boar Hammock who needed a doctor fast.

"Doc," said the cow hunter, "it's Mr. King's foreman. He's in bad shape. Mr. King himself sent me to fetch you."

Drew gulped the last of his coffee, grabbed his bag, and then called Anna to tell her where he would be.

Charlie, who was with Drew, let Mary Elizabeth know that Drew had left to go out to the King ranch.

Ziba "Buck" King was the biggest cattleman in south Florida and his men were a constant source of income for Drew, especially after a Saturday night.

Drew headed west on the bumpy sandy road and then down the cow trail paths he had learned so well. When he got to the Boar Hammock cattle pens, Buck himself was sitting on the porch of the cow house with some of his cowhands. He was at the side of the automobile before Drew even stopped.

"Come with me. My foreman's in a real bad way."

Drew followed King and found Bone Mizell, whose scarred body showed he had been stitched up many times. Strips of sheets had been placed over a gaping chest wound to catch the blood and, hopefully, stop it. Drew washed up and took off the strips.

"How bad is it, Doc?"

"Bone, how many times have you been cut in the same place?"

Bone took another swig of whiskey to kill the pain.

"I don't know, Doc. But this one's really hurtin'."

"It's bad, Bone, really deep. I can patch you up but you are going to have to take a vacation to heal. I don't want you back in the saddle for a while."

"Doc, you know I havta ride."

"Ride and die. Your choice."

Bone sighed heavily, then asked, "Did I tell you about Bill? I sent him up north. He never traveled anywhere until after he died."

"Yes, Bone," nodded Drew, who had heard the story now more than once. "That's a good story, but be quiet and try not to move."

Mizell's stories were legendary. His favorite was the one he had just tried to tell, of how a young rich northerner and an old cowpoke named Bill had both died on the Florida range. When the young man's family sent money for his remains to be shipped home, Bone shipped his friend instead.

Drew was glad at this point that Bone was passed out. The cut was extremely deep.

Drew stitched the wound and then walked out of the bunkhouse to where Buck was waiting.

"Keep him sedated for a while. I don't know if whiskey will do it. I don't want him to ride for at least a month. I hate to tell you but you best be looking for a new foreman. The liquor has gotten to him and he's old before his time. I don't think he can live very much longer."

"Don't say that, Doc. Drunk as a skunk, he can do the work of five sober men. I can't lose him."

A cowhand came running out of the cow house toward Drew, waving a picture that had been hanging on the wall above Bone's bed.

"Bone woke up long enough to say that he wanted you to have this."

Drew hesitated.

"I can't take that, Jeff. Bone is out of his mind in pain. He'll wonder what he did with it tomorrow."

"Go ahead and take it, Doc. Bone's got ample supply," said King. "This man from the north came down and painted him about twenty years ago. When Bone found out he was portrayed as the 'Cracker Cowman of Florida', he went and bought a blue million copies – gives them to everyone. Why, I have one hanging in my house!"

Drew took the portrait.

"This looks like the work of a man I once met. We even discussed the Florida cowmen he had sketched. He was a reporter, sketcher, and painter."

"Was his name Remington?" asked King.

"That's the same one. He sketched a picture of me playing catch. It's one of my treasured possessions. I have it framed in my office. I'll hang this up beside it."

The Seminole community was the last Drew tried to reach. He had been to the southern 'Glades enough to know that the medicine men did not like the white man's medicine. He also knew they still did not trust the white man. Drew, however, felt a connection with the Seminole because of Gopher. He hadn't seen Gopher in four years and the letters he sent to Brickell's Store in Miami to be delivered to him were sent back saying that he didn't trade with them anymore.

He knew there were Seminoles living in the Lakeport area because he had seen several trading at Beck's Store. Mr. Beck told Drew he might find them camped on Fisheating Creek or farther north in the Cabbage Woods, the largest stand of cabbage palms anywhere in the area. It was impossible to give him more directions than that because the Indians moved from place to place.

Drew followed a well-traveled path to the northwest and found an inhabited camp near a small creek that ran through thousands of cabbage palms. The grouping of chickees was the same as he had seen many times before, but instead of being surrounded by water, they had the palms and the open prairie.

As soon as he was out of his automobile, a stately Indian man, well over six feet tall, with snow white hair and mustache, approached. The distinguished Seminole introduced himself. He was the first Seminole Drew had ever seen with a mustache.

"I Cofehapkee. You call me Billy. Billy Bowlegs."

Drew's name was barely out of his mouth, when Billy Bowlegs turned and said something to a small boy. The boy scurried away quickly.

"Come!"

The old Indian motioned for Drew to follow him. They had gone only a few steps down a path when Drew heard a familiar voice from a few yards back of him.

"Doc! That you?"

Drew turned to see Gopher with the young boy.

As Drew and Gopher embraced, both exclaimed at the same time, "What are you doing here?"

The two friends sat down together with Bowlegs, who could speak English as well as Gopher, and reminisced about the past. Drew told Gopher why he came to Moore Haven. Gopher explained why he was living on the western side of the big water.

"I married Cofehapkee's niece. That's the way with my people. We go with squaw's family – Tiger Clan. Miss old places but like this one. Still can hunt, trap, and fish. Pa-hai-okee change and come dryer. Now build road. No good road. Sell my pelts some in Moore Haven."

"Still take hunters," Gopher said. "Cofehapkee take many long time ago. Railroad men and Presidents now go with him. Good money. I heard you marry, move. But heard no more after last visit. Father didn't come the next winter. Brickell said he died. Not know if plans change because of father or because of Great War. Hope you would come. Every time go to town, ask if new doctor in town."

"I did get married and I was a doctor in the war. I wrote to you several times and sent it to Brickell's Store as I did in the past, but they sent the letters back saying that you didn't trade with them anymore. I've missed you, friend. You'll have to come meet Mary Elizabeth. She has heard so much about you. We have a boy who just had his second birthday and we have another baby on the way. I came out today to see if I could assist in the medical needs of your people. Also to learn more about herbs."

Billy Bowlegs interrupted, "Own medicine and medicine man. We don't need any white man's chee."

"Cofehapkee," said Gopher, "is elder of our village. I'll work on him. He friends with many white, but likes Seminole medicine."

"I don't want to interfere with your ways," said Drew. "I want to learn from you and maybe you can learn something from me. I have learned so much from the notes my uncle left me about natural medicines and remedies he learned when he worked in Oklahoma. You have taught me a lot, but I want to know more."

As Gopher and Billy Bowlegs were walking Drew back to his car they passed a chickee where Drew saw a boy about two years old lying on a mat. The boy was crying.

"That my son, Doc," said Gopher. "He was burned week ago. It bad, not getting better. Medicine man done all can be done. Now up to Breathmaker. Not long to the Green Corn Dance. Get new medicine then."

"Mind if I take a look?" asked Drew.

Gopher led Drew to the boy, who was lying in his hammock. His flesh had been burned from the corner of his right eye to his chin and infection had set in.

"May I treat him?" asked Drew. "The infection has to be stopped; it can't wait until June."

Drew knew very little about the Seminole rituals except that the Green Corn Dance was the biggest annual event and was held in early June.

Gopher looked at Billie. He nodded.

From the black bag, which Gopher recognized, Drew retrieved a bottle of liquid, white gauze, and a little tube. Drew soaked the gauze in the liquid and washed the sore. Then he squeezed ointment out of the tube into the open sore. He then handed the bottle, the tube of ointment, and a box of gauze to Gopher to keep.

"Repeat what I just did three times a day. Wash the burns carefully and put this Unguetine on. It's going to take a very long time for this burn to heal. If you do what I say, you should notice a difference in a few weeks. I'll come back and check, if that is okay."

A Seminole woman in her mid-twenties came up to Drew with tears in her eyes and handed him a large straw basket she had made from sweet grass.

"Doc, this is Moon Flower, my wife. Take basket. Show friendship. You always welcome here."

As Drew drove down the sandy ridge toward home he said a prayer of thanksgiving. He had dreamed of living near Gopher for such a long time. He couldn't believe his good fortune. Through Gopher he would most likely gain the trust of, and have the chance to work with, the Seminoles.

Drew used the shovel, boards, and palmetto branches often. Without fail he thought of how dubious he had at first been about the advice that such strange items would be useful for him on a regular basis in his new surroundings. He forded creeks and prayed whenever he had to cross water on wooden planks that served as a bridge.

One of the best things about his travels was the opportunity to be outside close to nature. Wildlife and plant life were very different from one end of his circuit to the other. Birds were everywhere in abundant numbers. There was never an outing that he didn't encounter a snake or two. There was never a trip in which he didn't come in contact with something unusual.

One day he saw a flock of over fifty wild turkeys in an opening near a stand of cypress. Another day he saw at least that many deer in the same place. It was not uncommon to see panthers, bears, wild hogs, cooters, polecats, or foxes.

Sandhill cranes appeared often as he traveled across the open prairies. When he first encountered the sandhill cranes, he thought they were whooping cranes, because they had similarly long legs. Now he knew the difference and always enjoyed watching the red crowned sandhill. He especially liked watching the large bird in flight when its wings spanned almost seven feet and its long neck and dark gray legs extended straight.

All the while Drew was traveling around the area meeting people and trying to meet their medical needs, his practice in Moore Haven was growing steadily. His waiting rooms were usually full by 8 a.m. If he wasn't working in his office, he was on the road until past dark every night.

Often someone would come onto the Carter's front porch and knock on the window of his bedroom during the night.

Drew checked on the progression of his house each day before he went to work. By the first of June the outside of the house was finished. The inside was receiving its finishing touches.

Drew had paid extra for the wallpapering to be done. Mary Elizabeth made curtains for the living and dining rooms from Irish lace she had bought in Baltimore. Fabric for the rest of the windows came from Heard's.

The house was ready to move into by June 15. All that was missing was the furniture. When the household goods had not arrived by June 20 both Drew and Mary Elizabeth grew alarmed, thinking that everything they owned in the world had been stolen, was in a wreck, or sitting on a side track somewhere with a lost shipping order.

Every time he heard the train whistle, he called the stationmaster, who reassured Drew he would be notified when his shipment arrived.

Finally on June 29, shortly after two o'clock, the stationmaster called Drew.

"Your shipment is here. Will it be okay if Alfonzo Perry unloads it and moves it to your new house?"

"Of course! Alfonzo and I have already discussed the terms. Tell him I'm on my way!"

He couldn't contain his excitement. He looked into his waiting rooms and was glad to see the chairs empty.

"Miss Anna, cover for me. My furniture is finally here."

When Drew arrived at the station he found Alfonzo and his men already unloading the boxcar that had been side-tracked. When their three wagons were full, the men loaded Drew's Model T. By the time the procession arrived at the doctor's house, 20 men and boys were there to help unload the wagons.

Every box and piece of furniture had been marked as to their contents and what room they should be in. As one wagon was unloaded, Alfonzo or one of his crew would leave to get another load. By the time the third wagon was unloaded, Drew looked up to see a very angry Mary Elizabeth.

"Thank goodness this is a small town, Marian O'Brien came out to the farm and got me when she saw that you hadn't. I am probably the last person in this town to know that my furniture finally got here! This is my house, too, you know."

A sheepish Drew tried to apologize. He was saved only because Mary Elizabeth was soon caught up in the excitement of at last seeing her furniture, just as he had been earlier.

When the last wagon was emptied, Drew paid Alfonzo. As the muscular, black man turned to leave, he said to Mary Elizabeth, "Missus, my wife would be glad to help you with your things tomorrow if you think you needs her."

"I could certainly use some help," smiled Mary Elizabeth. "Please ask her to come around 8:30 in the morning."

After everyone had gone, Mary Elizabeth and Drew held each other for a long time. They had planned to work until the electricity went off at ten but Drew had forgotten to buy light bulbs. Reluctantly they closed the door of their new home and drove to the Carter's. Except to visit, this would be the last time they would make the trip down the bumpy road.

They were up early enough the next morning to eat with Charlie and Daniel. Mollie had a big breakfast waiting for them and had packed a picnic basket for lunch. She had agreed earlier to keep Thomas for the day.

"Don't worry about this young man. We'll be just fine. We might even walk to town this afternoon and pay you a visit."

Mary Elizabeth and Drew worked together at the house for about an hour before Alfonzo's wife, Josephine, came. Within a few minutes, five ladies from the church also arrived, ready to help with the unpacking. Drew slipped quietly away, knowing they could work much more efficiently without him.

His day at the office was slow, but he was called out to sew up a cow hunter's puncture wound. When he walked into the house a little after 5 o'clock, he was amazed to see what had been accomplished.

A woman, whom Drew didn't recognize, was putting the last of the china in its cabinet. Josephine was lining shelves in the kitchen while Mary Elizabeth was stocking the pantry with jars of food she and Miss Mollie had canned.

"Drew! Can you believe what we have done today? Walk through the bedrooms and see for yourself. I think all you need to do is to go to Heard's and buy light bulbs, kerosene for the stove and the lamps, and groceries from the list I've made out. You won't have to contact the ice plant. Alfonzo brought some ice an hour ago. I'll be glad when we have electricity all night so I can use my new Frigidare."

The enclosed back porch was still in disarray but the steps leading to the attic room had potted plants on each step. The attic room would be finished later as the family grew.

Drew walked into the master bedroom and saw that his parents' bed looked very good in the new room. Mary had coordinated everything in blue to match the blues in the wallpaper. At the foot of the bed hung Flora's quilt on a new quilt rack. The office that was designed to be his was now Mary Elizabeth's. A new typewriter he knew nothing about graced the desk. A four-door file cabinet completed the office equipment.

Thomas's room was set up next to the kitchen. His toys were in a toy box at the foot of his bed. The oak furniture in the front bedroom was from Drew's boyhood room.

From somewhere a phone rang, but Drew had no idea where to look for it.

"It's by your chair in the living room," yelled Mary Elizabeth.

When he picked up the receiver, the connection had already been made.

"Doc!" the voice shouted into the phone on the other end. "It's time for Mary's baby to come. Can you come now?"

"Frank, are you home?"

"No, Doc. I don't got a phone. I'm acallin' frum th' Bakers."

"Go home and I'll be over in a few minutes. Keep calm. You don't want to upset Mary. Boil some water for me."

Drew kissed Mary Elizabeth goodbye.

"I hope that this won't take long. I swear we'll spend the night together in this house tonight."

As he was leaving, the Carter's wagon pulled up with Thomas, supper, and the family's suitcases.

He drove to the Simpson's tar paper shack at the western edge of town and found the small house full of relatives who were ready to help. He shoved out everyone but Maggie, Mary's aunt, asking her to stay and serve as his assistant, and then went to the kitchen to check on the boiling water. If he didn't need the hot water for cleaning up the birthing process, he often needed it to get the house – or dishes – clean. He was determined to deliver babies in as sterile an environment as possible.

Five hours after Frank had first called, his wife delivered a boy. Two minutes later she delivered a little girl. Drew was caught off guard. He had never delivered twins without knowing beforehand that they were coming. During the examinations over the past three months, he had heard only one heart beat.

For once, Drew was not excited about delivering twins. He knew the extra burden of one additional child would be hard for the truck farmer, let alone two.

Drew left for home at eleven, hoping Mary Elizabeth would still be awake so that they could enjoy their first night together in the new house. He couldn't see any light coming from his house until he reached the front door. The lamp by the couch was still lit. Mary Elizabeth had fallen asleep on the couch waiting up for him. She woke up when he kissed her.

"Boy or girl?" Mary Elizabeth asked as she yawned.

"Both."

Drew placed his hand on Mary Elizabeth's stomach to feel the baby kick.

"Boy?"

"Girl."

Chapter 22

CHANGES IN THE AIR
September 1920

Because he wanted to see how many exotic plants would grow here, Drew soon filled up the yard with multi-colored crotons, single and double blossom hibiscus of different colors, bougainvilleas, azaleas, palms, and oaks.

A small citrus grove of lemon, grapefruit, and two types of orange trees Charlie had grafted from his own fruit trees were planted as well as a guava and a banana tree.

Drew pushed to get everything planted before the annual rainy season started. However, this summer temperatures rose to stay in the high nineties, and the rains did not come.

Not only did the Duncans' garden and yard dry up, so did the crops in the fields. None of the drainage canals contained any water. The large three-mile canal that connected Lake Okeechobee with Lake Hicpochee could be waded across. The big lake itself, naturally shallow, had dropped several feet. There was speculation that it was on the verge of drying up completely.

Hundreds of acres of muck lands burned day after day. The red glow of saw grass fires shown all over the night's horizon. Heavy, cream-colored smoke engulfed the town and the caustic odor caused respiratory problems in even the most hardy.

Because of the fires, Drew was busier than ever. Men were burned trying to put out the flames. Others suffered from breathing the air. The hot weather, combined with the odor of muck burning, also caused tempers to flare. Day after day they prayed for the rains to come.

One Saturday night, just before daybreak, Drew and Mary Elizabeth were awakened by loud shouts and banging on their front door.

"Doc Duncan! Doc Duncan! We's needs yo hep! We's bleedin' all over. We's been in a knif' fight an' we gots cut up purty bad!"

Drew pulled on his robe, slipped into his house slippers, and padded to the living room. As he reached the front door, he pushed the button to turn on the porch light. With one hand he pulled aside the curtains that covered the glass on the front door. With the other hand he automatically grabbed his bag from its resting place. The morning's darkness still enveloped everything and the porch light was not bright enough for him to recognize the faces of the two frightened young colored men sitting on the floor inside the screened-in porch.

As he turned the skeleton key to unlock the door, both men started shouting at once.

"Hurry, Doc! Hurry!"

Only when he got closer did he recognize the two men, sons of people he knew.

Blood from the cuts and gashes and the hanging skin on their faces indicated they definitely needed more than a bandage.

Before Drew could assess the damage, Mary Elizabeth was handing the men towels to soak up the blood that seemed to be flowing from every pore of their bodies. She had heard the shouting and the groans of the men from the bedroom and had instinctively run to the linen closet and grabbed an armful of towels and sheets before she headed to the porch.

Drew had seen plenty of blood from the countless knife fights he had encountered, but this was the first one that had ended up on his front porch. Blood was everywhere; however, there was no time to think about the mess or the reason behind it.

He reached into his bag and brought out some needles, tweezers, and scissors.

"Mary, go and sterilize these. I'm going to stitch these boys up right here."

Drew carefully removed the men's blood-soaked shirts and cleaned the wounds the best he could. Only when he placed clean towels over the wounds, did he realize how bad the situation was. Both had lost so much blood, he wasn't certain that he could save them.

As soon as Mary Elizabeth returned with the instruments, Drew administered shots of morphine to kill the pain.

As he worked, he asked Mary to call Tobias, a local Negro who had a car that served as emergency transportation for most of the folks who lived in the Quarters.

"Tell him to stop and pick up these boys' mothers, too, and bring them down here."

Between them, the two young men had one hundred and two stitches on their faces, necks, chests, arms, and backs.

When Drew finished, he walked around so he was squarely in front of the two and began to lecture.

"You both are damn lucky that you aren't going to the mortuary! You want to tell me now what took place?"

Just as James Albert was beginning to talk, his mother, Amanda, and Jimmie Lee's mother, Lucy Mae, came running up the walk as fast as their short legs could carry their enormous bodies. What they lacked in mobility, the two women made up for in screeching and howling.

Lucy Mae lit into her son.

"What's I's qwine do wit' ya, boy? I's pray ter dey Lord God above dat yo makes it. I's tol' ya 'bout dat jook. Ya jus' can't stay away cans you?"

Jimmie Lee protested.

"Tain' my fault, Mama. That nigger ain' nothin' but a low life yellow cheatin' dog son of a bitch!"

"Jimmie Lee! Watch yo mouth, boy. Yous ain' ter big fer me ter beat on yo backside. I'd gives yo w'at for if'n yous weren't so pitiful lookin'."

Tears were rolling out of her big round brown eyes on to her tawny brown cheeks.

"Anyways," continued Jimmy Lee. "We's wuz celebratin' en everythin' yesterday night at De Hide Away."

"Yea, I's knows w'at with. Moonshine and girls!"

Jimmy tried to smile.

"We's wuz playin' cards sometime this mornin'. James Albert won five straight games o' skin. No nig- body's dat lucky!"

"I's too lucky en I's didn't cheat!" a dazed James Albert moaned as he tried to defend himself.

"Jus' like dey daddies!" said Lucy Mae. "Day's de bes' o' friends 'sep theys goes crazy w'en dey gets in da moonshine."

"Take the boys home and keep them there until Wednesday; then bring them into the office so I can check their progress. They have both been seriously injured."

Both Lucky Mae and Amanda drew out crumbled dollar bills from a pouch at their waist and extended the payment to the doctor.

"Put your money back! I'll come out in a few weeks and get a slab of your delicious barbecue ribs in exchange for tonight's work. You just take care of your boys and try to keep them calm."

Drew shook his head as he watched Tobias drive away with the heart-broken mothers and their broken-bodied sons. He hoped the instructions he had sent would be enough to keep away infection.

Thankful Thomas had slept through all the commotion. Drew methodically began cleanup procedures, starting with the instruments that would be returned to his bag.

From needles to tweezers, to the stethoscope, each piece was sterilized and replaced with care, then the bag once more was put in its spot by the door, ready for any future emergency or routine call.

For some reason the low water level in the Okeechobee did not affect the good fishing. The owners of the commercial catfish houses shipped a record number of fish to their northern markets.

The fires also did not affect communities away from the muck lands. Drew was glad when he went to the west side of the lake because the air quality was so much better than in Moore Haven.

He rented a houseboat in Lakeport for Mary Elizabeth and Thomas to stay in to be away from the fires, but Mary Elizabeth insisted the smell wasn't that bad and she felt safer in her house than on a boat.

In August, when women all over the nation were celebrating that they had finally won the right to vote, there was little fanfare in Moore Haven. Women had been voting since the town was chartered three years earlier.

Mary Elizabeth had been part of the Suffrage Movement in Baltimore, so Drew wasn't surprised when she dressed in red, white, and blue for days after she read the banner headlines and news articles. Her mother wrote about the celebration in Rosemont and Mary Elizabeth wished that she had experienced the important event first hand.

August 20, 1920

Dear Mary,

I am so excited!

Although I know that you have moved to a liberated city and are probably not participating in big celebrations, what we women did here in Rosemont was beyond belief.

We ushered in the Women's Suffrage Amendment in a big way. Both the weather and the spirit of the day were glorious.

All of us ladies in town-and for miles around-dressed in our Sunday best. Most of us had bought new shoes and hats.

We met at the Presbyterian Church four blocks from the registration station. Female members of the town band led the parade. They played the "Battle Hymn of the Republic" and we marched together arm in arm down the street. We wore an American flags across our chests and women on the ends of each row carried large flags, which they waved as we marched.

The men, your father and brother included, stood on the sides of the street and jeered at us. That made our heads rise just a little higher for we knew we were making history. We knew that under the law we had the same rights as men.

The day was long in coming and I am so glad I have lived to see it. We plan to march together when we cast our votes in a few weeks.

I can't wait until November when I can vote for Harding. Imagine, I will get to vote for the next President of the United States!

Love,
Mother

On September 7, 1920, Mary Elizabeth cast her vote in the election the same as other women throughout the nation. It was just the primary, but Mary Elizabeth felt a rush knowing that this election was only the start of everything the Constitution promised to women.

When she dropped the paper into the ballot box she glanced up to see the former mayor of Moore Haven. The baby was very active. If the baby was a girl, she would be born into a world where women would be treated the same as men.

Chapter 23

AN ADDITION TO THE FAMILY
September 1920

The heat, the humidity, and her size made Mary Elizabeth miserable. She was anxious to have the baby. She was mad with everything and everybody.

"Fine doctor you are!" she screamed when Drew came in a few days later.

"You waltz into a house, deliver a baby, and then waltz out. This one is different, Drew. You helped make this one! You better not waltz out tomorrow unless this baby is out!"

Drew was glad to see her down on her knees scrubbing the kitchen floor when he got home Wednesday night. The next day he was glad to know that Dr. Mitchell was in town.

"Anna, call Dr. Mitchell and tell him I might have an emergency today and you'll send the more serious patients to him. I've got a feeling. Pray I'm right. I can't take much more of pregnancy!"

Anna laughed and called Dr. Mitchell. Mid-morning, Mary Elizabeth called Drew to come home.

"My water's just broken."

Excited as a first-time father, Drew announced to those in his waiting room, "I have a baby coming at home. If you need me, I'll come to your house this afternoon. If you think you can't wait, go to Dr. Mitchell. He's in town today."

With that he ran down the stairs, leaving his patients behind. He came within an inch of backing into Harry Sapp's truck as he left his office, yelled his apologies, and rushed homeward.

Two blocks later, he skidded into his driveway.

A scream from Mary Elizabeth greeted him at the door of their bedroom where he found his wife being comforted by Josephine. He quickly moved to Mary Elizabeth's side to reassure her, then he went into the bathroom to scrub his hands. While he was scrubbing, Mary Elizabeth had another contraction.

"Drew, they're coming faster and faster together. I don't think..."

She could not continue. Drew rushed to his wife's side and adjusted her into the birthing position. He could already see their child's head.

"You're right! A few more minutes and Josephine would have had to deliver the baby."

"Jo, please go and put some water on to boil. Then bring some cool wet rags to wipe Mrs. Duncan's face. I also need a tub and some towels."

After the contraction passed, Mary Elizabeth said, "Drew, I have so much more to do before I am ready for this baby.

"My dear, our baby doesn't care if you are ready or not, he is."

Josephine had just come back into the room with the tub and the towels when Mary Elizabeth let out the loudest scream she had ever heard.

"Push, Mary, push! Jo, please leave everything here by me and go check the water and bring it back fast!"

The baby slid into Drew's hands just as Mary Elizabeth's pain subsided. As soon as Mary Elizabeth realized her effort was finished, she asked, "What is it, Drew?"

"Mary, I think our little girl knew that her daddy was right here to greet her into the world."

"That's going to be the prettiest little belly button anyone ever had," he said, and wondered immediately if his father had said the same thing.

Mary Elizabeth checked her new daughter from head to toe. When she had finished, she smiled and said. "Let's name her Mollie after Miss Mollie. She's been so good to us."

"That's fine by me. Mollie is a nickname for Mary. So we are naming her for her mother, too."

Drew then took his daughter from his wife and handed her to Josephine.

"Josephine, please bathe this beautiful new baby and dress her in the clothes over there on the trunk."

Mary Elizabeth was soon asleep. Josephine laid Mollie in her cradle, left the room, and came back shortly carrying Thomas.

Drew looked up and took his son. "Where were you, big boy?"

Josephine answered for him. "I called Mrs. Robinson from across th' alley when Miss Mary's water broke. He's been stayin' over there."

Drew took his son over to the cradle to introduce the new baby.

"Thomas, this is your new baby sister, Mollie Elizabeth."

Thomas, looked at the baby briefly and then his eyes went to his mother. He reached for her and cried, "Mama, Mama!"

"Sh! Sh! Your mama is sleeping. We'll come back and see her when she wakes up."

Father and son left the bedroom and found that Josephine had two pieces of cake ready for them, one on the dining room table and one on the high chair.

"Josephine, I'm so glad that you were here today. I couldn't have done it without you!"

"Shucks, Doc, you do it all tha time by yourself."

"It was different today being my own. I'm glad the baby was so eager to get into the world."

Drew hesitated, then asked Josephine something he had just thought about.

"Do you think you can work for us five days a week for awhile?"

"Doc, Miss Mary an' I've already decided I would. I guess she forgot to tell ya."

Mary Elizabeth's parents arrived a week after the baby was born. As soon as she arrived, Hattie took over the running of the house.

To regain her strength, Mary Elizabeth was ordered to stay in bed for two weeks. The McRaes were glad to see the family but were especially delighted to see Thomas. He had changed so much in six months they couldn't believe it was the same boy.

The morning after the McRaes arrived, the clanging of milk bottles awakened them. Almost immediately they heard the patter of little feet as Thomas ran by their room and through the open front door. He continued running across the porch and straight through the open screen door, without stopping.

"Mr. Charlie! Mr. Charlie!"

Hattie gasped, afraid Thomas was going to fall head first down the steps. Both George and Hattie grabbed their robes and went to the front door.

Charlie introduced himself, "I'm Charlie Carter. You must be Mary Elizabeth's parents. You have some grandson there. We're quite good friends, you know."

"Yes, we're George and Hattie."

George couldn't feel anything right then but jealousy for the man who was taking his place as Thomas' grandfather.

"We have heard so much about you and your wife that we feel as if we already know you," George said.

"Well, you can't believe how very pleased we are to have your daughter and her family here with us. If you can bring Thomas downtown in about an hour, I can introduce you to a lot of folks. It will make you very proud to know how much your son-in-law is liked in this town."

"I'll try and make it if my wife and daughter don't have too many chores for me to do."

George went back into the bedroom to dress after Charlie left. Thomas was eating his breakfast when his grandfather sat down for his first cup of coffee.

As George sat down, Thomas reached over and hugged him and said softly, "I'm glad you're here, Paw Paw!"

George thought his heart would explode!

"Hattie, I think I'll walk down and meet Charlie. Drew can tell me just where to go. I'll take Thomas and we will both be out of your hair."

Hattie lit into her husband.

"We came to be with your daughter and now the morning after we arrive you are going to run off to only God knows where. I have a list as long as your arm for you to do."

"Mother, calm down," George interrupted. "We are just going to look around. I came down here to be with my grandson as well as my daughter. I'll start the list as soon as we get back."

"Just make sure that you don't talk to any of those fancy talking, high-powered salesmen. I don't want to live in this Godforsaken place, daughter or no daughter."

Realizing what she had said about her son-in-law's home, she immediately apologized to Drew but George ignored her apology.

"We just got here last night," he exclaimed. "You haven't even seen anything. How can you be so judgmental? And how can you say it's Godforsaken? I thought He was everywhere."

"This isn't Maryland and that will be my home always. Understand? You buy a piece of this muck land and you will live here by yourself."

"We'll see."

George laughed as he finished his eggs and toast. He loved his farm as much as she did. He didn't intend to leave his rolling hills.

Drew drove his son and father-in-law to the waterfront. George found himself mesmerized by the beauty.

"Dad McRae, I know that look! You see what I see here!"

The McRaes stayed with the Duncans until the first week in November. The Sunday before they left, Mollie Elizabeth was baptized during the morning worship service at Moore Haven's Methodist Episcopal Church, South. She was wearing a long white linen christening gown that had been made by her great grandmother. Standing up with the baby's family were her grandparents and the Carters.

Chapter 24

THE FIRE
Spring 1921

The spring weather was a carbon copy of the winter's. No person anywhere could have enjoyed a better climate. After the previous summer of heat, fire, and smoke, the people of south Florida gave thanks and hoped there would never be another season like the summer of 1920.

Moore Haven's land boom continued. Despite the drought and the muck fires, people were pouring into the area. Additional farmers came, followed by merchants who wanted their trade. Many fish processing and packinghouses were built for the booming catfish industry.

More and more buildings were being built in the downtown area. A few of them were made of brick but most were two-story wooden structures with tarpaper roofs. Most business owners had their shops on the ground floor and their residences on the second. They also had rental apartments that they used to supplement their incomes.

The growth of the Moore Haven area gave rise to a desire to become self-governing.

Moore Haven was sixty miles from Arcadia, the county seat of Desoto County. Because of the lack of good roads, it was a two-day trip. Not only did the townspeople feel isolated, they felt as though with the vegetables, cattle, and fishing industries growing at such a rapid pace, it was foolish to have to travel so far to transact county business.

Marian Horwitz O'Brien went to Tallahassee with a reportedly $20,000 to put in the right places to make sure Muck County would be carved out of portions of Palm Beach, Lee, and Desoto counties.

On April 23, Drew read the latest developments on the state level concerning the division of the counties in the *Moore Haven Times*. It was full of a challenge to Marian's plan on the formation of a new county. Andy Carter, editor of the *Times*, lead a faction who wanted to see only Desoto County divided.

Drew laughed to himself. How he loved small town politics.

This was the first Saturday afternoon in a long while that he had a chance to relax. He looked over at the fishing poles in the corner by the front door waiting for Thomas and Daniel.

The boys were digging for worms in the back corner of the yard where the food waste was buried. There the night crawlers grew long and fat. The boys were excited because they were going to Lakeport to fish and help Drew try out his new boat. Despite the low water level, reports indicated the fishing was tremendous.

Drew was vaguely aware of the ringing of the town's fire alarm. There had been so many alarms with all the muck fires. He kept ignoring the insistent clanging and wished someone would turn it off.

Then, the telephone rang. He wanted to ignore it, too. Drew reluctantly picked up the phone from the table beside his chair.

Mrs. Roberts, the operator, was so excited that her voice had become too shrill for Drew to understand what she was saying.

"Slow down, Mrs. Roberts. I can't understand you."

"Fire! Downtown is on fire! The whole town is going."

Drew immediately thought back to the terrible fire in Baltimore. The whole of Moore Haven wasn't as large as a neighborhood of Baltimore. He panicked when he realized that Moore Haven was built on the same combustible muck lands that had been on fire for so long.

"What's wrong, Drew?" Mary Elizabeth asked when she walked in and saw Drew's ashen face.

"Downtown is on fire!"

Drew kissed his wife as he grabbed his black bag from the door side table.

"I want you and the children off the muck as fast as you can get out of here. Go to Lakeport, Beck's store, until I come or you get word it is safe to come back."

As he ran, Drew could see black smoke ballooning over the trees in the direction of the business district. At the corner of Avenue J and 1st Street he saw people gathered around a woman stretched out on the ground.

"Doc, it's Mrs. Coleman! She is burned all over," cried Pete Blackshear, Mrs. Coleman's distraught landlord.

Drew checked the woman's pulse and found a beat. Then he ripped off her clothes, began to wash her off, and treat the second and third degree burns on her face and arms and first degree burns where her clothes had been.

Pete told what had happened.

"I heard a big explosion over the store and ran out to see what happened. Mrs. Coleman landed right at my feet. She had jumped from a window and was on fire. Luckily Alfonzo was delivering ice. He rolled her in the dirt to get the fire out. I started to run up the stairs to put the fire out, thinking it was small, but when I got half way up I could feel the heat and knew we needed the fire wagon. It was just a few minutes later that Bill, Noah, and J.D. arrived. They ran up the stairs with a hose."

"When they opened the apartment's door, they were beaten back by the heat. Others started throwing water onto the building but it was too hot to get close enough to do any good. The water from the fire wagon was of absolutely no help. I knew my store was a goner. Looks like the rest of the town will be, too."

Drew watched the fire as it leaped and grew from one tar paper roof to another, quickly igniting, then consuming, the wooden buildings of the downtown area. A black arm touched Drew. He jumped.

"Sorry I's scared you, Doc," Alfonzo was saying as he was getting blocks of ice off the ice wagon. "Thought you might be needin' these. Here's a ice pick, too."

"Alfonzo, is there any way possible that you could take some of this ice down by the elder bushes in back of the bank building? I think that will be a good place to work from."

"Also, could you go get bandages and supplies from my office?"

"Shore. I waz jest goin' to help with the water. I be proud to get your stuff."

"I don't know how much I'll need. Just load boxes into the wagon. Better go up the back steps because the fire could jump the street at anytime. Be careful. Here are my keys."

Drew pulled the dead skin off Mrs. Coleman's third degree burns and put ointment on what he could. Anna and her husband, Ronnie, arrived shortly. Anna ran to Drew's side. She was carrying a pile of blankets.

Ronnie ran to help fight the fire.

Marian O'Brien arrived about the same time and was soon helping both Drew and Anna.

"Marian," said Drew. "The best thing you can do right now is to hold Mrs. Coleman's head. Here's a damp rag to wipe it off."

He looked up to see his new hometown going up in flames. Men and women were hurrying everywhere. He could see a building on fire across from his office. He hoped Alfonzo could get in and out of his office before the fire leaped across the street.

Drew could see that merchants were taking their stock out of their stores. Anna and Drew left Mrs. Coleman with the former mayor and started to walk in the direction of the water brigades. They found several men who had been overcome with heat and smoke. They put wet compresses on them and helped them walk down to the elderberry patch. Drew then returned to the side of Mrs. Coleman, where Marian was still washing Mrs. Coleman's face. Drew checked her vital signs.

"Thanks, Marian. We've done all we can."

Marian carefully took Mrs. Coleman's head out of her lap. For the first time since he had met this strong-willed woman, Drew saw the former mayor cry.

No one knew who called him, but Mr. Parsons soon arrived with his funeral wagon. Drew covered Mrs. Coleman's body and put it into the wagon. Scores of people were brought for medical help.

Alfonzo returned with supplies and blankets.

"I'll go to the plant an' git some mo' ice. You is goin' to need it an' the peoples can use it to get cool."

"Thanks, Alfonzo," said Drew looking up at the tall husky black man.

Drew saw Clarence Busch, who had bought South Florida Farms from Moore, walking towards him in the fine suit that he always wore.

"Where is that fire truck?" Drew demanded.

Others chorused, "Yeh, where's that promised fire truck?"

Drew continued, "In case you forgot, we're talking about the one Moore promised us nine years ago – the one that would provide us with the best fire protection in Florida. The same one you have promised every year. The one you said was coming just last week! I've only seen the old wagon – which was antiquated before it even saw the muck lands. I don't think there have been too many days that it hasn't been in use somewhere this summer. Where in the blue blazes is that wagon now?"

Drew demanded an answer, as did most of the others in the crowd.

"Damn thing don't work," Busch muttered.

"You and Moore speak with silver tongues. Now he's gone and it looks like his town is going with him. How can you face us, knowing how you've lied?

"I ...I," Busch stammered.

He couldn't tell Drew and the others a good one cost more money that he had. Now his constant nightmare was a reality.

The fire was under control in about two hours. Drew continued to minister to people's needs for the next three hours. When the smoke had cleared, sixteen business buildings and five homes were in ruins and ashes. One by one the wounded began to leave with relatives and friends. After the last one left, Drew made his way down to the east end of the business district near the Lone Cypress.

Mr. Gram was out rejoicing that his store and home had been saved.

"Doc, it looks like we are a few of the lucky ones tonight. I only lost some rentals and your office wasn't damaged. I am sure grateful there was no wind. This thing could have been much worse."

"You're right, but that was too close for comfort. The building next to mine is nothing but ashes. What happened anyway?"

"Apparently Mrs. Coleman's gasoline iron blew up."

"I know that. At first I thought the fire was fueled by the muck, but as I watched it leap from roof to tar paper roof I saw those materials fuel it. Why did contractors use such building materials? Haven't there been enough city fires? We have less flammable materials now. Why weren't they used?"

"I guess everyone put profit first. A lot of those buildings were boom construction. That is going to change, my boy. I will be in front of the County Commission when it meets in Arcadia next week and make sure they set codes and they hire someone to enforce them."

"Meanwhile, what do we do in case of a fire?"

Drew changed the subject, commenting, "By the way, my lease will be up shortly. I've been there much longer than I expected to be. Is there room in the new arcade building for me? I would much rather be in a building that is concrete."

"There's a place with four rooms plus a big storage room. Are you sure you want to move? You current office is much bigger."

"I want a building that is better built and I really need to be downstairs. So many times people can't climb the stairs. It is hard to treat someone in the middle of the street. You remember just last week when that worker of yours fell and broke his leg, I had to set the splint right there on the bench in front of the drugstore with everyone inside and out gawking.'"

"With all the rebuilding that we are going to have to do I don't know when the arcade building will be finished, but you certainly can have those rooms."

"Send me the contract."

"Would you take me down to where my supplies are so that I can take them back to my office?"

When they returned to the elderberry patch, the supplies were gone. Drew wondered who moved them, but his question was soon answered when Alfonzo came riding up in his cart.

"Here's you keys, Doc. I put everything back where I found it except fo' the blankets. I is takin' dem home fo Jo to wash."

"I don't know what to say but thanks, Alfonzo. Also, thanks for trying to save Mrs. Coleman."

Alfonzo acknowledged him with a nod.

Drew walked into his house an hour later. Mary Elizabeth and Thomas were just finishing unloading the car.

"We had quite a caravan leaving town. We stayed at Beck's until we got word from town that it was safe to return. How bad is it, Drew?"

"Bad, but it could have been much worse."

"Sorry about the fishing trip, Son."

A few hours later, a nighttime thunderstorm rolled across the area. Hugging one another, Drew and Mary Elizabeth stood on their porch and watched as sheets of lightening virtually surrounded them in every direction. Drew thought that no other place on earth had such a spectacular show of light as did the Florida Everglades. The show was a common one for residents as the cool night air replaced the heat of the day. Even a youngster like Thomas appreciated the beauty of the lightening and watched the skies with awe, not fear.

Drew was at his office at dawn to check it out. He opened all the windows to let out the smoke. He turned on the fans so they would be ready to go on at ten if there was still any electric current. His office complex suffered only water damage with the exception of the west wall, which was scorched.

After restocking the shelves, Drew went out to assess the damage by the morning's light.

Clean up had already begun, and Drew pitched in to help. He returned home a little after noon to find his family just getting home from church.

After a light lunch, he and Thomas loaded up the fishing poles and got the can of worms that had been dug the day before and headed out to Lakeport to catch the fish that had been given a one day reprieve.

Chapter 25

GLADES COUNTY
Spring 1921

The smell of smoke lingered over the town long after the fire had gone.

It lingered in the piles of burned wood that had been thrown into huge stacks outside the buildings that could be repaired.

It lingered in empty lots where twenty businesses once stood.

It lingered in the faces of those who had given up and moved on.

It lingered in those who watched as friends left town and in those who fought to save the town.

The fire had burned away the enthusiasm everyone once had in building a new city.

Drew celebrated with others, however, when the news arrived from Tallahassee that the Florida Legislature had passed State Law 8513 which divided Desoto County into five smaller counties. Moore Haven would be the county seat of the newly created Glades County, the 58th county in Florida.

The first meeting of the county commissioners was held at the Moore Haven Electric Light Plant and lasted forty-eight continuous hours, from June 6 to June 8. The commissioners were resolved not to adjourn the meeting until they had a plan in place for many things that had gone lacking for so long.

Most people, Drew included, drifted in and out of the proceedings, but a few stayed with the commissioners for the entire time. It was easy to find out what had happened hour-by-hour, if not minute-by-minute, by visiting Mae's or Heard's.

Topics concerning the county were on the lips of everyone. A special edition of *The Times* was printed when the gavel sounded the end of the marathon session.

People were standing at the newspaper office's door to read the official news. Things had been discussed, debated, and discussed again so much that no one really knew what had officially been adopted.

The headlines read:

NEW COMMISSION
PASSES PLANS FOR GLADES COUNTY

New Fire Codes Established

Fire Marshal to be Hired

New Fire Truck Ordered

New Electric Plant to be Built

Drawbridge Planned Over 3-Mile Canal

Old School Will Serve as Temporary Courthouse

**Committee Appointed To Draw Plans,
Locate Site For New Courthouse**

Excitement again filled the air. Everyone had high hopes for this new county on the northern edge of the Everglades.

Moore Haven had only been chartered for six years and was the biggest town in the interior of south Florida. Now that it was the county seat for a new county, the prospects for a glorious future looked bright.

Drew and Mary Elizabeth decided to take a chance on establishing a new yard. All the trees had survived the drought, but not the shrubs. At summer's end the grass was as green as the Irish countryside and the shrubs were ablaze in brilliant colors that would rival any English country garden. Every afternoon there was a wonderful rainstorm that kept the air reasonably cool and the mosquitoes happy.

The rains continued through the summer and into the fall and soon filled up all the drainage canals in Moore Haven. The three-mile canal overflowed its banks. The business district was the only part of the town that was fairly dry but in order to get there, residents had to use boats for transportation. What a change this was from the previous year!

During this time, more of the farmers left. Three years of adverse weather conditions were too much for them to cope with. They had withstood the drought, but they couldn't deal with floods, too. Instead of bringing in three crops a year, only a few brought in one.

The O'Briens gave up on truck farming and Glades County politics. They moved sixteen miles to the east, to the southern shore of Lake Okeechobee where they began to lay out a new town on a sandy ridge.

A.C. Clewis, a banker from Tampa, and Bernard G. Dahlberg, from Chicago, were solicited to fund their project. The town's name was changed from Sandy Point to Clewiston. Having discovered that sugar cane grew exceptionally well on the muck, they soon established the Southern Sugar Corporation and Mrs. O'Brien used her influence to extend the railroad past

Moore Haven and into Clewiston.

Drew continued his travels to the outlying communities, but because of so much flooding, he left his automobile behind when possible. He caught rides to Citrus Center and Ortona on steamers of the McCoy brothers' Everglades Line or on the tourist boat, *The Crocodile*, which would travel through Lake Hicpochee and down the Caloosahatchee River. In Ortona, Drew would borrow a car to go to the cattle country, which included Muse, Palmdale, and Tasmania. To reach Lakeport he would ride on anything he could hitch a ride on.

His trips sometimes lasted for days because of the water.

The flood waters worried Drew. He knew that typhoid resulted from stagnant water. If typhoid fever did break out, it would spread like wildfire. He inoculated as many people as he could, but there was not enough vaccine to go around.

He tried his best to get more vaccine, but no matter who he contacted he couldn't get additional supplies. He knew the military had ample but they would not give it out. They contended that it wasn't for the general population. A typhoid epidemic on the heels of the drought and fire would be a certain end to the town.

When the rains stopped and the waters receded, boardwalks were put up so people could walk from place to place without getting into the water and the mud. In most of the residential areas a board was simply laid across the shallow drainage ditch in front of the house so people could get to the street.

The paved streets that had been the pride of the city lay in ruin. The asphalt paved marl curled up like fried bacon. The reek of the rotting bodies of small animals that had drowned during the high water was atrocious.

Mosquitoes were so severe that smudge pots were set up on every corner. Every conceivable item that would create smoke was burned in the pots, including oil, rubber, and turpentine. Layers of mosquitoes and flies plastered the screens. Palm fronds by the doors were used to wave away the pesky bugs, but the effort was mostly a futile one. Mosquito bars holding thin nets were pulled around the beds at night. Each room contained a bottle of Walker's Devilment.

Three Negro children and two white toddlers drowned after falling into the swollen waters of the canals and ditches.

Drowning was a constant worry, shared in the Duncan household where Thomas paid the price for his mother's apprehension. Mary Elizabeth went over and over rules about never playing near any canal and dreaded the day she wouldn't be able to protect him. She wouldn't let him go outside. The water was too deep. The insects too thick. The odors too strong. Day after day he sat on the window seat playing with his yo-yo or looking out toward the rainy skies with his kaleidoscope. The beautiful colors were no substitute for the outdoor activities that he yearned for. Coloring and building with his Lincoln Logs and Tinker Toys had become boring. His four-year-old legs

243

wanted to run.

Through the flooding and its aftermath no one became sick with typhoid. Drew was thankful and astonished. After weeks of studying, he realized the water had been part of the overflow of Lake Okeechobee to the Everglades and had not ever been stagnant. The cause of typhoid was stagnant water.

People blamed the Army Corps of Engineers for the flooding. They were accused of not operating the new locks correctly. The community did not want to hear the fact that nothing could have prevented the flood because every canal, drainage ditch, lake, and slough was full of water.

In the months that followed, a levee was built to the north of Moore Haven and extended to the east. The muck dike gave people comfort in having extra protection from the waters of the big lake.

Chapter 26

SEPARATION
November 1922

The only time in his life that Drew had worried about the lack of money was for a brief moment during his first trip to Miami. Money was something he took for granted like the sunrise in the morning. He had brought with him to Florida his inheritance money, the money from the sale of the family home and clinic, and the money he had made from his land speculation. His family was very comfortable financially – rich by the standards of most in Glades County.

Two and a half years later, that financial picture was totally different. Each month the record books verified that Drew's practice was drawing nearer to the red. Drew's paradise, Moore Haven and its people, had depleted most of their money. People were going broke, but still needed medical assistance. Drew treated them on credit. Most of it was never paid. He also traded his services for food and goods. Each month Mary Elizabeth had to go into their savings to make ends meet. She spoke to no one of the things that troubled her, for she had made a pledge to her husband and he was happy in this remote place.

Drew came home early one evening to find Mary Elizabeth sobbing.

"Mary Elizabeth, what is wrong?" he asked as he walked into the kitchen.

Mary Elizabeth dried her eyes on her apron and tried to smile for Drew. She hadn't heard him come in and didn't want him to know the agony she was experiencing.

"Mary, what is it? Did someone die? Your father?'

"No, Drew, no one died."

"Then what's wrong? I have never seen you this way before."

"Oh, Drew!"

She ran past him to the bedroom and flung herself on the bed.

"What's wrong with Mama?" asked a bewildered Thomas. "Why is she crying? I'm scared."

Drew hugged his son and patted his daughter on the head as she played with her doll on the floor.

"Don't worry. Everything will be okay in a few minutes," Drew assured his son.

Drew closed the door to their room and went over to the bed where his wife was sobbing.

"Mary, what is the matter?"

He tried to take her into his arms but she forced him away and just sobbed.

"Go away!"

"I will not! Tell me what is wrong!"

Mary Elizabeth just buried her head in the pillows. There was a knock on the door.

From the other side Thomas cried, "Daddy, I'm hungry."

"You haven't fed the children? What in the world is wrong with you?"

Mary Elizabeth sobbed that much more when Drew stormed out of the room.

He heated the vegetable soup left from the day before and grilled some cheese sandwiches. The preparation of that meal utilized the full extent of his cooking ability. Thomas set the table and poured milk. For the very first time in their lives, the children ate alone with Drew. He bathed the children and put them to bed with several stories and songs. Then he went to check on his wife who was now asleep. He took a bath and went into the living room to read. Mary Elizabeth came out several hours later.

"Drew, I'm sorry. I was so upset I couldn't talk. Will you let me talk now? When you came in tonight, you surprised me. I've been putting on a happy face for months. When you caught me crying, I guess that upset me even more. I never wanted to hurt you. I haven't said anything to you about money and I know now that I should have done so long before now. I've withdrawn our savings every week to make ends meet. I can't do it anymore. I don't know what we are going to do. We're almost broke. I don't know how we are going to live."

"We'll do fine. As long as my patients have eggs, chickens, hogs, fish, bear, venison, or whatever else they can trade me, we will never starve. We still have our stocks and bonds and the practice to draw from in Baltimore. How long can we go on with our savings that are in First Bank?"

"Tonight, maybe."

"What do you mean, tonight?"

"The bank closed today. We have lost everything."

"What! They can't do that!"

"They did. They had invested in the Moore Haven Sugar Corporation. It went broke, leaving the bank with no money."

"I knew their grandiose plans to produce sugar for candy factories they were going to build was a pipe dream, especially when they didn't have the right equipment...but I thought they recovered all that loss when they sent their sugar to the refinery in Savannah."

"I don't know about sugar. All I know is that the doors at the bank were locked. Gene Fuller, the head teller, was sitting on the bench outside with his head in his hands. He just kept saying, 'No more money. No more money'."

246

Mary Elizabeth started sobbing again. Drew took her into his arms.

"We'll make it through. I'll just sell the stocks and bonds. Things have to get better. People will start paying when they can. Hang in there with me."

Every thought and emotion Mary Elizabeth had hidden away deep inside herself came to the surface as she looked up at Drew. She began saying things that were inconceivable to him.

"I know that this place is your dream, but I hate it, Drew, I really do."

Mary Elizabeth pushed away from Drew and sat back defiantly.

"Little Ike and Thomas have been playing together every day since the Conrads moved into the house across the street three months ago. I thought it was wonderful for him to have a place to go on the days he couldn't play outside."

"Yesterday," Mary Elizabeth continued. "Yesterday, it all changed. Do you know what they found?"

Without waiting for Drew to answer, she continued, "They found white robes with hoods in a drawer. Ike said they weren't Halloween costumes. He said his daddy wears one to meetings. He said he wears it when he and his friends go to scare niggers and nigger-lovers."

"Thomas had no idea what Ike was talking about. He came home crying uncontrollably when he realized Josephine might get hurt. He asked me if you were a nigger-lover. He knows you doctor the Negroes."

"Did you explain everything? Did you tell him I hate that word and..."

Mary Elizabeth cut Drew off. Her frustrations kept pouring out of her mouth.

"Not knowing who my neighbors really are is just the tip of the iceberg. I hate the smell of the muck fires. I hate the rain and the standing water and the muck so deep that it comes halfway up your legs. I hate the smell of muck. I hate the smell of the drowned animals. I hate the mosquitoes that are so thick they coat the screens so black you can't see out. I hate the fact that someone has to stand at the door with a palm frond, broom or something, to keep the mosquitoes out whenever the door is open. I hate the frogs, the worms, the insects, the snakes, and the alligators. I hate the roaches that are as big as mice and the huge spiders that I have to leave hanging around to eat the roaches. I hate the fact that my children can't play outside for weeks at a time, and when they do I am in constant fear of the drainage canals."

Mary Elizabeth took a deep breath and then continued.

"Half my friends have already given up and moved. I miss the hills of Maryland. I hate that you are never home. I hate that the people in this God-forsaken place know you better than your own children. I just hate everything about this place!"

"Is there anything else that you hate?"

"I never want to taste a fish again. That's all those fisherman pay you!"

"Next time I will try to get them to give me cooter."

"That's not funny at all! And one more thing. I hate that you are always breaking the law."

"Mary, not that again."

"Yes, that again. You know good and well that it is against the law to buy whiskey and you do. You know you can get it legally from your medical supply houses but you insist on getting it from the bootleggers. That is criminal. What will happen to us when you are thrown in jail?"

"You know I need whiskey for my medicines! How many times do we have to have this discussion? You know how hard liquor is to get legally and the red tape that I have to go through. You also know that south Florida is called the leakiest place in America when it concerns that stupid law. I had a reprehensible ordeal dealing with the government trying to get the typhoid vaccine, so I will be damned if I will deal with them to get their permission to buy whiskey when it is flowing as free as the Caloosahatchee!"

Mary Elizabeth cut in.

"It's not only law, it's an amendment, a good one to boot. There are statistics telling how much alcohol consumption has gone down and how many lives have been saved."

"And who in the Hell took THAT survey? People get it anyway. Besides, most of my patients are bootleggers. I want to help them feed their kids."

Drew was extremely upset but he thought that Mary Elizabeth would smile when he concluded the argument with the mention of the kids. She always had before, but this time there was no a smile.

He continued.

"It has made law abiding, good people, criminals - and the fat cats richer- AND look at the gangsters! I WILL continue to get it from my suppliers until they repeal the law and I'm sorry that it worries you. Besides, if I'm thrown in jail, they will have to arrest 99% of this county. If a person isn't selling, he's buying."

"They will never repeal an amendment to the Constitution!"

"Well, they better build bigger jails."

Mary Elizabeth ran to the bedroom where she cried herself back to sleep.

In his living room chair, Drew fumed. He couldn't concentrate on the paper or a book and the radio static irritated him even more. He turned off the radio and the lamp. Leaning back in his chair with his legs stretched out on the ottoman, he thought, "Never a hint!"

Mary Elizabeth had always greeted him with a warm hello whenever he came home, no matter the hour. She was always full of exciting things the children had done in his absence, or the latest gossip she had heard from the neighbors. She had been the perfect mate. How dare she keep the money matters from him! But then again, he knew that the money wasn't coming in. He remembered how he had marveled many times about the way she had managed their finances.

The more he thought, the more his anger gave way to understanding. She had kept all of this from him because of her love for him. He had taken her for granted. He thought she shared his love for the 'Glades. The years had slipped away and she hadn't even been back to Maryland since they moved. He couldn't possibly get away, but there was no reason Mary Elizabeth and the children could not go to Maryland for a visit.

Drew checked on the children on his way back to the bedroom. Both Thomas and Mollie were sleeping peacefully in their beds. Looking at them, Drew wondered if they were happy. He had been so happy he never thought it would be any different for the ones he loved.

He tossed and turned all night. The woman who was beside him was more important to him than life itself. Was it time for them to throw in the towel, too? No! He couldn't do that. Things would get better. They had been through many other adversities. Things had to work out because he didn't want to have to choose between his family and this place that he loved so dearly.

The phone rang at 5 a.m.

He didn't want to go anywhere because he needed to talk to Mary Elizabeth.

"Please don't be anything major," he prayed as he went into the living room to answer the phone.

"Doc, I hate to call you so early but Andrew hasn't slept all night. I don't know what to do," Marge, the mother of a three-week-old, cried in the receiver.

"Does he have a fever?"

"No."

"Does he seem to be hurting anywhere?"

"No."

"Has he thrown up?"

"No."

"Are you feeding him anything?"

"I'm nursing."

"Mix some cream of wheat with water to make a thin gruel. He should take it. Even if he does, come see me later this morning in my office. I'll check out your milk content. I'm sure the cream of wheat will do the trick."

Drew saw Mary Elizabeth in the kitchen as he retraced his steps back to bed. He joined her there where she was preparing a sandwich and coffee for him.

"The coffee should be ready for you by the time you are dressed."

"I'm not going anywhere. Let's go back to bed."

"No. I'm up now."

"How did you sleep?"

"How was I supposed to sleep with you tossing and turning?"

"Mary."

"Drew."

They both spoke at the same time. Drew let his wife go first.

"Drew, I want to go home. Maybe I would feel better if I could just go home and be with my folks."

"I was going to suggest the same thing."

"Can you come with us? It could be a vacation. You need a break. You've worked almost around the clock six to seven days a week since we moved here. It is time for a vacation."

"Mary, I would love to, but I have three babies due next month and I just can't go. I'll make arrangements today for the train to take you and the children. When do you want to leave?"

"The sooner, the better."

There was bitterness in her voice.

Mary Elizabeth made arrangements for Bonnie Fisher, a bookkeeper for several of the merchants and the farmers, to take care of Drew's books. As Mary Elizabeth relinquished all of the records, she wished she had thought of Bonnie before. Maybe if she hadn't had all the stress of the books, she wouldn't be packing her bags to go home to her parents.

No one spoke a word as Drew drove his family to the depot three days later. Little Mollie lay asleep in the arms of her mother. Thomas knew that something was very wrong between his parents but he didn't understand what it could be. He didn't understand why he was going away without his daddy.

Drew kissed his wife as he helped her up the steps of the train. Mary Elizabeth didn't return the kiss.

As he lifted Thomas up to the train's steps, the boy grabbed him around the neck and squeezed him tighter than he had ever done before.

"I love you so much! Daddy, don't make me leave! I want to stay here with you!"

"No, Son. You'll be back very soon. You have fun on your Paw Paw's farm. Take good care of your mother and Mollie."

Thomas let go only when his mother reached out her hand to him. As the train pulled away, tears filled Drew's eyes. He didn't know if he should go to his office or slip away to be alone.

He didn't have to make the decision because it was made for him.

"Doc!" a young Negro boy yelled.

"Sure glad I seen yo' ca'. Miss Wanda be needin' you. She sent me to fetch you."

Life without Mary Elizabeth and the children was miserable for Drew. For days after they left, he would sit down to write his family whenever there was a lull at the office. He poured out his feelings but never mailed one letter. Eventually, he stopped writing altogether and threw away the letters that he had written earlier.

For the first three weeks he convinced everyone who asked that his family had taken a vacation back home to see Mary Elizabeth's parents. At the end

250

of six weeks Miss Mollie asked him what was going on. He lied and said that Mary Elizabeth's father had taken ill and that she was needed to help in Maryland. Drew grew more and more uncomfortable around Mollie and Charlie because he knew that Mollie had seen right through his lies.

The Everglades Bank collapsed sometime during those weeks. Since Drew had lost all his savings when the First Bank of Moore Haven went under, he didn't pay much attention to the new tragedy in the town. He was too caught up in his own troubles.

However, after the closing of the town's second bank, the town went crazy. Drew was glad that Mary Elizabeth and the children were not in town to witness everything.

Since the split up of the South Florida Land Company and the emergence of the Desoto Land Company, there had been two factions in town, each competing for dominance. Each company had had its own bank, its own newspaper, and rivaled the other for control of the bootlegging. Without the banks, the money was in bootlegging. Differences in allegiance became more prominent.

There was a feeling of desperation and distrust. Almost every man carried a gun.

The Ku Klux Klan, perhaps encouraged by local officials, became an extension of the law. White-robed men patrolled the streets in both small and large groups. Most white residents felt safer with the KKK on patrol. They knew the Klan would keep order one way or another.

The citizens of Lakeview were terrified. They had first hand knowledge that the Klan would shoot them without provocation. The lynching of Negroes had become a sport. The burning of the Negro town of Rosewood up the state had been reported with more detail than they wanted to hear.

During the day, only maids and others, who were vital to the needs of the white community, were allowed into Moore Haven. At night, the Negroes stayed home, on their side of the tracks.

Alfonzo continued to deliver ice, but he refused to let Josephine work.

Drew and Wanda improvised a temporary clinic in her front room to treat his Negro patients. He was met with hostilities every time he passed the Klan blockade at the edge of Lakeview.

Andy Carter, editor of the *Moore Haven Times*, was almost run out of town by a mob because he gave free space in the paper to the president of one bank who tried to explain the bank closure.

Wallace Stevens, the editor of the *Glades County Democrat*, in an attempt to calm things down, bought out *The Times*. He announced he would consolidate the two papers and move into *The Times* office. Apparently, there were people who didn't want peace. On the night before the move, *The Times* building caught on fire. In the charred ruins of the building, a human skeleton was found. Nearby was an empty gas can. It was rumored that a convict from Arcadia had been hired to set the fire and then someone made sure that he would never tell who paid him to do it.

A further confirmation that the fire had been well planned came when it was discovered that the new fire truck had not been able to get to the scene because sugar had been put in its tank. It took quite a while for tempers to quiet down.

Late one Saturday night after treating an unusual number of lacerations from the fights and brawls, Drew looked forward to collapsing in bed. As he turned the corner onto Avenue K, he could see an orange glow. Panic stricken, he drove faster.

"They've found the perfect way to get rid of me," he thought bitterly. "They've set fire to my house."

As he got closer, however, he realized that the glow came from torches held by a group of at least twenty Klansmen.

The doctor pulled into his driveway just as the mob approached. These hooded figures were not on a peaceful patrol of the city; they were angry and out of control.

Relieved that his house was not on fire, exhausted from his night's work, exasperated and lonely without his family, and annoyed with the intolerant attitudes towards Negroes, Drew stepped in front of the horde, a position no sane man would ever put himself in.

"Stop right there! Where do you think you are going? You have no business here this time of night!"

"Git out of our way, Doc, we got no argument with you."

Drew recognized the voice of Richard Timmons, whose right forefinger bore a bandage he had applied less than an hour before.

"Oh, yeh we do!" shouted a gruff voice from the back. "I don't like your hands touchin' niggers an' I do mean niggers no matter whatja ya want said round you. Ya touch them, God knows where, an' then ya come an' treat our families. Hit's jest not right."

The man continued as he pushed his way to the front. "I think hits high time ya know where you're livin'. I say whites take care of whites an' to Hell with them niggers."

Drew lashed out, forgetting that the Klan surrounded him.

"Curtis, you son of a bitch! Didn't I see you just this afternoon coming out of Shelia's front gate? In fact, I have seen you there many times! I don't think you were there to get your laundry done."

Curtis' fist hit Drew between the eyes, catching him completely off guard. While Curtis was reveling in the punch he had just thrown, Drew came back hard. He hit Curtis below the belt.

The troublemaker doubled over and fell to his knees.

There was a collective gasp from among the Klan. No one would have ever thought that the mild-manner doctor would hit anyone, especially in the groin.

"Now go home!" Drew shouted.

"Doc, most of us don't have nothing' against ya," Richard repeated. "Tha problem's down the street."

"Richard, I don't care to know what, when, or where. Nothing could be bad enough for twenty of you, mostly all drunk, to administer your justice at 12:30 at night. It's Sunday morning. All of you need to go home and go to bed. It will be time to go to church before you know it!"

A deflated group of hooded men dispersed.

Drew welcomed the chance to go to the outlying communities, especially when he had a chance to stay over night. His favorite place to go was the Cabbage Woods. He was always welcomed as the miracle medicine man.

Gopher's son had recovered within days of Drew's first visit and the people of the village gave Drew full credit for saving his life.

During his many visits Drew became acquainted with Lou Tiger, a beautiful young girl in her early twenties who wanted to learn English.

Her slanted black eyes laughed as she talked and there was a shyness about her that attracted Drew more each time he met her. She was very easy to talk to.

Lou was the daughter of the clan's medicine man and Drew was eager to learn all she knew about plants and their medicinal uses. She had gathered plants for her father for most of her life, and, though she was not allowed to learn the magic of the medicine man, she knew which plants were used and the time of year to gather them.

The tribe permitted Drew to learn about the plants because they knew to make the medicinal powers of the plants work, they must be administered with chants. Only Seminole medicine men were entitled to the chants and it took many years as an apprentice to be trained.

Dr. Mitchell stayed in town for a week, allowing Drew time to go with Gopher to the Big Cypress and to Pine Island. Gopher wasn't too happy when Lou accompanied them, but Drew wanted her to come because of her expertise in knowing and finding herbs and native plants.

After discussing the matter with Lou's father and others in the village, Gopher consented.

Things had changed in the lower 'Glades and in Drew's opinion, it wasn't for the better. The massive stands of cypress trees were almost depleted. Drew got a sick feeling when he realized that the shingles for his house had probably come from here.

"See how dry? All canals and drainage up by Okeechobee the reason. Not as many birds and animals,"

Drew had to admit that it didn't seem that the flow of water from the north was the same as it had been a few years ago.

Gopher stopped when he got to the place where they found dredges and road equipment. "Road from Miami to Tampa no good. Kill the Pa-hai-okee."

Drew wondered if progress and nature could ever co-exist without killing each other.

He thought of the new muck dike that had been built in Moore Haven to hold back the waters of the Okeechobee. This land needed those waters, but drainage canals and the floodgates were built to let the water out slowly. Why was that killing the 'Glades?

During the week in the 'Glades with Gopher and Lou, Drew found he couldn't stay away from Lou. They had first touched each other when searching for plants. The touch had been like fire. Drew knew he loved his wife, but this desire was like a thirst that couldn't be quenched. The pair slipped away to be together whenever they could. Beds made from pine straw and palm fronds proved to be comfortable and soft for their lovemaking. Sleeping next to her soft supple body make him feel young again. There was also a thrill in sneaking away and taking chances of being exposed.

Drew went to Gopher's camp as often as he could. He enjoyed hearing the Indians' stories, learning more and more about their herbal medicine, and being near Lou.

Gopher knew what was happening and tried to warn Drew of the danger. When Drew told Gopher that he knew what he was doing, his friend turned his back and pretended not to know about the love affair.

Drew also stayed busy attending community gatherings throughout the county. He took part in as many as he could. He grew to love chicken purlieu parties, peanut boils, cane grindings, and barn dances. He loved the music, dancing, and merry making as much as the food itself. Word circulated that the doctor's wife had left him. He had widows, spinsters, and young girls making passes and offering food. He often came away from the gatherings with enough food to last until the next one.

Drew also enjoyed dove and quail hunts with men from all over the county. He was staying busier than ever, which gave him little time to think about his losses.

Mary Elizabeth had been gone for almost three months when Drew received an invitation to come to a party in Clewiston at the home of Mr. and Mrs. John J. O'Brien.

Drew debated for days about the invitation because the people of Moore Haven had deep resentment toward the couple.

The O'Briens, who had been instrumental in Moore Haven's start, had left. Many felt betrayed. Drew didn't know which factor was resented most: their money; their manner of riding horses and acting like a lord and lady over their subjects; moving their enterprises to Sandy Point; bringing Negroes in to work their crops; being Catholic and bringing a priest in for services; or

254

starting the town of Newhall and filling it with retired British officers and their families who had strange customs.

The citizens of Moore Haven could have tolerated all that they didn't like about the O'Briens, but leaving Moore Haven and establishing their new town just sixteen miles away was a slap in the face. Many thought they should have used their money to develop Moore Haven.

The sugar company they were backing could have been based in Moore Haven. Whatever the case, the O'Briens were not at all popular in Moore Haven. Drew thought he might not be either if they found out he had attended a social gala hosted by the couple. He knew that if word got back to town he would be ostracized at best, lynched at worse. He finally just decided not to respond at all to the invitation.

On the night of the party, however, when he again faced an empty house, he decided he must go somewhere.

He almost turned on his heels to spend the night with Lou, but he decided a formal party would be a nice change. He could have called to inform his hosts that he was indeed coming but he didn't want to risk the exposure a call through Mrs. Roberts would bring.

Drew pulled his tux out of the closet, hoping the suit would still fit. After struggling for some time, he managed to get all of the buttons fastened and his cuff links in place.

As he approached the new hotel, he marveled at the transformation of the once barren sandy ridge on the edge of the lake. Lights were strung throughout the coconut palms that were throughout the lawn, giving the illusion of a fairyland. Drew drove into the circular drive, which was lined with Bentleys, Rolls, and large touring cars. Valets parking the cars looked at Drew strangely when he hopped out of his Model T. They didn't ask questions but before they parked the car, they looked towards the doorman to see if he turned Drew away.

Not finding Drew's name on the guest list, the doorman motioned to the valets to come to escort Drew off the property.

"Are you sure my name isn't there?"

Drew already knew the answer, but implied there must be a mistake and his name inadvertently omitted.

"Please call Mrs. O'Brien and give her my name," he insisted.

The doorman told the valet to summon either Mr. or Mrs. O'Brien.

"Give them the name Drew Duncan and ask them to come to the door. I think we might have a problem."

A few moments later, a very frightened and white-faced Marian O'Brien appeared at the door.

"Drew! Thank God! I have a man in here who is choking. He can't breathe. Hurry and help him!"

Drew was pulled into the living room where he saw a familiar face. Thomas

Edison, dressed in his usual white linen suit, was sitting in a chair gasping for air. A quick appraisal of the situation convinced Drew that he did possibly have something stuck in his throat. He grabbed the victim from behind and lifted up on his chest cavity. A small chicken bone came flying out of Edison's mouth. Edison coughed several times and demanded some water. Drew was relieved that this method of treating choking victims – one he had only read about – actually worked.

"Sir. Whatever you just did saved my life. I thought I was a goner! My name is Tom Edison and who are you?"

The elderly man paused. "Oh! Dr. Duncan! I didn't recognize you dressed up in that monkey suit! I am so glad that you came when you did!"

Drew had met Edison and Ford many times when they came from Ft. Myers up river via steamboat to Lake Okeechobee. He had seen them both a few times on the river property Mr. Ford had bought from Mr. Goodno.

Drew stayed with the famous man for a while to make sure he was going to be okay. They talked some, but it was hard, for Edison's hearing was nearly gone. Drew was self-conscious when he had to yell to be heard. He was glad when Marian came and pulled him away.

"Mr. Edison, please let me have Dr. Duncan now. He and I have been dear friends since his days at Yale."

The woman did know how to stretch the truth.

"Drew, daaarling. I didn't think you were coming. Thank God you did! I have a proposition for you. I want you to come work here in Clewiston. We have one doctor but we need more because we are about to grow. Don't you want to get in on it? Look around you. There is Mr. Edison, Mr. Ford, and Mr. Goodyear, all from Ft. Myers. The Vanderbilts are visiting me for a week from Palm Beach. They arrived on their yacht yesterday. Everyone here is famous or comes from old money as we do. These are your people, Drew."

"You've played the role of country doctor long enough. I have it on good authority that Mary Elizabeth left you because most of your patients don't pay and you are in debt up to your eyeballs. I'm offering you a chance of a lifetime. Come and work for me and live the good life again."

"Marian, I don't know where you got your information. Small towns do have a gossip grapevine, I know, but I am not even in the red. Mary Elizabeth is taking care of her sick father. I love Glades County and its people. If I had wanted high society I would have stayed in Baltimore. Thank you for your offer, but no thanks. I can see my way to the door."

"Well, I tried, didn't I?" Marian smiled, "No one can blame me for trying to steal the best doctor in south Florida away."

Marian paused, then shifted her mood, never acknowledging she had just lost getting Drew to abandon Moore Haven and move to Clewiston.

"Come on," she said, "enjoy the food and mingle. We have the best liquor that money can get. I think that's why most of my guests really like south Florida."

256

Drew did enjoy himself that night. It was as if he had stepped back in time. Almost everyone there had attended Yale or Johns Hopkins or they knew people who did. Many of the guests had known Drew's father from their winters in Miami. Before the night was over Drew was declining offers to practice in Palm Beach, Ft. Myers, and Miami.

As he was saying good-bye, his hostess enlightened him on more gossip from Moore Haven.

"Drew, is it true that you have yourself a squaw? You rascal you," Marian whispered.

"Where did that one come from?"

"Contrary to popular belief, I still have friends left in Moore Haven. They know everything that goes on."

"You can tell your friends, whoever they are, that they are wrong. I spend a great deal of time with the Seminoles because I am learning about their herbs and medicines. I have been a friend with one of them since I first visited Florida in '98. That's it, nothing more."

Drew had no idea that people knew about Lou. How in the world did they know? Maybe they were just suspicious of him because he was spending so much time at the camp. Drew was an emotional wreck as he drove home. He could pick and choose from any good practice that he wanted. He didn't have to be in a small town where everyone knew every move that he made. He could go somewhere where people didn't know or didn't care where he spent his nights. He could be wealthy again. What bound him to this land?

The next morning was not unlike any other morning in Moore Haven.

Charlie yelled through the door as he delivered the milk that he also had a lemon pie from Mollie.

As he drove to work, Luke Sanchez stopped Drew's car to give him a sack of fresh tomatoes that he had just picked.

Christine Franklin, with the twin boys he delivered a few months earlier, waved to him as he passed.

As he parked his car in front of Mae's diner, he saw activities at the docks and watched the egrets and the herons.

Drew knew that what attracted him to this place besides its beauty was its people.

He would stay here – but would he ever get his family back? When would he ever hear from Mary Elizabeth?

Since it was Sunday, Drew drove up to the Cabbage Woods to spend the day with Lou.

Mary Elizabeth and her children had lived with her parents for six months. Drew had called a few times but didn't say much and there were no letters from him.

Mary Elizabeth missed Drew – but then, she had missed him even when she had lived with him. She began to feel sorry for herself as she stared at the drawer of the dresser where she had kept all the letters Drew had written to her during the war. There were no letters to be tied up in a ribbon now. What had happened to them and to their love? Was it that he loved Florida more than he loved her? She did know that she hated Florida and she hated living so far away from the rest of her family.

Mary Elizabeth's family had been warm and friendly for the first two months she was there. Everyone in Rosemont and the surrounding farms had greeted her and told her they had missed her. Because of the warmth of their greetings, she knew she had done the right thing in coming home.

As time wore on, though, she could hear them gossip.

"What is going on?"

"Why is Mary Elizabeth staying so long with her parents?"

"Where is her husband?"

She even heard it whispered that she was divorced. She knew that if the rumor spread she would really be an outcast. She knew a few spinsters in the area, but there were no divorced women.

Little by little she spent more and more time alone up in her bedroom while her parents took care of the children. One afternoon Hattie persuaded Mary Elizabeth to go to the flickers with her and the children. Both George and Hattie were amazed when she consented to go.

"Daddy, aren't you going with us?" asked Mary Elizabeth as everyone climbed into the family's new Model T.

"No dear. I am going to stay here where it is quiet. A new issue of *The Saturday Evening Post* came today that I want to read. You go and have a good time."

George kissed his daughter goodbye and added, "I am glad to see that you are going out."

As soon as the car made the first turn of the long drive, George hurried to the kitchen. He turned the crank on the new wall telephone with his right hand while holding the receiver with his left.

When he heard the voice of the operator he said, "Madge. This is George McRae. Get me Drew Duncan in Moore Haven, Florida. Wait a minute. Not Drew. See if a Charlie Carter has a phone."

George hung up the receiver and waited for Madge to call him back. He read two articles in the magazine before the phone rang.

"George, I have Mr. Carter on the line."

Charlie was excited to hear George's voice.

"George! How are you? How's your heart? Was it a bad attack?"

"So that's the story you're getting down there. Well, to tell you the truth I'm not well at all."

"I'm sorry to hear that, I hope that Mary Elizabeth is a big help to you and your wife. We really miss her."

"Charlie, I'm not physically sick. I never have been. I am sick because my daughter is here with me and her husband is there with you. I'm at wits end and I don't know what to do. My Mary is miserable. She stays in her room with the shades drawn most of the day. The doctor says that he can't do anything for her. I'm afraid she is going to die. She misses Drew, but she is too stubborn to admit it."

Charlie, not really comfortable with either the conversation or using the new-fangled phone, shared news from his end of the line.

"Drew misses her too. He never smiles. People are talking about the change in his personality. You know how small town gossips are. He spends too much time with his Indian friend. There is some talk that he even has a squaw out there. We had him over for supper last week. Miss Mollie didn't mince words. She told him what was being said about him and told him to go and get his family. She was straight to the point about everything."

"Is he coming?"

"He said that he couldn't get away. He denied having a squaw. Mollie hasn't given up on him yet."

"Thanks, Charlie, for everything. I'll push things to happen from here. Things can't stay the way they are.

"Should I tell Drew that Mary Elizabeth is sick?"

"No, I'll give you a ring if it comes to that. Goodbye, Charlie."

"Goodbye, George."

George had just finished the magazine when the family returned home. Mary Elizabeth was laughing for the first time in a long time. He wanted to wait to talk to her but was afraid she would lock herself in her bedroom tomorrow.

"Hattie, will you please take the children into the kitchen for supper? Mary Elizabeth and I need to talk."

"Yes, Daddy. What do you want?" Mary Elizabeth said when the children were gone.

"What do you plan to do?"

"What do you mean?"

"I mean, what are your intentions? You came home for a visit and that visit has lasted for six months. For the past month you have locked yourself in your bedroom every day. Even if you don't think so, your husband needs you and so do your children. Your mother and I are too old to have a young family in the house. If you want to stay in Rosemont we'll look for a house for you to rent tomorrow. Then you'll have to find a job. It is going to be hard on you raising those children all alone and it's going to be hard on those children with you working all of the time."

George was really wound up from his talk with Charlie. He would have gone on and on but his wife appeared in the kitchen door.

"George, stop. You are upsetting her. You can talk tomorrow. It's late."

Mary Elizabeth ran up the stairs and slammed the door to her bedroom.

"I had to do something," said George. "I had to make her realize she can't go on like she has been."

"I know," Hattie said softly.

Mary Elizabeth stared at her closed door from the bed where she had been sobbing for more than an hour. She tried to cry more, but the tears would not come. She got up, washed her face, and dressed for bed. Then she went into the next bedroom where her children were sleeping. She kissed her sleeping daughter and then bent down to kiss Thomas.

"Mama, why do you cry so much? Why can't we go home?" questioned Thomas. "I miss Daddy and Whiskers. I want to go fishing and swimming. When can we go home?"

Mary Elizabeth took Thomas in her arms as they both cried. She then went back to her room and wrote to Drew.

May 15, 1923

> *Dear Drew,*
>
> *I love you so much and have missed you every day since we have been apart.*
>
> *I've been wrong to stay away so long. If you will still have me, I want to come home, as I now realize that my home is wherever you are.*
>
> *If you don't need or want me, I will understand, but I hope you will find it in your heart to forgive this foolish, selfish person.*
>
> *Anxiously and contritely I await your answer.*
>
> *Mary Elizabeth*

The next morning Mary Elizabeth met her father in the horse barn.

"I want to thank you for your talk last night. I'm surprised it took this long. I have decided to go home if Drew will take me back. I've written to him and will be on the first train south if I get a letter from him telling me to come home. If I don't hear from him in two weeks, I'll look for a job and a small house. May I borrow your Lizzy to go down to the store and mail this?"

"The mailman is due any minute. Just ride down to the mailbox. Get the mail when you give him the letter."

George prayed that it wasn't too late for his daughter to start over. Surely his son-in-law would not trade her for an Indian!

When Drew received the letter from Mary Elizabeth he read it and reread it. He couldn't believe she actually wanted to come back to him in Moore Haven. Would she still want him if she heard the rumors about him? Worse still, would she want him when she found out the rumors were true? What would people say to her when she returned? Had he really stayed out at the camp so many times? What had people said when they found out he had gone to Sheila's whorehouse to treat her for gonorrhea? What did the gossips have to say about that?

He decided not to write but to tell Mary Elizabeth face to face.

He arranged for Dr. Mitchell to take his patients while he was gone. He found it easy to get away, now that he wanted to.

A week later Drew was on a train to Baltimore. He went by the medical center and made a deal with Dr. Watson to sell the rest of his interests. He then went to the bank and arranged for the money from the sale to go straight into savings. He cashed in all of his bonds. With his money, his family could live well for several years. He decided to put half in a savings account in the bank in Clewiston and keep the other half in his office safe. He then borrowed a car and drove to Rosemont.

Life at the McRae farm was outwardly normal. Underneath the appearance it was anything but. Thomas cried every day about wanting to go home. Mollie cried because her brother did. It had been two weeks and Mary Elizabeth hadn't heard a word from Drew. She knew he had received her letters days ago. There had been more than enough time to respond. Had Drew forgotten her and their children? Did he care anything about them?

George was equally worried because Charlie's words echoed in his mind about the Indian girl. Hattie worried about everyone.

George was saying the blessing before the noonday meal when the doorbell rang.

"Someone timed that right," said George. "It must be the new preacher. Someone told him that you are the best cook around, Hattie."

"I'll see who it is!" Thomas yelled.

His feet made staccato taps as he ran down the hall that led from the kitchen to the front porch.

"Daddy!" Thomas screamed. "Daddy's here! Daddy's here!"

He opened the screen and jumped into his father's arms. The rest of the family ran to the front of the house. Drew put Thomas down as they opened the door to greet him.

Mary Elizabeth melted as she fell into her husband's arms. As he folded them around her, she knew that she would always be at his side no matter where they lived and no matter if she had to share him with the entire world.

After the family ate, Mary Elizabeth and Drew walked down the winding drive, up the road to the crossroads, and back again. Drew told her about the business he had transacted in Baltimore, about having saved Edison's life, the parties and gatherings he had attended, the trip to the Big Cypress with Gopher and what he had seen there. He told her about the new herbs and medicines the Seminoles had taught him to use. He also told her about new people who had moved into Moore Haven as well as those who had given up and left. He told her about everything that had happened in the past six months, but he wasn't brave enough to tell her about Lou Tiger.

The love Drew felt for Mary Elizabeth wasn't gone as he had thought it was. Being with her made him feel just as alive and happy as it had since the day that they met. He tried to forget about Lou and their love.

"Mary Elizabeth, I love you and have missed you so much. Will you come home with me now?"

Chapter 27

ALMOST TRANQUILITY
Spring 1924-Spring 1926

Life resumed in Moore Haven for Drew and his family with few changes.

Drew made a trip to the Cabbage Woods the day after his arrival home from Maryland. He and Lou talked for hours, but at the end, he made it clear that his family was first in his life. If there had been any talk of his activities during Mary Elizabeth's absence, he didn't know of it.

Drew hired Alfonzo to deliver his medicines and supplies to the outlying areas. He also made it known that he would make house calls only in cases of emergencies and babies. He was still on call twenty-four hours a day, but with the new arrangements, had much more time to spend with his family. There was time for picnics, swimming, fishing trips, baseball games, and social gatherings throughout the county.

He was a member of the Luncheon Club, Moore Haven's answer to the Chesapeake, and the Masonic Lodge, although his attendance at both organizations was poor due to his schedule.

Moore Haven was growing, even though it wasn't booming as it had been in the past. The land speculators were gone and the people who remained were hard-working individuals who were out only to make a better way of life for their families. Life, for the most part, was good.

Mollie and Charlie invited the Duncans out for a party on Sunday afternoon, September 17. It was to be a going away party for Daniel, who was leaving the next day to go to Oklahoma to work for his older brother, and an early birthday party for Mollie, who would be four years old the next day.

Mollie fixed a fried chicken dinner; the favorite of both little Mollie and Daniel. Mollie was blowing her candles out on the fresh coconut cake when Drew got a call to go to Lakeport to deliver a baby.

"I'm sorry, Mollie. I'll be with you tomorrow for your real birthday. I'll even help you pin the tail on the donkey at your party."

Drew gave his daughter a hug and his wife a kiss as he left. He came back in to ask Daniel to give his family a lift.

"Better be slow though. I don't want that bumpy road to cause that baby to be born before I get back." He wasn't worried because Mary Elizabeth wasn't due for another five weeks.

He got to the tarpaper shack at the edge of the Okeechobee at three o'clock. Ralph Bauman, a third generation catfisher, came out of his house to greet Drew. His apparel never changed. Like most of the other fishermen, he wore no shoes. His pants were rolled up to his knees and his wide brimmed hat never left his head. The only thing missing from his usual attire was the machete he always cradled in the crook of his arm.

Drew took a deep breath when he was inside the house. Repulsive odors hit his nostrils as he began to assess what was ahead of him. He moved through the dimly lit, dismal living room where newspapers were pasted on the inside wall to provide some insulation.

The chipped porcelain sink was barely visible underneath the filthy accumulation of food-covered saucers, plates, and silverware that had been thrown into it helter skelter.

The squalor did not end at the sink. Brown grocery sacks either half full of things yet to be put on shelves or things that were ready to be put in the garbage can sat on the cracked linoleum floor or on the counter. Empty tin cans and empty milk bottles coated with sour milk, as well as a multitude of empty beer bottles, were strewn about in disorder.

Jennifer Bauman was just starting her labor. This was her first child and the family had panicked with the first pain. Ralph, her husband, had ridden his mule to Beck's Store to call. Drew had no way of knowing how long he would be. He instructed Ralph and Jennifer to scrub down their home. It was one of his requirements when a baby was entering the world in a home of filth and squalor.

"Doc, do you think my wife should be doing this heavy work? She is about to have a baby."

"This work won't hurt her at all. I'm surprised that she hadn't already done it. Most women clean before a baby comes; it's just natural."

Then it dawned on him how clean his own house was. He had come into the kitchen that morning to see his wife cleaning the kitchen cabinets and changing shelf papers.

"Oh, no."

"What is it, Doc.?"

"I think I might be a father again soon, that's all."

Just before dark Drew went out to the Bouman's dock to fish. He always carried his rod and reel in his car for such emergencies. He didn't catch anything because others were nearby using dynamite to bomb fish out of the water. Nevertheless there were fish for supper.

"Doc, if I clean the fish, will that be enough payment for now? I'm a little short."

Drew became more anxious as the sun set in the west and Jennifer hadn't had more contractions.

"Jennifer, I am going to examine you to see how far along you are."

As she was getting into bed, her water broke and she had a hard contraction.

"Your baby is really on its way now," Drew told her.

He cleaned up the water and helped Jennifer change the sheets.

"You need to lie down. It shouldn't be long now."

At least he hoped that was true as he anxiously thought of Mary Elizabeth. A full harvest moon shown through the open window as Jedfrey Drew Bauman made his debut at 8:45 p.m.

Drew cleaned himself, Jennifer, the baby, and the room. He was in his car with a box full of black bass by 9:30. He pulled into his driveway just before midnight and knew what was happening inside when he saw Anna's Model T in the driveway. He prayed that he wasn't too late.

As he ran in the front door he heard a scream and knew he was in time. As he entered his bedroom, he saw Mary Elizabeth's legs up in delivery position. Miss Anna was there to deliver and Mrs. Miller, their next-door neighbor, was assisting her.

"Doc!" both of the women shouted in unison.

"Thank God that you are home!"

"You are minutes, if not seconds away from being a father again. Come take over."

Drew started towards the bathroom to scrub up. Mary Elizabeth let out another scream.

"Doc! Come now!" demanded Anna.

Mary Elizabeth continued to scream as she pushed. The baby's head emerged just as Drew traded places with his nurse. Two minutes later, at 12:01 a.m., Drew handed his second daughter to his wife. Susan Gail had been born on her sister's fourth birthday.

That afternoon Drew hosted Mollie's birthday party for 20 of her friends. He later told his friends how he handled the whole affair and that it was rougher than delivering a set of twins by C-section in a battlefield trench! He didn't mention the fact that he had the help of several mothers, Miss Mollie, and Josephine.

Mary Elizabeth was pleased that a few changes in Drew's schedule gave him so much extra time to be with his family.

One of their favorite activities was to go to the moving pictures every Saturday night. Mary Elizabeth loved Mary Pickford and was mad about Rudolph Valentino. At least once a month after church they went with several others on a picnic somewhere on Fisheating Creek. There they spent a lazy afternoon fishing, swimming, napping, playing cards, and talking.

The family also loved the radio. They had a big Stromberg-Carlson in the living room where they listened to news, sports events, and family shows.

Thomas and his father spent a lot of time together. Drew bought a bigger boat that he left tied up at the Carter's dock. By far their favorite activity was stargazing. Sometimes they would look from the boat or lie on the docks. At other times they would take the car and go out to an open field. The stars were so close that they felt they could reach out and touch them. Drew taught his son all he knew and then purchased books to teach him more. Thomas knew every constellation, in what season they would appear, and in what direction, and the stories and myths associated with them.

Thomas was almost as interested in baseball as Drew had been. Drew helped Thomas with his hitting and catching and they loved to go to the local baseball games.

Sometimes, when he was with Thomas, Drew knew he was the luckiest person in the world. How close he had come to losing him and the rest of his family was something that he tried not to think about.

As Thomas grew older, Drew reveled in taking him to watch baseball games in the Grapefruit League. He began to enjoy those games as much as he used to enjoy the regular season games of the Orioles.

He took Thomas to the spring practice of the Athletics in Fort Myers and made special arrangements for his son to meet the team and get an autographed ball.

He vowed he and Thomas would spend more time together next year. They might even take off a week to go to the training games in the Tampa and St. Petersburg area.

Mary Elizabeth said he was dreaming if he thought she would allow Thomas to miss that much school.

It wasn't long before heavy rains came again, just as they had four years earlier. The drainage canals were all full by the end of July but did not overflow as they had two years earlier. The people of the area were satisfied the drainage problems had been solved. They were also satisfied that the muck dike – five feet, eight inches high and forty feet thick at its base – was the answer to their prayers.

The third weekend of July Thomas went with his father, Gopher, and Gopher's son, Little One, for a week-long trip into the 'Glades. Both boys were delighted to be included. Although they had met each other on occasion, this trip forged a friendship that both fathers hoped would last a lifetime for both of their sons.

Deep in the 'Glades they fished, gigged frogs, and collected herbs. Thomas and Little One saw many birds and plants for the first time. Even though they were less than fifty miles from Moore Haven and the Cabbage Woods, it was a new world for both the boys. They saw no other people the entire week. Surprisingly, there was little rain while they were on their outing, although a storm hit the morning they started home.

Thomas couldn't stop talking about everything that he had seen and done down in the "real" 'Glades'.

"Well, Drew, you did it," Mary Elizabeth lamented. "You've taught your son to love the 'Glades as much as you do. When he does stop talking, he is pouring over your books. I think he knows every bird, animal, and plant that grows in Florida."

Glad the two were back from their trip, Mary Elizabeth snuggled up next to Drew and relished in his closeness. In spite of the rainy season and everything that seemed to come with it each year – the mosquitoes, the high water, the dead animals, the smell of rotting vegetation – Mary Elizabeth realized she had never been happier than at this moment with her three beautiful children and her very special husband.

Sally Settle

Chapter 28

THE HARDEST LOSS
August 1926

The sun came out the middle of August and remained out for a week. Thomas begged his mother to let him go play with his friend, Cal, who lived above his father's store not far from Drew's office. Mary Elizabeth caved in to her son's wishes. She felt sorry for him because he had been in the house for most of the summer.

"You can go if it is okay with Mr. Higgins. I'll call him."

Thomas was surprised, not believing that his mother was going to let him go. It was still wet and the snakes were crawling.

Mary Elizabeth picked up the phone and asked the operator to ring Jacob Higgins at his store.

"Jacob. This is Mary Elizabeth. Thomas is begging to come see Cal. He has been cooped up for so long. Is it okay with you?"

"Sure. The boys can help me put up a new shipment of clothes that has just come in. Then they can play outside on the walk or go upstairs to the apartment, if that's okay with you. Cal's been building a model town to go with his train set. It's quite impressive. He has been wanting to show it off to Thomas."

"Thomas, you may go, but Cal is helping his father at the store. You be sure and do whatever Mr. Higgins tells you to do. Be good. I want you home by five. One more thing, what do you do when you see a snake?"

"Mama, how many times do I have to tell you? Freeze and let it go by. If there is a gator, run zig zag. Don't play near the canals and ditches."

"Okay, come give me a kiss."

Thomas obliged his mother's request then ran to his room to get his father's Audubon book.

"May I take this if I'm careful?"

"Yes, but if anything happens to it your daddy will have us both shot, no questions asked."

Thomas ran out the front door and down the steps with the book. He turned to wave goodbye to his mother.

An odd sensation came over Mary Elizabeth as she watched her son ride down the street on his shiny red bicycle with the over-sized book in his front basket. She always had second doubts when she let him go out of the yard. At that moment Gail woke up from her nap and made herself known.

Mary Elizabeth shook off her fears and went to take care of her daughter. Throughout the afternoon and three piano lessons she continued to have an uneasy feeling.

Five o'clock came and Thomas was not home. By 5:30 Mary Elizabeth was caught somewhere between boiling mad and being worried out of her mind. She called the Higgins' store, but got no answer. Next she asked the operator to ring Drew's office.

"Joan, will you please try to locate my husband and have him call me immediately? It is an emergency. Also, can you find Jacob Higgins?"

Mary Elizabeth gave the girls their supper and tried not to upset them.

Mollie asked, "Where's Thomas?"

"He's with Cal Higgins. He should be home anytime."

Time dragged by slowly, even though Mary Elizabeth tried to keep busy. She was putting the last of the dishes in the cupboard when the telephone rang. She ran to the living room to answer it.

"Thomas?"

"No, ma'am. This is Joan Roberts. I can't find the doctor or Mr. Higgins. The Higgins' don't have a phone at home. What's wrong? Is there anything I can do?"

"Have you seen Thomas? He's been playing with Cal Higgins all afternoon and was supposed to be home by five. He isn't home yet and I haven't heard from him."

"It's only seven. He probably has lost track of time. You know little boys. He'll be home soon. Don't you worry. I'll call around to see if anyone has seen him."

"Thanks, Joan, I'm sure someone has seen him."

Joan Roberts did worry because she knew why the doctor's wife was in a panic.

The drainage ditches that criss-crossed the town and the big three-mile canal were every mother's nightmare. They were so inviting to children, especially on hot, humid days like this one. Several children drowned in them each year. She prayed the boys were safely playing somewhere.

Mary Elizabeth couldn't stand waiting at the house any longer. She called her neighbor, Sue Miller, to come stay with the girls. Keeping a lookout for her son and his red bicycle, she drove her new Buick down to the Higgins' store as fast as she dared. She was in tears by the time she reached the stairs leading to the apartment.

She ran up the stairs and beat loudly on the Higgins' door. She didn't wait for an answer but yelled through the closed door.

"Thomas! Are you still in there playing?"

Jacob Higgins opened the door.

"What wrong, Mrs. Duncan? Thomas's not here. Aren't the boys with you? They left the store a little before five to go to your house. They poured over that Audubon bird book all afternoon and were going to read some more at your house. I was about to go down to the store to call Cal to come home. Are you sure they're not at your house?"

"Of course, I am sure!"

Mary Elizabeth and the Higgins went down the block to Dowd's Drugstore to see if anyone there had seen the boys and when. Someone had seen the boys riding the bikes by the canal by the Moore Haven Hotel a little after five.

"Which way were they going?"

Mary Elizabeth couldn't believe her ears. Where were the boys going when they were supposed to be going to the house?

Within half an hour fifty men had gathered and then fanned out looking for the boys. Drew walked into the store about eight.

"Jim, I saw your lights and all of the cars. What's going on?"

He looked up to see Mary Elizabeth who demanded to know where he had been.

"Joan Roberts has called everywhere looking for you!"

"Why doesn't that woman acknowledge that Wanda has a phone? I was out with her delivering twins. It was a hard delivery and we lost one. Why? What's the matter? Why are you here? Where are the children?"

"Thomas. It's Thomas. He and Cal are both missing. They've been together all afternoon. He was supposed to be home over three hours ago and I haven't heard from him. They were last seen riding their bikes down the River Road by the canal. Oh Drew, what if..."

"Don't say it, Mary. Nothing has happened! Don't even think it!"

"Call Frank at the depot and have him check all the trains up the line. Those boys just ran away and when I get hold of Thomas, I'll..."

"But Drew, they were headed south."

"The farm. Has anyone checked at the Carters'? They are probably at the Carter's. They probably showed up at the doorstep at supper time and Miss Mollie fed them."

"Drew, Miss Mollie would have called."

Drew didn't pay any attention to his wife. He had gone to the phone on the wall.

"Mrs. Roberts, this is Dr. Duncan. Please ring Charlie Carter."

"Doc! Your wife is looking for you."

"Yes, Mrs. Roberts, she found me. Please ring Charlie."

"Have you found Thomas?"

"No."

The phone rang five times before Charlie answered it.

"Charlie, is Thomas with you?"

"No."

"Have you seen him this afternoon?"

"No."

"What's wrong, Drew?"

Charlie just heard a click in his ear.

"Someone take my wife home," Drew ordered.

"No, Drew. I'm staying with you."

"Who's with the girls and standing by our phone in case Thomas calls or comes home?"

"Sue Miller is there and she will call the drugstore or Higgins' store if the boys show up."

"Doc!"

Two men screamed as they came through the door of the drugstore.

"We've found two bicycles and a big bird book down by the Lone Cypress. What color is your son's bike?"

"Red."

"Cal's is blue with two baskets on both sides of the back wheel."

Jacob's voice was at the panic stage. The group that had crowded into the drugstore ran to the big cypress tree at the end of the street. There they found the bikes but no signs of the boys.

On the concrete wall of the locks was the book, *Birds of North America*. Drew picked up his book and looked at his sobbing wife.

A light rain turned into a downpour.

The wife of the assistant engineer in charge of drainage, Fern Flanders, was standing between the two women, holding their hands, and praying. Her house was within a few yards of where they were standing.

"Fern, please take my wife and Mrs. Higgins to your house," Drew suggested. "It's close enough that they can hear, but they will be out of this weather, too."

As soon as the women left, several men got into boats with a weighted net. They pulled it tightly between the boats and let it drop to the dark water's bottom. Others held lanterns and flashlights.

The net was thrown more than 20 times before they felt something big just beyond the floodgates of the locks.

Four men dived into the dark swirling water where the net had anchored.

A profound stillness fell over the assembled group. Everyone in the crowd of over 100 people hoped the net had hooked on something other than the bodies of two little boys.

For what seemed to be a lifetime, Drew and Jacob stared into the cold black, heartless water hoping against hope that what had been found would not be their sons.

"We found them!" the first diver yelled as he came up for air.

Twenty minutes later the two little boys lay on the bank of the canal.

Jacob Higgins stood motionless, staring at the lifeless body of his only child.

Drew started screaming, "No! God! You can't take away my boy! Don't punish me for my sins like this! I won't let you!"

He took his son into his arms and breathed into his mouth, trying to exchange his breath for his son's. Everyone in the crowd watched Drew in complete helplessness.

The crowd parted as Charlie Carter walked through them. Charlie bent over and touched his friend on the shoulder.

"Drew, our boy is gone. Let go."

Drew turned and looked into the face of his kind, old friend. Only then did he realize what he said was true. There was nothing more he could do.

Just then Mary Elizabeth and Jayne Higgins broke through the crowd. Taking their sons, both women held them close to their breasts, stroking their hair, and rocking them back and forth.

The night was still. The usual night sounds – the music of the crickets, the croaking of the frogs, the calls of the nocturnal birds – all were hushed.

The clouds parted and a full moon shown through the branches of the Lone Cypress. Somber shadows were cast on the faces of the heartbroken group as they silently waited for Mr. Parson's funeral wagon to arrive.

Two days later, funeral services were held for both boys at the Methodist Church.

They were buried in adjacent family plots in the new cemetery in Ortona. A shaken town stopped for the day to pay tribute to the boys and to their families, whom they all knew so well.

Chapter 29

REALIZATIONS
September 1926

Drew had dealt with death since he was a child working with his father. It was a fact of life. He believed with all of his being that life continued elsewhere after one's journey on earth was over. When an older person died he had comfort in knowing they had lived a full life. He thought of his grandparents, his parents, his Uncle Tyler, and Flora.

He had witnessed death on the battlefield. He had stood by young fathers as they buried their newborns in a shallow grave. Words did not come easily when the hopes of being a parent died with the child. Words also didn't come easy when he lost a mother in childbirth, a young man in some accident, or someone in the prime of their life to a fatal illness. The deaths that had been the hardest to witness over the years had been the deaths of children; yet there had been so many. Now he was facing the same thing and he didn't know how to cope. He had lost his Thomas. He knew in his heart that no man had ever loved a son the way that he had loved his.

Drew hated to go home, so he threw himself into his work. The house felt so empty when he walked through the front door without his son to greet him. Mollie and Gail hugged and kissed him, but it wasn't the same. He longed for Thomas. When he was home he had time to think and his thoughts were of one thing: Thomas.

He felt so much guilt. Everything was his fault – from moving here to the land of water, water everywhere, to taking Thomas deep into the 'Glades. Mary Elizabeth reminded him of his guilt every time he was with her. He felt it, although she said nothing.

Drew didn't want to think about his loss. He resumed going to the Cabbage Woods. Even in the arms of Lou, he felt no relief from his grief.

He justified his renewed relationship by saying that God had already punished him for this sin. There was no more to lose.

Mary Elizabeth ached more with every passing day. She had such a special relationship with her first born. His birth had made the war years bearable when Drew was gone. He was the one who gave her comfort when Steven was killed. She had watched him grow and had seen him becoming just like his father. She felt a deep sense of guilt because she was the one who watched him ride away, knowing deep in her heart she might never see him again.

She knew Drew blamed her as much as she blamed herself. But then again there was that book, that book that Thomas couldn't put down after he returned from the trip to the Big Cypress, the book that was lying on the banks of the canal where his precious body was found in the water.

Why was the book opened to the picture of the Great Blue Heron? Did the boys see one and then try to catch it? Why would they have done that? Thomas had seen the big birds as long as they had been in Florida. Why did he take such an interest that day? Why did she let him take the book?

Questions and guilt played over and over again in her mind. Mary Elizabeth watched her husband sink deeper and deeper into a shell. When he was at home, which wasn't that often, he just read, stared into space, or listened to the radio. He slept in his chair every night. The only contact he had with his daughters was a good night kiss if he happened to be at home.

He didn't talk to Mary Elizabeth and they hadn't been intimate since the drowning. She knew he was spending a great deal of time in the Cabbage Woods. Gopher was an extraordinary friend and Drew needed friendship. Mary Elizabeth wouldn't let herself believe the whispers she heard numerous times about Drew's squaw.

Nevertheless, she was glad when he was gone because he reminded her of her guilt every time she was with him. She felt it, although he said nothing.

She was determined to give a normal life to her daughters. They needed her and that was more important to her than contact with Drew or anything else. She vowed to love and protect them and make sure that they were never alone to even go near that deep waterway or the drainage canals.

School started the Tuesday after Labor Day. Mollie was the only child whose mother drove her to school and picked her up every day. The drainage ditch between her house and school was filled almost to overflowing with water.

As they rode past, Mollie could see her friends having fun playing and throwing sticks, rocks, and other things into it. She wished she could be with them.

Miss Adams was Mollie's teacher. Mollie thought she was so pretty and loved her short hair. She looked like the women in magazines and the moving pictures. She wished she could wear her hair in a bob instead of braids.

Mollie wanted to tell Miss Adams all about Thomas because Miss Adams had moved to town just a few days before school started and Mollie knew she didn't know what had happened to her brother.

The day before her sixth birthday, Mollie remained in her seat while her classmates hurried to Mrs. Parker's room for recess.

The two teachers rotated responsibility for the classes during the break in their classrooms. It had been impossible to go outside for a week due to the rain and the standing water. When Miss Adams asked Mollie why she didn't go out with the others, Mollie timidly walked to the front of the room. She wanted to tell her teacher all about Thomas.

The words were inside her head but they just wouldn't come out. Tears came, at first from frustration, then from something more. Her tears became uncontrollable sobs.

Miss Adams held Mollie in her arms and told her it was okay to cry. She seemed to know about Thomas already.

Sally Settle

Chapter 30

THE STORM
September 17-18, 1926

It was customary for members of the Women's Club to hold a welcome party for new teachers. Plans were made to have the party at the Peter Westergaard home on Friday, September 17.

Mary Elizabeth had held the position of social chairman of the club since January. This party fell under her leadership, but a special meeting had been called to see if she wanted someone else on the committee to be in charge of the function.

"I appreciate your concern," she told them, "but I must stay busy. I need to. If all of you are willing to help with a lot of the responsibilities, I believe I can continue as chairman.

The night of the party Mary Elizabeth left two teenage girls to take care of her daughters for the night. She left a long list of instructions for them. The main one was that they were not to leave the house under any circumstance. That was a bit foolish, she had to admit, because it had been raining for days.

The weather that day was particularly stormy and ugly. Some wondered if the party should be canceled. Others said that rain was a fact of life and that partygoers should just dress appropriately.

Mary Elizabeth was everywhere, making sure everyone had enough to eat and having a good time. A group of women gathered in one corner watching her.

"Look at her. She is so strong. I wouldn't even be out yet if I had lost my child only a month ago. I guess it is because she is a doctor's wife."

"Don't let that fool you, she'll come crashing down soon. I have seen it happen before. Parents act like nothing has happened and then all of a sudden they withdraw and you don't see them again for months. Sometimes longer."

"Yes, I wonder when that will happen to her?"

"Are you taking your children to the big birthday party she's giving tomorrow? Mollie will be six and Gail will be two. They say that Mary Elizabeth's going all out with pony rides and everything."

"I pray the rain will stop. Still, it's going to be awfully wet and muddy."

"Ponies aren't allowed inside the Woman's Club."

They laughed again.

"There's Mr. Charlie. Where is Miss Mollie? I have never seen them apart at a social gathering."

"She's on her way to West Virginia to visit relatives, but she stopped off to see her son in Orlando first. Thomas's death has hit her hard. The families are so close. You know, the Carters lost a daughter only ten years ago."

"Miss Mollie is such a dear person. I never knew she had a daughter. What happened?"

"I don't really know but the girl was around twenty. She died of some incurable disease. I heard that they tried everything over the course of five years. It was her health that first brought the family to Florida."

"Where is Doc tonight?"

"He could be anywhere."

"Like with the Indians?"

All the gossipers laughed.

"Now girls, we don't know if any of that is true. Anna Wright swears that it isn't, and she should know. She says that Doc has been a devoted husband and father since his family returned from Maryland three years ago. This has really been rough on him. I do know that all he does is work since the drowning."

"I think Anna is in love with the doc, too."

"Nonsense! I have never seen a woman who is so devoted to her family as Miss Anna. She just has a deep respect for Doc, that's all."

"Believe what you will, but I haven't seen him anywhere. My Jake says he doesn't even come to Mae's for his morning cup of coffee."

"He hasn't stepped foot in the church either."

"I hear he is really angry with God."

"Wouldn't you be? I feel sorry for them both."

In between their gossip, they watched couples doing the Charleston and enjoyed the night.

Fred Flanders, the assistant engineer for the Army Corps of Engineers, rushed into the room, making a trail of water across the floor as he headed for a small group of men on the other side of the room. He had not stopped to remove the raingear he was wearing.

As puddles formed around Fred's feet, the conversation became so animated that others moved closer to hear what he had to say.

"I just received a weather report from Miami," Fred panted. "There's a storm in the Atlantic that is supposed to hit there by the morning. I think we should get prepared. It might be here sometime tomorrow."

"Fred, I have lived here for eight years," said Bill Yates. "We've been through fires and floods. I can't count how many storms I've seen. I think we can handle another storm."

The other men nodded their heads in agreement.

"We have just learned to put our things on higher shelves and chase away all those varmints that come in to get out of the water. That's the price we have to pay for living on this fertile soil. My brother does the same thing in the Mississippi Delta."

The civil engineer continued his warning.

"I measured the water level of the lake at eighteen feet at six o'clock. It has been rising all day. The dike is only a few feet higher. I am afraid that the water will come over the top or burst through. There is just so much water pressure a dike can hold."

"Fred, you and your boys built that dike. You have used a lot of our tax and bond money. Now you are saying that it might give way. Don't you government boys do anything right the first time?"

"Even the strongest dike can weaken with so much pressure. I can tell you right now, I'm scared. I'm going back again to check for cracks or anything else that looks hazardous. Will any of you come with me?"

"What for?"

"To sound an alarm if need be."

"I'm not worried.," said Yates. "Just go out in all that rain and mud if you want to. I'll stay here where it's dry."

Fred turned to leave, "I'm telling you, boys, if you hear the fire alarm come to the dike quick!"

"Did you hear what Fred said, girls? I guess we'd better tell Mary Elizabeth to cancel the birthday party. It looks as if we will have rain all day tomorrow, too."

As soon as Fred left the Westergaard's house he ran into Drew, who was just getting out of his car.

"What's up, Fred? You look like a man on a mission."

"I am on a mission, but I'm glad to see you, Doc. Do you want to come with me? I hope to be back in about thirty minutes or so."

"Sure. Anything to delay going into that party. I really didn't want to go but I was making an appearance for Mary Elizabeth's sake. I'll drive if you want."

As the men got into the car, Drew asked, "Where to, Fred?"

"Just drive down to the pumping station at the dike. I want to check the water level. I'm worried because it's been on the rise all day. What have you been up to?"

Fred hoped the doctor would talk to him, because along with the rest of the town, he was concerned that he wasn't coping well with his son's death. He was glad when Drew began.

"I have just helped an old Negro woman live a little longer. She had a heart attack this afternoon but I was able to revive her. She should be around to celebrate a few more birthdays."

After a pause, he continued, "Fred, you've been around these parts for a long time. Do you believe in the local superstitions?"

"What do you mean?"

"Well, Hank Stewart was in from Lakeport this morning to get the cast taken off the arm he mangled when that horse threw him. He said the Indians were moving to higher ground and that's an indication a storm is coming. He also said the pollen is rising off the saw grass, something I've heard more than once is a sign of a bad storm. He was anxious to get home to move his family out and suggested that I do the same here."

"Also, I went to the Benbow brothers at their farm and they, too, said a big storm is coming. They said their animals were all restless and they were trying to secure things, just in case. Coming back into town, the sky was a most unusual pinkish color. It almost glowed."

"To top it all off, when I was out at The Quarters today, Wanda told me that a friend of hers, Luberta Kirksey, had such a bad feeling that something was going to happen that she insisted she needed to leave. She did, too. She and her children left on a train to Lake Wales Tuesday. What do you think it all means?"

"I don't know about all those superstitious signs," Fred said, "but the barometric pressure has been dropping all day. It is lower than I have ever seen it. It's got me concerned. You know the lower the pressure, the worse the storm; plus, I've gotten a report from Miami telling of a storm out in the Atlantic. It's due to hit there in the early morning hours. We'll probably get some of the wind from that."

Fred continued, "If we get much more rain, it will be too much. I'm afraid we'll be flooded again. Every lake, canal, and ditch is filled to capacity already. I have had instructions from Sam Elliot, the chief engineer – my boss – to keep the flood gates closed. There's no place for the water to go except over the fields and the town. Water is almost over the top of the dike now. We might have a prayer if they open the gates over on the east side tonight. They're closed now because people in the Ft. Lauderdale and Miami area don't want extra water in their canals any more than we do. I hope the officials come to their senses."

"Fred, this might be the wrong time to ask, but aren't we right in the flood plain? Was it a good idea to locate a town here? Is all this draining and diking doing any good? Is Mother Nature just getting back at us? She has taken so much from us from fires to floods, to..."

Drew's voice choked up at that point and Fred knew he was thinking about Thomas.

"Drew, I know you're concerned with the 'Glades. I wouldn't be here if things hadn't been researched. I think what we've done is a good thing. Most of the farmers know we are on a flood plain. They are growing crops on the richest soil in the world and, in a good year, they are delivering to market three times a year. We just have to put up with the bad to get the good. I don't think the 'Glades are in any danger of dying because of what we have done."

"Now that stupid road they have started to build again from Miami across to Naples is a different story," Fred continued.

Remembering Gopher's reaction to the road, Drew nodded his head in agreement. The time for retrospection ended as they approached the edge of the dike.

"Drive over closer to the shed. I need to get some lanterns for us so we'll be able to see." Fred pointed the way to the shed, which was hardly visible through the heavy rainfall.

It didn't take but a few minutes for Fred to find the lanterns and equip the two of them.

"Walk along the edge and see if you notice any water lapping over the top or if you see any cracks. If you do, yell. We'll meet back here and then we'll go down and cross the bridge to check near pump station No. 1. That's the weakest section of the dike. It was built across a slough. We have always had trouble there."

Drew braced himself against the stiff breeze as he walked far down the dike.

"Drew, we have a crack here," yelled Fred from his inspection point.

It didn't take but a few minutes for Drew to rejoin Fred where he saw the damage himself.

"We're going to have to sandbag or this dike will be history tomorrow," Fred said. "I don't want to think about what will happen if the force of eighteen plus feet of water is released on Moore Haven. There will be an explosion of water that will wipe out most of the town. I'll get bags and shovels out of the shed if you will drive over and sound the fire alarm. When the men come, tell them what is happening and to go home and get shovels. Send some across to pump stations No. 1 and No. 2. They'll find sandbags in the sheds. It's going to be a long night!"

Drew drove as fast as he could to the power plant where the town's siren was located. When he jumped out of the car he noticed that the water in the canal was lapping over the fish docks and was dangerously close to the power plant.

He ran into the plant, but just as he was approaching the room to the siren, it went off, more shrill and more demanding than any alarm Drew had ever heard. It was like a banshee that foretells the coming of death.

He found Ed Lundy bending over a crate, holding two wires down to the new fire alarm which had just been delivered and no one had had time to unpack. The siren continued its blast. Mercifully, Ed finally disconnected the two wires he was holding and the alarm stopped.

"That should bring them out," Ed remarked as he and Drew could finally talk.

"Doc, I found water lapping over the floor of the generating plant and down on the fish docks. I had to let the people know."

"Yes, I know you had to, Ed, but you have no business being out here in this weather with that arm."

Drew quickly checked over the stub of Ed's left arm that had been amputated only a few weeks earlier. Ed, an electrician, had accidentally touched a live power line and burned his arm so badly it had been impossible to save it. It was a miracle that he had not been electrocuted.

Ed connected the wires again.

It was almost midnight and the party was just coming to an end. People were getting on their boots and slickers when they heard the fire alarm go off.

"The fire alarm has never sounded so loud."

"It must be the new one that came in today. I wondered where Ed was tonight. He must have spent the night installing it and now he's giving it a test run to tell us to end the party."

The alarm stopped and everyone agreed that it was Ed, indeed, who was just testing the new system.

"I bet there are people who will want to string him up for pulling a Halloween prank like that."

"It really does work well. No one will ever miss that sound."

"I do dread Halloween. Do you realize how many times it will go off?"

People started streaming out of the house and into their cars. Two minutes later the siren was heard again.

"Wonder if there really is something wrong. Maybe lightning has struck something."

"Ain't been no lightn'. Must be tha muck."

"The muck's too wet to burn."

"Remember what Fred told us about the dike. Maybe there really is a problem. Let's go see what's going on."

The men crowded into several cars so their wives could double up and get home. When they got to the power plant they saw Dr. Duncan giving directions.

"Fred has found a crack in the dike," Drew said breathlessly. "He says not to panic, but we're going to have to sandbag. He has plenty of sandbags but only a few shovels. Some of you need to go round up more shovels. Those who live in the Park Avenue area need to go to station #1. That's the weakest part of the dike. There are sandbags in the shed. The rest of you need to go to #2. Now go get shovels or go to the pumping stations. It's going to be a long night, boys!"

Soon, all able-bodied men in town, including Negroes, were at work trying to save the town. They worked all night, side-by-side, filling bags and stacking them against the ever-widening crack.

They were in the rain so long they no longer felt the wasp-like sting of the intense rain. Often, though, when a sheet of rain moved past, they were so deluged that they almost choked standing there. Occasionally, the night sky became so black they could hardly see one another.

Squalls of strong winds made whitecaps on the lake and blew walls of water over the levee into the streets of Moore Haven. The volunteers were thankful the bags of sand were as heavy as they were. When a strong gale hit, more than one volunteer was blown off his feet.

Esther Klutts, whose husband was in Arcadia buying equipment for the movie theater he managed, heard about the men's vigil and organized a group of women to supply hot coffee through the long night. Working out of the waiting room of the train station, the women also made sandwiches from day-old bread from the local bakery.

At dawn, the exhausted men saw that their efforts had been futile. They had lost the battle with the lake water. The rain was getting heavier and the wind was coming in heavy gusts from the northeast across the lake. It would just be a matter of time before the dike would give way from the pressure of the wind on nineteen feet of water. The water was already two feet deep. The defeated men made their way back to town and to their homes.

Merchants went to work putting their stock on higher shelves, resigned to the fact that there would be another flood. Others took food and supplies to their apartments over their stores.

Some packed their cars and left town, but most stayed because they either had no place to go or had no desire to leave. They gathered in houses with other families for support or, knowing they would be isolated through the day and into the night, decided to have a long party.

Drew drove to the back door of his office, now located in the arcade building. Instead of putting things up higher, he loaded the new shipment of bandages and medicines into his Model T. He was especially glad that a supply of back-ordered alcohol had arrived Friday afternoon. He had a gut feeling that he would need it in the coming days to disinfect wounds. He made sure his medical bag was completely full, adding extras of everything, until he was barely able to close it. As the gusts of wind blew more often and the water in the street got deeper, he made several trips to the car with supplies.

He was about to grab other things when he heard a shout from the direction of the Lone Cypress.

"Tha dike's going! Tha dike's goin'! Tha- dike's breakin' crost tha canal."

"Must be by pump #1."

Knowing that the spill out would soon obliterate the entire levy, Drew hurriedly got into his car and drove the four blocks to his house. It was a long drive. He prayed his car would not stall out, as the water was getting higher and higher. Water lapped above the running boards. Debris flew against the car and odds and ends were hurled through the air. Periodically, chunks of muck splattered the windshield, making visibility even harder.

As he approached the corner to turn west toward home, movement to the east, toward the canal, caught his eye. The surging water pushed Mae's Cafe at the foot of the street from its foundation. The building began to float with the current, battering light and telephone poles, slowly twisting and bowing as it moved southward toward the Moore Haven Hotel.

The great Okeechobee was reclaiming her land.

Drew met Mary Elizabeth at the door carrying blankets.

Her eyes were full of fear and her voice full of anger.

It was only then that he realized he had never even told her where he was going last night.

The howling of the ever-increasing wind failed to cover the wrath in her tone of voice.

"I'm taking the girls to the clubhouse to be with other families," she cried. "Last night several of us agreed to meet there if the storm got worse. I have to be with someone. You seem to never, never be here for us."

"I'm so sorry, Mary. I'm so sorry. I was just getting to the party last night when Fred met me and I went with him to try to save the dike. It is really beginning to look bad."

In spite of the apology and the explanation, Mary Elizabeth found it hard to forgive him for not being with her during these last anxious hours.

"I already have everything over there for the girls' party and I'm taking a few more things in case we have to stay the night," she coolly responded.

Ignoring her attitude, he urged her to get going.

"The water is rising fast, Mary. Take the girls and go. I'm going to put up my car and then I'll be right over."

He scooped up both girls in his arms and carried them to the car. As Mary Elizabeth arrived with her provisions, he put a load of medical supplies in the back seat.

Drew yelled instructions to Mary Elizabeth. "Get someone to help you unload these boxes. I'm afraid we're going to be needing them very soon."

Drew knew he had to be fast if he was going to get to the clubhouse at all. He drove his car into the garage and ran into the house. He opened every window half way and opened the front and back doors.

He shuddered at the thought of the 19 feet of water that might soon be covering his house.

Having the windows open would keep the air pressure from building up inside the house and might keep the pressure of the flowing water from destroying the house by allowing it to run through.

The water was lapping at the back door as he prepared to leave. When he felt how fierce the wind was blowing and how deep the water was, he realized he might not be able to get through.

He had brought his bag with him, fearing that it wouldn't be unloaded from Mary's car. Knowing he would need both arms for swimming and holding on to things, he secured the bag with a necktie he had left in his pocket from the party the night before.

In no time he had made a couple of secure knots around the handles and dropped the makeshift rope with the bag attached around his neck. He hoped that his knots would hold.

By the time he had crossed the porch, the water was half way up his legs and the winds had increased in intensity.

Hesitating only a moment, he plunged into the fast-flowing river surging across his back yard. Faced with hurricane-force winds, combined with the swift-moving water, Drew knew the only way to get to the clubhouse was to grab onto trees and shrubs that had not yet been loosened by wind or water.

He pushed himself from tree to tree, a distance of only a few feet, but a distance that almost seemed impossible to bridge on more than one occasion. Once he had pushed off, he was able to swim to the next tree or structure.

He caught on to an orange tree next to the chicken coop. The children's cat, Whiskers, was crying forlornly from the roof, her sharp claws her salvation as she clung to the boards. Drew knew the scared little animal would probably scratch him to death, but he reached for her anyway. The cat surprised him by jumping into his arms and snuggling into his shirt.

The powerful winds whipped shingles and pieces of tin away from buildings and sent them flying through the air. Likewise branches and limbs cracked and fell around him. Once, a large branch trapped him momentarily, before floating on by.

A double row of pine trees that had been planted as a buffer between his house and the Women's Clubhouse gave him the last help he needed. Knowing the taproots of the pines were deep and would probably hold, he aimed first for those, then, tree after tree, inched his way between the two houses.

A 15-foot board flew through the air like a big spear that had been hurled, barely missing him. He was within five feet of the clubhouse porch when he was blown to the back of the property. He once again attempted to reach the clubhouse, but found the water too deep and too swift. He swam to a little tree not ten feet away and rested. White-capped waves attested to the wind's ferocity. A large limb from a nearby tree snapped and missed him by inches. The wind cut him like a knife, shredding both his shirt and his flesh.

He inched his way closer and closer to the house by swimming from tree to tree until he finally reached the back door. Ben Shorter and Jerome Potter grabbed him before the wind could snatch him again and pulled him into the kitchen.

No sooner was he across the threshold than the wind tore the open door from its hinges and hurled it across the yard.

"Thanks, boys. If my house weren't next door, I wouldn't have made it over here. I almost didn't anyway."

"We know. We were watching you and praying. Everyone is upstairs. The water is rising fast! Your wife sent us down to look for you and to get the girls' cakes she stored on top of the icebox," yelled Ben above the wind.

They found the cakes. One was covered with ants; the other, in a tight tin, was dry and pest free. Drew grabbed the three candles off the first cake and stuck them in his shirt pocket together with a box of matches. He was about to leave the kitchen when he saw some gaily-wrapped presents through the glass doors of the kitchen cabinets.

"Ben, take the cake. I'm going to see if I can't find a way to get these presents upstairs, too."

"We're staying with you, Doc, but if you don't hurry we're all going to drown," said Jerome, as he cradled four kerosene lamps and struggled to keep upright.

Drew put the presents and a box of matches in a big roasting pan.

"Let's go!" Drew shouted above the deafening sound of the roaring wind. He put the roaster on top of his head, again secured his medical bag around his neck with his tie, and waded through the house chest deep in water. The cat was still inside his shirt.

By the time they made it to the stairway, water was up above their chests. They turned just in time to see it pour through the open windows. Hyacinths, sticks, and several snakes came in with the water.

Drew thought to himself, "I'm glad someone opened the doors and windows here. If this ever happens again, I am not risking my life for my house like I have today."

Water was on the fifth step as the men reached the door to attic room.

"Drew!"

Mary Elizabeth ran to him when he entered the room.

"I was so worried. I have been watching you struggling against the wind and water. I didn't think you were going to make it."

Drew set the roaster on a table and took the bag from his mouth before his wife reached him. He held her while she sobbed.

Whiskers let out a loud meow as Mary Elizabeth squeezed Drew.

Mollie ran to get her cat from her father's arms.

The wet cat looked like an otter when she jumped out of Drew's open shirt. She was soon happily licking her mistress all over her face.

"Mary, we were able to save one cake. The other was covered with hundreds of ants. I have their presents too. Will you help me dry out my bag?"

"You need drying out yourself – and you are cut all over."

Mary Elizabeth draped a blanket around Drew, then got ointment and dry towels to dress Drew's wounds. She found a towel in her box of supplies and dried all of the instruments and put them into an empty box while water ran out of the bag, then, she put in more dry towels to absorb the rest of the water.

Drew was greeted by 15 of his neighbors who had decided to ride out the storm in the attic room. He smiled when he saw his crates of supplies stacked in the middle of the room.

"Dan, will you help me open these? You never will know when and if we will need the bandages."

The wind howling outside was demonic. As they hovered together, the refugees watched the sides of the house literally move in and out like an asthmatic with labored, uneven breath. They waited for the inevitable moment when the entire place would buckle under the pressure, listening all the while to nearby trees snapping like matchsticks. To make matters worse, the water had risen so much that it was running over the floor and, even though it was just before noon, it was as dark as a moonless night.

Most huddled in family groups, petrified and praying. Screams of hurt animals were interspersed with the screams of the wind. One of the overriding fears was that some of the cries that sounded like wildcats screeching in the night were not wildcats at all, but fellow humans, lost in the darkness. They could only hope and pray that the sounds were animals and not their neighbors. But deep down, they knew.

Finally, Drew and Dan felt compelled to walk over to the front windows. Through the darkness they could only see a wall of rain beating against the house. Limbs and tin were carried through the air by the wind. A big limb came crashing through a window on the east side of the room, sending glass everywhere. Luckily no one was hit by either the limb or the glass.

Outside, where visibility was less than fifty yards, those who dared to put their face next to an open window, peered out.

"Doc, didn't your wife park her car by the front steps? Look what's happening to it!"

They watched as the car half flew and half floated out of viewing range.

"Look!" said several at once.

"There's a house! Where did it come from?"

The group watched as the house was swept by the clubhouse. Had it been moving slightly differently, it would have hit them. Luther Sterns said in a very calm soft voice,

"That looks like it's my house."

Luther lived on the next corner up to the east. Drew and Ben returned to their families. Water continued to rise until it reached their knees. The children were placed on top of tables as the men started hammering at the slanted roof to provide an escape hatch.

There was a sense of relief as they broke through the top. The frightened group all crowded into the other end of the room to stay out of the gushing rain. Drew sat on a large round table with his arms around Mary Elizabeth and his daughters, listening to the wailing wind as it ripped at the trees and the house.

At last, the water quit rising, but the howling wind didn't subside. Drew feared that the roof would go at any moment. Worse still, he feared the house could be ripped apart or blown from the pilings on which it sat as it swayed and trembled.

All of a sudden, there was a loud pop and pieces of glass went flying everywhere. Every window on the north side of the house had been blown out. Almost everyone in the room was cut.

Mary Elizabeth, knowing that at any minute she could lose her remaining two children, became hysterical. Drew pulled his wife closer, attempting to comfort her.

Others in the room were ashen, thinking their fates were also sealed. They waited for the house to split apart.

Drew reluctantly pulled away from his family to assess the cuts. Only Caroline Lynch was seriously injured. He removed a large fragment of glass that was embedded in her cheekbone right below her eye. Blood poured profusely from the open wound. The cut took ten stitches to close.

Rain now poured in through the broken windows as well as the hole in the roof. They could plainly hear the shingles being torn away, one by one, as the wind howled and bit at the roof like a mad dog intent on tearing his prey into shreds.

The neighbors huddled closer and closer together. It was impossible to move anywhere in the room without getting wet. The children started singing old familiar songs and, when the adults joined in, the entire atmosphere of the room changed. Expressions of fear that had been on everyone's faces were no longer there.

Drew felt a peace come over him and wondered if others felt the same. Outside this room all his earthly possessions were probably gone, but inside he had his family. That was what mattered most in the world. He looked down at Mollie singing and petting her cat. Why they even had the family pet!

The wind stopped blowing that afternoon shortly after 3 p.m. The drenched survivors rejoiced they had made it through the storm. They carefully made their way to the broken window and looked out to survey the damage.

"Thank God! This nightmare is finally over," said Drew. "And we're all in one piece, we're high and somewhat dry, and from what I see in the boxes, I think we've enough food. Who wants to come with me to take a look outside?"

"I hate to burst your bubble, Doc," said Michael Hill. "This is just a lull in the storm. When I was 16, I was in the hurricane that hit Galveston. Everything was real quiet for a good while and people went outside and celebrated. Then the wind came again from another direction, worse than before. That's when most of the people drowned."

"Worse! You've got to be joking! How could it be worse?"

For the first time there was fear in Drew's voice.

"Daddy, I'm cold," Mollie said.

Drew sat down with the joy drained from him.

"Will you get me the pretty quilt?" Mollie asked,

"I'll see if there are any dry blankets left, Baby."

Mary Elizabeth had put the box of blankets on top of a chest of drawers that was high and semi-dry.

When Drew found Flora's quilt and wrapped it around his daughter, he remembered Flora's last words, "I's smile dow' from Heave' a' yo' chilluns."

Drew sat holding his family in his arms. He was at last at peace with himself and with God. Oddly enough the storm had drawn them closer together and allowed them to put closure to Thomas's death.

Drew listened to his friends at the windows describing what they saw.

"I can't see any land. It's one big lake. I can only see the very top of the Leggett's roof. I think I see Kevin and his wife hanging on to it! I can see several roofs but they aren't in the right locations. Some look like they are attached to each other. I don't see any bushes and very few trees."

"There are all kinds of things in the water: limbs, tin, wire, water lilies, and hyacinths."

Suddenly gasping, Ben exclaimed, "Oh, my God!"

Others reacted similarly; and several choked back tears with the realization of what the storm had done outside.

"What is it?" Drew demanded.

"Doc, the body of Joe Milton just came floating by."

About six o'clock, just as Michael had predicted, the winds started blowing again; this time from the southwest.

The group withdrew from the window and found places to sit that were somewhat dry, bracing themselves for more fierce weather. The roar was even louder than before, sounding like fifty locomotives coming through the house. Drew could only compare the sound to one thing, the terrible sounds of war – only these winds were louder.

The wind ripped away at the escape hole they had made and tore half the roof off. As potential lethal flying objects and rain blew into the room, the storm-weary group tried to find something to shelter themselves from the pelting rain. Drew tried to sleep. He had been up for over thirty-eight hours, but he still found sleep impossible. The wind outside sounded like a hundred steam whistles blowing all at once.

Every time the house shook, its occupants screamed. Sometimes the shaking was violent. They could only imagine what would happen next. For the next four hours the wet souls in the attic room shivered and held on to each other. Gradually the rain began to fall more naturally and, at long last, about 10 p.m., the winds stopped. Although they were aware of the change, they sat frozen in their huddles; not believing their day from Hell was over. The silence of the night overwhelmed them. The darkness of the night replaced the darkness of the storm.

When the rain stopped completely, a beautiful full moon shown through the gaping holes in the roof. Stars twinkled as if it was another night in paradise.

The women lit lamps the men had brought up from the kitchen earlier. The light gave a soft glow to the room where they had spent the terrifying day and would spend the rest of the night.

There ate some of the leftover sandwiches from the party that seemed to have been held weeks ago, but in reality had been only a day before. Cokes were plentiful because wooden cases of Coca-Cola were stacked to the ceiling for the Women's Club's functions.

After they ate, Drew said, "Now we can be thankful that we have all survived this storm. I know most of us are wondering and worrying about what we'll find outside tomorrow, but for tonight let's celebrate my daughters' birthdays."

He took the tin down from the high shelf where it had been placed and took out the cake.

"Girls, you'll have to share this cake, too."

He put on three extra candles for Gail. The group sang 'Happy Birthday' as the two girls blew out their candles.

"Hey, Doc! You have too many candles on that cake. I thought your girls were six and two today. I count ten candles," said Jennifer Moore.

Mollie said, "We are. We get an extra candle to grow on."

Jennifer grinned and said, "I always got an extra lick on my birthday spanking for that. Look around you. There are fifteen people ready to spank you."

Mollie was horrified at the idea. "Daddy! Don't let them spank me!" she pleaded.

"I think we will forget the spanking this year."

"I love you, Daddy."

Mollie gave her daddy a hug and a kiss.

"Mollie. Gail. Look what I have."

Mary Elizabeth pulled the roaster from the high shelf and took out the gifts. The girls tore into their packages. They both had dolls and doll clothes for them.

"The dolls are from your daddy and me. The clothes are from Miss Mollie and Mr. Charlie. Miss Mollie made them for you. She told me to give you a kiss and she would be thinking about you."

Mary Elizabeth gave each of her daughters a kiss.

Drew commented, "Bet she will really be thinking about us when she hears about the storm. I'd hate to be in her son's shoes trying to keep her from coming down here!"

"Oh, Daddy. Where's Mr. Charlie?"

"I promise to check on him tomorrow, darling."

"I think I have something else for you girls."

He reached into the side pocket of his bag.

"Mary," Drew whispered in his wife's ear, "where are the calico packages that were in my bag?"

She pointed to the shelf above his head. Drew reached up and brought down two presents wrapped in wet calico cloth.

292

"Sorry, but these were in my bag and got wet. I hope they will dry out. These are from Gopher, Moon Flower, and Little Boy."

The girls loosened the ribbon from the cloth. Inside each they found a multicolored cloth bracelet and a Seminole doll made from sweet grass and the fibers of the palm. They were dressed in the same fashion as the Seminole women and each had multiple rows of tiny multi-colored beads around their necks.

"They are so pretty! May I please go out and thank him?"

"Soon, I promise."

Drew hadn't completely told the truth and was having twinges of guilt. He had slipped the bracelets Lou had made in with Gophers' gifts so no questions would be asked. Gail held both of her new dolls tightly to her as she fell asleep in her mother's arms.

As Drew looked down at Mollie dressing her doll in different outfits, he thought, "This was a birthday for the history books."

Drew looked up as Jerome shouted from the window on the west side of the room.

"Come look! See that light way over there about a mile or so. What is it do you suppose? There aren't any two-story houses in that direction and everything else has to be underwater. Do you suppose it's a boat?"

Drew thought to himself before he made any wild guesses.

"Fellows, I think I know what it is. I'm almost sure that's a light at Charlie Carter's."

"I think you're right. That's about where his house should be. We have laughed for years about his house in the sky."

"He used his engineering skills to brace it, too. No little wind like the one we had today would blow that house down."

All the men laughed.

"I had the builders brace my house, too. I hope that did the trick even though I know my house is submerged, as is my office. Judging from where the water level is in here, I would guess the water must be about two feet above his floor."

"I guess we will never laugh at his tree house again!"

Through the darkness everyone kept watching the beacon in the south. It gave them hope and reassured them that they weren't the only survivors.

The attic's refugees were awake as the sunlight came through the roof and glassless windows. The water had receded several feet from the night before. In its place, inside the house, were six inches of mud and trash. All but the smallest children gathered at the northern windows.

What they saw was unbelievable. Absolutely no foliage was left. They saw friends and neighbors hanging on to roofs, chimneys, and limbs of trees.

Not five feet below them a woman with a baby tied to her floated into view.

"That's Mary Helen Crosby and her baby!"

Someone screamed, "They're DEAD!"

The women became hysterical when they saw their friend. She had helped Mary Elizabeth with the party Friday night. They had been with her less than thirty hours before.

It wasn't long before the horror intensified.

A lone man floated by holding onto a door. His clothes were torn to shreds and he shivered in the early morning wetness.

"What's it like out there?" hollered Preston Lynch. "Do you want to join us here?"

The man turned toward the voice but did not respond.

Only when he looked up did Preston recognize that the battered man was the teller at the bank. His face was expressionless and his eyes vacant.

"Julian, paddle over here and stay with us!"

Again, there was no response.

Instead, before their eyes, they watched the man slip off the door into the black water and go under. The horrors of the night had apparently been too much for the banker.

Sam Hogan summed up what they all already knew. "This is a horrible situation. I'm afraid the things that we all will face when we leave this room will be worse, but today is Sunday and we need to praise the Lord that we have made it through the storm and ask him to give us strength to get through the days of turmoil which are ahead of us."

Many in the group were reluctant to pray. They thought of their homes, crops, and businesses that lay in ruin. They thought about Mary Helen and her baby. They thought about all the others who had died in the past twenty hours. Why should they thank a God who would allow such tragedies to happen?

But, even those with their faiths shaken and their beliefs battered, joined together in a circle, holding hands while Sam gave a prayer of thanksgiving. Mollie sang *Jesus Loves Me*, following the prayer. The weary group spent the next half-hour singing songs of praise and thanksgiving. There was not a dry eye when Eloise Gorga lifted her high soprano voice and sang, '*Til the Storm Passes By.*

Chapter 31

STORM'S AFTERMATH
September 19, 1926

Anxious to get out to see the damage, the men opened the door to the stairway downstairs. When they saw only the top two steps, they knew the level of the water was just below 12 feet – the height of the ceiling.

Resigned to the fact that they were going no place soon, they ate breakfast – more sandwiches. As Drew ate, he watched Whiskers leap from the arms of Mollie to the rafters where she feasted on water soaked rats.

Mary Elizabeth had been through flooding before and knew what was above her head the minute Whiskers leaped. She dared not look up.

In the next two hours Drew watched the water as it slowly receded.

"That's what I was waiting for!" he shouted as he jumped up. "The water is below the sixth step and below the tops of the windows. I can get out of this house and into mine. I'm going to swim over to my house and check it out. I'll try to get into the pantry and bring back some canned food because it looks like we're going to be here for a while. Does anyone want to come with me?"

Sam volunteered to go.

"We can raid the pantry at my house, too," he said.

Both men cautiously inched their way down the treacherous, mud covered stairs and slowly eased themselves into the dark water. Although some light was coming in from the outside, it was not enough to help them detect everything in the water. They swam from the stairs to the windows, carefully avoiding debris and dead animals.

They quickly ascertained the best course to Drew's house and lost no time heading there.

As they were swimming over what had been the lawns that separated the Women's Club and the Duncan home, the biggest alligator Drew had ever seen was lying on a pile of rubbish in their path. He estimated the reptile to be at least fifteen feet long. Wondering if he had survived the storm only to be the meal of this creature, Drew was relieved to see no movement from the animal as they swam past him. The alligator seemed to respect the fact that the men were also survivors.

By the time they reached Drew's house they were exhausted from the current and from dodging masses of debris. They held on to the doorframe of Drew's former front door and rested.

"I know that 'gator, Doc," Sam panted. "Did you notice that he only had one eye? I was with Clyde Riley the day he shot his eye out several years ago; now people call the old gator One Eyed Riley. He's become somewhat of a legend and people sure get all excited when they spot him. I think he was so tired from fighting the storm himself that we were never in any danger."

"Well, I'm glad he didn't know you were there when he was shot. Tired or not, he probably would have had his revenge! I hope he doesn't recover his memory soon. We do have to come back this way!"

The Duncan's house was still on its posts and was almost intact. Drew could tell the water had reached the attic room, just as it had in the Woman's Club. He could not tell if the roof was still in place or not.

They entered through the front door opening, swam through the living room and dining room and into the kitchen.

They began to gather cans of food, now without any labels to identify the contents. They found four burlap bags on the top shelf and filled them half full with the cans. Drew fumbled through a submerged kitchen drawer and found a can opener.

As they started back through the living room, they saw two water moccasins coiled up together on the mantle. They had missed them on their first trip through.

"Don't even think that they were swimming in the room with us when we came in!" said Drew. "Let's not tell the women. Okay?"

They struggled with the bags of canned goods and returned to the clubhouse without incident. Mary Elizabeth welcomed her wet husband with a blanket when he walked up all but two steps.

"Is anything left in the house?" she asked in a weak voice. "I can see big openings in the roof from the window."

"Our house looks like it rode out the storm well. The front porch and front door are gone. I don't know about the windows and I know, as you said, we will have to have a new roof. I don't know what we can save inside. Time will tell."

Tears momentarily welled up in Mary Elizabeth's eyes, but she gathered her composure when she realized that at least all her family was still safe.

"Drew, we have our girls and one fat happy cat. Look!"

They both looked and saw Whiskers who was finishing yet another rat.

"Doc, are you ready to go to my house?" asked Sam, who was obviously anxious to check on conditions there.

"Just a second. Mary, what's in most of the cans in the pantry? They don't have labels anymore."

"Mostly vegetables."

Sam asked his wife, "What is in our pantry?"

"We have cans of meat and there are jars of vegetables, fruits, and jellies. I don't have any sacks though."

The women emptied the sacks and gave them back to the men. They

296

were promptly on their way to the Shrader house, which was just behind the clubhouse. Conditions were the same as they had been at Drew's. They found canned meat but found only a few jars that weren't broken. Sam thought he had found one intact but when he was lifting it out of the water, he sliced his hand.

"We need to get you back and get that treated and bandaged. I would hate to see you get an infection from that cut after you weathered the storm so well."

As they left the house, they saw a man at the edge of the garage, hanging on to a pile of wood.

"I'll go check on him," Drew volunteered. "I'll bring him with me when I bring the cans."

"You can't do both."

"I can make two trips. I want you out of this water as fast as you can. Have someone clean that cut the best they can. I'll be there shortly to look at it better. Now go!"

As Sam dog paddled on his side trying to keep his hand out of the murky water, Drew swam to the garage, leaving the sack in the branches of an orange tree that had been completely stripped of its bark.

Drew swam up to the man, calling out so he wouldn't startle him if he were sleeping. Getting no response, Drew reached out and touched the man's shoulder, realizing immediately he was dead. He turned the victim around just enough to enable him to identify the man as a farmer who had moved in with his family only a week ago. Whether the man had drowned or had died of fright or in some other way through the horrible night, Drew couldn't tell.

After a few attempts at trying to free the body, he gave up. The dead man's legs were tangled in the wood which held his lifeless body secure. There was nothing he could do, so, with a heavy heart, he retrieved the sack and returned to the clubhouse.

Sam's wife was drying his hand when Drew returned to the attic room. Sam questioned Drew with his eyes and got his answer immediately with the returned expression.

Drew medicated Sam's hand and then put in twelve stitches. As he wrapped it in bandages he said, "Sam, I think your swimming days are over for awhile. You need to stay here and keep dry."

"Mary Elizabeth?" Drew asked. "Do you mind if I go out to see what I can do? I know there are people who need me."

"When do you have to ask my permission? But how are you going to help anyone without supplies?"

"Remember our old rowboat? I saw that the shed hasn't been too damaged. I thought I would swim over and see if I could get the boat out. If I can, I'll come back here to get my bag and supplies."

To the others in the room he said, "I'm going to try and see if my boat floats. When I come back, I would like to have two of you go with me to see if there are people out there we can help."

"Watch out for One Eyed Riley!" shouted Sam as Drew started down the stairs. Drew heard Mary Elizabeth question Sam as he walked farther down the stairs.

Alone, Drew stared into the murky water, containing what seemed to be the remnants of the entire town. So much trash was in the water Drew thought it might be easier to hop from one pile to the next. He again swam the distance to his house, trying to avoid the debris.

Once again he swam past the gator. He rested when he reached the edge of his house, then swam to the back, past the bedroom, and on to the shed that was attached to the garage. Miracle of miracles, his old rowboat was hanging there just as he left it years ago. He swam to the boat, took it off its hooks, and let it drop into the water hoping it wouldn't sink from the water inside. Amazingly the boat was dry.

When it was on the outside of the shed, Drew pulled himself into it. A half dozen rats and squirrels scurried out of the boat as he sat down to row with the old oars still in their holders.

As he pulled out into the sunlight he saw two big black snakes coiled up together in the bow of the boat. He prayed they weren't cottonmouths. He looked again and saw that they were indigos. Like oil on water, their rainbow colors reflected off their sleek bodies.

He was too tired to push them out.

He rowed to the Women's Club and tied up to a post, then climbed the stairs to see if anyone would volunteer to go with him.

Luther Simmons, a very calm-mannered bookkeeper, and David Duffy, a strong husky farmer, were ready to go. The men helped Drew take his medical supplies down to the boat and Drew introduced them to the snakes, their companions for the day.

"I know we don't have water to spare, but we do have more than our share of food. Let's go back up and get some cans. Better yet, I left a lot over in my pantry. Let's go over there."

Drew rowed the boat back past the giant gator who was still resting on the rubble pile. He rowed the boat around his house to the back porch. It was closer to the kitchen than going through the front. They secured the boat next to a piece of what had been a part of the back porch, then moved slowly through the house where the water was still waist high, shuffling their feet to keep from being cut by some hidden object.

Drew remembered the moccasins and said, "We need to be careful. Anything could be in the water."

The only animals that were seen on that visit were a couple of black bass, each about six pounds each.

Finally, they managed to get to the pantry where they soon had emptied the shelves. After taking a supply to the boat, they scavenged through the drawers to find some sharp knives to use as can openers.

Before leaving the house, they rowed over to Drew's garage where they found a shovel and axe to take with them. Then they headed for a nearby garage apartment owned by Maude and Kevin Leggett.

"Hello. Is anyone up there?" yelled Drew.

Several faces appeared.

"Do you need food or medical assistance?"

"We're wet but we're fine," said Kevin's brother, Kirk.

"We have plenty of food. This is where Maude stores her canning. We took refuge here when the water started rising and have been thankful we were two stories up, but we haven't seen Maude and Kevin since the storm began. They were in their house over there the last time we saw them."

Drew remembered that he saw someone on the Leggett's roof the day before and rowed around the house to see if they – or anyone else – might have survived the storm by clinging to the roof. With a great sense of relief, they found both of the Leggetts on the roof. Both were completely naked and shivering from exposure and their bodies looked as if they had been flogged. Blood ran from numerous open cuts, blending with the dark water.

"God, Doc! I'm glad to see you," yelled Kevin. "Didn't think I'd ever see anyone in this world again."

A cypress tree that grew close to their house gave them a way to climb down to the boat, although the boat could just hold one of them at a time. Kevin held tight to his wife until David was able to pull her on into the boat. Drew gave the freezing woman his jacket, which also covered her nakedness. The crew then paddled over to the garage apartment where she was deposited, along with Drew, who stayed to dress her wounds.

David and Luther immediately left to go back for her husband.

As Drew and Maude climbed the steps the group inside gave enthusiastic yells of welcome.

"When you get something on her, try to get her as warm as possible. She was on that roof for this whole time. If you don't have anything dry, just huddle around her to give her warmth from your bodies. And get some hot food down her. Thank God you have a kerosene stove here."

Drew was waiting for the boat when it pulled up with Kevin. The doctor quickly applied salve to the worst of his injuries. He had found a blanket inside the apartment to use in covering Kevin.

"Tell them to take care of you the same as they are caring for your wife," Drew said as he and his two helpers rowed west.

One block looked the same as the other. Houses were off their foundations, some were washed down the block, and some were completely turned around. Several were so badly broken up that they looked as if they had exploded. Few roofs remained. Power and telephone lines were hanging loose, twisted, or completely down. None of the poles were upright. They were leaning at various degrees or completely down. Multitudes of trees were down with their massive roots exposed.

The men were led from one place to another by the cries of survivors, those either calling for help or the incessant sobbing of agony. They found people clinging to partial roofs and they found others in the limbs of trees. Almost without exception the survivors stared at their rescuers with glassy eyes, just one of the manifestations of disbelief of what they had experienced and lived through. All were cold and in need of food and blankets. Drew and his companions were able to provide food but not the blankets. They promised they would send rescuers back as soon as possible.

Survivor after survivor shared the horror of the past 24 hours.

Bodies had snagged in the branches of trees or were wedged between piles of debris. The rescuers stopped counting the dead after reaching one hundred.

They rowed up to a guava tree where they found Katie Smith, a young mother of three children.

"Doc! Where are my babies? Have you seen my babies?"

Her babies were all less than four years old.

The crazed woman was clinging to the tree but looked as if she would lose her grip at any moment. Drew reached out and tried to help her from the tree. When he touched her she recoiled and grabbed a small limb. She kicked and screamed at any rescue attempt he made. Understanding that she was in shock, Luther climbed the tree while Drew tried to soothe her fears. Luther pried Katie's arms from the branch and she fell into Drew's open arms.

They wrapped the dazed woman in a blanket and put her safely in the middle of the boat. Neither wanted to think about what might have happened to her children.

"Let's go to the Mayflower. Surely a hotel that large survived the storm. There should be someone there who can take care of Katie," Drew directed.

As they approached the Mayflower, Luther yelled, "Look! I believe the hotel has been turned around. That's the back porch that I see."

They rowed the boat close to the hotel and Drew climbed through an open window. Luther gently led Katie across the boat to the window, where Drew pulled her through to safety.

As soon as they were through the window, Drew witnessed another scene that would become commonplace throughout the next few days.

"Katie? Is that you? Is that really you?" a weak voice called from the corner.

Katie's husband, Harvey, limped over and took his wife in his arms, burying his head in her shoulder and sobbing.

"I'm so sorry I wasn't with you during the storm. We finished putting canned goods and groceries at White Star on the top shelves and when I headed home it was impossible to get through. I ended up spending the night with the Nortons."

"I kept trying to leave. I kept trying to get to you and the children, but

Mr. Norton wouldn't let me go. As soon as the wind quit, he couldn't stop me…but I don't have any idea why I'm here and not home."

Gradually, Harvey got himself under control, only to realize his children were not present.

"Where are the children?" he asked.

His wife's anguished look told him everything.

Drew's eye's swept the room as he asked if anyone needed medical assistance.

"Speaking for everyone," answered Linda McGuire, the manager of the hotel, "I think all of us who have been together since yesterday have faired pretty well. We're just exhausted, cold, and wet – nothing you can do for us. Harvey showed up just a few minutes before you arrived."

She continued, "He has a long, deep gash from his knee to his ankle. I was trying to clean it up when he saw Katie come through the window."

Drew sewed up a long cut on the side of Harvey's right leg as he held his crying wife. He reassured his wife that they would find their children. He sounded so convincing that Drew knew that Harvey believed what he was saying

The hotel's manager then began her story of the night of horror.

"Oh, Doc! We were scared to death when the building shook and turned around. As if that wasn't scary enough, the oil storage tanks from the Gulf plant floated toward us and barely missed hitting the edge of the hotel. I guess we are better off than most people out there. We at least have dry blankets and food."

"How bad are things?" asked a hotel guest.

"You won't believe it, Oscar," said Luther, but he was addressing his remarks to everyone.

"It's worse than anything I saw in the war. There are bodies everywhere. We've seen some that have been decapitated. But there are survivors. It's unbelievable that people were able to spend most of that storm on a rooftop and not be blown away, or hanging on to the branches of a bush. Dead chickens and dogs are out there. We've even seen dead gators, otters, fish and other animals that you think could weather a storm. The whole scene is impossible to describe."

After making sure no more assistance was needed, Drew, David, and Luther loaded the boat with more blankets and canned goods from the hotel. They then rowed to the high school just south of the hotel. As they approached the two-story brick building, Drew thought that the school building was probably the safest in town. Just as he began to wonder if anyone had thought to take refuge there, the blonde head of Andrew Southwood leaned out the English classroom on the second floor.

"Wondered who'd be the first to git out in this mess," the sometimes cowman, sometimes fisherman, all-the-time-no gooder, yelled. "Got food? My family's a mighty hungry."

As the boat pulled close to the school, Drew asked, "Andy, how many of you are in the school? Is anyone hurt?"

"We're all okay, Doc. It's jus' me an' my kin."

Ten little tow-headed children popped their heads out of the other windows. They were at least six feet above the boat. "We'll be able to throw some cans up, but we are too far from you to get blankets up to you."

"Throw th' stuff up, Doc. I'm a good catcher," shouted Mac, the oldest Southwood boy.

Five cans of vegetables were sent hurling to the window where the twelve-year-old easily caught them.

The men waved good-bye to the family and then headed northeast towards the business district. They passed the new courthouse that was under construction and were amazed to see gaping holes in the almost completed brick building. The storm's fury had blown away hundreds of cement blocks from the walls.

As they paddled down Avenue J, they found things essentially the same as where they had been earlier. They continued to give food to wet survivors and handed out one blanket per roof or tree.

"Let's go closer to that next house," Drew said when he realized they were near Anna's home.

Anna Wright and her family were sitting by a huge hole in their roof.

"Miss Anna!"

Drew was thrilled that his nurse was alive.

With a choked voice, Drew asked, "Do you need food, blankets, anything?"

Anna looked straight at Drew, a look of bewilderment on her face. She didn't respond.

Ronnie, Anna's husband, yelled down.

"No one's hurt. We're just wet, cold, and hungry."

Drew climbed the tree beside the house and opened some cans of food. He then put a dry blanket around his nurse. Anna still didn't say a thing.

"Anna, what is it? What's wrong?"

Ronnie spoke again. "Our Joannie isn't here. She spent the night with friends over on Park Avenue. We don't know if she made it."

Tears ran down his cheeks as he held his sobbing wife. Drew promised to keep a sharp eye out for Joannie.

"When we find more boats we'll send someone to take you to a dry place."

Drew and company helped as many as possible as they proceeded past scores of homeless and twice that many bodies.

"Stop a minute!" Drew demanded. "Listen!"

Luther and David sat motionless and tried to hear what Drew heard, but couldn't.

"Doc, what do you hear?" asked David. "I don't hear nothing."

"Exactly! There's not a sound anywhere. Not a bird. Not a frog. Nothing. Don't you find that strange? I knew something else was wrong besides the loss of life we've seen, but it has taken this long to realize what it was – absolute silence."

When they reached the Alamonte Hotel they found the roof was completely off and all the windows on the east side had been blown out. Hoping they would find more survivors inside, they tied up the boat and crawled through a window.

"Thank goodness you're here, Doc!" cried Alvin Beggs as soon as Drew was in the window. He acted like he was expecting Drew to come. "We need you real bad. Those of us who didn't get glass splinters in us when the window blew in, got hurt when the roof and the rafters caved in."

Drew went to the large dining room where he was met with a chorus of "Praise the Lord!"

Drew looked around and saw at least fifty wet, cold people. All were bleeding and bruised. Many of them were suffering from cuts that needed stitching.

"Leave me here, men. This will take a while."

"No, Doc. It looks like you need our help."

David brought supplies from the boat while Luther bandaged those who didn't need stitches. As Drew stitched and dressed wounds, he wondered how many more people needed him. There was as an immediate need for his services here today as there had been in during both wars in which he had served. This, however, was much worse. He could not detach himself from the wounded in the impersonal way he had in the field hospitals. These were his friends – this tragedy was personal!

When Luther, David, and Drew left the hotel they were empty-handed except for Drew's bag and one box of supplies. They were completely out of food.

From the Alamonte, David rowed the boat to the Moore Haven Hotel where they found the huge building completely blown off its foundation. They climbed through a lower story window and sloshed through knee-high muddy water, finding no one on the first floor.

Watching where they put their feet, the rescue team carefully climbed the stairs, avoiding snakes and rats that had taken sanctuary in the dry stairwell.

At the top of the steps, Drew looked up to see the sun shining through enormous gaps in the building's roof. Crowded into the rooms and hallway of the northern wing, they found almost one hundred cold and wet people. They may as well have spent the night outside.

Believing they were completely cut off from the pantry downstairs, they were in desperate need of food. Again the crowd was more than glad to see their rescuers. Drew used the last of his supply of bandages to dress cuts and abrasions.

Mrs. King, the hotel's manager, spoke for the entire group when she said, "I don't want to even imagine what is out there. The wind was so bad we felt this whole place move. We thought it was going to collapse around us. The roar and reverberation was horrible."

"I'm not going to spare words," said Luther. "It's indescribable. There are too many bodies to count. We stopped counting at a hundred. Houses have been blown off their foundations. The Mayflower is facing west now instead of east! This hotel was blown off its foundation."

Drew continued taking care of the wounded. David and Luther, after convincing several men that the floor was safe, took them and Mrs. King in search of dry linens and food. Piled in front of the linen closet's door was litter and rubble from the roof. David went down to the boat and brought back the axe and shovel. After an hour of chopping, pulling, and shoveling they were able to open the door. The roof above the large closet was still intact and sheets, towels, and blankets on all but the lower four shelves were dry. They gathered the linens and took them back down the hall.

"Boys, there's another linen closet directly under this one," said Mrs. King.

She paused as she remembered that water had reached the second floor a few hours earlier.

"I guess that won't do us much good, will it? But, if you can get to the kitchen pantry, you will find it stocked full. I received a train carload of canned goods Friday morning. Can openers are in the cabinet across from the sink. I would go down with you but I know what is swimming and crawling in that water!"

Ten men volunteered to go downstairs into the snake-infested water. They armed themselves with large pieces of wood. Although the water was knee high, everything on the first floor was fairly accessible. They carried cans and openers up to the hungry guests.

"Here, have a can of surprise for dinner."

Drew smiled slightly as he tossed cans that were minus their labels.

"Mrs. King, may we take cans out to others?"

When she heartily agreed, he continued.

"Now, may I ask one more favor? Would you be willing to tear up some of your sheets for me? I can use them for bandages. My supply is depleted."

Several men helped load the boat with cans and blankets. They would like to have gone on the rescue mission, but there was no room in the boat.

From the hotel, Drew, Luther, and David proceeded to the waterfront hoping to find usable boats. At the docks they found only mass destruction. The scene they saw was surreal – it looked like a war zone. All the docks were gone. Their remnants floated in the water like kindling wood. Most boats, those still recognizable, were sunk or were over on their sides.

One high-sided fishing boat, sitting upright, looked as if it had escaped damage. They paddled over, eager to have one more boat to help in the rescue efforts.

As they pulled up beside the larger boat, David grabbed its side to hoist himself aboard. The boat tilted and all three men screamed in surprise and fear. Hundreds of snakes were intertwined and knotted like earthworms in a can ready for a fishing trip.

A gaping hole was on the opposite side of the boat, apparently in just the right location for the snakes to swim through as they sought refuge from the storm and the current. They had anchored themselves to one another as they, too, became desperate to survive.

Not caring what species of snakes were in the boat, the rescue team found new energy to paddle fast. They had not found one usable boat.

The horror of the snakes was intensified as they looked beyond the shattered docks toward the area they knew was the main stream of the Caloosahatchee River. A swift current was sweeping bodies down toward Lake Hicpochee.

They paddled north to the Lone Cypress. It was still standing straight and tall, although bare of any foliage. Drew wondered how many storms of this magnitude the tree had withstood over the hundreds of years of its life.

Not far beyond the tree they saw a girl's body lying face down in the water near the railroad bridge. Her long blond hair was entangled in its gears. Drew knew instinctively it was Joannie Wright.

They paddled southwest to the business district. They could see that this part of town had weathered the storm the best. Since the big fire, most of the structures were now made of cement block. If made of wood, stricter building codes were adhered to. As they drew nearer, they could hear what seemed like a hundred voices calling at once. People were yelling from windows up and down the street.

"Glory to God!" shouted Drew. "I didn't think that many people survived in the whole town!"

The rescue team got out of the boat at Parkinson's General store, a new store that had been built of concrete after the big fire. Here they found the most fortunate refugees of their journey. Thirty-five people had taken shelter in the store's upstairs storage area. Half the room was filled with canned goods containing everything from meat to applesauce and milk. Most notably, all the cans had labels! Among many other things, crates of soft drinks and blankets were piled to the ceiling. Drew couldn't help adding some comic relief to the tragedy.

"You folks are living the good life. You're the only ones in town who know what to expect when you open a can. Also, you are the first dry people we have seen! Mr. Parkinson, we have food that we confiscated from Mrs. King. May we come back here and get more when we run out?"

"Of course, Doc. Do you need anything else?"

"We could use can openers, knives, and blankets, and any bandages, if you happen to have any."

Loaded down with what Drew had asked for, they floated down the length of Main Street. They could find no one in need of anything. Most of the merchants who lived over their stores were already in their shops trying to salvage what they could. Drew looked up to the place his first office had been, over Dowd's Drug Store.

"Look, if I had stayed there I wouldn't have had much, if any, damage. Let's go on down to the arcade building and check out my present office."

The boat stopped in front of Higgins' store. Drew called up to their apartment.

"Jacob, are you okay up there?"

Jacob could be heard but not seen.

"Doc, I dare not come out on the porch. We are alive if that is what you mean."

His voice didn't sound like he was happy about it. Drew made a promise that he would talk to Jacob as soon as possible. They had a special bond between them because of the deaths of their sons.

Drew had known what they would find long before they reached the arch at the entrance to the arcade. He wasn't surprised to find the water still standing about four feet deep in the long hall that lead to his office.

"Doc, you want to go in there?" asked David, who was rowing. "It's really dark and spooky in there."

"No, we won't go through the arcade. Let's go around to the back door."

Drew closed his eyes when they rounded the corner of the building.

His heart sank to his feet when David exclaimed, "Oh, my God!"

Reluctantly, he opened his eyes. It was worse than he had imagined it would be. There was a big gap where his office had been. The roof was completely gone and so were the north and east walls. If anything at all was left, it was submerged under water.

"Doc! Doctor Duncan!"

Drew looked up through his blurry teary eyes to see Nancy Watts, a heavy-set woman with very few teeth, and her four ragged children. They lived in the Higgins' back apartment and they all came running down the steps as Nancy yelled to Drew.

"Doc! I hope that you won't be mad at us because you have done so much for us."

Drew knew she was referring to the fact that she hadn't paid for their medicines or the birth of her last two children.

"What is it, Nancy?"

"Well, when the waters started really rising after you left Saturday, we broke into your office."

"Why are you telling me this? Look at the place. I never would have known."

"Well, my man said that the lake was a coming and that everything on ground level would be washed away. We was lucky to be on the top floor. He said that since we were so close and owed you so much, we should break in and git what we could. We couldn't git none of the big stuff but we did manage to git some. We made four trips before the wind picked up and the water moved in. We couldn't go no more. Do you wanta come up and see what we got?"

Drew was compelled to see what they had salvaged from his office.

"I know that this is selfish and we need to move on, but I need to go up there. If you want to go on, I'll swim and catch up."

"Don't be silly, Doc. We'll wait for you."

Drew climbed the stairs. One of the small bedrooms was filled with things from his office. The first things that caught his eye were his diplomas and pictures from the walls. There were also fans, the sterilizing equipment, lamps, and his medical books! He saw boxes of bandages and medicines of every description including the whiskey he had bought illegally for medicinal purposes.

He then walked through the kitchen to the front room. He wanted to thank Bill for saving so much. What he found was a man who had passed out on the couch. In his hand was an empty fifth of whiskey. Drew hugged Nancy and her children.

"Thank you so much; you have made me a very happy man."

"I'll be obliged if you would take one thing with you now."

"What's that, Nancy?"

"Take the whiskey. My man gets real mean when he drinks. Prohibition or not, he finds booze."

"Are you going to be okay when he wakes up and finds it all gone?"

"Sure. He'll be sober then," she lied.

Drew looked through the glass doors of the cupboards in the kitchen where they were standing. All the shelves were empty.

"Nancy, don't you have anything to eat?"

"I was planning on goin' to the store Saturday evenin' when Bill came in with his pay. Even though he came home early, the stores were already closed."

"Come with me and bring the kids."

Drew went into the bedroom, got the box of liquor, and carried it down the steps. Nancy and the children followed. Drew handed them a whole box of food, including canned milk.

"Make sure those kids get the milk."

Drew followed them back upstairs carrying blankets. He came down with the same box carrying needed bandages and medicines.

"Doc! Why did you give them so much food? They live on the second floor in a building without much damage. Not even the steps blew down. Look down the block. These are the only steps that I see."

"Boys, you know Bill Bennett."

"Yeah. He's a no good drunken S.O.B."

"Yesterday morning after I left, Bill and Nancy broke into my office. Nancy said it was to save my things and they did save a lot that could never be replaced. They also managed to get my whiskey. I think that was the real motive for the break in. It looks like Bill has been drinking since then. I doubt if he even knows we had a storm."

"So why did you give them so much?"

"There was not one can of food in that house! Those children's clothes had more holes in them than they had fabric. That's why. Maybe I did get carried away."

"It's okay, Doc. But why do you suppose that woman stays shacked up with that no good?"

"Who else would have her?"

"Luther! I don't believe you said that! I've never heard you be ugly before."

"These are not normal times. I see that you confiscated your whiskey. I'm glad he left a little. I sure can use it, for the victims, I mean."

Drew looked at his office again and wondered how so much damage could have been done to his corner when the stairs only a few yards away were not damaged. They headed back toward the hotel to get bandages.

As they passed in front of the bank building, voices shouted greetings from second story apartment windows. No one was hurt here either, and they also had enough to eat.

Nearer the hotel they met another boat. Bill Langton and his son, Bob, had found a boat floating by their house and had jumped in. They had just come from the northern part of town near the railroad tracks. Langton was in tears.

"We have just gone to Mama's. There's nuthn' much standing there. The house is gone. All we saw were my sisters, their husbands, and their youngn's bodies. We looked everywhere for Mama but we can't find her. Have you seen my mama?"

"No, but we promise to look for her. Are you hungry?"

"Yes."

Langton and his son took several cans of baked beans.

"We really could use that boat!" exclaimed David as they pulled away.

"Were you going to ask that man when he is so frantic over his mama?" asked Drew.

When they reached the Moore Haven Hotel again, Mrs. King handed them dozens of sheets that had been torn by the occupants of her hotel. Drew was more than appreciative as they retraced their trail and handed out food and blankets. They then went north as far as the railroad tracks.

Houses were completely gone. Only fragments of roofs, walls, and furniture gave any indication buildings once stood there. There were only a few hardy souls hanging on to whatever they could. They were grateful for the food, blankets, and bandages.

David exclaimed, "Look at the railroad track."

In awe, all three looked at the heavy steel track, twisted like a little girl's braids. Drew wanted to continue north to Lakeview but the food and supplies were exhausted. They would have to restock before going to the Negro section of town. As the boat turned back to the southeast, they saw movement along the railroad track northwest of them.

"What do you suppose that is?" questioned Drew.

"I think its people," said Luther in a matter-a-fact tone.

"Well, let's hope so!" said David in a more excited tone. That track bed would be a good way for those folks from the Quarters to get out. I wonder if they can get all of the way to Newhall."

"I pray those are people," said Drew, still straining to verify the sighting.

"I can imagine what we'll find in Lakeview. It's right on the lake and I don't think any building there would withstand yesterday's storm."

As they turned the boat back toward Parkinson's, all three looked at each other with somber faces, each knowing the body count in Lakeview would be high.

"We really need boats and some help. We've been going for hours and we haven't seen half of the town. We just can't do this by ourselves," Drew said with a yawn.

All three were exhausted but knew they must go on until they had relief. As the boat moved slowly back to Parkinson's, Drew thought of Charlie who had weathered the storm alone.

Was Wanda still alive? What was it like to the west? How did Gopher and Lou weather the storm in chickees?

He was deep in his thoughts when he heard the sound of a motor. He turned his head to see a small motorboat coming from the east. Excitedly, David rowed toward the sound of the motor. The two boats met each other not far from the Lone Cypress. The driver of the powerboat turned off the motor so they could hear.

"I'm Dr. Pat Collins from Clewiston. We heard Moore Haven had been completely wiped off the map. That appears to be right. Even your docks are gone, I see. Looks like some places I saw in France."

Drew noted, "It gets worse than this."

Then he asked, "What condition is Clewiston in?"

"We have extensive damage, but the ridge saved the town from flooding like this. A few injured, none dead. I came over to see if there was anything I could do. Others are waiting for word before they come."

Dr. Collins continued, "I've been asked to find out about Dr. Duncan. Do you know if he made it through?"

"He did." Drew smiled and introduced himself. "And you're the answer to my prayers! You won't believe what you will see. We've seen well over two hundred bodies and we haven't covered half the town."

"Your help is needed all right, as well as any others that can get in here. Would it be okay with you if these two take your boat back to Clewiston to get more volunteers and supplies?"

Dr. Collins paddled his boat close to Drew's, then stood up, holding his medical bag, indicating he was in agreement with the exchange. Drew and Luther held the boats together while Dr. Collins and David exchanged seats. Luther then climbed over to the other boat. They handed the doctors the medical supplies that Dr. Collins had brought with him.

"Don't disturb my friends in the front," Drew said quietly.

"Snakes!"

Dr. Collins began clambering to get back to his own boat.

"They are just harmless indigoes," said Drew as he calmed his new friend.

Drew wondered why anyone would come to the area and not know the difference between a harmless snake and a poisonous snake.

After another stop at Parkinson's and the hotel for canned goods, Drew suggested another direction.

"Let's head south, Dr. Collins. I need to check on a friend, as well as see who else we can help."

As they neared the auto bridge, Drew heard a young girl's voice and knew who it was before he was near enough to see the face.

"Doctor D! Doctor D!"

Only one person in the entire town called him that.

"Doctor D, look up here!"

With tears in his eyes he looked up and waved. The dead girl with the blonde hair he had seen earlier had not been Joannie. He would have good news to give to Miss Anna. Joannie was one of many on the bridge. Where did they all spend the past twenty-four hours?

They tied the boat to the bridge's railing and gave food away sparingly, not knowing how many people would have to rely on the food stored in Parkinson's, and for how long.

Joannie hugged her mother's employer.

"I am so glad to see you, Doctor D. We all were in the bridge tender's house during that awful storm. We were trying to get into town but when we tried to go across the bridge, he stopped us and took us to his house. Last night was terrible. Have you seen my parents? Are they okay?"

"They are, but they have been very worried about their blonde-haired princess. Come with us and I'll take you home."

After a glorious reunion at the Wrights, the two doctors continued southward where the death and destruction was similar to the other areas Drew had seen all morning. Dr. Collins, who was seeing the devastation and carnage for the first time, couldn't believe his eyes. Bodies were everywhere and people were clinging to whatever they could.

Animals, both domestic and wild, were sharing places with the displaced people. Frightened and exhausted dogs and cats, as well as opossums and raccoons, stared at the doctors with eyes full of fear and bewilderment. Hours in the rain and water had left their fur sleeked back and skin exposed. Most had multiple lesions and would probably not live.

The doctors stopped and assisted anyone who needed their help. Several people needed bones set. There was no way Drew could do it where they were. It was imperative that he find a dry place for a hospital. He could have used one of the hotels or the upstairs of a downtown building but they were either too damaged or too crowded. He knew the stranded would find shelter in those buildings when they could.

Drew knew he had found the perfect place for a temporary hospital when he stopped the boat at Charlie's. Seven steps were visible.

"Say! There isn't much water standing here, I wonder why?" Dr. Collins asked.

"Don't be deceived by appearances. This house stands twelve feet off of the ground!"

Drew tied the boat to the railing of the steps and walked up to the front door where they found it standing open.

They heard the sound of laughter coming from the kitchen along with the smell of frying bacon and coffee brewing. They let themselves in and walked to the back of the house where they found Charlie and ten other people.

Charlie was having a good time tossing pancakes in the air as he turned them over.

"Hello, Drew. I was wondering how long it would take you to get here. Sit down and eat. We have plenty."

Drew hadn't realized how hungry he was until he walked in the door and smelled the food. He pulled two chairs in from the dining room for Dr. Collins and himself.

"Charlie, this is Dr. Collins from Clewiston."

Charlie nodded his head toward the doctors as he continued to cook.

"How are my girls?" he asked.

"All are fine. They are still in the attic of the Woman's Club where we spent yesterday and last night. We had fifteen other people there with us. We all got wet and had minor cuts from shattered glass but that was the extent of it."

"How's your house?"

"It's still standing. Looks like it needs a roof, windows, and porches. I don't know what I can salvage from inside. We were one of the lucky ones. You won't believe the death and destruction out there, Charlie. We have seen well over two hundred bodies. What is worse, they are people we know."

For the next few minutes those who sat around the kitchen table were silent. They all had the same thoughts. Charlie poured water for all of them.

"Charlie! You have fresh water? Where did it come from?"

"The storm filled up the cistern."

"You didn't even lose the cistern?"

"Wish you had been with us last night," Drew said to Charlie. "The girls were able to have their birthday cake but the party was just a little different than we had planned."

"I tried to call but I think the phone lines were blown down early in the day."

"Were you okay here alone?"

"My son Paul was with me. He is worried sick, though, about his family in Sebring Farms. He has no way to reach them."

Dr. Collins said, "He's welcome to use my boat when it's returned from Clewiston."

Looking around the room, Drew said, "Charlie, how high did the water come up last night? Everything looks normal except I don't see your rugs."

"It didn't get too high. I tired my best to stop the water coming in the front and back doors but I knew it was a lost cause. When it came in and covered the rugs, all I could think about was Mollie and the way she will fuss when she comes home. I have them hanging out on the back porch now. But when the water came in I knew you folks in town were having it rough, especially with the wind. That wind was terrible. I never have heard anything like it even when I was a boy hiding in my basement with my family right in the middle of a Civil War battle. Yesterday afternoon I thought I was going to get blown off this high roost of mine. I opened all the doors and windows so the wind could pass right through. I guess that and all the bracing I did when we first moved into this house helped, too."

Charlie stopped briefly while he flipped more pancakes.

"After the wind died down the second time I lit my reading lamp and read until I fell asleep. I was hoping the light would keep some of the critters out because I knew I would have company when they found I was almost dry. I haven't seen any but I can hear them in the attic. I think I have a whole zoo up there. I can see my barn took a licking and my out buildings are all gone. I suppose my chickens and cows didn't make it either."

"Did you have your light burning all night?"

"Yes."

"We could see it through the darkness at the Woman's Club. Some watched it most of the night."

"That's what the others have said, too. That's why they came this morning."

"Charlie, could I ask a huge favor of you? This is the driest place around, although it isn't really close in. May I use your house as a hospital?"

"You can use this house any way that you want. I just wish Mollie were here. She would be a lot more help than I am. I'll get everyone who's taken refuge here to help move the furniture back to the walls. That will give more room."

"Thanks, Charlie. I'll go back to town and get the girls."

"Let me get Paul so he can go back to town with you."

When Charlie left the room, Dr. Collins commented, "You two have to be related."

"We are just good friends. He and his wife have taken my family under their wing from the night we first drove into town over six years ago."

"Let me check one thing out before we head back to town," Drew said to Dr. Collins and Paul.

"I want to see if I have any of Charlie's luck."

Drew rowed over in the direction of the Carter's dock.

"Can you see anything over there like a boat tied up to a dock? I don't want to get any closer because I won't be able to handle the current in the canal."

"Doc, there's nothing there but water and that one cypress tree," said Paul.

"Wait, I do see something. It's a boat tied to one remaining post and the bow seems to be lodged in the mud of the bank. It's under a ton of water hyacinths. Oh God! There are people in it! I can hear a baby crying!"

"Rope. We need rope."

They rowed back to Charlie's house. Charlie found several ropes that he had brought in the night before. The men knotted the ropes together and then tied one end to a post on the porch, then climbed into the boat with the long hemp cable and rowed out to the submerged boat.

Charlie and two other men from the house stood on the porch ready to pull. Paul tied the end of the rope around him and jumped into the raging water. He found the woman to be lifeless but her arms were still clutching her baby. It was a struggle for him to get the baby out of her grasp. Once he did, Drew gave the signal for the men on the porch to pull.

Paul gave the baby to Dr. Collins and held on to the side of the boat while Drew rowed it back to the house. Charlie came down the steps and took the baby.

"We'll keep her warm. Don't worry, we even have a wet nurse. This little girl is going to be just fine!"

Drew was glad that Paul was in the boat when they headed north. Even the overflow current was swift and he couldn't manage the rowing by himself. Paul took one oar while Drew had the other. Dr. Collins found a smaller one and paddled.

When the crew arrived back at the Lone Cypress, they met David and Luther with men in four more powerboats. Each boat held several large croaker sacks and boxes filled to overflowing with canned goods.

"Look, Doc. We have enough food here to feed and warm an army for a day at least."

One of the Clewiston volunteers addressed Dr. Collins.

"Doc, do you know where I can find a Dr. Duncan?"

"Here I am, young man."

"Mrs. Holt sent us. She said to come back for anything we need."

"That's wonderful. But who is Mrs. Holt? I thought I knew most of the twenty-two people in Clewiston."

She's some mucky de muck. I'm sorry, a wealthy widow from New York who came down to the Clewiston Inn when it opened. She likes fishing so much she decided to stay. She is building a big house up on the ridge."

"When this is all over, I will have to meet her and thank her. I wonder if she would sponsor a broke country doctor?"

"Doc, excuse me, but how can you laugh and make jokes at a time like this? Look around you. This is a disaster of the worse kind."

"You're young, but believe me some people have to laugh to keep from going mad when things are rough. Stick with me and you'll find me laughing hysterically at times. Most of my life I've been very serious and predicable. Some people might say I am now a little mad - and I do have a right to be. In the past month I have lost my only son and in the past twenty-four hours I have lost many, many friends. Both my house and my practice are under water; my boat has sunk; I don't know where one car is and the other is in a garage that is under water. All my chickens have drowned. Yes, young man I will be laughing today, tomorrow, and for many days to come."

"Paul, take my boat and go check on your family," said Dr. Collins. "There is an extra full gas tank under the seat in the stern. Good luck. May God be with you."

"Dr. Collins, will you take charge here?" asked Drew. "I want to get my family out to Charlie's."

"Yes. But you will need a powerboat to get back."

"Why don't you fellows continue to distribute food and blankets? Bring the more serious cases and broken bones to me at Charlie's. If you need my boat at any time, it's yours."

"Dr. Duncan!" a voice cried out from a block away. Drew turned to see two men sloshing through water that was now knee high.

"That's Dr. Mitchell. I wonder how he got here?"

Drew rowed his boat toward the doctor and the man accompanying him.

"Dr. Duncan! I am so glad to see you," said the water-soaked Dr. Mitchell.

"I'd get in the boat and sit down, but I don't think I have the strength to pull myself in. This is George Sebring. Mr. Sebring, Dr. Drew Duncan. We heard in Sebring that the dike broke just before the brunt of the storm hit. We came to see if anyone was still alive and what we could do. We'll survey the damage, go back to Sebring, and then get as many relief workers in here as we can muster. I'll be back to help as soon as I can."

"How in the world did you get in, Doc? I could see if you were in a boat, but you are walking."

"We made it in by car as far as Muckway and then swam the rest of the way."

"That's three miles, you must be exhausted. Let me take you to your office, Dr. Mitchell. I don't know what condition it's in, but as you can see the business section faired quite well."

"We are almost there. I want to look at it and go. I think that just by coming this far we can guess the extent of the damage."

Drew hailed down Luther in a motorboat to take Mr. Sebring and Dr. Mitchell back to his car, whenever he wanted to go.

"The train track is passable all of the way to Muckway, too. There should be a train full of help for you by tomorrow, Duncan. I'll send out pleas for boats, clothing, bedding, medicine, food, water, and other essentials. I'll also get undertakers and coffins," Mr. Sebring said as he shook Drew's hand.

"Tell all you see that Sebring is open for all who want to come. There's an army of volunteers who are already gathering things to send. There are also those who are setting up soup kitchens and the like for refugees."

Drew rowed his boat back to the Woman's Club where he lifted up the large snakes that had accompanied him most of the day and threw them in the water.

"Boys, your ride is over. I don't think my girls would enjoy your company."

He watched them as they swam toward his house.

"You're welcome to stay there and eat any critters that you see."

He called to Mary Elizabeth, who came to a window.

"I've come to take you and the girls out to Charlie's. It's the driest place in town. It comes complete with a stove that works, dry beds, and fresh water."

"Drew, I don't want to go out there," said Mary Elizabeth. "I'll stay here with the girls until the water goes down."

"I need your help. There is so much to do and I could use your help as my nurse. We're going to set up a makeshift hospital at Charlie's."

"I just can't take the girls out in that awful water."

Tears began to pour from Mary Elizabeth's eyes and Drew realized she was terrified that the girls would be drowned as Thomas had been.

Drew gently pulled her to him.

"Mary, you can do this. I came to get you because I want you with me. Can you do it for me?"

Still crying, Mary Elizabeth nodded. The fear, however, remained.

"Let's go get the girls and our things," urged Drew.

The group in the attic inquired about David and Luther. They also asked Drew to describe what he had seen. He told them everything but left out the names of the dead he had seen. There were too many friends and relatives.

"How's your cut, Sam?"

"I'll be fine, Doc. I sure wish I could go out and help."

"You should be able to get out tomorrow. The water is going down fast."

The men helped Drew carry Mary Elizabeth and the girls, as well as their few belongings, down to the boat.

As Drew picked up the oars, Mary Elizabeth asked, "May we please go by the house first, Drew?"

"Are you sure you really want to?"

"Daddy, look at that gator. He is bigger than you are!" Mollie exclaimed as they passed One Eyed Riley who was still in the same spot where Drew had seen him earlier.

"He's been there all day. I don't think he has moved a muscle."

"Don't tell me you swam by him this morning. Is that Riley?"

"One Eyed Riley, and over there are two of my boat companions. I made them give up their seat for you."

Drew pointed towards his house. Mary Elizabeth shuddered when she saw the big indigos on her window sill.

"If snakes and alligators are your friends, I know you have gone mad!"

Drew circled the house slowly.

"We could go in but there is still too much water."

He rowed up to the windows but it was too dark to see inside. He then headed the boat toward the Carter farm, forgetting that the loss of life was new to the eyes of his familiy. Mary Elizabeth told the girls to put their heads on her lap and close their eyes. She held them close to her.

Still frightened, but trying to be brave for the sake of her daughters, she suddenly flinched and let out a loud cry.

"What's the matter, Mama?" Mollie asked as she started to raise her head.

"Keep your head on my lap," Mary Elizabeth commanded. She had just recognized the lifeless body of Mollie's teacher, trapped in the elderberry bushes.

"Shh, Mollie. I'm going to close my eyes and not see anything else either."

She knew the bile in her throat would be hard to control if she saw another victim. She shut her eyes and prayed she wouldn't be nauseated.

When they arrived at the Carter's home, Charlie said, "I have the front bedroom ready for you and I pulled a little bed in there for the girls to share."

Leading them by the bedroom, Charlie said, "Come see the baby. She's brightened everyone's day. She is such a sweetheart. Do you know her name, Drew?"

"No, the Gibsons wanted a boy so bad that they didn't have a girl's name picked out. I haven't seen the family since the delivery early in the summer."

"We're calling her Joy."

"Let me take a look at you, Joy," said Drew as he took the baby from the arms of Glenda Baker who had become the baby's wet nurse.

"I think that you are going to be one rotten little girl here with all of these people taking care of you."

Only when Drew returned Joy to Glenda, did he realize he had not seen her three-month-old daughter earlier and saw no sign of her now.

"Doc, what will happen to her if her father is not found?" questioned Glenda. "Do you think I can keep her?"

Breaking down, Glenda described how the rushing waters had swept her daughter from her arms the night before. Drew looked into the anguished face and wanted to tell her she could keep the child, but he was honest with her.

"Usually they try to find other relatives. If they can't be located, the sheriff will handle it. I don't know how many other children are out there who have lost their parents. I don't know who will be in charge. I just don't know."

After brief pleasantries, Drew found his way to his old bed in Charlie's front bedroom. He was awakened by the sounds of motorboats. He had no idea how long he had slept.

The new arrivals were helped up the steps and welcomed. Mary Elizabeth directed the women in cleaning wounds and making bandages. Charlie was in charge of the kitchen.

Drew set countless numbers of broken arms and legs. Dozens of cuts required stitches. Those with broken ribs were taken to one of the three hotels where they were treated.

Drew couldn't spare bandages. His supplies were almost depleted when a boat arrived from Clewiston loaded with everything he needed. His work continued deep into the night.

The volunteers slept whenever there was a lull.

In the early hours of the morning, Drew was enjoying a cup of coffee when another boat arrived with two women, an odd looking older man, and a familiar looking man about Drew's age. Drew opened the door and welcomed them.

"What can I do for you? I am Dr. Duncan."

The middle-aged man took off his hat and said, "I'm Ed," and pushed rudely past Drew as if he knew where he was going. A thin middle-age woman with gray hair and wire-rimmed glasses introduced herself.

"I am Florence McBride. This is Julia Davis and Oscar Tubbins."

"We are nurses from Tampa General and Mr. Tubbins is a registered pharmacist."

Demonstrating her take-charge attitude, Florence went on to tell about the first relief train, its occupants, and contents.

"We're part of a relief team that has come from Tampa. We've scattered out all over town. We've brought doctors, pharmacists, Red Cross workers, newspapermen, and Legionnaires. We also brought a good supply of boats, food, medical and surgical supplies, cooking equipment, tents, and bedding. Make a list of what you need here and we will send a Legionnaire back to the train to get it."

Drew quickly made a list of food, more medicine, bandages, and bedding. Some of the men staying in the house accompanied the Legionnaire back to the train for the supplies.

"Drew!" Charlie called from the kitchen.

"Can you come back here when you get a break?"

Drew showed the nurses the patients who had been treated but needed to stay. He left instructions as to what they could and couldn't do. Mr. Tubbins found a spot and set up his portable pharmacy.

Drew went back to the kitchen, seeking a piece of the fresh-baked bread his nose told him had just been taken from the oven. Every muscle in his body ached as he sat down at the kitchen table.

As he poured Drew a steaming cup of coffee, Charlie asked, "Drew, do you remember my son, Ed?"

It was only then that Drew realized why the rude man he had encountered earlier had seemed familiar.

"I'm sorry I rushed past you awhile ago but I had to see about Dad," said Ed. "Mama's in Orlando and is sick with grief. When we heard this morning about the storm, I knew I had to get here, so I drove to Sebring as soon as I could and caught the first train south. My brothers called from Oklahoma in a panic and are waiting word."

"I'm glad you're here, Ed. I know you're relieved to find your dad. He has been so wonderful to share his home for shelter. How long can you stay?"

"If we don't hear from my brother, Paul, by morning, I'll try to find a boat and see about him and his family. I'll deal with that situation and then come back, hopefully with them. My primary responsibility is to get Dad out of here and take him to Mama. I'll be glad to help you any way I can until tomorrow."

Though there were now many volunteer doctors caring for the storm victims, they sent people who had to have stitches to Drew. They wanted them out of the water and mud. More people with broken limbs came, too. The house was overflowing with people, including those who did not require medical attention. Ed, Charlie, and Mary Elizabeth fed fresh bread and soup to everyone. Most were thankful for a taste of good, fresh water, too. The cistern at Charlie's was the only one left standing in town.

Paul arrived with his wife and two small daughters about two the next morning.

"Dad, it's a miracle they made it! The house blew away, but they had already gone out to the palm trees at the edge of the yard. They held on to the palm trees all through the storm!"

Paul suddenly realized his brother was standing nearby.

"Ed, what are you doing here?"

"You know Mama. How can you ask why I am here? I would have had to swim all of the way here, if necessary, to keep her from doing it. Frank wired this morning before I left. He and Daniel are sitting ready to come home if..."

"We can send word now that they can stay in Oklahoma. We're all safe!"

Charlie was overwhelmed with his good fortune. He had kept himself busy so he wouldn't have to think about the news he thought Paul would bring.

"I'm going to be on the first train out of here tomorrow to get to Clermont to Mary's family. Dad, why don't you come with us?"

"I don't want to leave. There's so much work to be done here, but I would like to see if Mollie is okay. I'll go to Orlando with Ed. I know she'll want to see me with her own two eyes. I know that she's been fretting."

"Fretting isn't the word I would use."

The Duncans said goodbye to Charlie the next day.

"Drew, the house is yours as long as you need it. I'll probably be back before you're into your house again. See you soon, my friend."

They were taken by motorboat to Muckway to catch the next train out.

Drew continued to work until early that afternoon. He had just gone into the kitchen to grab a sandwich when he heard Mollie call to him from the front door.

"Daddy, there are some men here who want to see you."

Drew greeted the new arrivals.

"Please come in gentlemen, I'm Dr. Duncan."

"How may I help you?" Drew asked, taking note that they were nicely dressed, although wrinkled and dirty.

"I'm Carlton Wells and this is Joseph Marshall. We are doctors who came in yesterday on the train from Tampa. We've been out since then treating people and getting them on trains headed north. We've also assisted in bringing the dead to a central location in what is left of the railroad station."

"Dr. Mitchell really needs you down there," said Dr. Wells. "He says you know more people than he does. If you could go over and assist him we'll take your place here."

Drew had been dreading this visit, which he knew would come.

"Let me get some things. My wife is here and will assist you and the nurses in any way that you see fit. We're in a friend's house so I would like for you to get my wife's okay before you do anything to the house or its contents."

Drew went into the kitchen to tell Mary Elizabeth what was happening.

"I don't want to do this, Mary."

"Go out on the porch and get Charlie's hip boots while I pack some sandwiches for you to take."

Twenty minutes later Drew was standing in the ruins of the railroad station putting name tags on many friends. After being identified, they were then carried outside and put in coffins.

"Doc, there are some niggers in the back. Do ya want to identify them or jus' wrap them up?" said one of the out-of-town volunteers.

Drew had slept only a little for the better part of five days and was in no mood to hear derogatory comments. Outraged, Drew lit into the man.

"Why on earth must these people be separated now? You bring them in here and I WILL tag them just like all of the rest."

"We can't put them in with the whites. You know that."

"I don't know that and if any more black bodies come in, you WILL bring them in here for proper identification. We will put the ones I recognize in coffins just like the others. Is that clear? If you won't do it then find somewhere else to work!"

Drew did not care at that point that the volunteers had paid their own way to help.

There were so many Negroes! Their homes were the closest to the lake so they took the full force of the water. There were only a few buildings, if any, in that section that were constructed well enough to withstand the force of the storm.

Drew wrote names on the tags of the first few Negroes that were brought in. The next dozen or so were not identifiable because of being out in the elements or having too many cuts and abrasions. He put an X on their tag and they would be wrapped in cheesecloth.

For the next hour Drew continued to tag those people who had not been looked at before. Each time he wrote a name, he remembered the person in some way.

Johnson, Johnnie. She was the one he had worked on only last Friday, only hours before the storm.

Adams, Shelia. He thought about her lonely, troubled life and how she had been with men.

Jones, Wanda. This was the hardest of all, this dear soul who had been uniquely connected to his beloved Flora and with whom he had shared so much laughter and many tears over the last six years.

There were so many children. They were the babies he had brought into this world. When he tagged the bodies of Katie and Harvey Smith's little blonde-headed girls he remembered how confident Harvey had been that they would be found safe.

Several of the children had been classmates of Thomas's who had cried at his funeral only a few weeks before.

The girl with the long blonde hair was someone he did not know. He hated to put an X on her tag as well as the others he couldn't identify.

Then there were his friends: the men who greeted him each morning at the cafe', women in the choir, the grocer, the train master, Ed Lundy's parents, brothers, and sisters. There were so many friends!

Drew hardly looked up when a large group of men arrived to survey the damage. When Governor John W. Martin shook Drew's hand it didn't impress him. It wasn't until much later in the day that he realized he hadn't been very receptive to the men who just seemed to look on everything and everybody as a curiosity.

A few days later, though, he didn't care how he had treated the governor when he read that Governor Martin had said , "Northern tourists shouldn't change their winter vacation plans because the damage in Florida was minimal."

Drew was furious.

Identification of the dead continued for the next three days. As each day passed the bodies became harder and harder to identify. There was no more concern for separating Negroes from Whites. At this stage in death, most of the bodies did not have much skin left on them. The horrific condition of the bodies worsened while at the same time, the smell became more and more appalling.

Drew passed out some of his alcohol and told the workers to drench their handkerchiefs in the liquor and tie the cloths on their faces to create a mask for their noses.

He went out with other volunteers to find more victims. They had to use big grappling hooks to grab the bodies submerged in the water and mud of the canals and ditches. Sometimes the hooks had to go down four to six feet in the mire.

On Thursday, the rushing waters subsided enough so that volunteers could go to Lake Hicpochee to recover bodies.

They were sickened by what they found.

Over 100 bodies were snarled among a mountain of debris that included mattresses, broken furniture, and trees. In addition to the human bodies, there were domestic and wild animals as well as a menagerie of birds.

The flow of the trash – and the bodies – had been stopped by the thick elderberry bushes and willows that grew in the shallow lake, else they would have washed on into the saw grass that was just beyond.

Other bodies were mired in the mud near the shore. Many were floating. Dead now for almost a week, the bodies were so bloated that the only way anyone could be identified was by some well known scar, a gold tooth, jewelry, or clothing.

The horror of the scene was magnified by hundreds of buzzards swarming down to tear into the flesh of the dead. Their grizzly calling went uninterrupted, even with occasional swipes of a paddle or the explosion of a gunshot into their midst. Occasionally, the giant birds flew above the boat, and dropped putrid flesh onto a volunteer.

Drew marked the bodies as they were put in boats. It was an almost impossible task. The decomposing bodies literally fell apart in the hands of those lifting them. The odor was overwhelming.

The scene and smell had been so horrible that most of the rescuers spent the majority of the time on their return ride retching over the side of the boat.

The one thing that made the effort somewhat rewarding was the anticipation of the free supply of liquor awaiting them at the foot of the Lone Cypress. Soon their senses would be dulled and the scenes of the day somewhat obliterated.

Drew's boat was the last of the group to arrive back in Moore Haven. A Captain Smith of the National Guard met them at the Lone Cypress.

"Sirs, we are commandeering all boats."

Drew was astounded,

"You're what? Are you crazy?"

"Those are my orders. We have brought trucks and are transporting everyone out. You need to get on a truck."

Drew, who was exhausted as well as sick from the smells of death, released his anger on the young guardsman,

"I'm not getting on any truck! I am a doctor. Why does someone think it necessary for us to go now? The water is almost gone and we need to clean up and save what we can from our homes."

"I have my orders, sir."

"Who's in charge and where?"

"Colonel Lowery. He's over in that white house by that old cypress tree. I believe you call it the State House."

Drew had never been as tired or angry as he was at that moment. He waded in the water to Fred's house and went in without knocking. He saw Fred, Sheriff Sam Richards, and County Commissioner Ed Frierson talking with the colonel. They all had red faces from arguing. Drew jumped right into the conversation to give them some relief.

"Colonel Lowery, I presume?" Drew didn't offer his hand. "Your men just commandeered the boats that we need!"

"Sir, you don't need the boats anymore. There are trucks waiting to take you and every other man, woman, and child out of here. This town is under Martial Law and will be quarantined as soon as everyone is gone."

"Why the Hell have you waited a week to come in here? For the past five days we've been working around the clock to save people and identify our dead. We've done it by ourselves. Now it is time to clean up and get our lives going again."

"Sir! I don't know who in the Hell you think you are but I am not having the same damn argument with every Tom, Dick, and Harry in this hell hole. You chose to live in this flood plain. Now take the consequences!"

"Yes, we chose to live here and we intend to go on living here. There is no reason to leave now."

"I will give you two reasons – looters and fresh water. You don't have fresh water and we are preventing a typhoid epidemic."

"We proved that wrong four years ago. People didn't get sick when the vaccines ran out and the government didn't care enough to give us any. We had more standing water in the Floods of '22 than we do now. This water is fresh water flowing from Lake Okeechobee south. There's no danger of disease."

"And are you some sort of an authority?" the colonel said in a very demeaning manner. "What kind of an authority on anything would live in a place like this?"

"I am just a country doctor, but I know what I know."

"And I know that all of you will be on the first truck out of here. Leave now or I will have you arrested...all of you."

"I am a state employee and I have as much right to be here as you do. I'm not leaving!" shouted Fred.

Sheriff Richards retorted, "I refuse to go and I can deputize anyone I want to. I will start with you, Doc, and anyone else who wants to stay."

Lowery jumped up out of his chair.

"I am the law and you will do what I say!"

The colonel shouted to the sergeant who was standing outside the open door.

"Sergeant, take these men, put them in the nearest transport, and get them out of my sight!"

"That won't be necessary. We're leaving, but you won't hear the end of this," Commissioner Frierson said. "We might be dirt farmers to you, but we do know people who..."

"Sergeant!"

As the men were leaving, Drew turned and asked Lowery, "Where are you taking us and when can we come back?"

"My transports are going to Sebring. Where you go from there is your business. I don't know when you'll be back. Anyone who comes back without authorization will be shot. There will be no looting under my command!"

"I do know the law and I'm staying," declared the sheriff.

"Stay! But only you, Sheriff. The rest of you, go!"

Drew turned to the sheriff as he walked to the waiting transport, "I promised Charlie I would take care of his house. It's in the best condition of anything around. I would hate to see the Guard go in there. They will be the only looters. If I give you the key would you look after it? Would it be possible?"

"I'll do my best, Doc."

The International Truck headed south to the Alamonte Hotel where the men were transferred to another transport.

Drew's family, Whiskers, and the others from Charlie's house were on this last truck out of town. Also on the truck was Bill Gibson, who sat alone in the back corner. Drew took Joy from the arms of her nurse and took her back to Bill. When he saw the baby he couldn't control his tears.

"We found her in a boat in front of Charlie Carter's last Sunday. She's been such a joy to all of us. In fact, we've been calling her Joy."

"Doc, thank you, thank you. Have you seen my wife?"

"She was with the baby."

Drew's expression told him what he needed to know. He held his daughter close and hummed, trying to hide his anguish from his fellow passengers. The tears though, streamed down his face.

Bill was not alone in his misery. Cries of grief came from all corners of the vehicle. Some, like Bill, were leaving without loved ones. All were being forced to leave what was left of their homes.

The weary refugees reached Sebring a little before midnight.

Chapter 32

SURVIVORS
October-December 1926

The National Guard truck carrying the last load of refugees from Moore Haven stopped in front of the Nan-ces-o-wee Hotel in Sebring. They were all shown to their rooms and told they could register the next day if they were going to make the hotel their temporary home.

Drew and his family, including Whiskers, fell into bed without baths. The next morning Drew woke before the girls. He went downstairs to make arrangements for the rest of their stay. Posted in the lobby were rooms and apartments to rent. He read every thing with interest. He knew he must find larger living quarters than just a small bedroom for his family.

"Dr. Duncan."

Drew could not place the voice and when he turned around, he could not remember the face either. He shook the hand of a stately elderly man.

"I don't know if you remember me, our meeting was so brief. I'm George Sebring."

"Yes, Mr. Sebring – Moore Haven's savior. I was amazed at the amount of help you sent and the number of people. Now, the National Guard has quarantined the town. But, I guess you already know that."

"Do you have any place to stay during this – sabbatical – if you will?" asked Sebring.

"No, I am just checking out the places posted here. Do you have any suggestions?"

"Yes, but you won't find it on the board."

"My house is empty and I would love to have your family stay with me."

"Thanks, but that is too much. I have three – uh two – little ones."

"I am sorry, doctor, I didn't know you lost family."

"My son was drowned in August; not in the storm."

"My deepest sympathy. The invitation's still open. I have a huge yard for the children and cool breezes off the lake. Besides, I don't see a nice place listed here. They must all be taken. You were on the last truck."

"And that was practically over my dead body," Drew said as he decided to accept Sebring's offer. "I need a quiet place to write some letters. I'll go back to Moore Haven as soon as I possibly can after I send my family to my wife's relatives in Maryland. There's nothing they can do at home for a while."

The citizens of Sebring did all they could to make the refugees as comfortable as possible. They collected clothing, toiletry products, toys, and other essentials.

On October 3, Captain James Albritton, who had been with the National Guard troops going into Moore Haven after the storm, led the survivors in a memorial and thanksgiving service which was attended by the people of Sebring and the ones who were calling Sebring their temporary home.

So many faces were missing. So many had perished; others had left to be with relatives in other parts of the country. With shrieks of delight, some found loved ones during the service they thought had perished in the storm.

Survivors clapped wildly when a proclamation was read thanking the people of Sebring for all the things they had done. Cries of agony were heard throughout the crowd as the names of the dead were read one by one. Some were hearing the names for the first time. When James Stevens sang, *Going Home*, Drew fought back tears, as did many in the crowd. Others, including Mary Elizabeth, let the tears flow.

The following morning, 15 to 25 men were allowed to go back to Moore Haven during daylight hours to see what they could salvage. All had to be given typhoid shots. Drew, who was in charge of inoculations, was one of the first to go.

The train was on its way at 5 a.m. At Muckway, the men were transported into town in Harvester transport trucks. Each volunteer was furnished a handful of cigars and a neckerchief. All were advised to use the neckerchief as a mask or to keep a cigar lit during the entire operation. The strong cigar odor would keep insects at bay and would, hopefully, mask the unpleasant smell of decaying flesh.

Water was still standing two feet deep in most places, but the big trucks were able to go through the water and the mud easily.

Drew covered his face in an attempt to mask the overwhelming smell of rotting animals and garbage, but, as horrible as the odors were, they were overpowered by the feeling of emptiness that permeated the city.

Less than three weeks before, Moore Haven had been a thriving community of over fifteen hundred people. Today, the men on the truck and men patrolling the watery streets were the only signs of human life. The only birds in the air were buzzards that were feasting on decaying flesh. Flies were thicker than mosquitoes had ever been. It was as if the whole town had died.

Drew had never experienced such bleakness.

There was only one guardsman at the station and Drew questioned the young man.

"Where have they taken all of the bodies we couldn't identify?"

"We took them to the Ortona Cemetery and buried them in a mass grave."

Drew's voice caught as he thought of all the families who would never have closure on this tragedy.

326

"That's probably the most tragic thing that has happened, yet," Drew said. "It's bad enough to know that a loved one is dead, but, to have one that was never found, is worse. They will guess forever if they are among the buried remains or if they are somewhere in a watery grave."

Luckily Sheriff Richards drove up just as Drew started to undertake the task of wading through water that still reached his knees.

"Give you a lift, stranger?"

"Sheriff, where did you get the truck?"

"It's mine. Darn thing just dried out! I saw you and wanted to let you know the Carter's house is safe."

"Good. Now let me check on mine."

"Hop in!"

As they drove through the town, it was hard to tell where the streets had been. Mud was over everything and houses that used to be landmarks were either gone or moved to new locations.

Drew said nothing. He was heartsick.

He didn't know if he could face seeing his own home again. When they reached it, he sloshed through water and muck half way up his legs until he reached the opening where his front door had been. He pulled himself up into his dark living room.

Two feet of mud replaced the water. He had been warned that snakes and other wild creatures were still everywhere seeking a dry refuge. Volunteers had been given lanterns in order to see in dark buildings and to keep the animals at bay. Cautiously, he went through each room. His head had known what he would find, but not his heart.

He gingerly climbed the stairs to the attic, where he found squirrels, rats, and mice. He didn't know what Mary Elizabeth had stored in the trunks and boxes. He decided to wait until later to find out.

Downstairs he was able to salvage a few dishes, silver, pots and pans, oil lamps, and a few other odds and ends. He found photographs in a tin box that could be saved. He thought that all of the old wooden furniture would be fine once it dried out. Everything else was a total loss. He put everything that could be saved into his bedroom.

His next order of business was to find something to serve as steps in order to get in and out of the house more easily. He found, tossed against a tree in the side yard, the front door that had been torn from its hinges during the storm. The once beautiful mahogany door served nicely as a ramp.

He worked until just after noon removing debris from the house and piling it out where the street had been, then headed to his office to see what he could salvage there.

Trying to walk through the deep muck was tiring as well as slow. It took him over an hour to walk the four blocks.

He wandered through the rooms that had been exposed completely to the elements for the past three weeks. Under a mass of fallen timbers and trash from the roof, he found his iron safe. He carefully turned the combination and prayed that it was air and watertight. The door swung open.

"Praise the Lord!"

All his insurance papers and the cash he kept in case of another bank failure were intact. He put the contents in a box that was also in the safe. He then drew a big X on everything but the safe, indicating to clean up crews that it could be removed and burned.

"Doc!"

Drew turned around when he heard the familiar voice.

"Jacob!"

The two men, eternally bound with the grief of their lost sons, squeezed each other's hands.

Drew was the first to speak.

"How did you get here? You weren't on the truck with me."

"I've been staying in Ortona. The Guard brought 15 of us in today. My store is a total disaster but the apartments upstairs are in pretty good shape. I have to replace the roof and windows but most things could be saved."

Pausing briefly, Jacob continued, "I went into Bill Bennett's apartment. Did you know he robbed you blind? His front room is full of empty whiskey bottles that came from your office."

"And how do you know the whiskey was mine? You know he was a runner for the bootleggers," Drew said. He knew what Jacob would say next.

"I found a bedroom full of your stuff. The room didn't even have a leak in the roof."

Drew laughed and told Jacob about Nancy and the children.

"They did me a great service when they broke in to get the whiskey. I'm sure they would have helped themselves to the contents of the safe if it hadn't been locked and wasn't too heavy to carry. That was the only thing left down there that I can salvage."

"Will you secure my things?" Drew asked his friend. "I'll get everything as soon as I can."

"I have an extra padlock in my apartment."

"Thanks, but do you think a lock will stop anyone if they want something bad enough? My bolts didn't stop the Bennetts. They were probably the first looters of the storm."

Drew paused again, bringing up another subject that was being discussed by most of the survivors.

"Uh, Jacob, are you going to stay or has this been too much for you?"

"I'm staying. Our losses were terrible but God spared our lives and our home. I'm not going to leave my son. This is home."

"I feel the same way exactly!" Drew said.

Drew waded back through the mud to his house. Until late in the afternoon he continued to carry things out to be burned. Two men from the Guard joined and helped him work. Together they took furniture out to the back yard so the sun could dry it. They wiped it down with cloths they had in the truck.

"We'll come back tomorrow and move all of this back in for you, Doc," said one of the young guardsmen. "And do you want me to get that car in your garage going again?" he asked. "I'm a mechanic when I'm not in the Guard."

"Mr. Ford built the Model T's to go through Hell and high water," noted the mechanic. "This should be a good test!"

The three men struggled together to open the garage door, then dug trenches for the car's tires and pushed the car out into the sun. They were just about to start working on the car when an Army truck pulled in front of the house. The driver honked the horn and shouted that it was time to evacuate.

Drew's two helpers continued to work as he hopped into the back of the truck.

He thought about his first encounter with the Guard and was glad Colonel Lowery had left others in charge of the cleanup operations. Everyone else he had met with the Guard had been cooperative.

"Is that all you found, Doc?" asked Wayne Buggs as he eyed the box in Drew's hands.

"Oh, I found quite a lot, but I stored it in my bedroom. Many things from my office are safe, too. How about you?"

Wayne pointed to a small sack.

"That's all. That's all I have left."

The broken man asked, "Doc, are you going to leave now? You've been through so much this past month. There's got to be a better place. What if a storm comes again? Are you going to do this again and again and again. I can't. I won't."

"I understand what you are saying, Wayne, but I've been assured a dike around the lake won't hurt the lower Glades. I'm going to lobby and fight for a bigger and stronger dike. A disaster like this one shouldn't happen again."

Drew continued, "There are places all over this country and this world where thousands of people are living on fertile land behind levees. I'm staying here because this is home. I lost many friends in the storm and I know others will leave. I also know many who are staying and they are going to need a doctor. I'll stay until they bury me beside my son."

The next morning Drew inoculated more men before they got on the train to go salvage their belongings. He then sat down on the veranda of Sebring's house, looking over Lake Jackson. In this peaceful setting he wrote letters to medical supply houses in Baltimore asking them to restock the order they had sent him in 1920.

He also wrote to his insurance companies to file his claims. Finally, he drafted a letter to the Bank of Connecticut.

Sebring, Florida
October 5, 1926

First Bank of Connecticut
New Haven, Connecticut

Dear Sirs:

I opened a savings account with you in the spring of 1898.
I've added to it through the years and my plans were to keep the
account for my children's education, but my plans have changed.
Please close the account and transfer the money to a certified
check, made out to Mrs. Thomas Drew Duncan, III.
Send the check in the enclosed addressed envelope.
Please include the note that is in the smaller envelope.

Sincerely,
Thomas Drew Duncan, III, M.D.

Drew watched Mary Elizabeth as she walked up from the lake where she had taken the girls to feed the ducks. Just as he sealed the last letter, she came up the steps with Gail. The breeze caught the full skirt of the yellow chiffon dress she was wearing. No angel could be as lovely as his wife was at that moment. Drew hid the letter as Mary Elizabeth sat down in the rocker beside the table where he was writing.

They both watched as Mollie twirled and danced among the flowering shrubs.

"Mary, why don't you take the girls and go to your parents? You can buy new clothes and things you need for the house and have everything shipped down. You can be comfortable there and be busy, too. We don't know when they will let us back in to live. When they do it's going to be a horrible situation. It's many times worse than the floods of '22. Mollie needs to be in school. I would feel a lot better with all of you up there and I won't worry either."

Drew talked fast for he didn't want Mary Elizabeth to get in a word and protest.

"Drew, do we have the money to start over?"

"You worry too much."

He pulled out the box from the safe, which included the insurance papers and money. He had a smile like a pirate showing off his treasure.

"Where did that come from?" Mary Elizabeth asked in amazement.

"My office safe! It didn't leak a bit! Now, let me tell you what I saved from the house."

When he finished, Mary Elizabeth asked, "Will it ever be safe to go back? So many are leaving. Drew, I'm afraid."

"It is scary, I'll admit. But we have put six years of love and work in building a practice and a home. It's the only home the girls know and Thomas is there. I just can't be a quitter."

"I'll go to Maryland for awhile, but only to prepare to come back."

The next day Drew put his family on a train heading north.

He was on the first one heading south.

The tracks had just been repaired so the train could now reach Moore Haven again. He joined the team of Red Cross workers who were allowed in to help the Guard with clean up operations.

A smile crossed his face as he looked down at the Red Cross Pass. What would Miss Barton and Uncle Tyler say about the fact that he was again joining forces with the organization they had loved so well.

Red Cross workers were allowed to stay in town past the sun-down curfew. Food was provided by the Red Cross to all who would work in the clean up.

Drew stayed alone at the Carter's home. Every day he joined clean up crews clearing, cutting, and burning debris in town. Every night he went home exhausted, but would spend a few hours each night getting the house in order until it was the way Mollie left it.

The Moore Haven Hotel again opened for business on October 18, soon after the quarantine was lifted. Most who came back stayed and had their meals there.

That same week people were allowed back in their homes, providing that they had running water, working toilets and proof of typhoid inoculations along with a health certificate signed by a doctor. Drew's signature appeared on a great number of the certificates.

It wasn't surprising to Drew that the majority of people decided to stay and live in Moore Haven, but he was surprised when he saw Wayne Buggs walk in for lunch.

"Wayne, I thought you were off to make your fortune somewhere else."

"No, Doc. I listened to what you had to say and then my wife said that she wasn't going to leave. The kids started crying when they heard us talking. They didn't want to leave their friends. So here I am. Besides, I have worked hard on my land. I own thirty acres of the best dirt in America. We started here eight years ago in a tarpaper shack and I guess we can build one again. I don't think a storm is going to drive me away. When did you say they were going to start building the new dike?"

Others echoed the same thought. All were anxious to rebuild.

Laughter began to return to conversations.

Every day Drew heard jokes about the storm. The three he liked best, he wrote to Mary Elizabeth:

1) The wind blew so hard, it turned a crooked line straight.
2) The wind blew so hard, it scattered the days around so bad that Sunday didn't get around until late Thursday afternoon.
3) The wind blew so hard, it blew a well out of the ground.

Most of the standing water had gone and only mud was left to contend with. Almost every day, though, at least one body was found and buried. Most wore nothing that could identify them.

One morning as Drew was leaving the Carter's home, he saw a bony hand protruding from the mud near one of the front pilings of the house.

A wedding band was still on a finger. Knowing it might be a way to identify the victim, Drew removed the ring. Inside was inscribed:

L.N. to S.B.J. 12-12-12

He immediately knew who the woman was.

During the first twelve years of the century, many couples had married so their wedding date would have the same month, day, and year. He had heard Lynn Newkirk laugh many times about pushing up their wedding date so they could have the last of the triple figures.

Drew dug up the body, rolled it in a blanket, and placed it in the back of the truck the Guard had loaned him. He then took it to the train station, where bodies were still being taken. Then he drove to Parkinson's where he found Lynn clearing and restocking the shelves.

"Lynn, may I see you for a moment?"

"Sure, Doc. What is it?"

"Come sit down with me," Drew said as he pointed to the only seats available, a couple of unopened crates.

"I know Sallie's body wasn't found and that's been really hard for you," Drew said.

"Doc, you just don't know. I just stay busy. It's so hard because we just lost the baby last winter. I don't know how to explain it to my boys."

Reaching out to touch his shoulder, Drew said gently, "Lynn, I found something this morning."

Drew took the wedding ring out of his pocket.

"This ring was on the body of a woman I found under the Carter's house. I think it belongs to you."

Lynn took the gold band in his fingers and looked at the inscription inside. Enormous tears ran down the big man's cheeks.

"We always thought being married on 12-12-12 was extra special. We never thought the date would be meaningful in such a way as this."

"Are you going to be okay?"

Lynn nodded. "Where is she? I want to see her."

"No, you need to remember her the way she looked the last time you saw her or on your wedding day. Where do you want her body sent?"

"Uh, Ortona, I guess. This is gonna be home and I want her close by. I am not a religious man. Will you saw a few words when we bury her?"

The next day Drew delivered the eulogy for Sallie Bane Jenkins Newkirk.

She was laid to rest not far from the massive grave of the unknown hurricane victims. For the family it was a very appropriate place. They were very thankful she wasn't with the unknown as they had thought for so long.

Dr. Mitchell decided not to return after the evacuation, leaving Drew as the only doctor. His medical services were needed more and more as the population of the returning citizens grew. He set up a temporary office in the Bennett's apartment when it was learned that they would not be returning.

Jillian Daughtery, trying to get the mud out of her house, disturbed two moccasins. She started chasing them around the living room with her broom, but then they turned and started chasing her. She fell down the front steps trying to get away. Drew had to set her right arm in a cast.

Cleanup was in full swing when another storm hit on October 30. Moore Haven got some wind damage and enough rain to hamper their cleanup efforts for one day.

Most people had little or no insurance to rebuild or obtain necessities needed to start over. The State Relief Fund provided $10,000 for cleanup and rebuilding and people from across the nation rallied in support of the flood victims. Two train carloads of horses, mules, and tractors were donated for replanting. Each family was given twenty-three Leghorn hens and a rooster. Money, food, sewing machines, furniture, and clothes were also sent. The Guard was in charge of distribution.

Daniel Lence organized and coordinated the efforts of the volunteers and the donations. The Lence-Baker Fund was set up to supplement the work of the Red Cross and the state. Drew was pleased with the Red Cross in the beginning but after state relief came, Red Cross support ended.

He was outraged when he heard radio accounts, read newspaper articles, and heard from friends in Baltimore that the Red Cross was concentrating their efforts on the coast where they indicated to the world that damage was much more extensive than in the interior of the state.

He wondered what direction the organization would be taking if he had headed the Red Cross efforts in Europe and had become the National Director. Would things be better or would he have been embroiled in the politics of the organization? He felt compelled to write to the people he knew in Washington.

Moore Haven, Florida
November 1, 1926

Henry Baker
National Disaster Director
American Red Cross National Headquarters
Seventeenth Street
Washington D. C.

Dear Director Baker:

I am writing to you today with a heavy heart.

I have been associated with your organization since the Spanish-American War and have known first hand all of the wonderful things you have done in both wartime and peace. It is hard to imagine that the same organization for which my uncle, Dr. Tyler Duncan, and his best friend, Miss Clara Barton, labored for so long to serve the needs of others, has failed when it came to the hurricane and flood victims of South Florida.

We have suffered from two storms this Fall; the devastating storm that struck us on September 18 and a second one that hit during our clean up efforts only two days ago on October 30.

We have heard and read of the fine job you are doing in Miami and Ft. Lauderdale. You should hold your heads up high because they did suffer massive destruction and death. Yet, you have forgotten your promises to help the people of the Lake region. Our damages were just as great, although the price tags were not as high.

We have homes, businesses, and crops that have been virtually wiped off the face of the earth. Our death tolls reached close to 300 and over 1,000 are homeless or have homes in bad need of repair. The people of the Lake region are the little people, the salt of the earth. We are the ones who will provide you the fresh produce on your table every winter. We ARE your winter's salad bowl.

They (We) need your help. I had the privilege of working with the volunteers on the first relief train on September 19. Red Cross nurses and volunteers worked around the clock with me in a makeshift hospital.

Three weeks later I was part of the Red Cross team that was allowed to go in to clean up. At the time we were assured of aid in the form of rebuilding supplies and funds. Furniture and stoves were also promised. We have seen nothing since the relief workers left.

Because of your empty promises, many of my neighbors have put up signs in their empty yards proclaiming:

"This beautiful farmhouse furnished by the generous donations of the American Red Cross."

The people across this nation have been charitable with their giving, but what has happened to the American Red Cross?

My uncle and Miss Barton spent months in the Houston area after the Great Hurricane of 1900 that hit Galveston. They were there to distribute food and

334

*clothing, and assist with the cleanup. They remained for
three months teaching people new skills. The famous
strawberry fields of Pasadena are testimonies to the
wonderful work your organization has done.*

*You were there after the San Francisco Earthquake,
the Johnstown Flood, the hurricane that devastated the
Georgia Sea Islands, the Baltimore Fire (I worked with
you there), and so many, many more. Why haven't you
been here for us?*

*Many veterans are here who saw you in action in The Great
War and there are women who helped you by handing out
doughnuts and coffee to the doughboys as well as saving peach
pits, making bandages and socks, depriving food from their own
families in order to feed the Allies, writing letters, and all of the
thousand of other things that were done on the home front. I
think they need to be repaid!*

*I have a newspaper friend who recently penned, "Everyone
has some cross to carry." The cross Moore Haven is carrying is
colored RED.*

*I have contributed monetarily to the American Red Cross
over the years, but this is a promise – If we don't get more help
from you, there will not be another penny from me. I will send
directly to those in need as so many have done for us!*

I look forward to hearing from you soon.

Sincerely,

Thomas Drew Duncan, III, M.D.

The Guard built the outer walls and put a new roof on Drew's office,
helped him relocate the supplies that had been confiscated by Nancy and her
children, and cleaned out one room so he would have a clean place to see his
patients. In between patients, Drew cleaned out mud from other rooms, did
minor repairs, and painted the walls.

When his new furniture and medical supplies arrived the middle of
November, he was delighted to see that it was Alfonzo who brought it from
the depot.

"We jes got in from Atlanta on yesterday. Dere's a lota work we's gotta
on de house. I's got de old truck goin'. I guess it jus' sat in de garage an'
dried out. I's didn't spen' but four hours workin' on it dis mornin'. Ain't dat
a miracle?"

"I've witnessed many miracles lately."

"Will yo wa't Jo to come back to work?"

"When will she be able to? There's still much to do at the house."

"She's says ter tell yo's dat if'n you's wants her to giv' her two weeks en den she'll glad to started.

"Two weeks then."

Alfonzo changed the mood of their upbeat conversation when he said softly, "Doc, you's knows Miss Wanda didn' make it."

Drew sighed, acknowledging the loss of the second best Negro friend he had ever had.

"Yes, I don't know what I'm going to do without her."

Alfonzo helped Drew set up his furniture and supplies. They were almost finished when Drew heard another familiar voice. He looked up to see Anna and Joannie at the door.

"Are you tired of loafing around and ready to come back to work?"

"Not just yet. We just came to get some supplies. There's still so much to do at the house. Is December 1 okay with you?"

"Great! In two weeks my right arm is coming back and so is Mary Elizabeth!"

"Doctor D, it looks almost like nothing has ever happened here. We're going to be okay, aren't we?"

"Yes, Joannie, we're going to be just fine!"

"I see you have your car in working order. It looks better than new."

"What are you talking about?"

"Isn't that your Model T parked out front?"

"I don't think so."

Drew walked down the arcade with Anna and Joannie to see the car in question.

"It sure looks like my car, but mine has never been that clean or shiny."

He went over and took a note off the windshield.

> **DOC**
> **SORRY IT TOOK SO LONG TO FIX.**
> **THE GUARD THOUGHT I SHOULD DO OTHER THINGS,**
> **TOO.**
> **MERRY CHRISTMAS EARLY,**
> **JOE DRAKE**

"It is my car!"

Drew got in and cranked it up.

"This thing is purring! I can't believe it! You two girls need a ride home?"

By the end of November the Red Cross had sent stoves, tables, and beds.

Drew thought it was too little too late. He never received an answer to his letter. He did read later that the organization was having internal conflicts and all the top officials had resigned. All of this happened in September and October.

Drew was still angry and vowed again not to send them another penny.

Most houses had been fixed up well enough to move back in and new construction was everywhere. He started working on his own house the day after the Guard cleaned the mud out of the attic room, chased off the unwanted animals, and replaced the roof. Electricity was also restored that day.

Mollie and Charlie returned the first week of November and helped Drew make the house livable again. Charlie rebuilt the porches and replaced the ceiling and windows. Together, Drew, Mollie, and Charlie stripped water-damaged wallpaper and hung new. When they were through the house smelled and looked brand new.

The first of December saw most of the businesses opened on Main Street. The general stores all had restocked their shelves. Clothing stores advertised Christmas specials in *The Glades County Democrat*. The White Star Grocery Store had signs in its windows telling the prices of milk, bread, and eggs.

Drew's office as well as the cafe, drug store, bank, gas stations, and barbershop were all back in business. The post office that had been extensively damaged opened its doors to full service again. The docks had been rebuilt and steamers were coming and going on the Caloosahatchee on regular schedules. Some of the fish houses reopened.

Late one afternoon in early December, Drew was stocking the last of his shelves when he heard a bell on the door of the Negro waiting room. He was shocked when he opened the door and saw Gopher.

"Gopher! It's great to see you. I'm sorry I haven't been out. I can't begin to tell you about the past three months. How did you fair in the storm? I heard the Lakeport area was hit pretty bad too."

"Been through many storms but that one worst. Many much older say same thing. Just move to high ground before the storm and went in bushes. Put blankets around us so we have protection from wind and could breathe. Just got back to the prairie. Came in to sell hides. Lou come, too."

Lou, with her eyes cast down, stepped out from behind Gopher. Seeing her made Drew's heart stop. His stomach was in knots.

Drew took Lou into his office while Gopher remained in the waiting room.

"It's been such a long time," Drew said as he took her in his arms.

Lou immediately pulled away.

Drew's eyes followed Lou's as she looked around his office with curious eyes. It was the first time she had been to Drew's white world.

Seeing him here made her feel very uncomfortable. It was not the same as when he was in her world. She knew that the decision she had made was the only one possible.

Backing away from Drew and his embrace, Lou took out a beautiful red jacket with patchwork colors of red, yellow, and black in the medicine pattern.

"Old one no good. This one keep you warm. I can not."

Tears streamed down her eyes. She also had a big grass basket and two of the largest dolls he had ever seen.

"For family."

She turned and ran out the door. Drew started after her, but Gopher stopped him.

"No. She must go. She loves you. Cannot stay any longer. She go to Oklahoma. Best for both of you."

Holding back his tears, Drew nodded. The two men embraced briefly before Gopher followed Lou.

Drew sat down at his desk and put his head in his hands. Lou was leaving behind her friends, her family, and everything she knew – because of him! He knew the woman who just left took with her part of his heart and soul. She had been there for him when he could talk to no one else. He ached knowing he would never see her again.

It was as if the winds of the hurricane had just blown through again, for he had lost one more precious thing.

He sat at his desk until long after dark thinking about Lou and their love. How could a man love two women? Lou had enchanted him. Whenever she was near, all reason, all morality, everything that he held dear, vanished. He slowly realized that Lou's leaving was the most precious gift she could ever give him.

The storm had passed and the rebuilding, with better materials, had begun. It was now time to rebuild his marriage and make it stronger than ever.

Josephine came back to work the same day the new furniture and other household goods arrived. Drew left Anna in charge of his office and stayed home to help set up the house.

"Look at dat piano! I's never seen one dat big! Will it fit in yo'r house, Doc?"

"I have just the place."

It was a struggle, but the men were able to carry the big piano to the attic room that had been decorated to be the music room.

Josephine followed, carrying a matching bench. As she put it down, an envelope fell out.

"Doc, here's a letter addressed ter yo'."

Drew sat on the cushioned bench under the windows to read the note:

My Darling Drew,

I was shocked when I received the bank check. I saw it before I found your note. I never knew about your secret savings account in Connecticut. I thought we shared all!

Thank you my darling. I don't know when I have ever been so touched.

My family convinced me that you really wanted me to buy a fine piano, even though I was quite reluctant to do so. I hope the other purchases I have made meet with your approval.

I remembered the dimensions of all the windows so Mother and I made the curtains. I am going to let you guess where they all go!

See you soon.
M.E.

The family would be home in less than two weeks and he was determined that the house be in top shape. Mary Elizabeth could sit and play her piano without having to worry about the house. Josephine interrupted Drew's daydreaming.

"Doc, I's 'ad dey men set up yo'r dinin' room en bedroom furnitur' en de marble top tables en your desk. Come en look."

"Wonderful, they look wonderful. I'm so glad that these things could be saved. They are old family pieces."

"But dey has no glow."

"They look good for what they have been through. I guess I should have someone refinish them."

"No sur, I's think I's have somethin' at home dat'll git dem a shinin' tomorrow, but now let's hang de curtains."

The next day when Drew returned home from work, everything was in place and the old furniture was gleaming.

"Josephine, what magic potent did you use on this furniture?"

"My mama gav' me some bottles of what she calls 'Bright'n'. I jest rubbed it on all over yo'r furnitur'. I's don't know all dat's it in it. I knows it 'as oil, lemon, en juice of some nut. My brother's trying ter find out w'at kind of nut."

"When y'all find out, get a patent, and then watch the money roll in. Y'all be in high cotton."

"My brother en I is tryin' our best ter do dat very thin'."

Drew stopped in front of the fireplace and looked up at Adam's painting of the panther above the mantle. "Where did that come from?"

"Alfonzo brought it from de train en hung it over de mantle right w'ere de old one wuz. Dere's another one of a sunset likes de one in yo'r office in de crate. I's didn't knows where I's should hang it."

339

Drew reached up to get a note that was stuck in the frame of the painting.

> *Glad to hear you survived.*
> *I had these paintings and thought that you might want to*
> *replace the ones you lost.*
> *Adam*

Drew told Josephine they could hang the sunset on the wall of the enclosed back porch. Then he went into his bedroom where the old family bed and dresser shone like new. On the dresser was a picture of him and Mary Elizabeth on their wedding day.

Drew looked at the picture and held it to his heart, promising himself that he would never again forget the vows he had made that day. Then he looked at the pictures of Mollie, Gail, and Thomas. Around the room hung samplers that had been created by his grandmother, his mother, and Mary Elizabeth. Many things had perished but Mary Elizabeth had taken many small things and put them in the attic before the storm.

Luckily the trunk in which she placed them didn't leak.

Drew looked to see Flora's quilt in its familiar place on the rack at the foot of the bed.

"Josephine, I have a better place for that quilt. Follow me."

Drew took the quilt off the rack and took it into the girls' bedroom. He and Josephine spread the quilt on Mollie's bed.

Mary Elizabeth and the girls arrived on the train after dark on Christmas Eve.

The first thing that Mollie said was, "Daddy, what's that horrible smell? It doesn't smell like home anymore."

Drew sniffed the air and realized the stench of death was still in the air. Then he laughed because the smell that Mollie associated with home was the smell of the burning muck that bothered him so long ago.

"Baby, your smell will be back. What you smell is what's left of the storm. I guess I have gotten accustomed to it."

"Well, I'm glad to be home, good smells or bad. It was so cold at Paw Paw's. They think it might snow for Christmas. I'm glad it doesn't snow here. May we go swimming tomorrow?"

"We'll see. We'll see."

Mary Elizabeth was delighted at the way the house looked.

"It's better than new, but where did you hide the piano?"

Drew led his wife up the stairs, "Your music room, Madam."

"Oh, Drew!"

She and Mollie sat down and played a couple of familiar Christmas carols. Drew went down to the living room and plugged in the new lights he had put on the tree.

Mollie and Gail ran into the living room and clapped their hands at the wonderful sight.

"Daddy, you saved our old ornaments! I love you, Daddy!"

Mollie ran and jumped into Drew's arms hugging and kissing him.

Drew felt a tug at his pants. "Me, too. Me, too."

Drew picked up Gail and carried both of his daughters into the dining room.

"Surprise!"

The Carters were there waiting with a big Christmas feast. After the meal Charlie shared his family tradition with them. When he had finished reading from the second chapter of Luke, Mollie asked, "Mr. Charlie, do all families read about Jesus on His birthday?"

After the reading, the families enjoyed Miss Mollie's gingerbread.

Drew thought it was almost as good as Mary Elizabeth's. Then he thought about the other recipes of Flora's. Were they saved? Mary Elizabeth seemed to read his mind and pointed one finger at her head. She had memorized them.

"Girls, it's time to hang your stockings because I think Santa might be on his way."

"You forgot, Daddy."

"What did I forget?"

"The poem, the poem you always say. You said a daddy gave the poem to his children on Christmas a long time ago. Will you please tell it to us? Please!"

Drew had hoped Mollie wouldn't remember. The poem was Thomas's favorite part of Christmas, with the exception of the presents. He always supplied the words Drew forgot or missed.

With a deep breath and a prayer that he could get through it without shedding tears, Drew began:

"Twas the night before Christmas and all through the house..."

Mollie supplied the endings to each rhyming phrase.

Drew carried Mollie to her room on his back, while Mary Elizabeth did the same with Gail. As soon as the bedroom light was turned on, Mollie squealed with delight when she saw Flora's quilt on her bed. She ran and laid face down, rubbing and loving each piece of fabric. As Drew and Mary Elizabeth tucked in the girls for the night, Mollie snuggled under the quilt of memories.

"Daddy, Santa doesn't have to come this year. I'm home with you and you have given me your special quilt. I don't need anything from Santa."

Gail, Drew, and Mary Elizabeth listened as Mollie said her prayers. Instead of the children's prayer she said by rote every night, Mollie prayed, "Thank you God for bringing my family safely through that terrible storm. Thank you that we are all home again safe and sound. Be with all who lost family and their homes. And thank you, God for Jesus. Tell him to take care of Thomas. I know Thomas is glad to have more of his friends with him, but we sure do miss them down on earth. God Bless Mama, Daddy, Gail, Grandma, and Paw

Paw, Miss Mollie, Mr. Charlie, and everybody. Amen. And, I forgot – Happy Birthday, Jesus."

Gail repeated, "Happy Birthday, Jesus."

At noon on Christmas Day the citizens of Glades County, and storm volunteers from as far away as Tampa, gathered in a small park near the Lone Cypress.

Members of the Moore Haven Woman's Club planted a small evergreen tree, a symbol of everlasting life. The tree would be a reminder to every one of the victims who had lost their lives in the Hurricane of 1926.

Children were given hand-made decorations to hang on the tree. Santa handed out presents to every child present. Members of the 116th Field Artillery of the National Guard had donated one paycheck to buy the presents.

A feast was prepared and served by several men of the community. Uncle Joe Peeples donated a beef that was barbecued and Lloyd Farnam and Buddy Fountain furnished sixty wild ducks.

Music played while friends shared their heartaches, joys, and triumphs of the past three months. People shared acts of heroism. In relating their stories, most were thanking those who had risked their lives to save them.

One such story was Mildred Long's experience in the theater.

"All of us who were in the theater that day would have surely drowned if it hadn't been for Jimmy Couse. We gathered there thinking it would be safe. We were petrified when the whole building started to disintegrate. We all knew we were about to die. Then we saw Jimmy just coming out of the sky to save us. He tied a rope on the Gram Building and jumped across the street to where we were. He tied a rope on the theater and we were all able to climb across and stay with him at the Gram's. We hadn't been there but just a little while when we watched the theater come crashing down and wash away. Thank you, Jimmy."

Many stood up and thanked Drew for his food and medical support.

Drew thanked Charlie for the use of his house as a hospital. Everyone laughed when he told of how in the midst of all the tragedies, Charlie was flipping pancakes just as though it was another day.

"His only worry was that Miss Mollie would be upset with the wet rugs."

Over half the crowd thanked Charlie for keeping his lamp lit all night. Like Drew and the others in the Woman's Club, its beacon of light gave them hope.

Fred Flanders and Ed Lundy were recognized for the warnings they put out.

There was a tremendous round of applause for Mr. Sebring, the volunteers, and the members of the National Guard.

W. E. Daniels, a dairyman from the Park Avenue section of town, relived his horrifying experience.

"I was out with my cows by the dike when I heard a roar. I looked up to see water gushin' through the dike. I started running. I reached an old oak tree 'bout the same time the water did. I climbed to the very top and hung on for dear life. I watched my house as it was submerged up to the roof. I knew my family was in there. That was the worse part; I knew I couldn't help them. Thank Goodness, they got up into the rafters and then on the roof. We all survived."

Many others related how they had endured the storm by hanging on to trees or their roofs. Others told of surviving on boats.

Although by now the horror of the storm was three months old, each story brought sobs and tears. The sharing of the grief was needed, however, and each story prompted another for long into the afternoon.

"Daddy, I'm so glad that we're home again," Mollie whispered as she felt the day was coming to a close.

"So am I," he said softly as he reached out and pulled Mary Elizabeth and Gail to him.

He looked across the crowd at his many friends. They all had endured so many losses during the past six years. Yet they were still determined to stay and pursue the hopes and the dreams that brought them to this frontier.

As the shadows of the evening began to flicker through the branches of the flat-topped cypress, he was aware of the lasting symbol the tree had become.

No matter that fires and floods attempted to destroy them. No matter that storms and drought ruined their crops. Just like the tree, they would continue to put down their roots here and hold steadfast to the soil that nurtured them. Their lives would be good, in this place and in this town, in the shadow of the lone cypress.

About the Characters

A great many of the characters that are included in this book were instrumental in the development of Florida in the early twentieth century. Dr. Drew Duncan meets them all as he discovers Florida and settles there permanently. To help the reader, the following, whose names may not be familiar, are identified:

Miami figures: P.J. Coates, photographer; Charles and Bella Peacock, early residents of Coconut Grove; Carl Fisher, developer.

Moore Haven figures: James Moore, developer and city founder; Fredrick V. Gram, real estate agent; John Dowd, drugstore owner; Dr. H. J. Mitchell; Mrs. Coleman; Andy Carter, *Moore Haven Times* publisher; Daniel Lence, chairman of Lence-Baker Relief Fund; Lloyd Farnam; Buddy Fountain; Jimmy Couse, lawyer; W.E. Daniels, dairyman; Wallace Stephens, *Moore Haven Democrat* editor; Fred Flanders, assistant chief engineer in charge of drainage; Fern Flanders; Marian Horwitz O'Brien, farmer, developer, first mayor, co-founder of Clewiston; Clarence Busch and George Horwitz, land developers; Mr. and Mrs. Peter Westergaard; Ed Lundy, electrician; Esther Klutts; Katie King, hotel manager; Cecil Parkinson, general store owner; One-Eyed Riley, alligator.

Glades County figures: Uncle Joe Peeples, cattleman and state representative;   J.L.Beck, general store owner, Lakeport; Buck King, cattle baron; Bone Mizell, King's foreman and cowman painted by Fredrick Remington; Ed Frierson, county commissioner; Benbow brothers, farm owners; Sam Richards, Glades County sheriff; Billy Bowlegs III, Seminole Indian guide for Flagler and U.S. Presidents; Luberta Kirksey, Lakeview resident.

Others: John Henderson, state land surveyor; Jake Summerlin, Florida cattle baron; John Martin, Florida governor; Colonel Lowery and Captain James Albritton, Florida National Guard; George Sebring, founder of Sebring; Fitzhugh Lee, American Counsel to Cuba; Henry Plant and Henry Flagler, railroad industrialists and developers; Hamilton Disston, Florida land buyer; Napoleon Bonapart Broward, gun runner to Cuba, Duval County Sheriff, Florida Governor; Jose' Marti', the "George Washington" of Cuba; Colonel Leonard Wood, commander of the 1st Volunteer Army in Cuba; Sidney Catts, Florida governor: Doc Abner, Okeechobee City doctor; A.C. Clews, banker; Bernard G. Dahlberg, Chicago investor; Sam Elliot, Chief Engineer, Army Corps of Engineers..

About the Author

Sally Settle is the granddaughter of Lake Okeechobee pioneers. As the daughter of a newspaper editor, her early life was touched early by local history, stories, and folklore of those who put their labor and love into making homes and chasing dreams on the edge of the Florida Everglades.

Ms. Settle holds a Masters of Science Degree in Library and Information Science and is a retired school library-school media specialist. She taught in Florida's public schools for 36 years. She has two grown children and a grandson.